I0604407

# The Power of Love

*A Tale of Time*

Ross J. Kinnaird

ISBN: 978-1-0686863-4-4

For more info on The Power of Love Series®

www.thepowerofloveseries.com

First edition: June 2024

First Print: June 2024

Edited by Imogen Howson

Cover by Ardel Media

*To Sarah & Debbie.*

*The term 'best friend' doesn't come close to defining how important both of you are to me. As a master of words, I'm afraid I fail at what should be the easiest of tasks. Yet, I know in my heart you understand what I cannot capture in writing.*

# CONTENTS


| 1 | The First World | Pg 11 |
| 2 | A Surging Threat | Pg 18 |
| 3 | The Enemy Within | Pg 33 |
| 4 | The Sacred Horn | Pg 44 |
| 5 | Of Love and War | Pg 55 |
| 6 | The Enemy's Whisper | Pg 69 |
| 7 | A Deadly Illusion | Pg 83 |
| 8 | The Beacon of Fire | Pg 98 |
| 9 | The Whispering Forest | Pg 110 |
| 10 | The Corrupted | Pg 120 |
| 11 | A Forbidden Love | Pg 128 |
| 12 | The Birth of a Greater Evil | Pg 145 |
| 13 | The Rightful King | Pg 160 |
| 14 | Sisterhood | Pg 170 |
| 15 | A Dying World | Pg 178 |
| 16 | The Machine of War | Pg 190 |
| 17 | The Price of Freedom | Pg 204 |

| 18 | A Truth Worth Dying For | Pg 216 |
| 19 | A Brother's Revenge | Pg 224 |
| 20 | A Promise Made of Hate and Blood | Pg 237 |
| 21 | The Meeting of the Twelve | Pg 245 |
| 22 | The Great Dawn | Pg 257 |
| 23 | The Face of the True Enemy | Pg 265 |
| 24 | The Rise of a New Queen | Pg 275 |
| 25 | The Mirrors of Time | Pg 282 |
| 26 | The Sweet Taste of Revenge | Pg 293 |
| 27 | Valahan Mogs | Pg 303 |
| 28 | To the Bitter End | Pg 314 |
| 29 | Anún Déil: the Flare of the Sea | Pg 335 |
| 30 | The Crimson Queen | Pg 350 |
| 31 | The End of Metal and Stone | Pg 361 |
| 32 | The Eradication | Pg 369 |
| 33 | The Invisible One | Pg 377 |
| 34 | Those Who Withstood the Evil | Pg 387 |
| 35 | A Tale of Time | Pg 402 |

# Chapter One

## *The First World*

∞

Coming back to my true self, my nature as one soul, one God, took more lifetimes than I could recount. So long it had been since my siblings and I had been together that their resounding power so close to mine overwhelmed me. In the aftermath of my awakening, the conjuring of my true power, Time, Soul, and Health floated next to me in the infinite vastness of the universe above Earth. There I stood, as I became conscious of who I was, Daniel's mind resisting mine, holding me to a past now gone.

Our greatest and most feared enemy, Nothing, was about to strike. It was imperative that I hasten my regaining strength and be ready to fight. As if time were both of the essence and yet irrelevant, my brother moved next to me and took my arm. The moment he touched my ethereal skin, every passing moment froze. In that fraction of a second, an eternity flashed before my eyes, an enchanting truth moving from one bearer to the next.

'Brother,' Time said to me, as his visions started to fill my mind. 'We are at the edge of our destiny, right between existence and demise. You need to know, before it's too late. The enduring existence of those brought to life by our mother spans countless millennia, bearing tales and truths unseen by eyes unfamiliar with the epoch before the Great War. Neither the exhaustive collection of the long-lost Radhal Daíuh, held within the crown, nor the enigmatic Ancient Mirrors themselves could contain the infinite knowledge tracing the annals of Runae's history. Yet, as I am the keeper of all that was, all that is, and could be, I possess the ability to hold this wealth of wisdom and share it with those wise enough to heed my lessons.'

'Why are you showing me all this? Why now?' I asked, before my brother could open up to a full confession. 'Did you know all of this was going to happen?'

'You are Love, brother. Don't you know every feeling, every emotion of every living being, deep within yourself? And yet,' Time added, before I could reply, 'have you ever stopped hoping there could be more? Do you ever fear there could be less?'

'Show me,' I whispered without hesitation.

Thus, Time's tale came to me, to us, in a time of turmoil, reaching its peak precisely when the world teetered on the precipice of chaos, when malevolence found opportunity in the God's vulnerability, his mind entangled in the memories of countless ages past.

This story emerged to show me the relentless assault launched from both without and within, as the adversary assembled his forces into a unified, relentless onslaught bent on conquest and obliteration. His intent was nothing short of eradicating every vestige, every testament to Creation's existence and perceived transgressions. With us Gods vigilant over our domains, the threat initially manifested as insidious whispers, insinuating themselves like creeping strands of malevolence. Yet, as the fabric of the universe frayed under his relentless assault, the sinister murmurs swelled into a mixture of despair and sorrow, announcing a new wave of suffering and unrest.

It is at this precise juncture that Time's tale converges with mine, with those of the other Gods, intertwining with our individual stories and uniting under the collective pain of all who endured the enemy's second coming.

∞

It all began with the creation of the first world.

After the cosmic explosion, after the birth of the universe, and Creation coming to life, the long, empty night came to an end. In the distant edges of space, hidden from Nothing's sight, the first God violated the existing, immutable order of things, initiating her inaugural act of creation: Runae emerged into existence.

Throughout her millennial existence, Creation continued her divine work, birthing matter from the void, expanding her creation to the furthest reaches of the universe. At each of the four cardinal points, she sculpted worlds teeming with life, interconnecting them as nodes, safeguarding her creations from the malevolent gaze of the King of Emptiness.

Shortly thereafter, four more Gods were brought forth, placed as sovereigns over their respective realms, vigilantly guarding the cosmic passages between worlds. In a mysterious dance of fate, Runae emerged as the inaugural world, yet it was the last to receive the protective mantle of its guardian, Time. It endured the rise of wickedness and the fall of its protector until liberation came at the hands of the carriers of Love, Daniel and Noah. Endowed with potent magic, Runae defiantly resisted the forces of darkness for aeons.

Its verdant hills and tranquil seas bore witness to the harmony of many races, each blessed with unique powers, existing in a delicate balance of light and shadow, under the watchful eye of their eternal master: the God of Everlasting

Existence. Crafted by Creation's hand, these diverse beings roamed freely, unified in peace.

To the Humans, renowned as the builders throughout the ages, a vast expanse of land stretched to the southwest, between the sea's embrace and the towering mountains. Their dominion expanded unchecked, marked by grand structures and monumental edifices, testament to their mastery in sculpting stone into awe-inspiring beauty. Yet, for a long while, they did not hoard their gift; with the passing centuries, their unparalleled engineering prowess shaped distant lands, leaving an indelible mark across the ages.

In the northern realms, the Leonty roamed untamed amidst verdant hills and parched plains, granted domain from the Cloudy Mountains to the eastern steppes. Possessing enigmatic powers, their females wielded a formidable magic, born from the depths of their powerful minds. As time wove its tapestry, the concept of a superior being evolved into veneration, and veneration into fervent devotion. The seven hills to the far west bore witness to their reverence, crowned by temples dedicated to the unseen deities who breathed life into their existence. From the Temple of Grace to the Temple of Time, the Leonty's hallowed ground stretched beyond limits, revealed only to those who ascended the heights of the Mogs Mountains.

To the far northeastern reaches, nestled between the rugged steeps and the vast expanse of the northern sea, the Garughals maintained their secluded existence. Intimately attuned to the essence of nature ingrained in their minds and souls, they possessed the remarkable ability to seamlessly meld with the roots of Runae at will. Often elusive and mysterious, they could effortlessly transform into any natural form they desired, a skill cherished and revered among their kind. Legend, whispered amongst the annals of Time, recounts tales of those consumed by an insatiable longing to merge with their beloved mother Runae. Their fervent desire led them to transform into trees and rocks, forever trapped in the embrace of their craved dream.

In the heart of the known lands, cradled between the formidable Firing Mountains and the vigilant gaze of the towering Mogs, the Valahans thrived in ceaseless industry, their endeavours driven by a relentless pursuit of raw materials at the feet of their colossal companion. Masters of mining and fearless in excavation, they played a pivotal role in fuelling the Humans' aspirations for greatness. As Time's memory serves, it was the Valahans who unearthed the very Flare from which all others would spring forth. Concealed within the deepest recesses of Runae's core, this primal force lay safeguarded by layers of rock and mantle until the day it was brought into the light, until the day its boundless power was revealed to the world.

In the vast expanse of the seas encircling the lands, the Aqualymphs ruled. Born of the very waters they inhabited, they possessed the extraordinary ability to absorb the life-giving lymph of their environment, sustaining their existence and adapting their form accordingly. Though capable of briefly traversing the land, their reliance on water for oxygen bound them to the depths of the underworld for eternity. Among them, a chosen Aqualymph held the revered title of Gatekeeper, entrusted with safeguarding the sacred passage—a solitary gateway nestled within a tiny island to the south, positioned squarely in the heart of the sea.

The sixth race, the only one who would eventually elude the Crimson Queen's sinister dominion, occupied a minute corner of Runae's vast areas. Though their stature was akin to that of Human children, their numbers were high and their strength formidable. Endowed with wings, they effortlessly bore heavy burdens, their flight as graceful as feathers. Naturally suspicious but inherently kind-hearted, they kept their distance from other inhabitants for much of their history. Adhering to the natural order, they interacted exclusively with the Aqualymphs, the eternal guardians of their world. However, as the Chomps were not very fond of the sea and their only friends were confined to its depths, it was only a matter of time before the two races became estranged.

# Chapter Two

## *A Surging Threat*

∞

In the yac eighty-three of the tenth millennium, a gathering of beings convened to meet their master, Time, deep within the wooded heart of the Garughals' home. They had been summoned by their protector and, responding to his call, two representatives from each race had promptly ventured into the mystical eastern lands. Arriving late to the meeting, three Valahans had just reached the forest's edge when two trees suddenly transformed into living beings. They were taken by surprise by the unexpected magic and stepped back, staring at the tall plants as they slowly turned into a new form. When the trees shed their foliage and roots, revealing themselves as Garughal guards, one of the Valahans, who was older and more weathered than the others, demanded answers.

'What's the meaning of all this? You should announce your presence. Instead you decided to wait for us, hidden in the shadows of your magic!' he shouted. His eyes looked like they had sunken and merged with his cheekbones. His old skin seemed pale, almost translucent.

'You are late, Vasheer, ruler of the Valahans,' one of the guards replied sharply, his head still partially distorted, with green foliage protruding from his ears.

'I'm late because this place is impossible to find. Let us in; we have important business to discuss!'

'Only two of you can pass,' the other guard stated, raising his wooden arm to halt the group's advance. 'It's the rule.'

'These are Varuk and Voishan, my sons. You see me, Garughal? I may be old enough to disappear into thin air if the Gods would allow it. But it's their will for me to keep going so I require newer eyes and ears to assist me with our master's commands…'

'Then you can stay behind if you wish. But only two shall proceed.' Foliage began to grow behind the stubborn guards, obscuring the road ahead.

'It's okay, father. Bring Varuk with you. He is the eldest. I'll wait here patiently,' Voishan replied, placing a hand on his father's shoulder, revealing thick hair on his skin.

As Vasheer and his son were granted access to the intricate Garughals' lands, an incredible sight unfolded before them. Stones shifted, trees parted to allow their passage, and hidden eyes watched them unseen. For Varuk, it was the realization of the tales his father had recounted. Between two hills, where the Gochi River cascaded into the sea, a majestic waterfall held a grand structure atop the rocks, concealed by foliage. An opening in the side revealed a rounded platform where many guests stood.

'Our numbers are finally complete. Thank you for joining us at this late hoc.' A tall, radiant figure spoke, cloaked and hooded, with two shining dots for eyes.

'What took you so long?' Arush, a Leonty male, stood from his seat made of roots and branches. His slim figure and broad shoulders partially obscured the presence of someone else.

'We don't spend our time praying and casting spells, Leonty,' Vasheer retorted sharply. 'We have work to take care of.'

'And this *work* has nothing to do with the excavation by the Mogs Mountains, does it?' Arush pushed back.

'Leave them be,' intervened the King of the Humans, a sturdy figure crowned and recognized among the assembly. 'They work hard not only for themselves but for all of us.'

'We Garughals are not seekers of glory in stones and artefacts. Do not distort our intentions with your vague words, King Lohan.' A large flower transformed its stems into a beautiful female of their kind. Her pink petals shifted into velvety skin as her arms moved gracefully to her side, her body seemingly rooted to the brown soil. Beside her, a male Garughal stood in silence.

'Friends, please, let's maintain focus. This is not the matter that prompted our gathering,' Time intervened.

'What urgent matter brings us together then? Speak quickly and be sharp!' Vasheer retorted, his skin flickering slightly in the presence of his summoner.

'Show respect to our protector! He is our everything, and we should address him accordingly.' A female Leonty spoke up, moving away from the shadow of her companions, her glowing red eyes conveying reverence as she cast a spell on the old Valahan, momentarily silencing him.

'This is unnecessary, Imperia,' Time interjected, releasing Vasheer from the spell's grip. Startled by the sudden magic, the Valahan fell silent and took a seat on one of the nearby chairs formed from a few trees. 'I'm not here to demand respect. I'm here to warn you of a looming threat—a threat emerging swiftly in the far west, near the Cloudy Mountains. It is gaining momentum not only here but in every world across the cosmos. I and the other Gods are summoned to confront something, someone who has lurked in the darkness for far too long.'

'Whom do you speak of?' a previously unnoticed Chomp interrupted, suddenly making his presence known with a pertinent question. To the gathering, he was nearly invisible, his stature seemingly reflecting the perceived irrelevance of his words, as if any contribution from his kind was considered as insignificant as his physical form.

'They are spirits—spirits forged from pure evil,' a voice answered. An Aqualymph, previously overlooked like the Chomp, shifted between air and water, her crystal legs emerging from the nearby waterfall as she spoke. On her head, a red crown made by corals and stones appeared as she moved close to the Chomp. 'They infiltrate minds and souls without the need to manifest in our reality.'

'Queen Eah.' Time's voice, though his face remained obscured, carried a gentle tone that hinted at a smile. 'Where is the Gatekeeper? I entrusted you to be accompanied by the one burdened with the solemn duty…'

'Whatever information you're willing to share, I'm confident I can relay it with equal urgency, my master,' the Aqualymph replied, her attention riveted on the Gochi River. Time briefly sought her gaze, his perceptive mind attuned to her discontent.

'How have they entered our lands?' Arush interrupted, his eyes locked on the Aqualymph, as if seeking accountability for the invaders' intrusion.

'They didn't enter through the node. They do not possess true forms,' Time explained. 'They were already present in these lands, sent by the King of Emptiness through magical means. However, there is a possibility more could materialize physically through the node.'

'Not under our watch!' Queen Eah asserted. In the recesses of her mind, she felt discomfort at the notion that her God would need and trust the Gatekeeper more than her. *After all, I'm the queen of the seas,* she thought.

'I am certain of it,' Time affirmed. 'And I trust you will continue patrolling the sea and its node while I am away, meeting with my siblings.'

'Is this why you summoned us? To inform us of your imminent departure from Runae?' queried Kasthor, the Chomp.

'Indeed, but there is more,' Time continued, eliciting full attention from the gathering. 'My brothers have been…researching, if that's the appropriate term. They have sought a more effective means to protect our worlds from the enemy. They have discovered that infusing their power with the very core of their protected planet enhances its effectiveness, allowing everything and everyone within it to absorb the power of its master, shielding them from within.'

'Is it truly possible? For you to honour us with such a gift?' Imperia asked, leaving the other Leonty behind as she walked close to Time.

'And I suppose your kind would like that, wouldn't you?' King Lohan stood up quickly, his hands clenched in disagreement. 'Do you not have enough power in your hands? Why are you craving more?'

'King Lohan is right,' another Human chimed in, supporting his ruler's question. 'This new magic, this power should be given to the ones who have none of their own…'

'And what would the Humans do with it? Conquer every land, from the frost side to the sacred waters?' the old Valahan quickly countered.

Time's idea was not received as he expected. In the recent yacs, something else had grown hidden as he came and went from Runae. Rivalry, quarrels, animosity had festered among beings who were not designed to be that way. In the depths of his mind, the God began to question the wisdom of leaving his beloved world unattended again. *Perhaps, sometime in the past, something wicked entered their souls, infecting them, depriving them of their kind nature*, he thought.

'Listen, all of you. This is a gathering of friends and allies. I'm not here to unfairly gift anyone. You are here to protect one another, to protect Creation's making. Whatever, wherever this magic is, it will be for everyone's safety. This power belongs to all of you; it's already part of the very core of this world. Through it and with my magic, we can defend our lands from the enemy.'

'Is there a chance this hidden power is connected with the recent events in the Firing Mountains?' King Lohan asked, suspicion still etched on his face.

'What happens in our lands is our business!' Varuk interjected before his father could speak.

'What happened in the mountains?' the Chomp asked, curious.

'I said it's none of your business.'

'The ground is shaking in the middle lands.' Imperia spoke, contradicting Varuk's statement. 'Something is moving from within the crust of our planet. It travels to the mines, at the back of the Mogs Pass.'

'It's not just moving,' Arush continued. 'It's cracking the ground all the way up to the Cloudy Mountains, passing right through the middle of our lands. There are whispers arising from the fractures, voices of an unknown will…'

'Varuk has spoken his father's words. Don't you know when to give respect to the kings?' The old Valahan moved away, dragging his son by the arm. 'This meeting is over!' With that, he left the group astonished as the two walked out of the Garughals' mansion, heading back to their home. As they disappeared from sight, Time briefly engaged with the Aqualymphs, preparing them for his upcoming departure. After ensuring that the rest of the gathering would respond to his next call, he bid a soft farewell and disappeared, quickly dissolving like early morning mist.

With pride, a strong will, and brisk strides, the two Valahans departed from the woods and reached the outskirts of the Garughals' domain, much to Voishan's surprise upon their early return. In a brief moment of astonishment, Time materialized out of thin air, his cloak billowing in the breeze with a sharp snap that jolted their senses. Assuming he had come to reprimand them and escort them back, Vasheer wore an expression of regret and sorrow. Despite his stubbornness and pride, he still harboured a deep-seated fear and respect for their true God.

'I heed your words, master. We always will, but please do not ask me to return and leave our people's affairs vulnerable. We make no demands of theirs; they should make none of ours,' Vasheer implored.

'I am not here to bring you back, King of the Valahans. I am here because I know what you are doing. I know where you stand in your endeavours,' Time responded cryptically.

'Where? What do you mean?' Voishan interjected, unaware of the contentious exchange that had occurred only moments earlier.

'You are on the cusp of a great discovery,' the God replied with a smile. 'Remember, I am the ruler of time. I can see the past and glimpse into some possible futures. And yours is becoming increasingly clear with each passing moment. The question is, how do we turn it into the greatest defence in Runae's history?'

'Defence?' Vasheer asked, puzzled. Whatever they had been excavating in the mountains, it seemed inconceivable that it could serve any purpose beyond erecting buildings and monuments glorifying the Humans. 'It's merely rocks and stones. Minerals, matter. How can it be transformed into a defence?'

'In the very place where you breached the mantle, where stone meets the seething liquid fire, there is something more, isn't there?' Time inquired, bending slightly so his piercing gaze could meet the king's.

'You said it yourself. You can foresee what we will uncover. Since we haven't found it yet, you must tell me!' Vasheer demanded.

'Very well then. Consider this my directive: cease all excavation, every digging, and exploration,' Time commanded, prompting startled glances among the three Valahans. 'Just until my return. I must be present when it is brought to light. Let me be unequivocal: halt all activity until my return.' With that, Time departed as abruptly as he had arrived, leaving the lingering imprint of his dazzling eyes in their minds and his admonition echoing in their ears.

As if anticipating the Valahans' inability to keep their promise for long, Time kept his absence short and soon returned, appearing within their own lands, nestled at the feet of the towering mountains. The rugged ridges transformed into their familiar homes, thousands of caves emerged from the rocky slopes, extending from the peaks down to the barren lands below. Each cave entrance was guarded by a sturdily carved stone door, adorned with engraved words on the head jamb: *Valahans vhosn atun vrath*, translating to the common tongue as: *May the stones protect all Valahans.*

Time materialized right at Vasheer's doorstep. With the large star Erion unable to penetrate the depths of the caves, the God was the only radiating power that had ever walked their lands, shining brightly in the darkness of the silent space. After he knocked three times on the stone, another sentence glowed, flickering at his touch. *Vasheer Fláir Do Méh.* Moments later, a voice echoed the same words from within the house.

'Does Time require a password to enter your protected abode?' the God inquired, his face displaying a bashful smile.

'We have been expecting you for so long, but surely not now, not here…' Vasheer replied, his tired face emerging through the opening of the heavy door.

'I am Time, my friend. How can here and now not be right?' the God countered, stepping inside, his head still veiled by the hood.

'You and your riddles... Do you wish to go now?' Vasheer asked, donning a large woolly jacket.

'If it's not inconvenient for you...'

'Inconvenient? As if we were not eager to resume our work... Let's proceed. The faster we do this, the sooner we can return to our business with the Humans,' Vasheer said, firmly nudging Time out of the house, unafraid of seeming impolite.

'What business is this I hear of? Involving the Humans...' Time inquired, walking alongside the king as they approached another stony door adjacent to his home.

'*Vasheer vónt ushnat,*' the king whispered. The imposing door creaked open, releasing its grip. 'You have been absent too often and for too long. The Humans are closing the gap to the east, between the Mogs Pass and the Leonty hills.'

'Father!' Varuk emerged at the entrance, clad only in his hairy skin. 'Time? Your presence here means only one thing. Let me inform Valiah that we are heading to the depths. The children may become anxious if they don't find me when they wake up.'

'Vasheer...' Time redirected the conversation. 'About this matter with the Humans...'

'The winds are changing, my master. The king has made his decision. He seeks to safeguard his people by erecting walls and gates around their lands. And for this, they require our invaluable labour.'

'Protecting his people from whom? How has evil already reached so far south?' Time's voice echoed, his eyes briefly flashing as he delved into the most recent chapters of their history, searching for the enemy's movements.

'Define evil…' Vasheer replied, stepping aside after his son joined them outside. 'Rumours suggest they believe their neighbours have succumbed to malevolent spirits. The Leonty have endured this threat at their doorstep for far too long.'

'Why not come to their aid, then?' Time pondered, his thoughts reaching back into the depths of the past.

'Because of their magic! They genuinely believe the Leonty's power is turning into something sinister. In the darkness of night, the Humans convene to plan something far more intricate than stones and walls.'

'This cannot be allowed!' Time's voice reverberated through the cavernous expanse they had just entered.

Everywhere appeared tinged with red and orange hues, as if blood and fire had seeped through the layers of Runae's crust, filling the very matter with the same fiery heat that streamed beneath the surface. Like glistening diamonds scattered across a desert landscape, spikes of metal and grey stones pierced through their path into the depths below. The road wound like a giant serpent coiled upon itself, drawing countless circles, one layer below the next, in an endless loop. Finally, after a painstakingly long journey, the three companions reached a colossal rocky barrier. As if testing its solidity, seeking out an invisible weak spot, Vasheer trailed his weathered hand across its surface, causing it to tremble.

'There it is… Right here,' he whispered. In an instant, it vanished, giving way to a wide opening where paths branched out amidst the surging flames and dividing fissures. Crimson and purple liquid poured from the walls and seeped through the cracks in the ground, resembling the fury of a bleeding star.

'You must understand there is purpose to our presence here, but I implore you to reconsider engaging in this perilous effort any longer,' Time advised, advancing further as his hands rose into the searing heat, causing the flowing lava to slow to a halt.

'If we had your guidance and your power, we could delve much deeper,' Varuk remarked, pondering how his master's magic could aid them in their restless excavation.

'Just beyond that pathway, near the dark abyss, amidst fire and shadow. At my age, I dare not trust my legs. Please forgive me if I stay behind,' Vasheer explained, stepping aside to allow his son to lead the way, indicating to Time the precise spot where their enormous excavation had ceased. To either side, the lava had melted and dragged the ground into an immeasurable hole, leaving a vast, dark opening before them. Between the God and the other side, a narrow pathway remained. Halfway across the precarious walkway, Varuk halted.

'We must proceed with extreme caution. We can traverse it, but the intense heat makes it impossible to hang around.

Now that your magic is in place, perhaps we have the time to explore what lies beyond that barrier?' The Valahan gestured, summoning his magic against the obstacle ahead. The wall shifted, revealing two more layers behind it, as if supporting each other. In the centre, an intense light pierced through, as if the rock had absorbed the largest ruby in the universe, held captive amidst layers of metal.

'And so you've found it. Mother's secret. The very heart of the planet!' Time exclaimed, his eyes widening as his hands pressed against the scorching wall.

'The heart? What is it?' Varuk inquired, his thoughts already racing ahead, envisioning the discovery of the most precious stones they could ever hope to possess.

'It's power. Pure power. Only the Gods can wield it. Forged to sustain this world, it breathes life and magic into every being that walks these lands. With Runae facing the threat of destruction, it is time to unearth its power and bestow it upon the people. There is no value in keeping it hidden here, only to see it destroyed along with you all.'

And thus, the great discovery, the most anticipated excavation, was made. The Valahans assisted Time in retrieving the object they needed most, and in return, they were to receive a portion of it. As Time's tale recounts, the Great Flare was soon brought to the surface and ignited with the power of the mighty star, Erion. Time's magic froze each atom's heartbeat, breaking down the Flare into its minuscule components and reassembling them into six precious gifts. Its once-solid form now ablaze, it transformed into fire, the same fire that had concealed it in secrecy for millennia, safeguarded within the deepest recesses of the Mogs Mountain. One by one, the races of Runae convened with Time in council. The concealed, protective Flare passed from one bearer to the next. In exchange for safety, they vowed never to wield any of the six stones against each other, holding them as a beacon for the protection and preservation of Creation's making.

While Time's narrative delves into the creation of the Flares, it leaves uncharted the depths of his prescient knowledge. As the sole master and controller of the wheels of past, present, and future, we are denied the opportunity to scrutinize his decisions, shifts, and actions. Whether predetermined or not, whether his will perpetually outpaces every event in the universe or he is merely a skilled manipulator of probabilities, remains a mystery. What is certain is that the decision to share the power with the inhabitants of his protected world was not unique. It was echoed among by the other Gods, by me, and whether we chose wisely or not, that is a tale for another time.

# Chapter Three

## *The Enemy Within*

∞

One yac had passed since the creation of the six Flares, and the God of Runae had once again disappeared from sight. Concealed between space and reality, he desperately sought to glimpse the myriad possible futures, searching for the one where Nothing would be defeated. Too many iterations of the same end played out before him. The universe seemed destined to the same fate over and over again. In all those wandering paths, one constant remained: he was not the harbinger of the long-awaited triumph. In every iteration of his future, he found himself defeated and imprisoned by evil in an eternal, magical chamber. Yet, as he obsessed over his primary concern, much more eluded his infinite mind.

In the lands to the southwest, the Humans clamoured for conquest with a growing fervour. Their rightful share of Time's magic, their own Flare, appeared weaker than the others, an intolerable situation that added insult to injury for all they had achieved and become. Already the only kind with no magic of their own, they found themselves discriminated against once more. Growing weary of being confined within the very walls they had erected against the Leonty, the fringes of the crown's realm seethed with unrest. King Lohan and his sole heir, Romohan, sought to validate their plight as victims of an encroaching malevolence lurking deep within the Leonty's hills. They demanded an audience with the Aqualymphs, who were the first to voice concerns about an emerging threat in the Cloudy Mountains.

In the yac hundred of the third millennium, at the turn of the warm Fohalt season, two Humans traversed the pass towards the southern coast, nestled between the Aqualymphs' Sea and the Chomps' land. Swiftly descending the hills, they maintained a cautious silence. Their mission had to remain secret; they divulged nothing to those they encountered along the way. Unannounced and ahead of schedule, King Lohan and his son Romohan reached the shoreline, their boots splashing into the sacred waters as if they were demanding an audience with the inhabitants of the deep.

Moments later, a towering wave rippled across the sea, merging the azure expanse with the violet sky in an ethereal union. Within the swirling vortex, the guardian of the node revealed herself to the intruders. Emerging from the mystical embrace of the elements, her presence slowly materialized. Her legs took on the sandy hue of the ground beneath her, while her chest and arms became adorned with the verdant foliage of the sea. Finally, her crystal face appeared, her countenance a radiant testament to the celestial realms, her eyes gleaming with the luminance of distant stars.

'I am Aura, the Gatekeeper and guardian of the passage,' she declared with the solemnity of reciting a ritual prayer. Then, her tone shifted abruptly. 'King Lohan! We did not expect your arrival until another rhoc. Why do you enter our lands as if they are yours to command?'

'I am here for urgent matters. Matters that cannot wait another rhoc. Please, lead me to your queen,' the king insisted.

'I am certain arrangements can be made, but you are aware that our lands are not hospitable to your kind. There is much work to be done before we can allow your presence in the depths of our kingdom,' she replied, and with a snap of her fingers, the Aqualymph vanished, replaced by two more of her kin.

Crafted from the same crystalline water, they retained their true form and remained unresponsive to the visitors. Instead, they intertwined their liquid arms and gestured in a circular motion, conjuring a transparent bubble right in between them. As if they had experience in that kind of magic, the king and his son entered the sea without hesitation, the water swiftly rising to their chests as they stepped into the magical void created by their hosts. Enclosed within a sphere of pure air, the four submerged into the blue depths and vanished from sight.

With the swiftness of dolphins, the two Humans glided through the layers of deep water, following the trail left by the Aqualymphs. As the surroundings dissolved into a dense blue matter, the guests breached an invisible barrier of magic and entered the realm of their hosts. Amidst coral and stone structures, sprawling buildings dotted the submerged landscape. Vegetation swayed gracefully to the silent melody of the numerous Aqualymphs darting in every direction. At the heart of a vast expanse, a crimson tower radiated against the azure backdrop, proudly marking the queen's residence.

As they neared the regal entrance, Aura presented herself to King Lohan and Romohan once more. Her hands gracefully gestured towards the interior, silently beckoning them to enter. When the bubble containing the Humans touched the still-closed doors, the surface shimmered and became intangible, as if transcending existing reality. The king and his son passed through the hard, pinkish coral as effortlessly as a mirage dissolves. On the other side, the vast body of water receded, draining to an imperceptible below, leaving only a large puddle slowly rippling on the stony pavement. With the space now filled with air, it was time for the Humans to disembark and move freely.

Driven by determination to address the queen, King Lohan strode ahead fiercely, leaving the lengthy corridor behind. Atop a grand staircase, an empty throne awaited, a precursor of potential disappointment.

'The queen is not here?' Romohan inquired, his gaze wandering around the enchanting spectacle unfolding before him, his first encounter with such magic.

'Oh, she is here,' Lohan replied, his eyes darting to the left of the vacant throne. 'Queen of the seas, I have an urgent matter to discuss. I could not wait for our agreed meeting. I trust you understand,' he continued, subtly inclining his shoulders—a gesture of respect, though tinged with the persistence of his ego.

'And tell me, Lohan, King of the Humans, does Time know of your request for an audience with the guardian of the passage?' Queen Eah materialized before her guests, her feet seemingly anchored in the gently undulating water on the ground. Her legs took on the colours of the surrounding corals and stones, followed by her body and arms. Finally, her face emerged, her cerulean eyes framed by golden sand, a crown fashioned from shells adorning her regal visage as the Queen of the Aqualymphs.

'Time is nowhere near our lands, my queen,' Romohan said, his gaze fixed on the ground, hesitant to meet her eyes. At the mention of *my queen*, King Lohan gave his son a disapproving glare.

'I know why you are here, and I cannot assist you with what you are about to request.' Queen Eah's words were measured. With a slow pace, she advanced towards the front of her throne. The gentle rustling of her gown's elaborate train, crafted from pebbles and shells, added an air of tension to the room, unsettling her guests.

'I know you have witnessed the growing threat of evil in the west. It is no coincidence that it has chosen that particular place amidst all the lands in our world. It festers, feeding on those who conceal dark magic in their veins!' the king declared.

'There is no evil within the heart of the Leonty. And you too possess magic, thanks to our God,' Queen Eah replied, settling onto her throne. Her eyes briefly flickered as if sensing another presence approaching from afar.

'Magic? Is that what we've been granted? With the Flare, their powers have only grown stronger. The Valahans have been endowed with strength. The Chomps have been gifted with invisibility. They elude us at every turn. Even the Garughals now possess the ability to transmute matter permanently. They can shape the world at will...'

'And we have been granted little more than you, King,' the queen exclaimed. 'Our ability to venture beyond the sacred waters is merely extended, but not to a life-altering degree. Isn't that so? You, on the other hand, have been bestowed with the power of a new science. Some might call that magic.'

'Bending the laws of matter and harnessing pure energy. But what good is such a gift if we cannot defend ourselves? It is time to wield it in defence of our lands and eradicate this threat,' Lohan asserted.

'So, what exactly have you come here to request? To seek validation of your stance? Perhaps an alliance with my people against them?' The queen swiftly descended from her throne, closing the distance between herself and her guests. In their minds, the sudden shift in her manner hinted at an impending confrontation. King Lohan was poised to speak once more when another Aqualymph materialized beside them.

'My queen, someone has entered our lands, through the node!' Aura's eyes conveyed fear as she addressed her queen. The other two fell silent, stunned by the revelation. In their minds, threats loomed large and fast.

'How? Only the Gods possess the ability to pass through. Act swiftly. Take the guards with you and escort this unwelcome guest to my presence. They can join the other two here. As for you, you are strongly urged to remain here; our discussion is not yet concluded.' The queen pivoted and knelt upon the water's surface, her crystal fingers dipping into the liquid. Unseen by the king and his son, she initiated her magic, conjuring a formidable defensive barrier along the shorelines above. Stretching from left to right, as far as the eye could discern, a dense grey fog enveloped the node, obscuring the midlands from view.

Shortly after, Aura and several more Aqualymphs emerged on the surface. On the small, rounded island, a Human with white hair and a white beard stood motionless, his eyes fixed on the emerging barrier.

'I am Aura,' she introduced herself as soon as she took form. 'The God of this world has tasked me as Gatekeeper. We did not anticipate any visitors. This gateway is open only to the Gods. Who are you?'

'My name is Lëogan,' the man replied, attempting a wry smile amidst his unkempt beard. 'I am here because my world is in danger. I have come to seek help.'

'What world do you speak of?' The Aqualymph regarded her guest suspiciously. Something felt wrong.

'Earth. We are under attack! We require your assistance, your power, your magic to combat the enemy…'

'If his words hold truth, we must bring him before the council,' another Aqualymph suggested.

'Yes, please. I must speak with them!'

Like King Lohan and Romohan before him, the new guest plunged into the seas with haste, guided swiftly by the Aqualymphs towards the queen's home. In their urgency, all security measures seemed to be overlooked. To the king's surprise, the stranger was ushered to the queen's domain with considerably less resistance than they had encountered earlier. Before he could voice his objection, Eah spoke.

'Who are you, and how did you enter Runae?' she inquired.

'I am Lëogan, and I come from Earth. I approach you all bearing news of a looming threat in the distant skies—an enemy of our God is waging war against us. The evil has deployed a formidable army with the intent to erase us all. I have come seeking help,' the stranger replied.

'Tell me, Lëogan…' The queen hurried her walk along the corridor, her steps quickening. The king, observing the unequal treatment, bristled with indignation. 'You appear Human, yet you are not. What are you?'

'Our kind differs from yours. Do not be deceived by appearances. Listen closely to my words,' Lëogan cautioned, his eyes gleaming with a dark energy. An invisible, magnetizing force emanated from his presence. 'A grave danger approaches not only over my world but yours as well. Something malevolent is coming…'

'It is already here, you fool!' The king erupted, weary of being treated as inferior. 'The enemy has already infiltrated our lands, amassing strength in the west and spreading fast!'

'It is…' Lëogan's expression betrayed a hint of satisfaction. He had acquired the knowledge he sought. To lend credibility to his fabrications, he needed to quickly find something that could resonate with the fears of those beings. 'I'm afraid my arrival may be too late then. If his forces are already among your people, there is little you can do.'

'If there is a threat, we will meet it head-on!' The queen's response was sharp, igniting Lohan's fury.

'So you are prepared to heed the counsel of a stranger in matters of conflict, yet you hesitated when I, King of the Humans, sought your aid in driving back the Leonty from the Cloudy Mountains,' he accused.

'Do not give in to anger, my king,' Lëogan interjected smoothly, his voice carrying an unusual authority. 'Your wisdom in seeking alliances in times of crisis is commendable. I trust you are all in agreement. Action must be taken.'

'And action shall be taken!' The queen's declaration caught Aura off guard. Aqualymphs rarely engaged in disputes, let alone discussed the prospect of war with the inhabitants of Runae. Feeling the weight of the queen's sudden shift in behaviour, she felt compelled to deviate from protocol.

'My queen, this is madness! It is neither wise nor our duty to entertain thoughts of conflict and warfare. Perhaps we should consult our God before making any decisions?' Aura asked, earning a disapproving glare from Queen Eah.

'It is natural to feel the burden of a such responsibility…' the stranger began, before the queen could speak. Whatever influence he wielded, it seemed not as effective against a simple Aqualymph like Aura. 'There will be a time to report to your God, just as there is a time to act. That time is now.'

'Agreed,' King Lohan exclaimed. 'We shall march to the northwest hills. We assume we have your approval and support?'

'Indeed, you do,' the sovereign affirmed, leaving Aura stunned. 'Prepare for war. With the power of our Flare, we will depart these lands for as long as necessary to aid our ally in need. When we are done with our enemy, we will discuss how to defeat yours,' Queen Eah turned around and extended her right hand towards Lëogan. 'Come with me,' she invited. 'I'm truly eager to know any additional details you can provide.'

As the stranger took her hand, the two vanished in an instant, leaving a trail of vapour in the room. The king and his son exchanged resentful glances. Though they had achieved their objective, the queen's behaviour felt disrespectful. In the depths of their minds, they both acknowledged her as an ally, albeit one whose commitment was destined to be short-lived.

# Chapter Four

## *The Sacred Horn*

∞

Mareen, it's me. There is something urgent I need to discuss with you,' Aura whispered from behind a red, rocky wall. The Aqualymph's fear was escalating rapidly, her concerns palpable in her trembling voice. She felt an urgent need to warn the others about Queen Eah's perplexing decision to abandon the sacred waters in support of the Humans. Though Aura knew no one would dare challenge the sovereign's decree, she was certain they all shared her deep apprehensions, particularly the one she trusted most.

'Aura? What's wrong? Is it the node again?' A large square face emerged from the dark water, Mareen's form coalescing amidst the swaying vegetation behind him.

'Not again, but it does concern the node and the stranger we escorted to Queen Eah. Something feels wrong…' Aura's body dissolved momentarily, only to reappear next to her companion, amidst thick brown bushes. 'I fear our policy of non-intervention has been forsaken…we are on the brink of war.'

'You must be mistaken. We've sworn to eternal peace!'

'King Lohan and Queen Eah have decided to march westward. They're preparing for war against the Leonty.' Aura's voice dropped to a whisper, her words muffled by her own magic. 'I'm convinced it's connected to the stranger who crossed the node. Our queen was adamant against the king's proposal. Then, before my eyes, the stranger spoke of an imminent threat, a danger from other worlds and within our own. I swear I felt a dark magic emanating from his very words.'

'So you believe he enchanted them with some sort of spell? That's impossible. Queen Eah is the most powerful being among us. Her magic cannot be overshadowed by a mere Human.'

'He's not Human, Mareen. The queen herself questioned his identity, before he clouded her mind with falsehoods and deceit. We must act swiftly…' But before the two Aqualymphs could devise a plan, a deep, thunderous sound reverberated through the space, causing their bodies to ripple between realities. A deafening blast had been unleashed from a towering spire within the queen's domain, signalling an urgent summons to all inhabitants.

'The sacred horn of protection? It's been ages since we last heard it…' Mareen murmured, his gaze fixed on the distant azure depths. 'I'm afraid we've run out of time.'

'We need to warn the others, we must!' Aura declared urgently, her body blending seamlessly with her surroundings, leaving a trail of white in her wake.

'My love, please be careful!' Mareen's words fell on deaf ears as Aura disappeared from sight in an instant.

For millennia, they had existed in a state of perpetual peace and patient waiting, but now time was of the essence. With a rush of determination and dread, Aura propelled herself to the surface, emerging beside the tiny island at the heart of the sea. Drawing upon the raw elements of the earth, her limbs formed swiftly. Gazing skyward, she sought the divine presence of the God, hoping for guidance in a time of danger. Yet, to her dismay, Time remained elusive. A dense, grey fog shrouded the landscape, obscuring the midlands from view. Queen Eah had deployed the final line of defence to shield their world from danger, but the enemy had already infiltrated their ranks.

Granted an unusual and prolonged audience, Lëogan stood in silence beside the queen, her face stern, her crown aglow with crimson light. As Eah paced the chamber, torn between hesitation and resolve, the empty throne awaited her touch. Visibly challenged, she debated whether to remain indoors or join the other Aqualymphs who were rapidly gathering outside. At the second blast of the horn, she swiftly exited, conjuring a transparent bubble behind her with a deft gesture. Lëogan's carriage awaited him, ready to carry him across the sea safely.

As Eah passed through the towering red doors, a hushed murmur rippled through the depths. Many questioned why the horn had been sounded, what the meaning of the stranger's presence beside their queen was, his feet hovering above the dank ground within the ethereal bubble. 'Who is he?' some whispered. 'Why would our queen be in the company of a Human?'

'Silence!' Eah's voice thundered, its depth reverberating across the waters. 'My dear Aqualymphs, we face a grave threat looming beyond our borders. Dark magic seeps from the northwest, creeping down from the Cloudy Mountains into Leonty's territory. It seems they are making no effort to resist it. Their very essence resonates with an unrelenting evil, fuelling its advance and jeopardizing our hopes for peace. We pledged to our God to safeguard the passage and our world. We must act, now!'

'This is not our concern,' an Aqualymph objected.

'The Humans will handle it; isn't this the reason they erected walls around their lands?' another chimed in. In the midst of the crowd, Aura reappeared, darting among them, attempting to draw closer to the queen.

'Lymphs, my dear brethren,' Eah's voice rang out above the murmurs. 'We cannot rely on Humans alone to face this dire threat... We are all keepers of this world; we must defend our friends and allies.'

'Why do you speak of allies and defence?' Aura challenged, her fists clenched, her dissent plain on her face. 'We are bound to the waters. We swore to Time we would never abandon our home and our realm. Our place is here, between Runae and the worlds beyond the node!'

'Do not venture in a false sense of entitlement, Aqualymph…' Eah's gaze narrowed, her tone stern. Beside her, the stranger's lips moved slowly, a fleeting grin crossing his face. 'You have long held the mantle of Gatekeeper. You have long believed it's your duty to safeguard us all. Remember whom you address! Why do you suppose our God bestowed upon us the power of the Flare? Why would we need to endure beyond the sacred waters if not for this very purpose?'

'The Flare was given to us for one purpose alone: to survive on the surface as we watch over the passage on the island,' Aura retorted, her fury mounting. At last, she was certain Queen Eah had been deceived.

'Quiet!' the sovereign snapped, her hand outstretched, a whirling thread darting towards the defiant Aqualymph. Before its power could reach Aura, Mareen materialized next to her, his arm intercepting the punitive spell, causing him to flinch in pain. A vast chasm formed around the two Aqualymphs. Horrified by the queen's actions, the gathering quickly dispersed, leaving a palpable silence in their wake.

'I see…' Eah continued, her tone unwavering. 'Does anyone else wish to voice their dissent?' But an abrupt hush had settled over the assembly. 'Very well. Prepare for battle.

We depart from our lands at the rise of Erion.' After a brief pause, the queen whispered to an Aqualymph standing resolute by her side, 'Take them away. This may be their final act of rebellion. To the Avalian Deep!' Her last words rang out, eliciting a collective gasp from the assembled crowd.

Four large Aqualymphs moved towards Aura and Mareen, swiftly trapping their wrists in shimmering green ligaments. Bound by the chains of magic, their bodies were rendered immobile. Dragged away from the mass, they were escorted to the eastern side of the queen's keep, where eternal captivity awaited them. With terror in their eyes, Aura and Mareen exchanged a knowing glance. They understood the fate that awaited them beyond the sovereign's abode. Towering above the crimson spikes and rocky foundations, a profound abyss lay gaping. Its depths, shrouded in mystery even to the Gods, symbolized eternal oblivion.

'No, stop!' Mareen cried out as they neared the edge of the threatening void.

'Brothers, this is madness,' Aura pleaded, her voice tinged with desperation. 'Consider this carefully. When was the last time we condemned one of our own to death? When did we ever impose the Judgment of the Silent Sea?'

'It is the queen's decree. You know this, Aura,' one of the four Aqualymphs retorted.

'Corhal, hold on...' another interjected, his determination faltering under the weight of doubt. 'This feels wrong. There's no coming back from the Avalian Deep. If this is a mistake, we cannot undo it…'

'Listen to Thalamea, brother,' Mareen urged. 'First the sounding of the sacred horn, then the call to war, and now this? Aqualymphs fighting against each other?'

As if Mareen's words had pierced the guards' veil of certainty, the magical restraints around their wrists faltered, their luminous glow dimming suddenly. Sensing an opportunity amidst the confusion and fearing they might not persuade the four Aqualymphs to defy the queen's order, Mareen acted swiftly. With his arms spread wide, he broke the spell and swung his hands across the water, freeing Aura from her confinement.

'Go now,' he urged. 'Warn those in the midlands!'

As Corhal quickly returned to his duty, his arms danced through the water, conjuring whirlpools aimed directly at Aura. Mareen, his mind clouded with confusion, shoved Thalamea aside with urgency. With two more guards closing in, Mareen tapped into the depths of his magic, morphing from one form to another, creating shimmering spheres of power that encased them in a protective barrier.

But Aura, unwilling to stand on the sidelines as her beloved battled alone, surged forward, her movements a blur of grace and determination. With a flick of her wrist, bolts of energy crackled through the water, colliding with the approaching guards, sending them reeling backward.

As the clash intensified, Mareen's transformations grew more intricate, each shift accompanied by bursts of arcane energy that illuminated the depths. Aura, her resolve unwavering, unleashed torrents of power, the currents swirling around her in a dazzling display of elemental mastery. The underwater skirmish raged on, a symphony of magic and might echoing through the depths. With every twist and turn, the combatants pushed themselves to the brink, their fates entwined in the swirling currents of battle.

Flashes of light danced through the dense waters, striking Corhal and the other guards, momentarily stunning them. Despite their mastery, Aura and Mareen had erroneously counted on Thalamea's hesitance to join the battle, allowing him to slip from their attention. Moved by a renewed sense of duty as a queen's guard once more, he banished his doubts and, with a swift motion of his right hand, caught Mareen off guard, unleashing his magic directly at his neck. A bright green rope materialized around Mareen's shoulders, squeezing tightly around his throat, rendering him inert. Unable to shift shape once more, Mareen lost his balance, his gaze locked on Aura as he plummeted into the deadly abyss.

For a brief moment, they all stood frozen, Aura's eyes fixed on the spot where her beloved had stood, shock gripping her.

'I didn't mean it, Aura. I swear!' Thalamea cried out. 'I was only trying to stop him...' As his words reached her, Corhal and the other guards closed in on the startled Aqualymph.

Within her fractured soul, an overwhelming rage and sorrow surged forth. The sour taste of desperation and loss spread rampant. With each beat of her heart, her anger raced at the speed of her growing power. Her eyes blazed with an intense fire as her arms shot outwards, fingers splayed wide as if to grasp hold of the very fabric of reality itself.

In a blaze of brilliant light, a torrent of energy erupted from her outstretched hands, engulfing the guards in its searing embrace. The waters shone bright as the blast rapidly spread, tearing through the space unchallenged. The guards, caught in the maelstrom of Aura's wrath, were torn asunder by the sheer power of her vengeance, their forms disintegrating into countless droplets that swiftly merged and vanished within the azure depths.

With a heavy heart and her mind echoing with pain, she dissolved into the water, swiftly swimming towards the towering spire in the keep. If Mareen intended to warn the people of the midlands, she would follow him in death by carrying out his command. Unseen by the countless eyes within the queen's home, Aura navigated through the rooms and up the winding staircase. To her surprise, no one patrolled the ascent. As she breached the rocky doors, they sealed shut behind her, revealing a figure standing within the small space. His white hair and beard contrasted starkly against the large, purple horn beside him, their gleam accentuated by the dim light of the chamber. A wicked smile played across his lips as he greeted her, his grip firm on the sacred tool.

'I see you resist not only my magic,' he spoke.

'And I see the queen has granted you full access in her keep… Who are you?'

'You know my name, don't you?' Lëogan countered, his hand softly brushing the edge of his protective bubble, as if inspecting its strength carefully.

'What are you? How can you turn our queen's magic against her own kind?' Aura refused to yield. There was no time to play her enemy's game. She needed answers promptly.

'Strange powers are at play in this world…the Humans of Earth possess none of their own. They are merely…sophisticated animals. How is it that you wield all this magic?'

'I have no time to indulge you with tales from our world. Tell me, who are you?'

'I'm finding it strangely difficult to read you. Please, explain it to me. Is this a peculiarity of your kind or just yours? Never mind, give me time and I'll know which levers to pull…'

'Why have you come here?' Aura demanded.

'You see…it's hard to trick someone who can see ahead… Our enemy on Earth is weak, predictable. You pull one or two strings, you kill one or two Humans, and you can be sure he will present himself to us, right in our hands. A foolish God moved by Humans' foolish emotions. Yours, on the other hand, is more, well, pondered. Our advance from within your lands has been slower than my master required. So, to answer your question, I'm here to…speed things up,' Lëogan explained, a sinister grin spreading across his face as his figure slowly grew larger and darker. It was as if he had brought a second stranger into their lands, a wicked presence looming within his power.

'Whatever you or your master are planning to do, you won't succeed!' Aura exclaimed defiantly. 'Tell me, do you know what fate befalls creatures who are not Aqualymphs when they lack our protection? Show me who you are!' Aura's hands surged forward, her power seizing the very essence of Lëogan's protective bubble, tearing it asunder. With a snap of her fingers, the shield dissolved, leaving the stranger grappling against the oppressive weight of the sea.

To her surprise, Lëogan's form resisted, his silhouette contorting into a dark, grey shadow. His limbs stretched, his visage twisted into a mask of pure despair. Before Aura could launch another assault, the spectre vanished, leaving behind a cloying scent of deceit.

Alone in the dim chamber, she approached the horn, her heart hammering in her chest, her mind echoing with Mareen's final words. With all her strength, she pressed her lips to the reed, unleashing a colossal wave across the sea. Mighty ripples surged towards the surface, multiplying with each passing moment, until they intensified into a deafening, earth-shaking roar as they met the warm air. From the nearby coast to the distant Garughals Forest, down to the realm of the crown, a chilling warning echoed across the land.

# Chapter Five

## *Of Love and War*

∞

Seeking refuge, Aura concealed herself behind massive, submerged rocks along the sea's edge. The bright blue waters stretched endlessly, the towering cliffs at her back merging with the land to the southeast. Remaining perfectly still, she blended into her surroundings, her presence all but invisible. In the distance, a flurry of activity signalled the imminent departure of the queen and her brethren. Despite the impending march to the west, Aura held her ground, pondering her next move. She found it inconceivable that the Flare could sustain them beyond the safety of the sea. The prospect of enduring the arduous journey into the midlands, far removed from their natural habitat, filled her with dread. In her eyes, the queen's decree amounted to nothing short of a death sentence for their entire kind.

As the queen's army assembled and prepared to depart, bolstered by their sovereign's unwavering authority and Lëogan's insidious magic, the sea emptied of all but memories. With her mind consumed by Mareen's fate, Aura raced towards the precipice of the abyss. There, she unleashed a desperate cry, her voice echoing into the depths of the Avalian Deep, swallowed by the void below. Amidst her anguish, a glimmer of hope flickered—a faint sparkle in the depth below, teasing her senses.

'Mareen? Please...' she implored, her words swallowed by the vast emptiness. 'I'll find a way to rescue you, I swear it! Even if I must plead with the Gods themselves.' The weak light flashed against the dark void three times, a new, unknown magic struggling to emerge. 'Hold on, my love. Please, don't despair. I'll return to free you.' Yet, the desperation she felt was not his—it was hers.

Seeking help from the only ones she could trust, Aura emerged from the sea through the thunderous cascade at the eastern cliff, entering the Gochi River. Amidst the seven hills, where the stream curved towards the Garughals' lands, she surfaced. Unable to discern the shielded Chomps, Aura lingered on the riverbank, yearning for help. Suddenly, a female Chomp materialized before her, suspended in the air by delicate wings. It was as if she had appeared out of thin air, her rounded face flushed red, her chunky hands clutching two large baskets. Startled by

Aura's sudden presence, she let out a yelp and dropped her goods on the ground.

'Don't be afraid, Chomp. I'm Aura, a creature of the sea. I'm looking for Kasthor. It's essential that I speak with him,' Aura assured, her voice carrying a sense of urgency.

The Chomp swiftly gathered the scattered items, her eyes reflecting curiosity mixed with caution. 'You've travelled far from your home. Aren't you bound to the waters?' she inquired, her hands deftly collecting the fallen goods.

'I am indeed. I can't venture further inland. If I follow the stream ahead, it would lead me too far from your home. I hoped to find your kind here, but sadly, my eyes fail to discern your village. Please, find Kasthor and bring him to me. It's of utmost importance,' Aura implored.

'Is this related to the great roar we heard? It echoed even within our dome,' the Chomp queried, a hint of concern in her voice.

'Yes, it was my doing. I wish I could explain further, but time is of the essence. Please, hurry!' Aura pressed, a sense of imminent danger creeping into her words.

Without another word, the Chomp darted away, disappearing beyond an invisible barrier. Aura knew she had little time left. Uncertain if the Chomps could aid her, she had turned to them for their renowned kindness and their proximity to the sea. If they failed to assist, her only recourse would be to journey to the distant Garughals' land. But dwelling on future possibilities served no purpose now; she had to act swiftly, before her queen's folly became irreversible.

As the sun began its ascent, three Chomps emerged from their protective dome. Aura, on the verge of abandoning hope and heading north, paused as Kasthor's voice echoed through the clearing.

'Are you still here, Aqualymph?' Kasthor called out, his eyes straining to discern her transparent form.

'She was here, by the dock… Her name is Aura, I believe,' another Chomp chimed in, approaching the spot where they had met the night before. Beside the two stood a third, smaller Chomp, silent and observant.

'I'm here,' Aura announced, her form slowly solidifying. Green tendrils snaked up her limbs as her body absorbed the earth's essence, her features taking on hues of deep brown. 'I was about to head upstream to seek aid from the Garughals.'

'There's no need,' Kasthor interjected, drawing closer. Unlike his companion's earlier reaction, his response to the Aqualymph's presence was more composed. He was well acquainted with her kind. 'This is Treekan, my son. He's never seen an Aqualymph before...'

'Kasthor, please, there's no time for introductions,' Aura urged, her gaze fixed on the western hills.

'There's always little time these days… If only the people of Runae were more like us, embracing peace and tranquillity,' Kasthor lamented. 'But I digress. I've just returned from a meeting with Garúth in the Garughals' realm. They won't help you. They won't help anyone...'

'If they knew the queen's intentions, they might reconsider,' Aura insisted, quickly outlining the impending threat.

'Queen Eah? What is she planning?' Kasthor's gaze bored into Aura with a mix of concern and scepticism. Under their sovereign's guidance, the Aqualymphs had become  as reclusive as the Chomps, wary of the world beyond their watery sanctuary.

'King Lohan asked for our aid in a war against the Leonty. He claims they pose a grave threat to our world. My people have forsaken the safety of the sacred waters and now venture into the perilous midlands,' Aura explained, holding Kasthor's attention captive. After a brief silence, he stepped closer to her.

'If your words are true, our choices are few. We may convene the council, but it's doubtful it will prevent any conflict,' Kasthor murmured, his voice heavy with concern. 'Who's going to oppose the two sovereigns' decision?

'Father, can't we ask Time to intervene?' Treekan interjected.

'It seems our only option,' the third Chomp added solemnly. 'If your queen can walk on land, wielding such formidable power, what can we do to stop her? We can only remain within our protective dome.'

As she understood the gravity of the situation, Aura's expression darkened. 'You may still be able to help. Speak to Vasheer. I cannot reach the Valahans alone; there's no water route to their kingdom…'

'I just met Vasheer. He accompanied me on my visit to the Garughals,' Kasthor divulged, drawing Aura's attention.

'Why did you meet with them?' Aura inquired, her curiosity piqued. The sacred horn had been sounded only recently, indicating that any interaction with the Garughals must have been for another significant reason.

'Because of our Flares.' Kasthor's tone grew hushed as he gestured for Aura to step away from the other two Chomps. Whatever he was about to reveal, it seemed meant for her ears alone. 'Something is happening to the stones. They emit a different glow now. The nights grow brighter because of their flames. Whatever is causing this change, it's rising...'

'You suspect Time is granting them greater power? To confront the emerging threat from the Cloudy Mountains?' Aura's gaze shifted eastward, as though she could see beyond the countless miles ahead, yearning for more information.

'That's precisely what Vasheer implied. He spoke of whispers echoing from the mountain peaks, slithering through rocks and soil, seeping into the surrounding lands. Someone is calling out from within their summit.'

'This provides yet another reason to act swiftly. We must understand the cause behind these developments. I will approach Garúth and request the use of the Beacon of Fire.'

'He will never consent,' Kasthor cautioned. 'You underestimate the Garughals' transformation since obtaining that power. Their minds merge more deeply with the earth each rhoc, their hearts growing as cold as stone.

Nevertheless, my son and I will set out immediately to share your information with the Valahans.'

'Thank you, Kasthor,' Aura whispered, placing a reassuring hand on his shoulder. Though a fleeting smile touched her lips, fear and sorrow still overshadowed any glimmer of hope. 'Take the Path of the Hundred Lakes, avoiding the King's Road. Evil lurks in the outskirts, especially now with the crown's army vacating the city. You never know what savagery it may unleash.'

With a final warning, Aura disappeared into the frigid river, her resolve steady despite the looming darkness ahead.

Venturing to the far west, just as the giant red Erion vanished beyond the Mogs Mountains, the Aqualymphs entered the Humans' kingdom. Emerging from the sacred waters, they penetrated the lands under the shield of their Flare. In the heart of the kingdom, the citadel stood as a beacon of power and authority, its walls looming tall and formidable against the backdrop of a darkening sky. Within its confines, the air crackled with anticipation and tension as soldiers, clad in armour and bearing weapons, gathered in the great hall.

Torches flickered against stone walls adorned with ancient banners, their colours faded but their symbols still carrying the weight of history. Amidst the clamour of voices and the clangour of armour, the king's presence commanded attention, his stern visage a testament to the gravity of the impending conflict. Yet, despite the looming shadow of war, there was a sense of camaraderie and revelry among the soldiers, a last moment of respite before they marched into battle.

Echoing his people's renewed sense of security, King Lohan greeted his new ally with outstretched hands and a smile. Queen Eah stood before him, a formidable force with unmatched power, the most sought-after guest in this time of need. After indulging in an evening of extravagant celebrations, the king extended an invitation for the Aqualymphs' sovereign to join him in a grand feast and libations. However, unable to sustain their forms through Human means, the queen graciously declined and led her kind to the nearby Frost Lake.

'I believe you should stay with the Humans, beside King Lohan,' she said to Lëogan before departing. 'I trust my own judgment and power to guide me to success. Unfortunately, I can't say the same about the king. Please, lead him to…wise decisions.'

'So I shall,' he promptly replied. Staying behind with those easily swayed by deceitful words was what he was truly after.

Tables groaned under the weight of hearty feasts and barrels of ale, and the air was thick with the scent of roasted meat and smoke. Amidst the noise, the king's voice struggled to travel the short distance between him and the queen's counsellor.

'So tell me, do you indulge in Human pleasures and revels, or are you like those Aqualymphs, staying apart and subsisting solely on pure water?' Despite their newfound alliance, a lingering contempt tainted his voice.

'I do, but my mind is preoccupied with the threat we are facing… Thank you,' Lëogan replied, stretching his hand to accept a golden cup filled with a purple liquid from Romohan's hand.

'There are serious reasons to be worried, but not now. This is the grand feast before the war. Celebrate with me, my friend.'

'A wise king like you knows that celebrations are more appropriate once the threat is eliminated. What is your strategy? I can tell you, in my world, the enemy has spread rapidly and corrupted the souls of every living being.'

'The Leonty possess unimaginable magic…' Romohan interjected, his eyes filled with rage and alcohol as he sat beside his father. 'Their females, they are the worst! They have the power of the mind. They can enter your head just by looking at you, make you do things, or even kill you if they wish.'

'Have they? Have they already done that?' Lëogan inquired.

'I'm sure they have. Not to us. We have walls protecting our people, shielding us from their power.' Romohan's voice grew low, almost like a whisper, amidst the loud music and the voices of many celebrating. 'Time's Flare is giving us the knowledge we need to push them away. We have discovered and developed this secret technology that can emit invisible waves capable of bringing flesh and soul to their demise.'

'Incredible!' the other replied, his eyes narrowing to two black, sinister lines. 'I'm sure you can use it wisely to bring the enemy to its knees.'

'The device is too large to be carried around,' the king explained. 'These…scientists, as they call themselves nowadays, say we can't move it. The machine was built inside the Great Chapel, not far from here, in the heart of the city.'

'Incredible, indeed… Incredible,' Lëogan repeated. 'With the right action and at the right time, I'm sure you will be victorious.'

'You should stay here, with us, by my side. I think you would be a great Aver,' King Lohan said, smiling.

'The ones who delivers my father's command...' Romohan added, noticing a doubtful expression had appeared on the stranger's face.

'Romohan, did you share our plans with the General of the Guards?' The king asked, punctuating his question with a loud burp. 'We need to ensure his division is ready to attack from the Farohals while we proceed from the front, through the hills.'

'I have, Father. Kareesto insisted we should avoid the Whispering Forest. If I didn't know better, I'd say he is afraid of the magic that runs through those woods.'

'Witches and false prophets!' his father exclaimed, his fist pounding on the wooden table. 'We should have exterminated those wicked Humans. If it wasn't for your mother…' King Lohan's voice trailed off, his drunken expression tinged with regret as he averted his gaze.

'Don't worry,' Romohan interjected, his voice steady. 'I've already told him that this is the only way we will free those lands from evil.'

In the eyes of the Humans, the plan of action was flawless. They would attack the Leonty from two fronts, and a third force would descend from the Mogs Pass, with the Aqualymphs moving unopposed by the Valahans, right down to the steppes. However, unbeknownst to their bloodthirsty minds, their most trusted general was engaging in a clandestine conversation with the very enemy.

Inside an ancient house nestled within the northern outskirts of the city, where the wild revelry of celebration faded into a hushed whisper, Kareesto sought solace in the embrace of his beloved, Vertatis. Illuminated by the soft glow of a solitary candle, her mystical beauty seemed to radiate with an ethereal luminescence, her captivating ruby eyes mirroring the inner turmoil that consumed them both.

As they lay side by side upon a weathered, crooked bed, Kareesto's touch traced gently along Vertatis's green skin. The wooden door and windows stood firmly shut, enclosing their intimate haven and safeguarding the dangerous secret they shared. In the flickering candlelight, passion and desire intertwined with every movement, their bodies drawn together by an irresistible force.

Amidst the impending dawn of war between their disparate worlds, their hearts beat in unison against the turbulent tide of fate. Yet, beneath the veil of their forbidden embrace, a palpable sense of urgency lingered in the air, casting a shadow over their fleeting moments of comfort.

'You need to leave the city now,' Kareesto whispered urgently, his grip tightening around Vertatis's arm as he imparted his dire warning. Passion, love, and fear mixed as he stood up.

'Come with me…' Her hands moved over his bronzed skin, tenderly caressing his face. His emerald eyes mirrored the shade of her own skin as he gazed at her, his emotions clouding his vision.

'I am the Great General, Vertatis. I have twenty thousand men relying on me to lead them into war… A war against your people. How can I escape such a dire fate?'

'We can flee from our worlds, together. Leave behind our families, our homelands. Seek refuge where they cannot find us.' Vertatis hurriedly dressed herself, her movements fraught with urgency.

'They, you mean my king and your fearcel?'

The soft desperation in the Leonty's eyes transformed into displeasure at the mention of the latter. 'My jailer, you mean. The one I despise above all else. In this impending war, he is the one who truly deserves to face its consequences.'

'Listen to me…' Kareesto grasped her shoulders firmly, locking eyes with hers. 'My soldiers and I will advance through the Whispering Forest. The witches may attempt to halt our progress… I have no intention of resisting them. If my army succumbs to their enchantments, it may provide us with an opportunity to halt this war…'

'But you said the king will march through the northern gates while Queen Eah descends from the Mogs Pass…' Vertatis queried as they made their way towards the door. With a sweeping motion of his arm, Kareesto concealed her features beneath the shelter of his ample cloak. 'We knew this day would come,' she murmured, her words heavy with resignation. 'There is no escaping.'

'My dear, please. You must return home and do as I have asked…even if it means returning to the one you despise the most.' He sighed as they vanished into the dark fields of the outskirts, their forms blending seamlessly with the shadows, unseen by prying eyes.

'While he'll watch my every step, exploiting my power for his own gain. Don't you see? It's individuals like him who stoke the hatred of your people towards us. I refuse to go back to him, only to be used as a pawn in your people's war.'

'Vertatis, look into my mind. You can see that I speak the truth. Please, hurry and warn your sisters. Tell them to seek refuge near the temples. The king has vowed to spare those structures, deeming them sacred to the Gods. Run and hide. If our love is destined to endure this trial, we will find our way back to one another.' After casting furtive glances to the left and right, Kareesto forced open a heavy door nestled within the northern walls. With a final, desperate look, Vertatis moved away, poised to flee.

'Kareesto, I came here for a reason far more important than us,' Vertatis said, her voice barely above a whisper, her eyes searching his for understanding. 'There's something you need to know…'

Caught off guard by the solemn tone of her voice, Kareesto's brows furrowed in concern. 'What is it?'

'Promise me you'll come back to me. You have to come back to me,' Vertatis implored, her voice trembling with urgency. 'We are bound together by far more than desire now. This love is not just the beating of two hearts any more. There are three of us now.'

Confusion clouded Kareesto's expression as he tried to make sense of her words. Before he could respond, Vertatis turned around and disappeared over the large gates, a final red flash appearing in her eyes. Kareesto stood there, stunned, as the weight of her revelation settled heavily upon him. With a troubled heart and a confused mind, he walked back to the camp where a multitude of soldiers were chatting loudly, their anticipation for the rising of a bloody star palpable in the air.

# Chapter Six

## The Enemy's Whisper

∞

In the early morning of the marching day, the crown city bustled with activity as soldiers prepared for battle. Kareesto, at the head of the largest group, cast a lingering gaze towards the far northern gates, his thoughts consumed by the recent escape of the enemy through those very doors, undetected.

Meanwhile, within the heart of the city, an air of tension hung over the palace as the king's delayed arrival raised eyebrows among his soldiers. Romohan paced impatiently, his anticipation mounting with each passing moment. Beside him, Lëogan observed the scene in stoic silence, his mind undoubtedly pondering the implications of the king's tardiness.

Deep within the large palace's labyrinthine corridors, concealed within layers of walls, a clandestine meeting unfolded in a secluded room. King Lohan entered, flanked by two trusted advisors, followed by a regal figure whose demeanour bespoke irritation at the abrupt summons.

Inside the chamber, shelves groaned under the weight of ancient tomes, their weathered pages a testament to the countless hocs spent in research by the assembled scholars. As King Lohan approached one of the tables, his hand tracing the lines of an open book, the gravity of the moment hung heavy in the air, foreshadowing the fateful decisions that lay ahead.

'So the entire collection of the Radhal Daíuh is powerless in the face of our needs... All these centuries amassing knowledge, to what end? To collect dust?' King Lohan's voice echoed with frustration, his gaze sweeping over the ancient tomes that lined the shelves.

'My king, we have been recording the witches' prophecies as closely as we could... But since you have cast them away, we have lost access to their most recent visions. If we had...'

'You know well the reason why they were exiled in the Whispering Forest,' the king interrupted sharply, his eyes flashing with irritation.

'The same reason why you need them now, my lord...' the other replied, unafraid to challenge the king's decision.

'Perhaps our beloved Queen Shahara still has access to their magic?'

'Watch your words, priest!' the queen's voice sliced through the tension in the room. 'Is this why you brought me here? To hear about your end? The end of our kingdom?' With a pointed glance, she signed for the men to leave.

Alone with his consort, King Lohan faced her squarely. 'I've listened to your words many times,' he began, his tone tinged with defiance. 'Even after you confessed your origins, I kept my promise as your fearcel. And yet your words remain the same…'

'And they won't change only because you are scared,' the queen replied, closing the door firmly behind her.

'You told me if we had a son, this would not happen.' His voice softened a little, betraying a hint of vulnerability.

'Yes, it's what I told you, many times.' Her patience wore thin. 'I saw the kingdom in ruins. The throne empty. A threat surging from the temples. One of them, a female of their kind with green skin and red eyes, was going to bring us to our end.'

'And a son would change that…that's what you suggested,' the king pressed, his doubts evident.

'I told you everything I saw. With the rise of this threat, there is also hope.' And her hands took his. 'A man is sitting on your throne. Dark hair, eyes bringing the blue of the sea and the green of our lands together… He's going to rule the whole of Runae through peace and love. I can still see him in my mind. Many allies accompany him. Even the Chomps are by his side.' Shahara's voice wavered with emotion.

'And you are certain that is Romohan you saw?' King Lohan's scepticism lingered in the air. Their son looked nothing like the man she had described.

'I saw one of us. It could be Romohan's son, for all we know. I asked you to keep my people in the city so I could look for more details... But you cast them away, too preoccupied with the legitimacy of your bloodline.'

'Rightfully so! If the truth had come out... If it comes out...' King Lohan's voice thundered with suppressed anger as he took his hands away from hers.

'There was no other way. You could not produce an heir... What else could we do to make sure what I saw would actually happen? As long as you had no son of your own, it was clear that the omen was to be believed...' Her words cut through the tension like a knife.

'For our sake, I hope you were right, Shahara.' With a heavy heart, the king turned and left the room, his footsteps echoing down the corridors of the Radhal Daíuh.

No long after, Lohan stormed out of the palace and walked next to his son. As if he carried too many thoughts and worries to be able to express them all, he murmured something incomprehensible to those who stood by. A shining, golden item flickered in his hand as he moved closer to Lëogan.

'There. It's official now. Not that it'd really matter in a time like this, but you are one of us now. Stay by my side and be victorious.' Without adding anything else, the king pressed the golden pin against Lëogan's chest. The usual pompous formality of investing someone as the Aver had been forgotten. The small crown, symbolizing the bearer of the king's word, shone briefly as Lëogan gazed at it. There, right where a Human's heart would be, the malevolent void he carried instead was endowed with new power.

With almost half of the army marching north, by the time Erion rose in the purple sky, the king and Romohan had reached the gorge in between the Mogs Mountains, their walk fast, their hearts filled with rage. Their heels pierced the hot ground, heel to toe in quick succession; the bitter sound of war accompanied them.

Lëogan stared at the towering peaks of the mountains, envisioning the Aqualymphs darting through the rugged highlands, threading a path between the imposing rocky walls. In the depths of his mind, a labyrinth of schemes and ambitions unfurled, a maze of machinations yet to be realized before he could return triumphant to his master. For where Runae's God had ventured remained a mystery. If indeed he had returned to safeguard his beloved realm, there would be no power Lëogan could wield to oppose him.

'You seem troubled,' King Lohan remarked, perched atop a majestic lion-like creature, its strong limbs and robust frame carrying the weight of the regal burden without falter.

'Let me share a tale with you,' Lëogan replied, a sly smile dancing on his lips. 'The world from which I come from, though vaster in scale, is younger than yours. Teeming with life of every type, it also harbours an evil so dark that it eclipses even your own. My master has waged a tireless battle against the encroaching enemy, yet they persist— resilient, indomitable. There is a truth, a revelation, that may disturb you,' he continued, his voice lowering to a sombre pitch, shadows swirling within his eyes.

'As a king, my friend, the only disruption to my peace is the peril my people face daily at the hands of the Leonty. Speak plainly; I must know,' King Lohan demanded.

'Very well,' Lëogan pressed on. 'Their magic emanates from a singular source… Reflect on it, and perhaps it will not surprise you. There is a reason why you, the most deserving, were not bestowed with extraordinary gifts by your God. Instead, He endowed others with magic—the same magic that festers at the fringes of your domain, a malevolent blight poised at your doorstep like a creeping disease.'

'If you imply Time is behind this, you are mistaken,' Romohan interjected, drawing a reproachful glance from his father.

'We came to this bitter realization too late. That is why I fled to seek help here. Little did I know you hosted a deity of your own—here, condemning you to a fate akin to our own miserable end.'

'What happened to your world?' Romohan inquired, his scepticism tamed by the strands of Lëogan's dark sorcery.

'The restless threat of greed, power, the craving of conquering every corner of the universe came to us, to devour under the pressing violence of making. Many of us were sent to put an end to it, but those Gods—those sworn guardians who pledged protection—proved to be the architects of our downfall. They are the creators of this calamity, and they will not rest until we have annihilated each other, until our very essence is extinguished. How else do you think the evil infiltrated your realm?' Lëogan posed the question with a chilling certainty.

'Unless Time allowed it,' King Lohan interjected, realization dawning. 'I suspected he had other motives when we demanded fair treatment. He dismissed our requests, our pleas…'

'Because, deep down, he knew you would uncover the truth in due course. He dared not grant you power that could be turned against him, could he?' Lëogan's hand brushed against Lohan's arm, infusing his enchantment deep into the king's flesh. Gifted with the dark power from the greatest evil, Lëogan fulfilled his nature as a Harpy, once again called to carry out the deeds of a more terrifying master. With his influence fully unleashed, his grand design began to unfold. Just as he had wrought havoc upon Earth for centuries, he now wielded his sorcery again, ensnaring minds to serve his insidious will.

With no further inquiries reaching his malevolent ears, Lëogan once more fixed his gaze upon the distant peaks of the mountains. His thoughts were consumed by the meticulous planning of his next move, a cunning grin creeping across his face as he envisioned Queen Eah's impending entrance into the Valahans' domain. Meanwhile, dozens of miles away, the queen and her Aqualymphs glided along the narrow road carved into the mountainside, their movements soundless, their forms invisible. They traversed like spectres, their sights set on what lay ahead.

Contrary to her soldiers' expectations, Queen Eah steered her course towards the residents' domain, diverging from the path leading to the temples as they reached the turn of the Mogs Pass. 'My queen, why do we venture into the caves? The road to the temples lies that way...' an Aqualymph questioned, materializing beside her. She remained silent for a brief moment before her gaze drifted towards the multitude of caves dotting the ridge.

'There is something I must attend to first. Follow me. And keep your voices hushed. The Valahans are not known for their hospitality.'

The unseen army infiltrated the stony realm with stealth, leaving no trace of their passage. Their progress remained unimpeded as if they glided like a gentle breeze over the sea. At the culmination of the lengthy path, their advance came to a halt before a colossal wall crafted from rock and metal. Embedded within its surface, countless iron fragments shimmered like a vast, sparkling ocean, their enchantments stirring at the presence of Queen Eah. Before her scrutinizing gaze, a sequence of cryptic words materialized, each letter aglow as if infused with life by the touch of the towering Erion.

'*Valahans vhosn atun vrath,*' the queen whispered softly as she deciphered the welcoming riddle. '*May the stone protect all Valahans. May the key grant its master the wished passage...*'

'Why must we offer anything to those who are not our equals?' an Aqualymph questioned, shifting between air and grey dust as his form coalesced beside the wall.

'What key?' chimed in another.

'The Valahans are our equals, Ahoester,' the sovereign replied, casting a brief glance at the one whose arrogance had momentarily overshadowed reason. 'Though their means may lack ethereal power, their hearts and minds are as weighty and solid as the stones they are so in love with. To them, material holds the only true value. Yet, I do not see this as a flaw…' She drew nearer to the mystical words, inspecting them closely.

Moments later, her form radiated with a brilliant light. Within her grasp, the Flare of the Sea gleamed with intense sapphire luminescence, its core fluid, its edges undulating like waves crashing upon each other. As Queen Eah approached the wall, she declared, 'Behold the Anún Déil, the Flare of the Sea, presented to all Valahans as a testament to its wielder. Grant us entry!'

At her words, the sturdy rocky barrier began to shift, its surface gradually turning white before dissolving entirely after a pair of luminous pulses. A colossal opening stretched before the Aqualymphs, the path descending into the depths of the Mogs, its end vanishing into the unknown. Beyond the range of the queen's formidable sight, a speck on the distance approached, soon joined by another. Initially appearing as two identical Valahans, both sons of Vasheer emerged to welcome their guest.

'Queen Eah, here, in the depths of the mountains?' Varuk exclaimed, his shock palpable.

'How?' his brother hastily added, both momentarily forgetting the customary courtesy extended to guests. Caught between surprise and reluctance to entertain visitors in their abode, the brothers exhibited the notorious rudeness characteristic of their kind.

'Varuk, Voishan, I must speak with your father. I am not here to linger. Our journey has one destination only—the Leonty's land. However, it is imperative that I talk to him before taking action against an adversary I wish not to confront.'

'I see…' Varuk conceded. 'There is no greater reason for granting you entry then. But,' the Valahan continued, raising his hands in a resolute gesture before the regal Aqualymph, 'only you.'

'Is this hairy creature daring to challenge our advance?' one of the Aqualymphs beside the queen interjected. 'Do you realize who you're speaking to?'

'Silence!' Queen Eah exclaimed sharply. 'You will heed the directives of those kind enough to welcome me into their home.' She regarded the insubordinate soldier with suspicion, sensing a subtle shift in the collective wills and hearts of the purest beings on Runae, as if a silent transformation had begun. Aura's warning words echoed in her mind once more. *Am I responsible for this change in them all?* she wondered.

After a brief shake of her head, she turned to Varuk and took his hand. Together, they embarked on a descent into a realm vastly different from the serene depths she was accustomed to—a realm where the tranquil blue waters were supplanted by the furious flames of the mines, where the calming blue hues shifted to searing reds, and where the fluid landscape transformed into a suffocating, rigid prison of stone and metal.

The long road ahead branched into smaller paths that wound in every direction, creating a labyrinth of caves and turns, dark alleys, and flickering passages. Soon, the trio arrived at a vast opening. An enormous, flat courtyard hung in the hot air, enclosed by two bridges made of black stone—the embrace of the mountain in its colossal arms. Below, streams of lava boiled with raging heat, releasing fumes and steams that rose all the way to the walkways.

A multitude of Valahans bustled about the courtyard, their minds and hands absorbed in the tasks they loved. Many pairs of eyes followed the two brothers and their guest as they crossed one of the bridges, murmurs of surprise trailing in their wake. The presence of an Aqualymph in their domain was an unprecedented sight for them.

'Father is not home,' Varuk said as they traversed to the other side of a wide fissure, the sound of rocks breaking off the walls echoing faintly in the distance. 'He is at the cave on the west flank. Follow me...'

'It is quite reasonable, if I say so myself, to wonder when all this will find its end...' Queen Eah remarked as they turned onto a smaller road to their left. 'After all, there is only so much you can extract before the Mogs will collapse

in on themselves… Or perhaps your plan is to merge with
the very mountains, even changing your name? The
Valahan Mogs…'

'We have barely scratched the surface…' Voishan replied
with a smile, dismissing the notion. 'Here we are, this is the
west flank…'

A space twice as large as the one they had just left opened
up before them, a constellation of homes and monuments
rising from the stones and rocky walls. Their original shapes
shifted, their surfaces taking on the appearance of façades
and buildings, blending yellow, red, and grey hues into a
majestic tableau. At the centre of the colossal beauty a tall
tower spiralled from the ground to the ceiling, its peak
melding with the mountain's surface. In the heart of the
architectural marvel, an opening hosted a large stone, a
tribute to the object of the Valahans' veneration, left there
for all to admire.

'The Murán Déil…' Queen Eah let out, her gaze fixed on
the relic. 'The Stone Flare, right before my eyes…' A flicker
of uncontrollable desire danced in her heart. The precious
stone resonated with the one she carried, as if they yearned
to be reunited once more in their original form — the Flare of
the Sea pulsating within her soul.

'Father!' Varuk exclaimed, breaking Eah's reverie. 'We
were going to the caves to see you…'

'I was informed of an intruder passing through. I guess I
know who they referred to,' Vasheer remarked as he
approached his regal guest with a slow, tired stride. 'Queen
Eah… If I didn't know the difference between reality and

smoke, I'd say you were just a peculiar figment of my imagination.'

'Father,' Voishan interjected hastily. 'The queen is here to see you. It's important.'

'Indeed it is,' the Aqualymph added. 'Is there somewhere the two of us can exchange our greetings in a more...appropriate setting?' Her eyes flickered towards the Murán Déil once again. The strange attraction was swiftly turning into seduction. She needed to move away.

'Appropriate?' Vasheer chuckled. 'Follow me. The comfort of my house is the best I can offer.'

The interior of Vasheer's home looked no different from anywhere else Queen Eah had cast her gaze. From the heavy stone door to the furnishings inside, everything was carved from the very space the Valahans had claimed from the mountain. Without softening his words or manner, Vasheer gestured towards a square, uncomfortable chair beside a long table and said, 'What is it that you want to discuss?'

'It's not what I want to discuss, but rather what you have to tell me that I don't already know...' Queen Eah replied as she dusted off the hard surface before sitting down.

'How would I know what you know and don't know? Have you learned your cryptic ways from Time?' The old Valahan retrieved a small brown bottle from a shelf and poured a viscous, yellow liquid into two stone cups. 'Here, to give you strength against the heat...'

'I have to say, I'd love to breathe the fresh air of the sea right now. This place is unbearably hot. But I'm afraid your means won't do for someone like me. Anyway,' she continued, pushing the cup away, 'you are accustomed to the depths of Runae. You know the tongue stones and fire talk in their relentless movement within this world. What did they tell you?'

'You are not asking about the Mogs' thoughts. You are asking about the whispers that came here from the Cloudy Mountains…' Vasheer's eyes narrowed to thin lines.

'I am,' the queen replied, falling silent.

'Something is stirring in the high peaks of that distant land. Voices of the evil we can't see slide through the cracks, under the ground, to surface here, where our world's scars are cut open… The Murán Déil is keeping them confined, but they are indeed getting stronger, every passing rhoc.'

'What do they say?' The Aqualymph remained still, yet her ears journeyed beyond the suffocating room, outside Vasheer's home, away from the mountain. As she closed her eyes, she attuned herself to the whispers Vasheer spoke of, searching for a signal, a hint.

'They are calling for someone… It has no name, it has no face, but its hovering voice is clear. In the rustling of fire and metalwork, we can hear the same words, over and over…'

'What do they say?' Queen Eah repeated, her presence growing brighter. Her form shifted from vapour to smog and dust. Her magic resonated with the tale Vasheer spoke of, causing her to flicker.

'They say, "Come to me. The one who has the power, come to me…"'

# Chapter Seven

## *A Deadly Illusion*

∞

The long journey from the crown city had drained Vertatis's energy to the bone. Her feet were swollen, her heart pounding in her head as she reached the Temple of Wisdom. Just as she arrived, a large group of Leonty emerged from behind the lowest hill, shouting and pushing each other in fear. The news of the king's army marching towards their home had reached them swiftly, outpacing Vertatis's intention to warn her sisters. She hurried inside the first temple, seeking someone she trusted. There was more than just news of an imminent war to share; her deepest secret could only be entrusted to those she held closest. Among the towering pillars, amidst light and shadows, Vertatis ran as fast as she could, yet unable to reach her destination. Suddenly, a fellow female of their kind greeted her.

'Stop running, sister. You're already in the naos.'

'Illusiō? Why are you using your magic against me?' Vertatis asked, panting, her hands moving as if trying to dispel a foggy vision from her eyes.

'It's not against you. You were followed. He's been searching for you for two days. He must have seen you enter our lands at dawn,' Vertatis's sister replied, her eyes blazing red like fire in the darkness.

'Chiron suspects something…' Another Leonty appeared from nowhere, her body shrouded in a dark cloud. 'But your fearcel is so stupid he thinks you've been conspiring with the Humans against us all. He doesn't realize your motives are… simpler than that.'

'Don't call him that. Fearcel…he's nothing like it. He only wants my power. And stop judging my motives, Umbra. You forget I can discern if you're speaking the truth or not. I know you understand me more than you show.'

'How can you love one of them? It's beyond comprehension,' Umbra remarked, her magic dissipating into the air. The temple and its naos reappeared before their eyes as the sisters moved closer to Vertatis.

'The Humans are mobilizing against us,' Vertatis revealed. 'They're on their way. It's only a matter of hocs before they arrive!'

'We've heard. Your news is late, sister…' Umbra replied.

'What else is there?' Illusiō inquired, placing her hands on Vertatis's face, her eyes fixed on her sister's, sensing something more was about to surface.

'I'm expecting… and it's not Chiron's…' Both Illusiō and Umbra recoiled in shock, taking a few steps back.

After a moment of stunned silence, Umbra's magic surged forth, enveloping the paved ground in a grey, dense shadow. As if night had suddenly fallen, she cloaked the area in her protective magic. Underneath the concealment, the secret Vertatis had just divulged hung heavy. Loving a Human was risky enough, but bearing a child of such forbidden union was not only prohibited but also deadly.

'How many times have we told you to stop seeing him? How many times have Umbra and I warned you about how dangerous this was? Even with the looming threat of war, you continued meeting the Human…'

'If the others find out, it would be your end and the end of this…thing you are carrying,' the other one added, their voices echoing off walls of pure grey illusion, adding to the anguish of the one burdened with the dreadful affair.

'The others can't know. Please, I beg you!' Vertatis cried out.

'How will you explain it when it shows?' Illusiō pressed.

'If we even get to that point…' Umbra interjected. 'Your loved one is coming to exterminate us…'

'I'll tell them, but they can't know it's not Chiron's. I think…I can feel her. I can feel her nature. It's a she. A female who won't carry our magic because her blood is

Human…' Vertatis confessed, moving closer to Umbra and clutching her hands tightly.

'You know our law. The reason we can't mix with any other kind is because of our very magic. We don't know what could happen. She might be born with no power, or she could turn out to be the most powerful being on Runae. Regardless,' Illusiō continued, 'we need to get to our sisters and warn them about their advance.'

'We need to bring them to the Temple of Time,' Vertatis insisted. 'Kareesto said the king won't destroy the temples. We will be safe in there. Trust me, as I trust his word, completely.'

With nothing more to add and urgency rushing their steps, the three Leonty departed from the Temple of Wisdom. Shielded by Illusiō's magic, invisible to the many rushing around preparing for battle, they made their way to their eldest sisters. One by one, the seven siblings gathered together. Little explanation was given; they were merely warned about the king's imminent arrival. Vertatis's indiscretion was kept hidden by the two trustworthy Leonty who, with magic and resolve, made no mention of her mistake.

'Sisters, go and hide,' Illusiō instructed before they could proceed to the temple. 'Our males need as much help as they can get.'

'No, please. We need you!' Vertatis pleaded, her hands gripping her sister's arm tightly.

'You have enough magic of your own. They need me. Don't worry, nothing will happen to me.'

'Why are you going to their aid? They have done nothing but abuse us,' Umbra objected sharply, her hand firmly grasping her sister's arm.

'The Humans are coming for us, not them. Who do you think they will go after once all our males are gone?' Illusiō released herself from Umbra's grip and turned around, running swiftly towards the edges of their land.

Unable to contest their sister's decision, the small group departed from the village, making their way towards the temple atop the highest hill. As they entered the sanctuary of the Gods, a shrill sound pierced the air. A horn of peril echoed from the distant lands to the south, signalling the clash between the crown's army and a handful of Leonty.

Arriving too late and in insufficient numbers, the residents were unprepared to repel the invaders. Less than fifty Leonty moved together as a unified group, while the king held his vast army in check, his hand raised in the air, awaiting the order to attack. In his mind, the difference in numbers felt unjust. Deep down, he knew it wouldn't be a fair battle. The overwhelming numerical advantage of his forces almost made him ashamed to label it a war.

'Surrender to me now, and your lives will be spared!' he shouted. 'There is no disgrace in conceding victory to an adversary you can't defeat… You have no army and no way to oppose me. We are here to liberate these lands from evil. Join us, and you'll prove you are no enemy to the peace we long sought.'

'Peace?' a male Leonty retorted, his face displaying clear anger. As he stood with his shoulders close to a few others, the group hid someone behind them. 'You talk of peace, yet here you come with a full army against us, seeking to conquer the lands our God has given to us!'

'You have been warned many times,' the king said sternly. 'But you continue to dabble with the great evil growing at your doorstep. From the Cloudy Mountains, they whisper of blood and death. They have charmed you, turned you to their side. And you have let them. It's time we cleanse these lands of your sick magic.'

Before King Lohan could give the order, a cold breeze swept from the enemy towards the invaders. Racing swiftly across the ground, it reached the front line, enveloping the soldiers' feet, legs, and bodies. Along with it, a multitude of voices began to speak, enchanting their minds against each other. To their eyes, anyone beside them transformed into Leonty.

The enemy had infiltrated their ranks without their notice. Under the stunned gaze of the king, the soldiers began to fight among themselves, screaming and swinging their swords wildly. Human blood spilled across the field as they turned against each other, their minds controlled by a single Leonty. She stood behind a few males of her kind, her eyes flashing with a red light, her hands stretched in the air.

'In the name of God, what's happening?' King Lohan exclaimed, horror etched on his face.

'Someone is wielding dark magic across the field,' Lëogan replied, pointing a finger at the small group of

Leonty. 'I can see through her deception. She is standing right behind them.'

'Romohan!' the king commanded, and his son quickly extracted a golden arrow from his quiver, aiming at the unseen foe.

'I can't see her! It's all a grey cloud!' Romohan replied in frustration.

'Let me help you,' Lëogan offered, stretching his arms. With one hand covering Romohan's eyes and the other pointed at the Leonty, he dispelled the illusion. Suddenly, the field cleared, and the king's son could finally see the source of the power. She stood firmly on the green soil, her hands clasped to her chest, her eyes wide open, shining with a deadly red light. Without hesitation, he released the arrow. Swift as a golden shooting star, the arrow of death found its mark.

'Illusiō!' a Leonty screamed. Covered in purple blood, her eyes frozen in the eternal greyness of death, she dropped into his arms, her magic extinguished instantly.

A desperate roar erupted from the group, mingling anger with pain, sorrow with wrath. Another female Leonty emerged from the midst of the uprising crowd, walking slowly. The green shade on her face had paled with age and the rising agony. She appeared much older than Illusiō, yet her determination was unwavering. Floating between her arms, a red stone spun frenetically, flashes of crimson light darting around her incessantly. Her fiery eyes shifted to the one who now lay dead, tears streaming down her face, dispersing like dew in the early morning air.

'My daughter…my innocent, sweet daughter…' she sobbed, leaving her kin behind, her magic surging rapidly. 'You came here to dictate who's evil and who's the enemy. Let me tell you this: anyone who inflicts suffering as you have made me suffer now deserves to face the very evil they fear the most! Fear me, Hypno, the one who was gifted with the Róshen Déil!

Raising her hands to the sky, the old Leonty unleashed the Flare gifted by their God. Countless red droplets left her face and body, her tears transforming into a bloody mist moving towards the king. As it rose from the ground, enveloping the army from behind and above, the soldiers and their leader vanished into an impenetrable fog. Screams of pain and terror reverberated through the air as those trapped within her spell witnessed their darkest nightmares come to life. They fell to their knees, hands clutching their heads, hearts racing too fast to resist. One by one, they collapsed unconscious to the ground.

The king and his son, shielded by Lëogan's power, remained unharmed but immobilized. Behind them, many had met their end at the hands of their own comrades, with many more destined for the same fate. It was a harrowing spectacle, the most dreaded nightmare unfolding before King Lohan's eyes. A small group of seemingly vulnerable Leonty had brought an entire army to its knees with the sheer force of their minds.

'She is using the power of their Flare!' Romohan shouted to his father.

King Lohan stalled at the edge of Leonty's domain, harbouring a secret hope for rescue. Initially resistant to the idea, he conceded to the overwhelming power possessed by the enemy. The Humans were too numerous to tally, yet they had been effectively thwarted by only two Leonty. From the far side of the hills, right under the vigilant gaze of the Mogs Mountains, the Aqualymphs turned their charted course towards their ally, leaving the temples behind.

A resounding roar, like waves breaking against the shore, echoed through the expansive space, heralding the arrival of Queen Eah's soldiers with a blend of magic and fury. The Leonty turned their attention away from the king to confront the unexpected party. Taken aback by the Aqualymphs' advance inland, they stood frozen in place. 'How did they breach our borders?' one shouted. 'Are they here to aid us?' 'They must have learned of the Human threat and come to intervene!' another speculated.

To their astonishment, the well-rewarded neutrality of the Aqualymphs was forgotten as the impartial, powerful kin turned against them, descending from the heights and wielding their magic against the unsuspecting group. Like a torrential river overflowing its banks, the Aqualymphs surged forth, their assault swift and devastating, colliding with the enemy in a fierce onslaught.

Walls of lethal water propelled their adversaries into the air, scattering them across the battlefield in lifeless disarray. Amidst the sudden betrayal, Hypno kept the Flare aloft, resisting the magic clashing against her, her formidable power keeping the Humans immobilized. Lost in her grief, the Flare bearer failed to anticipate the magnitude of the attack. Her focus remained fixed on the king as her magic collided with Lëogan's in a futile struggle for dominance. Desperation, grief, and a soul-crushing feeling of injustice fuelled her rage, rendering her blind to the arrival of a supreme force.

Just a few steps away, a crown made of red corals shifted between realities. Sets of eyes shone with a bright light as a deadly swing darted at her back. In an instant, Hypno vanished, engulfed by a massive wave of white energy. Upon the ground, the Flare fell onto the verdant grass, while a trail of purple blood served as a grim testament to Queen Eah's rapid triumph.

Awakening from their surreal reverie, the soldiers rose to their feet, unharmed and untouched. The afflictions of Illusiō and Hypno had been nothing more than elaborate deceptions of the mind. The Leonty had never launched an attack; the casualties, mere mirages of the mind, served as a sobering reminder of the power of deceit.

'Where is the rest of your army?' Queen Eah asked, her form solidifying before the king. In her hands, the Leonty's Flare shone brightly.

'Kareesto is leading the attack from the west. We were not expecting them here, at the walls,' King Lohan replied, his gaze shifting to the soldiers, who exchanged uncertain glances.

'They had two females in their ranks…' Romohan added. 'Their magic is truly terrifying.'

'And yet they didn't lift a finger against you, I see…' The queen turned away, the Flare dissolving in her arms. A flickering shadow appeared at her back, as if she had doubled her presence, a dark copy following her closely. 'We should move forward. If what I see is true, I don't anticipate any challenge coming our way.'

The Aqualymphs transformed into misty fog once more, dissipating into the air. Before the king could speak, they moved away, heading towards the temples. In his mind, Lohan began to realize a staggering truth: the queen had not come to help and support his kind. There was no parity between them. Compared to his ally, he felt as weak and as devoid of power as he was against the Leonty. As if Lëogan could read his mind, he spoke:

'Sir, she took the enemy's stone…' But the king remained silent.

'Father?' Romohan called, his concern evident.

'We can address this matter once we've dealt with the enemy,' the king retorted sharply.

'I concur…' Lëogan murmured, his words hissing like a hungry snake, fixated on his prey, '…but I must question who else might easily be labelled as your foe, my king. After all, this is your quest for liberation. Whatever spoils of war are obtained, they should rightfully be yours.'

Once again, Lëogan's words seemed prophetic as events unfolded. Before the king reached the temples, the Aqualymphs had penetrated the inner lands, encountering no resistance. The Leonty residing in the hills greeted them with open hands, mirroring the reaction of the group before them. Believing the Aqualymphs had come to rescue them from the Humans, they refrained from fighting back and avoided deploying any magic.

'As I mentioned earlier,' Queen Eah stated upon the king's arrival, 'there is no threat here. They are not the danger you claimed them to be.' Behind the multitude of Aqualymphs, the alleged enemy remained silent, fear gripping their hearts.

'Tell that to those who witnessed death firsthand as if it were tangible!' Romohan snapped.

'Keep your thoughts to yourself!' the queen retorted angrily. 'I did not abandon my throne to entertain your paranoia, nor to indulge the whims of a king's son. King Lohan, the true enemy lies far beyond these lands, deep within the Cloudy Mountains. That is where we must journey. Your army may continue north with us if you are prepared to lose your soldiers. However, I advise against it. The adversary we are bound to face is not of flesh you can pierce or bones you can break.'

'So be it,' the king agreed, catching Romohan off guard. Before he could interject, Lëogan placed a hand on the young man's shoulder, silencing him. 'We will secure this place while you advance. Once you have rid the mountains of evil, return to me. There is much we need to discuss. For the sake of Runae's peace, we must ensure we stand united.'

'Do as you please,' Eah said dismissively, making a brief, half-hearted attempt at a bow, before turning and departing, followed by her loyal followers.

As the Aqualymph dissolved into thin air, King Lohan gazed at his son, his thoughts traveling back through space and time. Shahara's words echoed in his mind, mixing fear with anger. She had sworn Romohan would sit on the throne one day. If they had promptly removed the threat of a rising Leonty, they would still see that bright future unfolding.

With Queen Eah's betrayal, his quest stood at the edge of failure. His heart had long settled in the comfort of rightful hate and prejudice. Craving revenge against the dark magic that had long oppressed his people, he was determined to find someone to blame, and that someone was right there, finally in his hands.

When it became clear that Kareesto had been delayed somewhere in the Whispering Forest, the king ordered his son to gather all the Leonty by the first temple. Lohan was sure he had lost his general and a great portion of his army at their hands, *'possibly tricked by some evil sorcery in the deepest of the woods.'* Whatever had happened to them, they were going to find out after they had dealt with the enemy. Not long after the Aqualymphs had disappeared behind the hills, the Humans resumed the hunt. In the heart of the Leonty's home, hatred and war reignited.

For three rhocs, the invader pushed inland, killing and taking prisoners. The enemy resistance was formidable but indeed not magical. The females of their kind, the ones who could change the fate of their race without moving a finger, stayed hidden from sight. By the time the king advanced to the Temple of Grace, at the sixth hill, the Leonty had surrendered. Having lost more than half of their males, the rest were imprisoned or left behind to die. And so the first Runan Daíl—what the Humans called the First Cleanse, was enacted.

As part of the armistice, the Leonty were brought under the rule of King Lohan, with their lands becoming his domain. From the Aqualymphs' Sea to the Cloudy Mountains, they could finally rule the entire west. With the Valahans to their east flank and the deserted steppes to the north, the Humans finally felt safe. However, fuelled by the undying fear of a still-standing prophecy, and under Lëogan's suggestion, King Lohan demanded full control over the lives of those who had survived the war and were kept alive, their magic to serve their new master.

Every power, every female Leonty who showed signs of magic, had to be listed and registered in the ancient Radhal Daíuh. An entire new section was built in the core of the large library where every enemy's name could be recorded. Their identities, their relatives, and their powers were all to be collected for the king to know and dispose of as he pleased.

As Time's tale says, the fall of the Leonty at the hands of the Humans and the taking of their Flare by the Aqualymphs marks the end of the old era and the beginning of the *Fóer Aldú*—the Decline. From that moment, every event listed in his tale seems to follow one path only, with all scattered pieces of time and history taking their rightful place in a much larger event: the Great Dawn.

From the Aqualymphs' return to the sea, their minds deeply changed, their souls irreversibly corrupted, to the birth of Una, who would become known as the Crimson Queen, the flow of events was set towards one outcome only. And yet, my brother still floated in the sky above Runae, his eyes fixed on a soon-to-become future, trying to change it, trying to save it. In his infinite wisdom, he had narrowed his focus to only one exact moment, becoming blind to the many horrible events happening on the planet he had sworn to protect. Those same events, one after another, were going to become the very reason why Time himself could not escape from his own demise.

# Chapter Eight

## *The Beacon of Fire*

∞

Even the fury of the majestic waterfall could not dissuade the concerned Aqualymph. Aura ascended the cliffs of the eastern seaboard in an instant. She knew, deep down, that the Garughals would not welcome her unannounced intrusion. Emerging from the Gochi wellspring, she bypassed the imposing guards stationed on the western perimeter. A vast courtyard lay silent before her, its stones slick with the myriad droplets dancing in the air. Above, a towering structure reached towards the heavens, its form obscured by dense vegetation, seeming to struggle beneath the Garughals' formidable shrubbery. At its pinnacle, a radiant flame danced with divine energy. Aura's gaze was drawn to it, halting her advance.

Abruptly, the branches enveloping the tower stirred, signalling that her presence had been detected, and whispers of an intruder began to circulate.

'Gorah grou-th, Aqualymph,' intoned a deep, resonant voice. 'Ish-roghat, aharut,' another voice chimed in.

'I could offer apologies, but I suspect you know who I am,' Aura responded, addressing an empty space at the tower's base. 'I must speak with Garuth; it is urgent!'

As if every facet of nature could perceive her, Aura scanned her surroundings, her eyes flitting over the profusion of foliage, stones, and trees. After a brief pause, a nearby tree uprooted itself, its branches retracting swiftly. Taking on a humanoid form, the Garughal approached the unwelcome visitor.

'You have not been granted entry, Aqualymph. This marks the second unbidden intrusion in quick succession. Return to the river and retreat to the sea whence you came,' the former tree intoned, pivoting to resume its natural guise.

'I am more than a mere Aqualymph. I am Aura, the Gatekeeper. Take me to your master; I urgently need to confer with him.' Yet the Garughal remained unmoved, anchoring itself in the earth, its arms outstretched and a verdant crown adorning its head. 'Is this how you honour and serve your God? Your Flare was bestowed upon you to safeguard this realm, not to forsake those who seek aid in its preservation!'

'Lower your voice, Lymph.' A male Garughal appeared from behind the tower. His movements were slow, as if burdened by age and weariness. His face appeared distorted by the intertwining knots and blossoming stems of flowers. 'You are a stranger to lands, soil, trees, and our dear nature. You don't know how unsettling your frantic behaviour is to us… Kasthor was here not long ago. Garúth has already conveyed to him that we cannot intervene in whatever troubles you. I detect his scent lingering on your skin… Did you think your magic could wash it away as you traversed the river? Return home; we cannot offer assistance.'

'Do not turn your back on me, Garughal!' Aura exclaimed as another one was on the verge of departing, leaving her feeling hopeless. 'As the Gatekeeper and protector of the node, as an Aqualymph, I demand to be heard.' Her form swayed in the humid, mist-laden air, and the myriad droplets fused, forming a growing puddle beneath her feet. As if her power permeated the very fabric of space, the waterfall slowed to a halt, then reversed its flow, cascading back into the courtyard. Swiftly inundating the hardened soil, it roused a multitude of Garughals from their slumber. Amidst the ensuing panic, a towering tree, its bark thick and its crown bowed, trembled, its shape shifting with haste.

'Stop, stop it, you stubborn Gatekeeper,' Garúth implored, his body morphing into that of an elderly man, his back now curved akin to the tree's bowed head, his expression weary and pained. 'There is no need to use your power upon us. Do you realize how long it will take to dry all this water? What is it that you seek now?'

'You heard the Sacred Horn, did you not?' Aura held her magic in check, the water frozen in place, her resolve unyielding.

'Indeed, we did. Even the termites themselves heard its call. And now they stir, plaguing us. For that, we thank you…' Garúth's voice trailed off, filled with exhaustion.

'And yet, you persist in inaction. You conversed with the Chomp as well, yet still you defer this matter to others,' Aura lamented.

'What would you have us do? We are Garughals. Our power is linked with the very nature of this world. Whatever peril you warned us of, there is nothing we can do to prevent it,' the aged Garughal replied, settling onto a newly formed wooden bench conjured by his touch with a tree root.

'Allow me to look through the Beacon of Fire.' Aura's demand was sharp, causing the old man to startle, nearly losing his balance. The surrounding vegetation stirred as if caught in a sudden squall, the Garughals clearly displeased by her request.

'You know the decree, Aura. One Flare for each kind. No more.'

'I'm not asking you to give it to me. I'm asking you to let me use it,' Aura stated, withdrawing her power, the water swiftly receding into the earth. Seating herself beside Garúth, she continued, 'I don't possess my own Flare.

Queen Eah took it with her, along with those of my kind. They are moving against the Leonty, alongside the Humans.'

'Dear Time! Is this tied to the Horn?' Garúth inquired, taken aback.

'Yes, it was me. I sounded it,' Aura confirmed, surprising the Garughal. 'I had no choice. Queen Eah is no longer herself. A stranger has breached our world through the node. Instead of expelling him or presenting him with the deadly embrace of the Avalian Deep, she has welcomed him as her advisor. There is a sinister magic surrounding this stranger; the same magic that persuaded her to join the Humans in their war.'

'This is indeed unsettling,' Garúth murmured, rising to his feet. With a sweeping motion of his hands, several Garughals reverted to their true forms and rallied to his side. 'What do you seek to uncover in the Beacon of Fire?'

'I wish to perceive through the eyes of Mother Nature. Your Flare grants you access to the countless sensations and insights of Runae. I believe we could glean invaluable knowledge by delving deeper… I need to know what's happening to our world,' Aura explained.

'And delve we shall. Bróhat, Raruel,' Garúth commanded two Garughals nearby. 'Inform all guards at our borders. No one enters without my authorization. Allow access solely to the Chomps if they seek an audience. No exceptions!' With that, he gestured for Aura to follow him towards the tower. After a moment of hesitation, fearing separation from her beloved waters, she acquiesced.

The ascent was swift. Infused with renewed vigour and urgency, Garúth ascended the winding stairs in a whirlwind of motion, spiralling upwards to the summit. Finally, they reached a small, circular terrace. In its centre sat a large dish atop a short pedestal. Within, a flame burned with a vibrant orange light, yet emitted no warmth. As they drew closer, Garúth's feet transformed into roots firmly anchored in the paved ground. His hands morphed into verdant tendrils, enveloping the cold flame with a protective embrace.

'Aqualymph, place your hand on my shoulders and hold tight. We are entering the realm of every matter,' the Garughal commanded. Aura promptly complied, positioning herself beside him. As her fingers made contact with his wooden skin, her body transformed into steam.

Their souls melded with the ground as they entered the Flare and its essence in an instant. It was as if they could exist both there and everywhere simultaneously; their senses heightened, their awareness spanning across the vast expanse of the land. They traversed the steppes, climbed the mountains, and delved into the valleys. Their essence flowed alongside the planet's lifeblood; they beheld the sea, the crown city, and the towering Mogs.

Diving within rocks and metal, they descended through the Valahan caves, sensing the presence of the many residents and the light footsteps of two strangers whose walk was lifted by wings. Nearby, Kasthor and his son journeyed along the mountainside. Scores of caverns dotted the landscape, their stony doors sealing the Valahans' dwellings securely.

'Where is everyone?' Kasthor pondered aloud, his gaze fixed on a towering, upright rock. At its peak, a radiant sequence of words shimmered brightly. 'Treekan, my son. This is Valahans' magic. We cannot enter or summon them without the code.'

'And you don't know it?' Treekan inquired anxiously, his eyes scanning the sprawling canyon below.

'I can't decipher Valahania,' Kasthor admitted. 'Vasheer!' His voice reverberated through the silence, causing a few small stones to dislodge from the walls of the mountain, tumbling to the ground. 'This place seems hotter than I recall… What are they doing to the mountains?'

'Can't we continue onward, father? Perhaps we'll encounter someone further along?' Treekan suggested.

'We could, but we must not approach the Mogs Pass without their consent. Valahans can be quite territorial. They are very protective of their treasures and possessions; they may mistake us for thieves,' Kasthor cautioned.

'And are you not?' a voice interjected from behind them. A stout Valahan stood at the entrance of a cave, his hairy hand clutching the heavy door. His large brown eyes peered out from beneath thick eyebrows, his expression inscrutable.

'Varuk!' Kasthor exclaimed, his smile masking a flicker of concern. 'I hoped to find you or your father. I need to see him.'

'Father is in the mines with my brother. Your arrival is unexpected, to say the least. When was the last time a Chomp ventured beyond their dome?' Varuk queried.

'Not long ago, in fact. I have just returned from the Garughals' lands. I was there with your father when he visited Garúth to discuss the strange behaviour of our Flares. On my journey home, I encountered the Gatekeeper. The Aqualymph requested that I speak with Vasheer in her stead,' Kasthor explained.

'We heard…' Varuk responded. 'Funny enough, something else unusual occurred not long ago. Someone unexpected ventured from their lands to see my father. Now, with a Chomp arriving at our doorstep, it's two marvels within the span of a rhoc. Nonetheless, allow me to escort you to him. It seems everyone wants to speak with my father lately…'

Amidst his efforts to be gentle and watch their steps carefully, Varuk guided the two Chomps down to the mines, where a multitude of Valahans delved deep into the planet's roots. It was the first time Treekan beheld the legends he had only heard of, his astonishment palpable as they entered caverns of staggering size and were engulfed by the searing heat emanating from the scorched earth. Overwhelmed by the fiery atmosphere and the reverberating clang of metal against rock, he remained silent.

Eventually, after traversing the fiery depths and enduring the deafening clamour, the trio reached the deepest recesses of the Mogs Mountains. Before them, a large hole stretched from side to side, a perilous path spanning its breadth. Across the stone bridge, Vasheer stood immobile, his attention fixed on Voishan, who wielded the Flare's magic to breach a massive, stubborn wall. Spotting the unexpected visitors, Vasheer promptly traversed the narrow walkway, his face betraying a flurry of doubts and inquiries.

'If this isn't strange—meeting you twice in a few rhocs, and now seeing you in my home,' he exclaimed. 'You must be Treekan. I recall your father's tales about you and your unique talent…'

'I can't deny it's, well, unusual, but unusual circumstances require changes in behaviour,' Kasthor replied, smiling. 'You must forgive me for entering your lands without warning. I understand you're occupied, but we come at the behest of the Gatekeeper.

'You, my friend, are not the only one who has been dealing with an Aqualymph lately. Oh, just give us time to get comfortable in my house, and I'll tell you…Voishan!' he shouted across the bridge, capturing his son's attention. At the sight of Kasthor, Voishan's eyes widened, and the magic of the Flare suddenly shut down. 'Your former fearcel, the one you let go…to my disappointment…' he quickly added, whispering in the Chomp's ear, '…is here!'

Ignoring Vasheer's request to wait, Kasthor's news preceded that of his host. By the time the three reached the Valahan's home, the Chomp had already shared the reason for their visit.

'Impossible!' Vasheer replied, as they stood in front of his house. 'Nobody can enter through the node… How could that be true?'

'I possess very limited information.' Kasthor replied as they entered the dark, hot abode. 'What I do know is that the Sacred Horn sounded as a warning. Aqualymphs and Humans are mobilizing against the Leonty, believing evil has seized their lands and hearts.'

'I'm afraid you came a long way to tell me something I already know, something you might not entirely be accurate on,' Vasheer replied. For a few moments, he fell silent, his eyes darting across the room, settling on the table where Treekan sat next to Varuk, suspicion creeping into his mind.

'What's wrong?' Kasthor asked, trailing after the Valahan around the house. 'What are you looking for?'

'Our spell is impenetrable…and yet, I feel the presence of someone. Something sinister is crawling the walls. Can't you hear it?' he asked, pressing his hairy face against the warm stone.

'What are you talking about?' Kasthor chuckled. Before he could say more, the old Valahan pressed the Chomp's face against the wall, taking Treekan by surprise.

'It's Garughals' magic! What is he doing? Why is Garúth trying to enter my kingdom without permission?' Vasheer whispered, as if expecting the Garughal himself to hear his words. 'That's three now. First Queen Eah, then you, and now him…'

'Queen Eah was here?' Treekan interjected from across the room. 'How? I thought they could not leave the sacred waters.'

'She's traveling to the Cloudy Mountains to confront the evil herself, to face it, perhaps defeat it,' Vasheer replied, returning to the table.

'So she's not aiding the king against the Leonty?' Kasthor glanced at his son, momentarily doubting Aura's words.

'Not at all. I've told my friend Lohan...' Vasheer paused, letting the implication of choosing the word 'friend' instead than 'king' sink in, '...many times, they pose no threat. Personally, I harbour great antipathy towards them. All that devout worship, all that fervour. I've encountered the God myself several times, but you don't see me kneeling and praying. As you're aware, we discovered the Flares together!' Once again, Vasheer's tone betrayed arrogance.

'The Humans act on their superstitions, father. You should not entertain their desires to expand west any longer,' Varuk interjected. 'Queen Eah and other Aqualymphs are far above their squabbles. I believe it's safe to assume they will liberate the Cloudy Mountains from evil and free us all from this burden.'

'Do you see it?' Vasheer exclaimed, jumping from his seat and pointing at the enormous amount of dust sliding on the grey floor. 'Garúth?' he called.

'Father, it's just the tremors from the mines...' Varuk's hand moved to rest on his father's shoulder. 'You are just tired... This idea of yours to break through the west flank of the Mogs Pass is driving you insane...'

'I'm not mad! The old bark is here!' he shouted. 'Show yourself, you crooked tree!'

Though the Chomps' mission proved fruitless, Vasheer's instincts were correct. His words had not fallen on deaf ears and muted walls. Through the very essence of fire and stone, Aura and Garúth trailed into the fiery depths, alert to a subtle indication of their next destination. Unnoticed by the multitude within the mines and perceived only by their king, the two departed, their spirits speeding through the Mogs Pass, their course charted on the cold, treacherous peaks at the edge of the seventh hill.

# Chapter Nine

*The Whispering Forest*

∞

Like flashes of intense light, colours danced before Aura's eyes as she traversed the vast expanse propelled by the Flare's power. Within her mind, electrifying waves of energy and sound surged, melding with the smallest creatures' heartbeats beneath her feet. She sensed Erion's warm embrace upon the foliage, the gentle caress of the breeze whispering across the lowlands and over the crown's towering walls. Somewhere, beyond the convergence of the north gates and sprawling west, the sound of thundering steps reverberated across the field.

The multitude charging towards the nearby woods gradually slowed their pace upon reaching the forest's edge. Amidst them, a singular heartbeat pulsed with a resolute rhythm, distinct from the rest. As Aura and Garúth drew nearer, the figure poised to venture into the dangerous land came into focus. A towering man with stormy green eyes, bronzed skin, and broad shoulders removed his helmet, revealing a cascade of golden hair. He was accompanied by a retinue of soldiers, who halted their march, apprehension tainting their features.

'Stay silent,' he murmured, his gaze sweeping over the ashen faces of his men. 'These are treacherous lands. This forest harbours no sanctuary for the faint-hearted or feeble-willed. Its trees dwell in perpetual twilight, straddling the line between wakefulness and slumber.'

'My lord Kareesto,' a soldier moved closer, his voice barely above a whisper. 'Are these the Garughals of which we've heard tales?'

'No, Eoshín. They are the antithesis. The Garughals, akin to us, are stewards of our Mother Nature. This, however, is Nature unleashed, defying its silent disposition,' Kareesto replied, gesturing for his troops to divide, signalling with a sweep of his hands. 'It is said the ones who were cast away from the crown city have made of this place their dark domain, amplifying the shadows within…'

'The Witches of Fárahal!' another soldier exclaimed. A ripple of murmurs spread swiftly through the ranks. They were numerous, armed, and formidable, yet faced an adversary capable of striking down many without ever revealing themselves.

'My general,' someone interjected, brow creased with concern. 'If this is what lies ahead, why divide our forces? Shouldn't we proceed together?'

'United, we present a formidable threat. Apart, we may appear to be of no danger to them and slip through unnoticed,' Kareesto explained, his heart weighed with uncertainty. Leading his comrades through a realm of magic and peril, he concealed conflicting desires. Two divergent futures loomed before him, both fraught with anguish and despair. If they traversed the Whispering Forest unscathed, an assault upon the Leonty was inevitable—his beloved and her kin would face the king's wrath in its entirety. Should they falter in reaching the temples, thwarted by the very magic he simultaneously yearned for and feared, Vertatis might yet endure.

Several feet away, the second in command, who had just received the order to move further west, was openly questioning Kareesto's decision. 'This is absurd,' he muttered to the followers trailing behind him.

'He's trying to keep us alive, Captain Lóran…' another soldier countered, the surroundings growing darker with every step they took.

'He's trying to keep *them* alive, you fool,' Lóran retorted, his anger palpable.

'So it's true, Captain… He's truly involved with the enemy? One of their females?' another soldier queried, shoving aside his comrade, a gesture that underscored their collective distrust of their general and anyone allied with him.

'It's true, all of it. Who do you think he's been meeting in the secret of the night? I'm telling you, he's been feeding information to the enemy for who knows how long. And now, he's deliberately stalling us, prattling on about magic and danger as if we're children. We're soldiers, damn it, soldiers of the king!'

'We should side with King Lohan… What do we do?' a tall thin soldier interjected, betrayal simmering in his eyes.

Moments later, shouts echoed from deep within the woods. From afar, Kareesto turned his gaze towards the chaos, straining to discern amidst the dense foliage and rising mist. Half of his army was charging northward, their voices raised in fury against their perceived foe.

Ghostly forms flitted among the trees, weaving through the shifting dance of light and shadow. Too swift and insubstantial for mortal eyes to grasp, they scattered the soldiers in fear, vanishing into the depths of the woods, ensnared by an unseen foe. Strong in will and skilled in combat, Kareesto stood firm, his senses poised for the imminent threat. With a deliberate motion, he drew his sword, holding it steady before him, prepared for whatever darkness lurked ahead.

A chill wind swept across the rusty ground, slithering over Kareesto's shoulders and coiling around his neck. Lips materialized from the formless grey mist hovering behind him.

'You've come a long way from home, General,' the spirit whispered, its voice a spectral echo. 'Your feet tread these lands heedless of danger, yet your heart betrays you. It is the green-skinned one you seek, not those you once cast aside in pursuit of glory and pride.'

'Who are you? Reveal yourself!' Kareesto demanded, his gaze darting frantically from tree to tree, seeking the unseen adversary. All he could discern were the panicked shouts of his retreating soldiers, their cries swallowed by the forest's shadows. Some screams ceased abruptly, their souls ripped from their bodies in a flash. The sickening crunch of bones and sinew being torn from joints echoed through the air.

'You know who I am… You yourself dragged me and the others through the walls. Do you not remember?' The malevolent spirit took shape before Kareesto, manifesting as an old woman with flowing hair and a sinister grin. Time and sorcery had rendered her skin a sickly pallor, as though afflicted by a dreadful disease.

'You are one of the Fárahals…' the general replied as he briefly looked at a young soldier whose eyes widened in terror. He lay on the cold ground, his back against an old tree. Petrified by the manifestation of that dark power, he could barely breathe.

'Not just one of them… I'm Meeriah…' And the old woman smiled. She knew her name would bring the painful reality of the past right into Kareesto's mind. 'How's my sister? Is she still enjoying her granted immunity?'

'The queen is fine. What do you want? We have done no harm. My soldiers have done nothing.'

'Oh but this is not our making, my dear…' she said; her voice sounded as she could sing every word in the most menacing way. 'This is!' And a green dart flashed in the air, against the tree next to the soldier. To his surprise, the evil's magic had not aimed at him. As he looked at his hands and body, relieved at being alive, a branch of the old tree swung in the air, curving as it turned thin, its end piercing his chest. With his smile still printed on his face, he briefly looked at his general and died.

'Now,' she continued, undisturbed by her own cruelty. 'Do you know my beloved sister is not the only one with the gift? I can tell you a prophecy of my own, if you wish…' But Kareesto didn't engage, his eyes fixed on the young soldier. 'Very well. You'll get what you want, Kareesto, son of Aldush, the Crown Sunrise, the Great General. She'll come to you, very soon. She carries the fruit of your forbidden love, and yet she won't get to be a mother… And love will turn into the greatest evil. Red eyes, and a terrifying power that will erase us all…' After a brief pause, Meeriah moved in front of him, her face and body finally taking full form. 'I could prevent this from happening, right now, right here. After all, who's going to miss the Crown Sunrise when there won't be anyone to mourn your early departure?'

A green glow emanated from behind the Fárahal, slithering along the cold soil, lifting leaves and dead branches. With it, the Whispering Forest turned its gaze upon the one she desired dead. The ground began to tremble, slowly giving way beneath Kareesto's feet. Petrified by horror and magic, he remained rooted in place, his eyes transfixed on the slow demise that awaited him. Alongside the dark magic, another power silently traversed the space. Two souls, shielded by the fiery Flare, darted from place to place.

'Garúth, hold steady, we must intervene,' Aura urged, her essence weaving through the dense fabric of the forest, blurring the line between reality and enchantment.

'What can we possibly do? The two of us against this magic?' The Garughal's form flickered amidst the shifting branches as they raced through the natural tapestry. 'This place teeters on the brink of consciousness. Remember, Aqualymph, they were marching against the Leonty…perhaps we should simply let it unfold.'

As they melded with the earth, the duo traversed the soil, the Flare's energy igniting magical sparks in their wake. Drawing upon the essence of life, the trees stirred, their branches swaying menacingly against the unseen intruders. A mournful groan reverberated through the darkness, punctuated by the cries of those struck, flung, and upturned.

Many soldiers lay prone on the ground, their souls departing the realm of the living, while others found themselves ensnared in thick branches, limbs held tight by strong stems, their hands broken at the wrists. Some vanished suddenly, swallowed by the earth, while others were turned over, their feet entangled in dense, green ivy cascading from the treetops. In her desperate bid to halt the war, Aura bore witness to another conflict unfolding before her eyes, her anger burning within her like a raging fire.

Determined to wield the Flare to bend nature's will, the Aqualymph delved into the mind of the towering tree beside Kareesto. Tasting the bitter tang of death, she released the fallen soldier from the tree's lethal embrace and extended its branches towards the witch. To Meeriah's astonishment, the long-standing companionship had turned against her, seizing her wrists and coiling around her neck.

'What sorcery is this?' she murmured, gasping for air. 'Let me go!' she demanded, her eyes widening as she glimpsed the arrival of two strangers. They darted through the woods, unfazed by the fury of the forest. Their green skin and feline grace left no doubt: the prophesied Leonty had arrived.

'He must die…' the witch exclaimed, her voice strained as she struggled to free herself. In a swift sequence, ten figures arose from the ground, mirroring her form. The witches of Fárahal materialized around Kareesto. With a collective raise of their hands and the invocation of a ritual prayer, bushes bristling with thorns sprang forth, their brown needles piercing the vulnerable spots in the general's armour, drawing blood that stained the grey metal of a vivid red, reminiscent of the eyes of the figure looming in the distance.

'No! Stop!' Vertatis cried out, rushing towards her loved one, with Umbra hastening her steps alongside.

'He marched against your kin. How can you plead for his release?' one of the witches challenged.

'He is not the one who gave the order,' Umbra interjected, scanning the undergrowth for Kareesto's faltering form. 'Whoever you are, there is much you do not know… He has been trying to save us.'

'Release him! He is my daughter's father!' Vertatis's heartfelt confession laid bare her desperation. Stunned by the sudden revelation, Aura paused the Flare's magic, allowing Meeriah to break free from her wooden confinement.

'You are the one I foresaw...' Meeriah's voice was a hoarse whisper, her throat ablaze with agony. 'You are the harbinger of death that will befall us all...'

Before the witches could retaliate, Umbra's magic surged forth, shrouding the surroundings in an impenetrable darkness that transformed day into night. A dense fog rose forth from her form, enveloping the witches and rendering them blind. Within the swirling mist, sparks of magic danced as the two Leonty moved beside Kareesto.

With tears streaming down her dark green face, Vertatis pressed her hands against his neck, desperately attempting to staunch the flow of blood.

'There is only one thing he is guilty of,' she cried. 'Falling in love with me, his enemy. I can see in his mind the honest truth of his feelings. He is pure in his heart; he would never come to harm me or harm my sisters...' And Vertatis gazed at the exact spot where Garúth and Aura stood, invisible. 'Please, help him...'

'You see us?' the Garughal let out, surprised. Their bodies were left behind, by the Beacon of Fire. In the woods, their spirits still moved unseen.

'I see the truth behind magic and lies. I see your minds as if they were here, please help him...' And the fire in her eyes sparkled with pure power.

'Is it true then? You and this Human have a child?' Garúth asked. His voice betrayed his anxiety at the news of that omen, but his power moved slowly on the ground to help them. A large string of leaves formed in the air, surrounding Kareesto's wounds, covering them with the healing power of their oil.

'Not yet,' Umbra spoke. 'My sister is carrying the child. She should be born before the end of the yac. I doubt we will get to that. King Lohan has entered our lands, together with the Aqualymphs.'

'Are they at the temples? The Aqualymphs?' Aura asked, finally revealing her presence, her voice showing anticipation.

'Only the Humans. The others left for the Cloudy Mountains. We saw them disappearing over the Temple of Time when our sister Jestha felt Kareesto's mind in hers, sensing the threat of imminent danger. Vertatis feared for his life, so she ran here, and I followed her.'

'Take him away, hide him somewhere. Leave the witches to their fate…' Aura said, sharp.

Before the two Leonty could share anything else, Aura's and Garúth's presence grew small and eventually disappeared. In the Aqualymph's mind, Queen Eah was the one she was after. If her sovereign had decided to face the evil in its own home, there was a reason. Reassured by the idea they owned the Garughals' power, they sped through the Leonty hills, unaware that the queen was now holding not only one Flare but two.

# Chapter Ten

## *The Corrupted*

∞

Concealed from view, the grey ridge and its majestic mountains were veiled by dark clouds. Descending from the lofty peaks to the verdant valley below, an ethereal mist permeated the air, crackling with electrifying energy. Like minuscule specks confronting the towering menace, Aura and Garúth paused momentarily. Despite their keen senses, any trace of the Aqualymphs' passage had been erased by an overwhelming sense of foreboding. The Garughals' Flare faltered, leaving them adrift in a world devoid of nature's whispers.

'This stillness is unsettling,' the Garúth remarked. 'I sense nothing at all…'

'They had to be here…somewhere close by, perhaps they have climbed to the summit.' Aura's energy flickered within the fog, casting feeble shadows amidst the low-hanging clouds.

'Aqualymph, I'm not sure if we should venture further.' Garúth's silhouette moved across the damp ground. 'The Beacon of Fire may not shield us adequately in this desolation, so far from home.'

'If Queen Eah could wield her Flare to endure beyond their bounds, so can we. We've come too far; we must find them. We must discover what's befallen our world.'

Once more, the aged Garughal found himself heeding the Gatekeeper's call. Their souls glided over the cold rocks as they ascended the mountains like a gentle breeze. Amidst the rugged terrain and dense fog, their senses waned, their connection to magic slipping as the malevolent lands sought to reclaim them. Near the summit, Aura halted, her companion's presence nearly imperceptible. With fear clutching at her heart, her distant physical hands clung tightly to his arm, though the Garughal remained elusive.

Suddenly, a fierce gust surged from the nearby peak, heralding a chilling sense of peril. Voices carried on the wind, animated and urgent. Recognizing her queen's voice, Aura pressed onward, reaching her fellow Aqualymphs moments later. A vast stone plateau stretched before her, encircled by towering spikes. Amidst the gathering of sea creatures, Queen Eah stood at the centre, her form obscured by shadows. With her hands resting on a round well, a strange liquid swirled within, its black hue reflecting the queen's visage in an eerie inversion.

'I finally found the one who can lead my quest against this abomination…' a deep whisper resonated from within the well. Queen Eah remained motionless, her lips sealed shut, yet her mirrored twin spoke in her stead. 'You've come to bestow upon me great pleasure. You creature of defiance…you could indeed be the one I need to rid the world of these Gods…'

'Who are you?' the queen inquired, her voice struggling to break free. The surrounding Aqualymphs trembled with fear.

'I am everything… I am before and I will be for eternity.' The viscous, dark liquid quivered.

'Why have you come here? What do you desire?' an Aqualymph exclaimed, fear driving his words. Suddenly, his ghostly form flickered, his eyes widening in terror. In the presence of the horrified onlookers, the Aqualymph disintegrated in an instant, leaving behind a faint trail of smoke. Untouched by the unexpected act of terror, the queen looked back at her reflection and repeated the exact same question.

'I want every matter to return to me. I want your God on his knees, weakened and trapped until the day I can obliterate him from existence!' the voice thundered, causing the courtyard to quake.

'And what shall I gain in return?' Eah continued, surprising Aura. She couldn't fathom the words that had just left her queen's lips. *Why is she entertaining a deal with the enemy we swore to repel?* she thought.

'I am the true sovereign of the past, present, and future,' the voice replied. 'In my eternal wisdom, I foresaw a creature of this world approaching me with your very same question...and I would bestow upon her the ultimate authority. I would entrust her with full dominion over this world until my return.'

'I want it!' Queen Eah declared, a swirling darkness consuming her eyes. 'I want them all! I want every Flare, every ounce of power in my grasp. I desire to break free from our eternal imprisonment beneath the waves!' Her voice resonated deeply, reverberating through the darkened space. Her soldiers recoiled, their hearts pounding with the same horror gripping their minds.

In an instant, the well crumbled, its stones disintegrating into dust. In its place, a vortex of black water churned, rapidly expanding. Engulfing the queen, whose screams mingled with laughter, the suffocating clouds parted where she stood, and a swirling force descended upon her feet.

'No!' Aura's voice echoed, recognized by those pressed against the rocks, their fear palpable. 'You cannot have her!'

'The sweet sensation of freedom...' Queen Eah exclaimed, disregarding Aura's presence. 'Ah, the allure of letting it all go...corruption is not the foe today; it sets me free...'

'May the gift of my God shield this land and its people from evil.' Garúth's shadow materialized beside Aura. His hands placed on the rocky ground, his essence permeated the earth, spreading through the space, lifting heavy stones and breaking the very foundation of the mountain plateau.

Two opposing forces clashed in the midst of the turmoil. From below, the Garughal pushed against the fierce power descending from the sky while a blast of dark energy clashed on their heads, inside their minds and hearts. In the midst of the confrontation, Queen Eah wavered between realities, light and darkness vying for dominance. Sensing her queen's dangerous contact with the evil embrace, Aura rushed forward, her spirit melding with the swirling energy, holding her tightly. At the touch of the two Aqualymphs' bodies, a fleeting spark ignited within, followed swiftly by a resounding explosion.

'You wield the Beacon of Fire in your hands...' Queen Eah's figure grew darker with every surge of energy. 'Give it to me. You can no longer protect this world...'

'My queen, please,' Aura's voice trembled with anguish, her suffering evident in her expression. 'You cannot bear such immense power. The enemy is manipulating you. Return to me. Return to the sea...'

'Give me the Flare!' the queen's demand echoed, her voice resounding throughout the surroundings. Another surge of power erupted from the duelling pair. From the Cloudy Mountains to the vast expanse of the Mogs, down to the dome of the Chomps, a blinding flash tore across the landscape. A devastating shockwave rippled through the land, shaking the very foundations of every living being's existence.

Cracks cleaved from the mountain's peak all the way down to the Leonty's hill, shaking Runae's crust with violent tremors. The wicked quakes reached the temples, causing some of them to crash upon the soft grass, billowing white, thick dust into the warm air. King Lohan's and Romohan's faces paled amidst the debris as they scanned the Cloudy Mountains for their ally. Between them, Lëogan remained unmoved, a wicked smile curling upon his lips.

The evil he had purportedly come to warn against and vanquish had enacted its move; the plan unfolded as foreseen. In his diabolic mind, he eagerly anticipated the return of a queen reborn in darkness, seduced and corrupted by the power unleashed by Nothing upon her world.

In the aftermath of destruction, Queen Eah emerged from the settling dust. Her face shrouded by the looming threat of the enemy, her soul gradually succumbing to a malevolent transformation. The seeds of a great affliction that would plague all Aqualymphs began to spread, corrupting the very ground beneath her army. Their future as spectral beings unfolded before their eyes.

With the Aqualymphs' Flare gripped in her right hand and the Leonty's in her left, she turned, revealing a horrifying duality. Her crown lost, her long hair seemed to be woven from both light and smoke, as if she was accompanied by the same twin entity she had glimpsed in the well. After being challenged by the one she had believed long banished to the depths of the Avalian Deep, Aura's opposing power had trapped her at the edge of becoming.

Stuck between her current state and the potential for a darker transformation, she stood at a precipice of choice.

The presence of the dark magic had dissolved. The one who spoke of power and destruction was gone, and so was her chance to be the one he had chosen. 'But he has seen the future,' she whispered. 'He claimed to have seen the one who would hold power in Runae. He will find a way to return to me; I am certain of it.' With resolve in her heart, she departed, leaving the sinister peaks behind, her followers trailing behind. As they journeyed homeward, a trail of emptiness lingered in their wake, clinging to their evolving souls.

Far away, Aura's and Garúth's bodies had detached from the Flare, their souls swiftly reclaimed by their owners as the Garughals' towering structure began to crumble. Shaken by the power surging from the distant land, its foundation and the courtyard beside started to collapse.

In their rapid descent, right before falling unconscious, the warriors felt the gentle embrace of branches, deployed by Garughals for their rescue. As they landed onto the ground, stones and dust poured like the same waterfall nearby, while the Beacon of Fire plunged into the depths of Gochi River like a speeding bullet.

Their determination to halt the war between the Humans and the Leonty had transformed into a desperate race against time, and against an evil too powerful to oppose. As Garúth's words echoed in Aura's mind—'What can we possibly do?'—she regained consciousness, finding herself lying beside the Garughal on the dusty ground. Her ethereal form flickered, hovering just above the surface. They had faltered. The war had not been stopped, and the enemy's advance remained unchecked. Instead, they had borne witness to the perilous convergence of two formidable forces—the malevolent and Queen Eah's. *Did we succeed?* she pondered before slipping once more into unconsciousness.

# Chapter Eleven

## *A Forbidden Love*

∞

Human troops marched relentlessly, their footfalls echoing from the lowest hill to the revered Temple of Time. Under King Lohan's decree, they dragged each Leonty patriarch, regardless of age or stature, to the Temple of Wisdom. Fear of invasion mingled with the palpable panic of a world trembling beneath their feet. Amidst the fissures tearing through the soft earth and the collapse of their dwellings, fathers and sons, elders and youths alike, were forcibly brought before the monarch, a grim prelude to the impending betrayal awaiting them.

At the king's behest, they were pressed to divulge the names and abilities of their daughters and sisters, their futures uncertain as shadows danced across the land. Many hesitated to speak, their hearts torn between loyalty to kin and the dread of what refusal might bring. Some, driven by desperation, resorted to falsehoods, weaving intricate lies in hopes of shielding their loved ones from harm. Yet, Romohan, spurred by his father's command, stood resolute, his resolve unwavering as he lined up a small contingent of Leonty at the temple's feet, issuing a final ultimatum.

'Confess now,' he proclaimed, his voice carrying both threat and promise, 'and you will be reunited with your kin. His Majesty is merciful and just. We seek only to understand and safeguard those gifted among you.' But beneath the veneer of clemency, the Leonty sensed the harsh reality of their plight. They had been invaded without mercy, their sanctuary violated by the savagery of humanity. Rumours of Illusiō's and Hypno's demise cast a dark cloud over their thoughts, foretelling a grim fate yet to unfold.

As the numbers of the soon-to-be-enslaved grew, lined up, brought to their knees, pushed and hit with cruelty, two Leonty moved at the edge of the Whispering Forest, their terrorised gaze fixed on the unfolding event.

'Hold on, sister,' Umbra said, her voice tinged with fear, as she halted at the forest's end. In their arms, Kareesto lay unconscious, his skin slowly regaining its hue, yet his vitality remained elusive, his very breath a whisper against the chaos. 'The Humans advance up the hills,' she observed, her eyes fixed upon the Temple of Truth. 'They are entering the hallowed halls…'

'It won't be long before they reach the seventh hill and our sisters,' Vertatis replied, her full attention on Kareesto as she set him down gently. Her sister's eyes blazed crimson, her obscure power guiding them swiftly through the fields between the woods and the Temple of Time. A hazy veil unfurled along their path, distorting reality itself, where the highest hill lay barren and the temple atop it vanished from sight. With freedom to move unseen, the two lifted the general back on their shoulders and pressed on, urgency lending wings to their steps. In mere moments, they reached the safety of the Leonty sanctuary. Stepping into the temple, they were met with the bewildered gazes of four more Leonty emerging from the naos, their faces etched with shock and confusion.

'What's the meaning of all this?' Ecne questioned, her grip tightening on Jestha's hand.

'He is the one whose fear I heard loud in my head,' Jestha interjected, hastening towards her sisters.

'Yes, yes,' Umbra replied, her tone urgent. 'Cease your magic, sisters. We will explain everything, but first, let us tend to this burdened Human.'

'Vertatis, where are you?' A male voice echoed from outside the temple. A Leonty frantically scoured the hilltop, searching for an entrance to a temple that had vanished from sight. 'Umbra, let me in, it's urgent!'

'Protheux?' another Leonty's voice called out. Mementhya raced outside, her senses guiding her swiftly through the towering pillars, beyond the reach of Umbra's enchantment. Free from her sister's spell, she appeared before her brother. 'Protheux, you must not linger here. This sanctuary must remain concealed. Come inside, follow me; I know the way back by heart.'

'Vertatis,' he exclaimed upon joining the group inside. 'Chiron has been taken to the king. I fear he will trade your life for his own. He will reveal your powers, all of yours!'

'What else is there?' Jestha pressed, sensing the weight of her brother's fear.

'Some soldiers said Illusiō and our mother have been killed at the wall.' And his face turned away in sorrow. 'I don't know if it's true. Mother had the Flare with her; she wouldn't falter, would she?' His sisters couldn't say a word, agony squeezing their hearts. 'If Chiron tells them about you, all of you…'

'He won't,' Vertatis replied, her tone laced with revulsion and anger. 'I know him too well. All he craves is my power—his only means of continuing to amass fame and glory in the eyes of the Valahans. My power has served him well so far; he won't let it go. Now, brother, there is something I have to tell you.'

Vertatis stepped aside, unveiling a Human body lying on the cold floor behind her. Kareesto was gradually emerging from his slumber. With gentle hands tracing his face, she gazed at him with eyes brimming with love and magic, as the full truth began to unfold. In the silence of that concealed sanctuary, her secrets unfurled before Protheux and her sisters.

The love and desire they both surrendered to hadn't blossomed immediately. Once more, Vertatis had found herself dragged to the lowlands on the fringes of the crown city by her hard-hearted fearcel, Chiron. There, they encountered two Valahans and a handful of Humans for business discussions. Even if reluctant to fulfil her despised duty, Vertatis was ready to guide him towards the most advantageous deal.

Inside an old tavern, the two Leonty sat at a worn wooden table, waiting for someone's arrival. The derelict interior seamlessly blended with the neglected aesthetic typical of the outskirts. Amidst the noise of loud and drunk patrons, who moved about with an air of ownership, three Humans engaged Chiron and Vertatis in conversation. With their mouths adorned with scant remnants of teeth, and their hair tangled with the leftovers of countless meals, the Humans radiated an unpleasant odour, adding to Vertatis's discomfort. Draped in a voluminous cape with a hood concealing her features, she averted her gaze from them, resisting the urge to delve into their thoughts, lest her magic be inadvertently exposed.

'When are they coming? We don't have all day. It's a long way back, we need to leave before Erion-dúl,' Chiron said to the Humans, referring to the two Valahans who were late to their meeting. His eyes pointed at the rusty front door as it swung open. To his disappointment, two male Chomps walked in instead. Attempting to approach the dirty counter, one of the small, winged creatures pushed through the chaos. Right behind, the other one followed closely, holding a smaller Chomp in his arms.

'Kasthor?' an old Human with a long grey beard let out in surprise from the other side of the counter. 'I haven't seen you in yacs! I thought your kind had decided to just...vanish from the face of Runae.'

'Very funny...' the Chomp replied. 'My fearcel, Faróel, and I are headed to the crown city to register our son's name in the Radhal Daíuh. He is seven now, look at him!'

'Seven yacs already,' the Human replied. His voice sounded rough, and it carried a thick accent. Scared of it, the little Chomp hid in his other father's arms.

'We know dark times are ahead, and it's risky to abide by the rule,' Faróel said. 'Everywhere there are rumours of hate, dark magic, and upcoming wars. The crown is getting more and more intolerant of anything that is not in their customs. And we know they are not particularly fond of our...kind of love... But the law says we need to register Treekan in the books when he turned seven.'

'The crown...' The Human's expression twisted in disgust, and he spat on the floor a few inches away from his feet. 'What do they know? Look at how they treat us...and we're Humans. Well, do what you have to, but I suggest you leave the city as soon as you're done. Whoever you love or what you do in your own lands, it's nobody's business. Valahans, my friends, what can I get you?' he shouted across the counter after two large males walked in.

The expected guests had all arrived. Soon, conversations and agreements began. Vertatis's hand was placed on Chiron's leg, patting it ever so slightly every time one of their counterparts lied or tried to persuade him to believe they had offered the best deal. At one stage, one of the Humans said:

'I'm telling you, it works! All you have to do is to put it around your neck; it will protect you from evil spirits, especially the ones that hide in the Cloudy Mountains...' And Vertatis's hand moved again.

'Please, Margoul,' Chiron replied, smiling. 'We know this is junk... But don't get offended,' he continued before the other interrupted him. 'I still think we could make it work if Vaisha here could add some stones to it, you know, to make it prettier? It might sell well...'

'I think we should revisit our first idea, the one about that special material that is popping up everywhere in the lands,' Vaisha said. 'That silver is special, nothing like this rubbish! If you polish it well, you can see things when you look at it...' And Vertatis's eyes glanced around, her hand still. Whatever he was saying, he wasn't lying.

'If it's everywhere, I don't think we could sell it for much...' Chiron was buying time, waiting for his fearcel to give him a sign.

'It is, but its form is too raw,' the Valahan replied. 'I have one here, look at it and tell me what you see...' And a shiny, flat grey stone appeared in his hairy hands. With his palms stretched towards the two Leonty, the Valahan showed unexpected excitement.

Pulled by curiosity and a sudden, almost imperceptible detection of magic, Vertatis joined Chiron in the inspection of the newly found treasure. Finally turning her head towards the table, her eyes fixed on the small stone. If

Chiron could discern nothing but a highly reflective material, Vertatis's keen affinity for magic of any form made her suspicious. The Valahans had unearthed something decidedly unusual.

Forms and shapes moved inside the stone, distorting her face as her double stared back at her, akin to a mirror. Behind her contorted figure, six more moved. Whatever magic the Valahan had discovered, it was revealing her sisters as they appeared in the past, displaying places and events she had already experienced. The mirroring stone was showing remote events.

Before she could fully comprehend the unimaginable power before her, several Human soldiers burst into the tavern, their laughter and shouts filling the air. Spotting the two Chomps at the counter, they began hurling derogatory words, verbally abusing them.

'What have we here?' one started, snatching a glass of brownish alcohol from a customer's hands. 'Two feathers?' Kasthor winced at the word but turned his head away, seeking to avoid confrontation.

'And they even produced another one? Who's this little monster?' another soldier jeered, moving in so close that the Chomps could smell the dirt and booze festering on his body.

'Let them be,' someone from the counter interjected, but their plea was quickly dismissed. At the far side, Vertatis stood up, ready to move and offer her support to the Chomps.

'What are you doing?' Chiron asked, pulling her hand. 'Get back to your seat and don't attract their attention!' Yet she refused to heed his reasoning, her heart pounding and her ears filled with dread.

'Leave them be,' she implored, stepping between the soldiers and the Chomps. 'Why do you come here and spew such hateful words? Surely there are better pursuits for your time?' Beneath her hood, her visage betrayed her anger, her eyes aglow with a fiery hue. Chiron and his associates, sensing trouble, hastily stowed away their illicit goods, retrieving them from the worn table and concealing them within their bags. Amidst the chaos, one item remained unaccounted for—the stone still rested in Vertatis's grasp.

'A woman stands up for a pair of Chomps, no less,' a soldier jeered, his hand reaching to pull down Vertatis's hood. The tavern fell silent, a collective gasp echoing through its timeworn walls. There stood a Leonty with shining red eyes, a female harnessing her formidable power.

'Tell me, Joleer,' Vertatis addressed him, her tone laced with an eerie familiarity. At the sound of his name, the soldier visibly quivered. 'You're quick to identify kindred spirits, aren't you? Why not share with your comrades here about…Garion, was it? The commander of the eastern ranks moves your heart, turning lust into fire…and yet you are ashamed of it…' Fear gripped the soldier; the Leonty possessed knowledge of his clandestine affairs, secrets he had guarded with utmost care.

'Do you hear this creature?' another soldier interjected, his voice filled with contempt. 'Evil speaks through her! We

Humans aren't afflicted with such a curse. Everyone knows it.' With a forceful grip, he seized Vertatis's wrist, drawing her closer, spittle flying from his mouth.

'Enough!' a man thundered from the front door, his hair gleaming in the dim room, a mix of white and gold. His dark skin and golden eyes exuded warmth that reached Vertatis's heart. 'Why do you seek trouble?' he demanded.

'She can't help it, my general. She's a Leonty, one with dark magic. Trouble follows her like a shadow,' the soldier retorted, his grip on Vertatis firm.

'I was addressing you, Fadaur. Release her!' Kareesto intervened, moving beside Vertatis with a stern gaze fixed on his soldiers. 'Chomps,' he addressed the trio, 'the outskirts are no place for your kind. I suggest you head to the east wall; there you'll find Humans with kinder hearts.'

Without hesitation, Kasthor, Faróel, and Treekan rose and exited the tavern, their troubled faces fixed on the dirty floor. Meanwhile, Vertatis's power shifted to the general, delving into his mind uninvited. Amidst the chaos, the beauty he radiated in that squalid place shone through in his thoughts. Their eyes met as Vertatis delved deeper, navigating his emotions, fears, beliefs. The general's mind was enchanted by her beauty and the strength she had displayed. Thoughts of admiration surfaced, mingling with desire in a potent blend of attraction. She glimpsed deep into his heart, sensing his newfound feelings for her. In that moment, between hatred and challenge, love blossomed between Vertatis and Kareesto.

'Are you here alone?' he inquired, as he glanced across the crowded tables. Amidst the bustling gathering, his eyes homed in on the other Leonty and the two Valahans. While the presence of the mountain diggers was not out of place, the sight of two Leonty venturing into the crown domain was indeed unexpected. Before Vertatis could respond, he extended an invitation. 'Please, accompany me.'

'I'm not here to cause any trouble,' Vertatis replied once they had stepped outside. A few inebriated Humans lay sprawled on the ground, their unkempt appearance adding to the squalor of the scene.

'You should not be here at all. The outskirts are not safe for anyone, especially for your kind. You should leave immediately,' Kareesto replied as he took her arm and guided her to the back of the tavern. His hand could only feel her wrist, yet he envisioned himself touching her, running his fingers over her velvety green skin.

'My will is not my own. I was forced to come here. I'm not free to do or go anywhere without my fearcel,' Vertatis explained, sensing the general's intentions manifesting in her mind through magic and desire. 'You might not know what my obligations are, as a Leonty, as a female. But I can assure you, I wouldn't be here if it were up to me.'

'Your eyes are of unspoken beauty,' he confessed. 'Who are you? What magic envelops you?'

'I'm Vertatis,' she stated, locking eyes with him. Golden stones clashed against his dark skin and sandy hair. 'My mind allows me to see the thoughts of others, understanding their truth, perceiving their lies.'

'Can you read mine now?' he whispered.

'You can touch me, if you want,' she replied, smiling.

Their love ignited then, fast, burning like a raging fire. For two yacs, they met in secret, in the crown city, at the Leonty hills, and everywhere in between. Concealed from prying eyes, shielded by the myths of the Whispering Forest, they found solace in each other's arms, consumed by passion and desire. It was his pure heart that captivated Vertatis the most, his power and position as a general mattered little. She desired him for his true essence, his soul untouched by deceit.

Yet, that pure soul now faced a slow, ignoble demise. In Vertatis's arms, he lay silent, wounded. His entire battalion had perished in the Whispering Forest, and now he found himself in the hands of their enemy, in the hands of the one who carried the fruit of their sin.

A heavy silence descended as Vertatis recounted their story, their unstoppable love. Though her siblings' initial reaction was one of shock and fear, they had already borne too much weight in their hearts to let horror dictate their words. While Umbra had time to process the magnitude of her sister's actions, Protheux was hearing it for the first time. However, his love for his youngest sister, Vertatis, was so strong that he could not bring himself to feel anything but sympathy. Eventually, after a long silence, one of her sisters spoke.

'There is still a way out of this,' Lethya said. 'I could make you forget about him; I could make all of you forget this ever happened…'

'No!' Vertatis replied firmly. 'He is everything I wanted. He is everything to me.'

'Sister, there was no future for the two of you before, and definitely there won't be one now that the king is taking over our lands.' Protheux said, moving beside her, his arms around Kareesto's back. 'We can't let them find him anywhere near. They won't listen to reason. He will be executed for treason.' And he lifted the Human and placed his body on his shoulder. 'I'll bring him back to the west wall. I hope he'll find a way to survive all this.'

With tears flowing, Vertatis leaned in to kiss Kareesto's face. His eyes briefly moved as her dark green lips found his, upside down. On the verge of awakening, he felt the Leonty's love reaching his heart, healing his wounds from within. Desperately trying to open his eyes, he wanted to tell her that he knew, that he was ready to risk his future and be with her for the rest of his life. But the scars inflicted on him by the witch still held a fierce grip on his body. And so Protheux left the temple and the protection of Umbra's magic.

It was only a matter of moments before the Humans reached the top of the seventh hill. Guided by Chiron, they had narrowly missed Protheux leaving the temple by a mere coincidence. As he had warned, Vertatis's fearcel had surrendered to the king, and he was now ready to hand her and her sisters over, the harsh sentence ready to be imposed mercilessly.

The six sisters could no longer hide. Despite Umbra's magic shielding the Leonty's whereabouts, and led by

Chiron, the soldiers sensed their proximity. The absence of the entire temple was a clear sign of magic at work. Persisting in hiding would only signal defiance, a risk too great to take, with death looming as the consequence. Eventually, Umbra's power dissolved, and before the Humans' eyes, the white columns and the entire temple reappeared.

Brought down with the rest of their kind, they endured questioning, inspection, verbal abuse, and threats. In the eyes of the king, Umbra was deemed the most dangerous, her abilities a direct threat to his plans of domination. Vertatis, conversely, was portrayed by her own fearcel as possessing the most useless magic.

'She can merely discern if I'm lying to her or not. A power that only complicates matters for me, her cherished one. She is naught but a hindrance to you, King Lohan,' he remarked at one point.

'Either way, this one's name must be written in the books!' Romohan demanded, his tone firm and authoritative. His gaze briefly met that of his father, who looked visibly concerned. For some reason, the notion of a Leonty possessing the ability to uncover lies unsettled him deeply.

'My king,' Lëogan interjected, 'you can spare as many as you want, but I believe the one whose power we saw spreading wide, should be brought for...further inspections...' His sinister power acted upon King's Lohan's will and yet, it failed to foresee the greater threat they were about to leave behind. Unseen by the many judging eyes, another magic had begun to envelop Vertatis's ability, shielding her from within. In the not-so-distant future, that same magic would face Lëogan once more, deep within the heart of the Humans' kingdom, challenging him through the hands of the most terrifying evil Runae would ever witness.

'So we shall,' the king replied, triggering a loud opposition from Umbra's sisters.

And so, the time arrived for the Humans to depart from the hills. Following the signing of an armistice between the king and the surviving elder males, the army marched south, taking Umbra along. Behind them, a trail of sorrow, grief and anger followed. The king had brought the seven hills under his domain. The Leonty's lives his, their powers under his control, names built up in the newly built section of the Radhal Daíuh.

Countless Leonty were recorded in the library, detailing each female with magic running through their veins, along with their family members, connections, and whereabouts. One by one, every Leonty magic became known. One by one, they were going to follow Umbra's same horrifying path.

Near the west wall, over the Whispering Forest, Protheux laid Kareesto on the soft green grass. As he turned away, the general stirred awake. His eyes struggled to focus, and he whispered his beloved's name.

'Forget that name, forget what you felt for her,' Protheux said without turning back.

'Where is she? I must tell her I know…I must tell her I want to be the father of our child.' Kareesto attempted to rise to his feet, but his legs betrayed him, sending him crashing back to the ground.

'I know you love her, and I know she loves you.' The Leonty finally glanced back at the Human, compassion mingling with fear on his face. 'This is why you will never, ever seek her out. If she manages to survive your king's madness, she will never risk her life and the lives of her loved ones for you! Do you understand?'

'I tried. I tried to delay my army as much as I could…I led them to their deaths in the forest. I have already sacrificed them and sacrificed my life, my honour for her. Please, don't let it all be in vain.'

'Your actions may have spared her life, just as hers may have spared yours. Do not ask for more. If I ever catch sight of you setting foot on our lands again, I will send Lethya against you. If you beg now, perhaps I may send her regardless. She will erase any memory of my sister from your mind and your heart. But I understand you may wish to spend the remainder of your days cherishing her sweet memory. And that is the only mercy I am willing to extend. Once again, Human: forget about my sister!' And with that, Protheux walked away, leaving him behind.

Lying on the grass, Kareesto wept, his tears flowing as if they could drown the land with the power of his despair. Just earlier, he had stood behind that very wall, Vertatis in his arms, concealed beneath his cloak. Once the greatest general of the mightiest army, he now lay defeated, separated from the one who mattered most. Love, prestige, and future all lost in an instant. Their forbidden love, destined to remain forever concealed, had turned into a painful punishment. Yet, Vertatis's face remained etched in his mind, her touch like a balm on his wounded body. In his heart, he could not let her go.

'Never,' he vowed, attempting to rise once more. 'I will never…'

# Chapter Twelve

## The Birth of a Greater Evil

∞

'Come with me!' Chiron's voice boomed, echoing through the doorway of his home. His elongated, green face bore a determined expression fixed on Vertatis, whose pregnancy was unmistakably visible.

'Please, Chiron, let me stay. It's getting close; I don't want to risk it.' Her voice quivered with fear.

'I said, come with me! Or do you want me to tell the Runers they can have you too?' The threat, repeated with cold insistence, aimed to compel her into action, but Vertatis resisted.

'They got two of your sisters already. Illusiō has been dead for a hundred rhocs now, and Umbra…well, you can bet she is dead too.'

'Stop it,' she cried out. 'They are my sisters!'

'Do I need to remind you that you and Jestha are still free because of me and Hicarus? If you weren't bound to us in the sacred union, they would have turned you into priestesses or sent you to the crown city. Is this what you want? It's this or the Humans.'

Once again, Chiron's menacing words had their intended effect. There seemed to be no way out for Vertatis. Somehow, being his fearcel represented a form of freedom. While her power was tempered by her obedience to him, she was not enslaved in a life of servitude by the temples, nor was she deported to the crown city to meet her premature death. Yet, in her mind, Kareesto's face resurfaced, a constant reminder whenever Chiron invoked the threat of her name still being written in the Radhal Daíuh. Burdened by the pain of carrying both her physical and emotional burdens, she struggled to comply with Chiron's demand. Eventually, she relented, and they both made their way to meet two Valahans at the edge of their lands.

As they had done many times before, Chiron was exploiting Vertatis for his own gain. His ambition was to rise above others by amassing wealth through trade with the mountaineers. In their negotiations, he consistently stayed one step ahead, with Vertatis discerning the truth behind their words with remarkable clarity. Seated outside a grand wooden structure bustling with Valahans, Humans, and Leonty alike, they engaged in trade discussions with the merchants.

'I'm telling you, this is pure miltosh. Easy to shape but impossible to destroy once water has been poured in,' a Valahan named Vrost explained confidently.

'And the more water it gets, the stronger it becomes,' the other trader chimed in, his gaze fixed on Vertatis, who turned away, her eyes ablaze.

'It's different from the others; I'm not sure the Runers will pay much for it...' Chiron commented, sliding the small bag containing a silvery, shining dust away across the table.

'They have been sent by the crown for two reasons: keep all of you under scrutiny and repair the God's temples. If they want to rebuild them, they'll buy it and pay you handsomely,' Vrost assured him.

'Hey, you,' the other Valahan interjected, leaning closer. 'What are you looking at? Turn around and show me your face...'

'Leave Vertatis alone,' Chiron intervened, concern evident in his voice. 'She's not well; can't you see she's pregnant?'

'Vertatis,' the Valahan persisted, reaching out to touch her arm. 'There are many rumours about you. Are you not the one who put a spell on the general's mind?' Vertatis's heart raced as she anticipated what would come next.

'You're the one who knows the secrets, aren't you?' the Valahan continued.

'What are you talking about?' Vrost questioned, shooting a puzzled look at his companion.

'She's the one who reads minds. I've heard she can hear things you'd never say in the open.' To those words Chiron's mind raced as he struggled to contain the situation.

'It's not her. That was her sister; she's dead now,' Chiron interjected, his words mingling with nervous perspiration. 'This is my fearcel.'

'Chiron.' Vrost rose to his feet, pushing his chair aside. 'Have you been bringing this evil with you all this time so you could read my mind?'

The trading ceased abruptly, tensions escalating as accusations flew. The Valahans were prepared to leave and spread word of a Leonty openly wielding her power, against Human law, without Chiron's control, and for their own gain.

'Vrost, please, use reason,' Chiron pleaded. 'Vertatis was spared by our king because she wasn't a threat. The only power she has is over me; I can't be separated from her. She's with me because I fear she could give birth to our daughter anytime soon...'

Deeply affected by Chiron's false words, Vertatis felt a surge of emotions, her eyes flashing red once more. Amidst the turmoil storming in her mind, she suddenly felt a soothing warmth emanating from within, calming her fears and doubts. As if her unborn child spoke to her, the silent soul urged her not to be afraid, assuring her that she could relinquish her magic if she chose to.

'If what you say is true, you don't mind?' Vrost pulled Vertatis's arm, forcing her to face him. To his astonishment, between the olive-green eyelids, he found only two simple yellow eyes staring back at him. Somehow, Vertatis's magic had vanished in an instant.

'I'd say we go, and you pay us this time…' Vrost's voice was a menacing whisper, his narrowed eyes drilling into Chiron's.

Forced by their threat, Chiron reluctantly agreed to pay for their silence. With a firm grip on Vertatis, he dragged her away, the journey home shrouded in tense silence. Vertatis couldn't discern if Chiron had fully grasped the gravity of the Valahan's insinuation. To her, it seemed he was more preoccupied with the loss of a profitable deal and the extent of the rumours surrounding her powers in Runae. Somehow, the mention of a general had slipped by unnoticed.

Upon their arrival home, Chiron's heavy hands pushed Vertatis through the door, causing her to fall to her knees. He hastily gathered some belongings before leaving, his parting words dripping with disgust. 'Thanks to you, I have to walk all the way to the Mogs Mountains and fix the mess you made… I'll return in two rhocs. You better be done with that daughter of yours when I'm back. You owe me!'

A few moments later, Vertatis and Jestha convened at the Temple of Grace. With the help of Protheux and a few loyal males, they devised the rescue of their sisters from the clutches of the Runers. Under the cover of darkness, the five sisters sought refuge in Jestha and Hicarus's home, where they immediately recounted the recent events.

'It's true, sister...' Protheux confirmed, securing the wooden windows shut. 'I've heard he was brought to the king. He must have confessed, as there's no other way the truth about you two would come out.'

'He would never!' Vertatis protested.

'What about that counsellor? The one who was made Aver of the King?' Hicarus interjected. 'I've heard he has powers of his own. He might have compelled him to tell the truth.'

'If that's the case, why not kill him?' Lethya pondered, tending to Vertatis's legs and applying a warm oil on her skin. 'Sister, the nuartíl is turning pink. Any moment now...'

'King Lohan is keeping him alive for a reason,' Jestha remarked, passing a large basket of white sheets to her sister Ecne. 'Whatever that reason is, I hope it worked the same for Umbra. I'm really worried she might not be coming back, ever.'

'We should worry about the real risk here. What if this...daughter of yours turns out to be the one in the Humans' legends? By the look of that oil, it's going to be tomorrow.' Mementhya's harsh tone carried the same fear all of them had in their hearts. Vertatis, however, remained steadfast in her confidence.

'Una... Her name is Una,' she said with a smile, caressing her large tummy. A few dark lines had lately started to appear from her hips up to her chest, like black ink running on her skin, forming marks of many different shapes. 'She is the first, the only one born out of a love that has never existed before. She is good, she is strong, I can tell...'

'She is marking your body like an old Garughal's bark,' Mementhya insisted. 'She is branding you with a dark power. She will brand all of us...'

'Stop it!' Protheux exclaimed. 'There are very few Leonty left we can trust. Let's not allow division to enter our home, our family. Chiron has no idea. After all, this...little one, Una, may be one of us. We will address it when the time comes.'

'Protheux is right,' Hicarus let out. 'It's getting more and more difficult even to bribe the Runers. They have been watching all of us closely. These Human priests who came from the south have taken full control of our temples. For the next while, we might not be able to pull any of you out of it, not even for a few hocs. Your sister Jestha and I will stay by your side, Vertatis. The rest of you, keep this quiet and don't make any trouble. Something terrible might happen,' Hicarus urged as he stepped outside the house, scanning the dark landscape. If the four sisters were to safely return to the temple, they had to ensure nobody would be around to witness their departure.

Like a flash in that very same stormy night, a few hocs later Una was born. To Vertatis's and Jestha's joy, the little creature was one of their own. Her flesh was green, and her short hair was hard and thick. However, it was clear from the first moment Vertatis laid eyes on her daughter that

Kareesto's blood ran in her veins. Una had a strange, pale face; a pink veil covered it like a second skin. Jestha had made the same comment several times.

'Don't worry, sister. She is going to get darker as the rhocs pass by.' Hoping it was a mere sign of birth distress, she kept dismissing the dark omen. Cheered by the idea of Chiron being in the Valahans' lands for another rhoc, both she and Hicarus kept their confidence high.

It wasn't until the first light of the rising star that they realized their hopes had been misplaced. The little Leonty lay on a large bed, her hands moving on her eyes as if she tried to find relief from a persistent burning feeling. It was then, as the three Leonty looked at her and smiled, that Una opened her eyes for the very first time. Two shining rubies gleamed in the early morning darkness, bringing horror and desperation to their hearts.

She was definitely a Leonty, but with it, a terrifying future was quickly unfolding. She had magic running through her body, a power mixed with Human blood. Whatever the legends said, Una was already taking all the steps to fulfil Mementhya's prophecy.

In his fascinating tale, Time spoke with emphasis of that specific moment. He called it *my very first mistake*. The truth is, among his many qualities, humility was the least prominent. It's hard for me or for my siblings to truly understand what it means to be able to see the past, the present, and the future in a never-ending flow. Every move he made, every decision he took, he did it conscious of what would happen next. His actions were pondered to the extreme, to a point where mistakes were impossible. And yet, his words spoke of missteps, even without mentioning Una's birth. As if the cosmic power of fate had brought two events together, a few moments after Una was born, on the other side of the universe, a celestial being was torn asunder.

Our cherished sister, Health, had fallen under the attack of our enemy, the omnipotent force she wielded across the universe collapsed. Immortality, once a universal privilege, became a distant memory. Every living being found themselves exposed, unprotected, cursed with an invisible sentence, a relentless countdown hurtling them towards an inevitable end.

The defeat of our sister reached Soul, Time, and me in an instant. As my brother hovered in space near Runae, sifting through countless possible futures, he sensed Health's magic dissipating, its power fading from the surroundings. Whatever had befallen her, its implications were of incommensurable proportion. Unable to remain passive, he extended his arms, his power escalating in tandem with his desperation. In that pivotal moment, a green clepsydra materialized before his radiant form. As my brother's magic extended beyond its limits, a greater wave of energy emerged from the cosmos, channelled through the hourglass; a burst of boundless magnitude erupted from his spot, reverberating across the small planet and reaching the scorching Erion. The celestial bodies' movements ceased, their surfaces locked in a singular point, halting the flow of time itself.

As Runae's rotation slowed, streaks of green and purple illuminated the skies, a fierce battle between light and darkness ensued, blending night and day into a disconcerting loop. Penetrating lands and matter, the majestic, terrifying dance of celestial powers travelled from the high mountains to the Valahan caves. From the sea to the Leonty's temples, the sign of a new omen manifested.

Nearby, three Leonty huddled together by Vertatis's bedside, gripped by terror. Their eyes remained fixed on Una's face; her crimson gaze sent shivers down their spines, plunging them into a frenzied state.

'It's all true!' Jestha exclaimed, her voice tinged with panic.

'It's not her doing, sister. I can't sense any power...' Vertatis reassured them, cradling her daughter in her arms.

'I've never seen something like this,' Hicarus observed, peering out from a tiny window. 'What are the chances this could be a mere coincidence?'

'Hicarus, please, find my brother,' Vertatis pleaded, clutching Una tightly as if she could shield her from the world. 'I need him here before Chiron returns. If he sees her eyes...' Her words trailed off, prompting Hicarus and Jestha to exchange a fleeting glance, their intentions momentarily stalled. After Vertatis implored them once more, the two hurriedly departed.

The speed at which the Leonty sought Protheux was inconsequential. Vertatis's desperation weighed heavy in their hearts, but it wouldn't hasten their journey. Not long after their departure, Chiron strode in. His expression stern, his gaze immediately fell upon the little one cradled in Vertatis's arms. For a brief moment, they locked eyes, long enough for Chiron's venomous thoughts to crystallize in his mind.

'Is it a she?' he inquired, shutting the door behind him.

'Yes. Your daughter couldn't wait for her father's return...' Vertatis replied, gently laying Una on their bed, bracing herself for what was to come. Sensing the tension crackling in the air, she knew his fury would soon be unleashed upon her.

'And I thought you couldn't...of all your sisters, you, the one who can only speak the truth...I thought you couldn't lie. Move, I want to see her eyes!' Chiron's voice boomed, his face mere inches from Vertatis's.

'Leave her be, she needs to rest...' Vertatis protested, her words barely a whisper. But her resistance only seemed to enrage Chiron further. With a violent shove, he sent her crashing to the floor. Upon catching sight of Una's crimson irises, his fury erupted unchecked.

'How? How did you manage to deceive me? When did you learn to harness your power and wield it against me?' he demanded, whirling around and striking Vertatis in the stomach.

'Leave her alone! She's your daughter!' Vertatis cried out, tears streaming down her cheeks.

There was no room for argument. Chiron seethed with fury, his mind racing through countless scenarios where he stood to lose everything he held dear. If what the Valahans had told him was the truth, if Una indeed was the offspring of a Leonty and a Human, an unthinkable, terrifying future loomed before him. Even if she were undeniably his daughter, Una's burgeoning magic posed a dire threat. Once her abilities were uncovered, he could no longer conceal her or Vertatis from the Humans. His entire livelihood would crumble, reduced to ashes.

'You sicken me,' he spat, his voice dripping with venom. 'You swore she had no ties to darkness. You swore she wasn't like you. But here we are. You birthed a monstrosity! She's a monster, just like you!' Yet, as Chiron hurled his accusations, Una lay on the bed, oblivious to the cruel words her father hurled.

'I didn't intend to deceive you,' Vertatis pleaded, her voice cracking with desperation. 'Something has halted my powers. Since our daughter's birth, I've looked at her and seen nothing but an ordinary being, like you...'

'You lied to me, Vertatis, you lied!' he roared. With a brutal kick, he sent her crashing to the ground once more, purple blood staining the floor. 'Do you want to provoke another war with them? Do you? Don't you understand how difficult it is for me to shield you, to ensure they remain ignorant? I assured the king that your powers were my sole concern.' After a tense silence, he made his way to the door. Before departing, he delivered his final decree. 'You know the laws of the Humans. I won't have any more trouble because of you. She'll die today!'

Terrified by Chiron's intentions, Vertatis summoned her strength, the pain in her body fading in comparison to the grave danger ahead. She scooped Una from her bed and rushed to the Temple of Grace. She couldn't wait any longer for Protheux. As she ascended the long staircase, her brother emerged from behind the towering pillars. The moment his eyes met hers, he knew Chiron was the one responsible for the marks she carried on her face. Anger suddenly mounted in his heart.

'Don't fret, sister,' he reassured her, his voice laced with fury. 'The Runers are at the fifth hill, grappling with the sudden change in the sky. The temple is deserted; the others are inside. Hurry now, I'll stand guard here. If anyone dares lay a hand on you again, I swear I'll kill them!'

Vertatis entered the naos finding her sisters on their knees, diligently sweeping the floor strewn with dust from the latest shockwave that had emanated from the Cloudy Mountains. The trio was taken aback by her sudden appearance, sparking a fervent discussion.

'You must help me, sisters This is my child,' Vertatis implored, her desperation palpable. 'I cannot allow them to harm her.'

'Vertatis,' one sister began, 'this is the law. For them, any of our kind harbouring magic is seen as malevolent.'

'She is one of us. If she is condemned, then so are we.' Ecne finally spoke.

'They will not spare her,' Lethya insisted. 'We wrongly find comfort on being kept enslaved here as priestesses, instead of prisoners in the crown city. But we could be gone any moment. We could be taken away once they are finished with the ones they took already. Can't you imagine what would they do to her, especially if they discover her Human heritage?'

'She needs to die,' Mementhya declared. 'Do not despair,' she quickly added as Vertatis stared in terror. 'She needs to be dead *to them*. We will ensure the Humans remain oblivious to her existence. We can keep her with us, at the temples, and claim you lost your child at birth. Lethya!' She suddenly looked at her younger sister. 'You will keep erasing her from Runers' memories. The three of us will raise her. In a few yacs, when she is old enough, she will join the other orphan children. Nobody would ever know where she came from.'

'But you know what they intend to do... They aim to confine you here for the remainder of your days. I will never lay eyes on her again, my baby...' Vertatis lamented.

'It is the only recourse. They will groom her as a priestess. And if she lacks our kind of magic, one day, perhaps you can reveal the truth to her,' Lethya reasoned.

'Why must I suffer such a terrible fate? Why must we endure this agony?' Vertatis cried out.

'It is the law, sister. The same law that shields us from the enemy lurking within. There is no alternative... It's either them or the darkness in the Cloudy Mountains.'

Whether Time's first mistake was about Una or merely the halting of Runae's revolution is unclear. Yet, in the grand scheme of things, it hardly matters. From that moment onward, events became inexorably intertwined, like a chain reaction sealing the fate of Runae and my brother's destiny for epochs to come. Still, Time remained steadfast in his belief that it was all destined to unfold that way. Despite his decision being the very catalyst for his centuries-long enslavement, he maintained, *there was no other way.*

# Chapter Thirteen

## *The Rightful King*

∞

Ten rhocs had passed since Erion had frozen in the sky, its sudden halt casting whispers of a second war across the crown city. The Humans, fuelled by anger and fear, planned their final raid northward, spurred on by the unexplainable events unfolding in the skies above. Death, an unfamiliar spectre, haunted their thoughts.

'This is incomprehensible to me,' Romohan mumbled, his mind ablaze, tears tracing down his cheeks. He stood vigil by his father's bed, his gaze fixed on the distant horizon through the large window. Below, guards patrolled the white walls, murmuring about the strange lights above.

'This is the darkest of magics; there is no other explanation!' Queen Shahara exclaimed, her grief morphing into rage. She sought someone to blame, a tangible face for her sorrow.

'I never imagined such a fate… He was here, in his chambers, by your side, by mine. How could death reach him here?' Romohan's voice wavered as he sat beside his departed father, his hands tracing the cold contours of death.

'You know that the cruellest powers can traverse lands and skies,' Lëogan interjected from the corner of the room, his body engulfed by the shadow of the walls, the golden pin on his chest gleaming proudly. 'The magnitude of this tragedy bears but one name…'

'Those vile creatures! Plotting in the darkness since the day we purged their lands from evil.' Romohan's fists clenched, his body quivering with anger.

'And they shall answer for it,' Queen Shahara declared, her hand resting on her son's shoulder, her resolve hardened by Lëogan's counsel. 'I've lost my fearcel, my other half. Let them pay the same price…let us root out these monsters from our lands.'

'But before you act—' Lëogan moved to close the grand doors, his words meant only for their ears, '—there are matters that demand attention. Firstly, the problem of the crown. I know it feels premature,' he continued, pre-empting Romohan's protest. 'But a kingdom without its king is vulnerable. You don't need further complications.'

'My son, he is right. I know we never imagined this day would come, but your father is gone...' The queen's voice trembled, tears staining her pale cheeks once more.

'What else is there?' Romohan's tone was heavy, his gaze fixed ahead. Lëogan's words had struck a nerve.

'The one lurking in the depths below... We know his deeds, his potential plans once the City is stripped of its defenders.'

'Why should the fate of a dishonoured soldier concern us now that we are grappling with the loss of our loved one?' the queen asked, perplexed.

'If we are to believe Kareesto lay with the enemy, we can safely assume he will try to carry their deeds once the city is empty. There are still many soldiers loyal to the traitor, sworn to serve him beyond the will of their new king,' Lëogan replied, moving closer to the other two. With his voice reduced to a mere whisper and his eyes gleaming with a dark light, he concluded, 'Who knows what truths he will uncover and use against you, King Romohan...'

'My father made his wishes clear,' Romohan interjected sharply. 'He was our greatest general, deserving of Herrdúr's justice. Once we deal with the Leonty, the tribunal will see to his punishment as the law demands.'

'Very well then. We may need to expedite the transfer of the crown. You must be seen as the king when we journey north. Allow me to shoulder this burden, my king.' With a sweeping bow, Lëogan exited the chamber.

'Mother,' Romohan called, striding towards the open window. 'Whatever magic they've wielded against my father, it may be beyond our grasp. Inform the guards on the walls that I require their finest scout to rendezvous with Queen Eah.'

'Do you truly believe it wise to involve them again? They've already claimed the spoils of war that rightfully belonged to your father.'

'I see no other magic that could contend with…this…' Romohan replied, his hand pointed at the one who had fallen. 'We'll depart for that godforsaken land once my beloved father has been laid to rest in his eternal chamber.'

For beings blessed with immortality, the passing of the crown was less about succession and more about the aging of the mind. While time eroded their physical forms like all others in Runae, their lives stretched to infinity. Yet, unforeseen events in the cosmos had stripped away their eternal youth, leaving them vulnerable to the passage of time. King Lohan, unprepared, met his end, his immortality shattered by the waning magic of Health.

Two rhocs later, the old king's remains lay in the large chapel below the Radhal Daíuh. Following a majestic, drawn-out ceremony, Romohan retreated to the library, his mind challenged with the recent events. Despite the crown city being thronged with Humans from every corner of their kingdom, no representatives from other races had come to offer their condolences to the new king. While the absence of the Garughals and the Chomps was anticipated, the vacant seats reserved for Vasheer and his sons, as well as Queen Eah, stoked his fury.

The three soldiers dispatched to the Aqualymphs' Sea had not returned, their absence heralding the arrival of a chilling new reality. Romohan would have to face the battle alone. The allies who had barely remained faithful to his father had seized the opportunity to sever ties with the Human kingdom. In the hushed expanse of the grand library, he paced restlessly, his face lightened by large candles, his shadow religiously observed by a few old men.

With bald heads and their stout bodies swathed in brown vests, they had promptly abandoned their weighty tomes upon Romohan's entrance, dropping to their knees in a gesture of reverence. Moments later, the imposing doors swung open once more, admitting Queen Shahara and Lëogan, their voices rising in an animated discussion.

'I fail to see the relevance of dredging up events from the past,' the queen declared, her words rushed before Romohan could draw near enough to overhear. 'My people have been exiled to the Whispering Forest. There's no need to unearth old secrets.'

'Yet someone still possesses the ability to peer into the past, my queen,' Lëogan countered, causing her unease. 'I require access to the crown's Vetitus, specifically the section concerning the malevolence residing near the temples.'

'Sir, the Vetitus is an extensive compendium of rules and practices,' the librarian interjected, his voice barely audible. 'Might I inquire as to the nature of your search?'

'That's none of your concern, priest!' Queen Shahara interjected sharply. 'And address him as your Aver, not "sir".' Behind her, Lëogan silently moved his lips, subtly guiding her words.

'This way, my Aver,' the librarian acquiesced, his demeanour suddenly diminished. Head bowed and shoulders hunched, he led the trio to a remote, chill corner of the vast library before departing, leaving them alone.

'I fail to comprehend the necessity of seeking out these individuals,' Romohan remarked as they traversed the labyrinthine rows of books. 'I have no need to identify them. My father subdued them without such knowledge.'

'My king, you remember well what their females were capable of, just the two of them,' the Harpy interjected. 'There's a reason why your father initiated all of this. We must ascertain who might oppose your rightful rule.'

'I am my father's son; none can challenge my authority,' Romohan asserted, shoving the hefty tome Lëogan had retrieved back into its place, stirring up a cloud of thick dust. Queen Shahara averted her gaze, her discomfort palpable beyond the swirling grey particles.

'You'll be heading to war soon, my king. But before you do, there's something you must know. Something I learned from your father and have kept to myself out of duty. But I won't reveal it here and now,' Lëogan interjected before Romohan could inquire further. Snagging a crimson tome adorned with a golden binding, he continued, 'This is the one. Let's return to the palace. Queen Shahara will disclose a painful yet pertinent truth.'

One hoc later, the red book lay open on a large table in the council room. Protected by the privacy of the thick walls, the secret unfolded. Lëogan's finger moved fast across the pages, his dark eyes twirling with a hungry magic. He craved the only name that mattered, the name of the one who King Lohan had left behind, confident the threat of the Leonty had been successfully removed.

'I still don't understand what you are so eagerly searching for...' Romohan let out. 'Why does it matter? We are about to eradicate that evil kind out of our world once and for all.'

'Queen Shahara,' Lëogan said, his gaze fixed on the dusty pages before him, 'I believe it's time to reveal the truth to your son...'

In the privacy of Romohan's home, compelled by the Harpy's power and against her own will, the queen finally disclosed a long-kept secret from the depths of history, a time when King Lohan found himself incapable of producing an heir. Her son listened in disbelief, his eyes locked on Shahara.

'I understand this may be difficult to accept, my son,' she continued, moving closer and taking Romohan's hand. 'But there is more you need to know to grasp the reasons behind your father's and my decisions. Romohan,' she added, her voice gentle yet firm, 'I'm a Witch of Fárahal.'

'One of the exiled, deranged people?' Romohan's eyes widened in shock.

'We are not deranged,' Shahara retorted, her tone carrying a mix of defiance and hurt. 'I am not mad. Your father banished them, cursed their names, to ensure that nobody would ever uncover the truth we glimpsed in our visions. Of course, he would never exile me, his fearcel. I was to bear you, the rightful king, in my womb and carry the burden of that secret in my heart for the rest of my days. However, we can no longer keep the truth hidden from you.'

Before Shahara could continue, Romohan withdrew his hands from hers and moved to the other side of the room. A wide opening led to a spacious terrace, offering a panoramic view of the sun-drenched landscape stretching across the horizon. Despite the late hoc, Erion glowed brightly, its radiance indicative of a superior magic they could not grasp.

'Did you do it because the law dictates that a king must have an heir within three yacs?' he asked, turning around to face the interior of the room.

'The Wise Ones were unequivocal: your father was incapable of siring children of his own. There was no other recourse but to secure an heir through alternative means, and so we did—because *we had to have you!*' Queen Shahara declared, her voice firm with conviction.

'Then why did he never tell me?' Romohan cried, his gaze falling to his hands. With each revelation, his sense of identity crumbled. He wasn't the son of a king; he was the son of a witch. His aspirations of a lasting kingdom were supplanted by the weight of an enduring curse.

'Because it was irrelevant,' the queen replied, 'Because it is still irrelevant.'

'It matters, Mother,' Romohan retorted, stepping back into the room, ready to confront her. 'Why didn't Father take another wife then?' he demanded, his voice tinged with accusation. 'Why did he keep *you* by his side, knowing what you were? Why risk everything further? No woman is worth that much…any other could have fulfilled the purpose of giving him an heir,' he shouted.

'Because I was the one who had the vision!' Shahara snapped, her weariness palpable. 'I was the one who foresaw the consequences of not having you. I saw a Leonty, a female, rising to conquer and destroy. But I also saw a Human king who would confront her and bring about her downfall. He is the one destined to reclaim the throne, ushering in the peace we all yearn for. It had to be you! I was granted that vision so you could be the one who would save us all.'

'I am not his son; I am not the rightful king!' Romohan seized his mother's arm, pushing her against the cold wall. Fury and bitterness surged within him, clouding his judgment and drowning out reason.

'Romohan!' Lëogan's sudden shout reverberated through the room, his voice carrying an ominous weight. A dark shadow swept across the space, enveloping the trio in its sinister embrace. 'You are the King of the Humans. Beyond these walls, the truth remains hidden. We would never have divulged it under different circumstances. But now, as you prepare to march into the lands of the Leonty, you risk getting too close to the one who can expose it all.'

His eyes turned pitch black, and with a wave of his hand, the Harpy lifted the large book without physical contact. Its pages fluttered wildly before coming to an abrupt halt, halfway through. An eerie thread slithered across the words and names, gradually obscuring them from view, one by one. Amidst the now-obscured pages, only a single name remained visible: Vertatis.

In that moment, Romohan felt a surge of heat in his hands, while Shahara's body began to glow red, pulsating with the unleashed power of ancient magic. Tremors wracked her limbs, her eyes rolling back as if possessed. Then, with a voice that seemed to emanate from another realm, she spoke, her words echoing with an otherworldly resonance:

'Gone are our days when he finally walks among our spirits… He bears the power of a God, his soul intertwined with another's, his heart that of a warrior. The crimson evil is slain by his hand, but his heart redeems her from her sins. The one who does not belong, surges as the new king of a reborn life…'

# Chapter Fourteen

*Sisterhood*

∞

Lethya's magic had been at work for twelve rhocs, shielding her sister Vertatis and the little one from the Runers' memories without issues. Hidden inside the naos, mother and daughter remained undetected from anyone who could harm them and, above them all, from Chiron's malevolent intentions. Twice they had been seen by their Runers, and both times Lethya had erased their presence from their minds, sending their recollections of the events down into oblivion.

As Protheux had promised, he had been watching over his sister by monitoring Chiron's every move, following him everywhere he went, as Vertatis's fearcel restlessly looked for her, determined to give her up to the Humans. On the thirteenth rhoc, Chiron had suddenly left the hills to go down south to the crown's walls. Like a stubborn shadow, Protheux had followed his every step, all the way to a few abandoned barracks where Vertatis's fearcel secretly met with three Human soldiers. He stood only a few feet away, hidden behind the cracked wall of a derelict building, when he heard the other one whispering of a deadly secret. Chiron had been informing the Humans of the Leonty's every move in exchange for a long-desired wealth. Amongst the many pieces of information he had passed on to their ears, the mention of Vertatis's and Una's names worried Protheux the most.

'Are you sure it's her?' one of the soldiers asked, his closed hand left hanging in the air. 'What we're paying you is more than we agreed… and now you're saying your own fearcel is the one?'

'It's her!' Chiron didn't hesitate. 'Tell your king he can come and get her out of my sight. Her and that monster she had. I suspect she has your general's blood running in her veins.' At those words, a few golden coins dropped from the soldier's hand to his, ringing as they touched his palm.

'This is the last payment. If what you say is true, you're better not going back to the hills. We are about to leave the crown city. After all, if what you say is true, there is no greater sin than the one happening within your home,' the soldier concluded, turning around and hurrying back to the city.

Without hesitation, Protheux left the walls and ran back to the hills, fear hastening his feet. Several hocs later, he was walking inside the Temple of Grace, his agitated voice recalling what he had heard.

'Vertatis, we need to get you out of here,' he pushed.

'How, brother? The Runers will be here soon, and so will the Humans, if what you say is true,' Lethya replied.

'It is true…' Vertatis interjected, her eyes shining red. 'So they are coming, again…'

'They are coming for you, for her,' Ecne let out, worried.

'I can't erase the memories of them all; it's beyond my reach,' Lethya added. 'But there is a way I could make it work. You are not going to like it, sister…'

'What is it?' Protheux asked, hope regaining its strength.

'First of all, we need to tell them what we agreed on. Una is dead. We knew she had a dark power and, in respect of the Humans' law, we killed her as soon as she was born,' she replied. Vertatis looked at her, worried. 'In this way, I can focus my power on one memory only. If they see the little one, I will be able to remove her from their minds, no matter how many there are. Eventually, when she is old enough, when nobody would suspect she is related to you, we can introduce her to the Runers. But you, sister. You need to leave, and you need to leave right away.

'No!' she shouted. 'I'm not leaving my daughter!'

'Vertatis, you knew this was the only way…' Ecne moved beside her, their eyes meeting as they teared up in desperation.

'I hoped I could have more time with my child. I've lost Kareesto, I'll lose my daughter too,' Vertatis cried.

'And your sisters, at least for a long while,' Protheux added, making Vertatis's heart plunge into her stomach. 'But I won't leave your side, I promise. We can both run away.'

Before the siblings could agree on a detailed plan, Jestha stormed inside the naos, her face sweating, her eyes brightening with a red light.

'They are coming! The crown's army passed the walls a few hocs ago; they will be here soon… Sister,' she added, taking Vertatis's hands. 'I see his raging mind too; he is close!'

There was no time for questions or debate. Chiron was furiously moving towards the entrance of the temple. Determined to have Vertatis in his hands before the army arrived, he shouted, 'Where is she? Where is Vertatis?'

'She is not here,' Ecne replied, emerging from the shadow of a large pillar. 'We've told you this before; your fearcel fled after we killed your daughter…'

'Enough with your lies, shut up!' Chiron interrupted, punching her in the face, making her fall on the white, cold floor.

'Chiron!' a large Leonty exclaimed from inside the temple. 'Raising your hand against an old one, against your own kind.' His shoulders large, his green legs made strong by prominent muscles, his eyes were fixed on the aggressor. After helping his sister to get up, he moved closer.

'Protheux, I'm here for your sister and that monster she calls a daughter. Step aside and let me have her,' Chiron demanded, pushing him away, his ears pointed at the cry of a little Leonty coming from inside the naos. 'I knew she was still alive.'

'I've warned you before. You have been using and abusing my sister for long enough,' Protheux replied, his words barely passing through his teeth, his right hand on Chiron's neck. 'Walk away and keep your mouth shut, and no harm will come to you.'

'Brother, let him go,' Vertatis pleaded, emerging accompanied by her sisters, Una still tightly hidden in her arms. 'Do not spill blood here, in the temple of our God, please.' But there was no prayer that could sway Chiron from his course. His will was consumed by pride and rage; he swiftly broke free from Protheux's grip and lunged towards Vertatis, his hands frenetically aiming at Una, determined to end her life. Before he could reach them, Chiron was seized and slammed against a pillar.

'In one way or another, I'll have them dead,' he hissed, his anger transforming his green face into a mask of purple madness. But Protheux's love for his sister was as unyielding as the promise he had made to her. His hand moved swiftly, unchallenged, and Chiron's neck snapped; his body collapsed lifeless.

'Give the little one to me,' Lethya demanded, her hands already reaching for the little Leonty. 'I swear to you, no harm will come to her.'

'You two, run. Ecne, Mementhya and I will take care of him,' Jestha added, her gaze fixed on the lifeless body lying at their feet.

Tears and pain welled up once more as they briefly embraced. The five sisters knew in their hearts that this might be the last time they saw each other. Their future teetered precariously on the edge of a blade; they parted ways, the distant echoes of war reaching their ears. The soft touch of Una's little hand was the last thing Vertatis imprinted on her mind as Protheux pulled her away from the temple, sprinting towards the Whispering Forest.

The enemy surged into their lands with the unstoppable force of a landslide. Amidst the cacophony of screams and cries, the Leonty fell by the hundreds under the relentless onslaught of heavy metal. There was no escape, no reprieve; only death awaited them.

The battle was short-lived. Rendered defenceless, some of the male Leonty fled over the hills, towards the mountains, while the rest of them turned against their own kin, mirroring the sinister deeds of Chiron. They offered up their daughters, their fearcels, their mothers to the enemy, like sacrificial presents in exchange for their own survival. With no negotiations, no truce to be brokered, the betrayal of their loved ones was their sole recourse. Amidst the carnage of death and the consuming flames of their homes, a line of Leonty knelt in terror, their trembling forms held in place by their male counterparts, as they were handed over to their new masters.

Lëogan's gaze swept over the scene of terror, searching the faces of the afflicted for the one he dreaded the most. As the Runers dragged the last of the hidden Leonty from the temples, King Romohan joined the Harpy, beseeching him to identify the chosen one. To his astonishment, the Aver found himself unable to discern the precise magic he sought. Arrayed like commodities for the taking, the four sisters stood motionless, their eyes tightly shut, tears streaming down their cheeks as they braced for their inevitable fate.

'There are seven of you in Hypno's line,' he began, his tone measured but laced with a sinister undercurrent. 'Two of them perished long ago, yet I see only three before me. Where are the other two?' A dark gleam flickered in his eyes, hinting at the depths of his suspicion.

'Vertatis and Lethya met their end just several rhocs past, after Erion ceased its descent behind the mountains,' Jestha responded, her voice barely above a whisper, her gaze fixed on the ground.

'Lies…' Lëogan countered, a sly smile playing at the corners of his lips. 'The one you call Chiron would beg to differ… Where is he?'

'He departed some time ago, heading south. We cannot say when he will return,' Ecne interjected, her words tinged with desperation as she clung to their fabricated tale, knowing their very lives hung in the balance.

'Very well, let see if this impresses upon you the gravity of falsehoods spoken to your king,' the Harpy declared, a silent signal passing between him and a nearby soldier. In one swift motion, the soldier's blade fell, and Ecne's head tumbled to the ground, a chorus of screams erupting in its wake. In the throes of anguish and fear, Jestha's and Mementhya's eyes snapped open, revealing the telltale crimson glow of magic.

Determined to shield the little one cradled in her arms, Lethya remained steadfast, her own magic suddenly amplified by a silent power, cloaking her presence from the prying eyes around her, rendering her and Una invisible. Before the Humans could comprehend her presence, she would erase their memories in a relentless loop, her power stretched to its limits in her efforts to protect Una.

'We seek only the one known as Vertatis, and her alone,' King Romohan declared, his voice echoing with authority. Unbeknownst to the cold-hearted Humans, the unbreakable bond of sisterly love that bound the seven siblings transcended their grasp. Lethya clung to the vow she had made to Vertatis, persistent even in the face of impending doom. A few moments later, Jestha fell to the cruel blade as their last sister, Mementhya, was chained and carried away. Their ultimate sacrifices etched into the annals of their tragic tale.

Undiscovered, cradled within Lethya's arms lay the key to her amplified abilities, Una unknowingly bolstering the Leonty's power and resisting Lëogan's dark magic. In that coincidental alliance lay the seed of a triumph that in the near future would prevail against their formidable foe.

# Chapter Fifteen

*A Dying World*

∞

The warm, babbling waters of the Gochi River provided a melancholic backdrop to the sombre gathering of Chomps near its banks. Aura encountered the group, their wings drooping with grief as they recounted Kasthor's sudden illness. Desperation tinged their voices as they implored the Aqualymph for aid, seeking any magical remedy that could restore him to health.

'I'm afraid this is a battle I don't know how to fight. I wish I could return to the sea and seek counsel from my queen, but sadly, you know it's beyond my reach,' Aura lamented, her translucent visage betraying her sadness.

'Could you not attempt it? So much has happened... Perhaps the queen will listen,' one Chomp suggested.

'I've already risked much. Since that day in the Cloudy Mountains, Queen Eah has changed drastically. A dark shadow looms over my kind, a transformation I cannot comprehend. It drives them from the depths more frequently. Moreover, with the queen wielding not one but two Flares, I dare not bring her closer to a third. Especially now, as their nature seems to veer towards something malevolent.'

'Can't we seek aid from the Garughals?' Treekan proposed tearfully.

'After the tower's collapse and the Flare's descent into the river's depths, Garúth and I are hardly on amicable terms. But that won't deter me. I can navigate the river's currents to the waterfalls once more. I understand your reluctance to leave your dome, and I advise you to limit your excursions outside,' Aura advised empathetically.

'If a greater war looms, our Flare may be our only salvation. The supposed master of our world, the one holding the key to our Runae, is nowhere to be found. Why?' Treekan's distress was palpable. He had grown up hearing tales of the God's heroic deeds, yet now faced a world abandoned by its supposed saviour.

'Where the Key master has gone, I cannot say. But let me confer with our allies to the east. The Garughals may possess knowledge of a hidden magic within nature that could aid Kasthor.'

'Please Aura,' the one called Faróel pleaded, his voice heavy with desperation. 'I understand we're asking a great deal of you… My fearcel and Treekan are my everything. In times of need, Kasthor was the one we turned to, the one every Chomp trusted. I would journey to the Valahans myself to seek a remedy, but I cannot bear to leave Kasthor's side…'

'I'll do my best to help. Please, wait for my return. I'll hasten as best I can,' Aura assured them before dissipating into the chilly embrace of the river's current, leaving the Chomps to anxiously await her return. Terrified by the fading of their once-enduring vitality, their only hope lay frailly within the wisdom of Aura's kind or the magic of the Garughals.

As the Aqualymph approached the fringes of the Garughals' domain, she was struck by an unnerving silence that enveloped the once-vibrant surroundings. The harmonious whispers of those attuned to the rhythms of nature had fallen silent, replaced by an eerie stillness that spoke of desolation and despair. Aura could hardly believe her eyes as she emerged from the waterfall's embrace, greeted by a dying landscape stretching before her.

Once-vibrant trees now stood tall but lifeless, their once-green canopies replaced by barren branches. To her right, the remnants of the old tower lay in ruin, its stones scattered across the courtyard. As she cautiously made her way forward, expecting to encounter the Garughals who guarded the sovereign's home, she was met with eerie silence. No one emerged to challenge her presence; not even a leaf stirred as she took shape, and the once-thriving land seemed to wither before her gaze.

Moving past the crumbling structures, Aura ventured deeper into the grove, her mind racing with thoughts of what could have transpired since she had last been there. Her hand reached out to touch one of the few remaining trees, its trunk still faintly retaining some semblance of life. With closed eyes, she tapped into her magic, probing the tree's inner core for signs of vitality. What she discovered filled her with shock: the tree was hollow, its life force drained to the brink of extinction. It stood on the verge of collapse, a stark testament to the devastation that had befallen that once-thriving woodland.

'This cannot be,' Aura murmured, her voice tinged with disbelief. 'What happened to you all? What happened to this place?' In response, a faint rustling called behind her, the sound of dead leaves stirring in the wind.

'Our master is gone,' a voice whispered, barely audible yet laden with sorrow. 'And we are going with him.'

'Where are you?' Aura turned, her gaze fixing on a small bush quivering in the shadow of its larger neighbours. Its leaves had wilted, and its roots bore an uncanny resemblance to Human feet.

'The lights in the sky descended upon us, and we could not withstand their approach,' the bush lamented.

'What lights?' Aura's heart raced with foreboding, her fears of a dire fate growing with each passing moment.

'The aging, death…' the Garughal whispered, its voice barely audible. 'We Garughals naturally merge with nature as we age, becoming one with our beloved world when our time comes. But this…this came too swiftly, too unexpectedly. We had no chance to transition. We were not ready… Those closest to their Gahál-Aidír had already lived many yacs beyond their time, and they transformed into lifeless trees instead.'

'This cannot be!' Aura exclaimed, her voice trembling with fear. 'How, why is this happening? And how many of you remain?' But the bush, now rooted to the ground, remained silent, its transformation complete. Behind her, another presence stirred in the air, carrying with it a chilling aura of malevolence. 'Who's there? Show yourself!' Aura demanded, rising to her feet.

A familiar scent wafted through the air, yet it was tainted with darkness, leaving a trail of ominous magic in its wake. 'Who are you?' Aura repeated, her heart racing with unease.

'The sea is disgorging the dead and the living alike…' came the reply, catching Aura off guard. Though the voice was familiar, its identity remained elusive to her. 'I was among the many long dead, freed to join our queen…but I was drawn to you instead.'

'Did you do this to them?' Aura questioned, her voice tinged with accusation.

'She's about to emerge from the sea once more, seeking greater power…' The incorporeal, dark form flickered, struggling to manifest itself before Aura, caught between light and darkness.

'The Beacon of Fire,' the Aqualymph blurted out. 'It's still at the bottom of the river, an easy reach for those who can traverse the waters.'

Without hesitation, Aura departed from her spot. Though bearing the heavy burden of the Garughals' fate in her heart, her mind fixated on the looming threat ahead. *It's all my fault*, she thought. *If only they still had their Flare safeguarding their lands…and now Queen Eah can sense its power coursing through the water stream.* With a swift leap down the waterfall, Aura resumed her true form and plunged into the river's depths. As she reached the riverbed, she beheld the gleaming golden stone of the Flare. Its power surged through her, enhancing her senses, guiding her consciousness along the river's bottom. Through the power of the stone, Aura's sight grew unlimited, speeding towards the distant horizon where the river met the sea. There, she witnessed Queen Eah and her legion of Aqualymphs speeding upstream.

'She will be here soon…' The same voice Aura had heard in the woods spoke to her underwater. 'Please, go…'

'Mareen?' Aura's voice trembled with emotion. Empowered by the Garughals' magic, she could perceive the essence of the being beside her. Her beloved had returned from the Avalian Deep. 'I can't believe it. How is this possible? How did you free yourself from the endless night of the Deep?' she asked, moving next to him. As her figure came close to his, a whispering chorus of anguish and torment resounded in Aura's mind, confirming Aura's worst fears—that Mareen, too, had succumbed to the encroaching darkness. 'You are changing, just like the rest of them…' she murmured, reaching out to touch him.

'She knows you're here,' Mareen interjected. 'You must retrieve this power from the waters, now.'

'The queen can traverse the lands freely now. Wherever I go, she will follow,' Aura replied.

'Then every moment you keep it from her is a moment of hope. Go, my love. Be the one you promised to be, a Gatekeeper from every evil. I cannot hold back this darkness much longer. But I needed you to be safe…before I let it consume me.'

Mareen trembled in the waters, stirring the sandy foundations beneath the Flare. Lifting himself from the ground, he pressed his hands against the radiant stone, igniting it with a blaze. His malevolent shadow loomed behind him, writhing in agony as if attempting to break free from the Aqualymph's form. Through the Flare's magic, Aura glimpsed her companion's true essence once more. His eyes locked on to hers, conveying a love undeterred by darkness. In that fleeting moment, Mareen affirmed his unwavering commitment to her, standing by her side. 'Go!' he bellowed, propelling her towards the surface.

Aura ascended through the warm waters like a missile until she burst into the open air of the Garughals' courtyard. Close behind her, a horde of Aqualymphs converged on the spot where the Flare had stood, only to find it gone, stoking Queen Eah's fury. The Gochi River contorted, its waters pulsating with violent energy. In spasms of power, the

Aqualymphs materialized on land, their forms resembling countless droplets suspended in the humid air.

At the front of the evil mist, Queen Eah took shape. Absorbing the sandy, white dust of the Garughals' ruins, her form appeared quickly. Her limbs and arms contorted like thousands of bricks badly assembled, her face looked deformed, her eyes stretched to the sides. What once was a shining red artefact made of corals, her crown shone of a grey, dark metal.

'The traitor of her own kind eludes me once more...' the queen murmured. 'Aqualymphs. Hunt her down and bring back that defiant Lymph!' Her army surged forwards like an advancing, hot steam, infiltrating the depths of the Garughals' domain and seizing every last vestige of lymph lingering in the land. Energized by theft, corruption, and sacrilege, the Aqualymphs rapidly succumbed to darkness, their once-free wills enslaved by malevolent power, transmuting them into spectral slaves.

With the multitude of enemies closing in behind her, Aura found herself with little distance to spare. At the edge of the Garughals' territory, she stood at a crossroads, faced with a crucial decision. To the west lay the arid expanse of the steppes, a harsh landscape leading to the hills of the Leonty. Turning south would lead her to the scorching Mogs Mountains, where fire and heat threatened to consume her very essence. Whichever path she chose, she knew the others would soon catch up.

Pausing at the small crossroad, where the mountains parted to reveal a narrow passage between their towering peaks, Aura weighed her options. Her gaze lingered on the blistering Erion to the south, her concern growing for her waning magic. *How long can I continue to evade capture without the revitalizing touch of water?* The lakes near the crown city were too distant, and the nearest access to the Gochi River lay with the Chomps.

That was her best option. Aura had to make her way towards the only place she trusted, the sole land where the elusive power would shield her from sight. With a final glance at the scorching sun, she mentally counted the precious moments she had left before she would transform into a dark spirit. Fearful that she might not be able to breach the formidable dome of the Chomps, Aura closed her eyes and clutched the Garughals' Flare close to her chest. Suddenly, her soul detached from her body, sinking into the earth and traversing through soil, trees, and sweltering air.

In the span of a few fleeting moments, she found herself standing before a small house atop a hill. Its door stood ajar, while the front windows, low to the ground, seemed to convey a sombre countenance. Inside, the air was heavy with the sounds of sobbing and whispers of despair. A young Chomp emerged onto the porch, tears streaming down his face, his wings drooping low, cheeks flushed with anguish. Moments later, Faróel appeared, following in the wake of the distraught youngster.

'Treekan, my son… I know it's difficult to understand. It's difficult for me too,' he said, gently running his hand over Treekan's head.

'Why is this happening, Father?' Treekan's voice quivered, and as he spoke, a breeze swept between them, causing the grass along the porch to sway.

'Faróel…' a voice called out. 'Faróel, can you hear me?' The two Chomps were taken aback, their eyes narrowing to thin slits. Something was materializing before them. From the small steps at the front, a bush began to move, its roots lifting from the brown soil, its branches stretching upward.

'What's happening?' Treekan exclaimed, instinctively moving back towards the front door.

'It appears to be Garughals' magic. Garúth?' Faróel inquired, stepping forwards to shield his son.

'Garúth is dead,' the bush stated. 'It's me, Aura.'

'Dear Erion, how?' Faróel drew closer. 'How did you manage to breach the dome? And why are you using this kind of power?'

'The Garughals are all gone!' Aura revealed. 'I retrieved their Flare before Queen Eah could claim it. The other Aqualymphs are pursuing me, far from here, near the Red Pass in the mountains. My only hope of evading them is to seek refuge within your dome. You must permit me entry when I arrive…'

'But you're already here, aren't you?' Treekan interjected, his confusion evident.

'My spirit is present, channelled through the Garughals' Flare, but my physical body remains elsewhere. I must return now and reach this location in the flesh. Please, act swiftly! And Faróel, Treekan, I'm profoundly sorry for your loss…' With that, the bush abruptly ceased moving and collapsed to the ground, lifeless.

Aura's eyes widened. Her spirit re-entered her body as she found herself encircled by a multitude of Aqualymphs. Their forms flickered, wavering between ethereal steam and ominous smoke. One of them seized the Flare from her grasp, his expression filled with disdain.

'You couldn't have been more foolish,' he remarked, his voice whistling. 'This belongs to our queen. And you…you belong to the Avalian Deep…'

The Aqualymphs advanced on Aura with synchronized movements, their collective will focused on her like a singular force. With arms raised and faces twisted by dark intent, they closed in, leaving her with no escape. The end of Aura's desperate bid to elude her queen's judgment, to prevent her from seizing the Garughals' Flare, had come.

Queen Eah materialized from the swirling mist, her once-noble form twisted beyond recognition. No longer infused with the essence of earth and nature, her renewed shape was sustained by darkness and corruption, casting her soul and body into a grim shadow.

'You have defied your queen for far too long, Gatekeeper,' she declared, her voice laced with the chill of impending doom as she closed her hand around Aura's neck. 'Your arrogance blinds you to your duty and disrespect. Cease your futile resistance. You cannot shift nor prevail against me. You couldn't before, and you certainly cannot now that I possess three Flares.'

'This is madness,' Aura managed to choke out, her voice a mere whisper of defiance. 'You have surrendered to evil…'

'What choice do we have in the face of such relentless adversaries?' Queen Eah countered, her tone dripping with bitter resolve. 'We must adapt, we must raise our stakes to match the darkness that threatens to consume us. Now, join me, or die!'

'I swear my allegiance to one God, and to Time alone I shall answer. You, my queen, have strayed from the path by the hands of our very foe. I shall never yield to you…'

'Very well. You have chosen death!'

Queen Eah's hands ascended into the sky. Above her rapidly expanding form, three Flares materialized, swirling fervently. Their melded hues of orange, red, and crystal blue pulsed as her gaze locked on to the one she had condemned. With a gesture towards the defiant Aqualymph, Queen Eah made the earth tremble, rending asunder. Its wide mouth disgorged torrents of subterranean waters. Amidst the swirling azure torrents, crimson droplets darted towards Aura.

Before the Gatekeeper could confront the colossal onslaught, a grey shadow interposed itself between her and the queen's sorcery. Mareen materialized briefly, his smile a bittersweet farewell to his beloved as he propelled her to safety, shielding her from harm.

His parting words whispered for Aura's ears only, echoing with urgency, 'Run, my love…'

# Chapter Sixteen

## *The Machine of War*

∞

Vertatis and Protheux had barely entered the Whispering Forest when she abruptly halted, collapsing to her knees in agony. Clutching her head, she groaned as her mind reached out across the distance, sensing a disturbance that filled her with dread. All around them, an endless expanse of dark trees stretched in every direction, their gnarled forms looming like silent sentinels of the forest. The air was thick with the palpable presence of the fallen Human soldiers, their restless spirits haunting the surroundings with their anguished cries. Vertatis felt their presence weigh heavily on her mind, each scream echoing through her consciousness like a relentless barrage.

Amidst the eerie stillness, the memory of her and Umbra carrying the unconscious Kareesto reverberated loudly in Vertatis's thoughts, a vivid reminder of the perilous journey they had undertaken together.

'What's wrong?' Protheux spun around, closing the gap between them. His hands tenderly cupped her pale face, his touch a comforting anchor amidst her turmoil. The colour in her eyes shifted, swirling into a deadly red reminiscent of the blood recently spilled at the temples.

'We made a mistake, brother,' she cried out.

'Is it Una?' His concern was palpable as he helped her to her feet.

'No, I can still sense my baby in my heart, in my mind,' she replied, her voice trembling. 'But the others...I fear for them, I fear for my daughter. I see death everywhere I look. Here, in this place where many of them fell, and at the temples...'

'Don't jump to conclusions, sister,' Protheux urged, his tone soothing yet filled with apprehension. 'Your power has its limits. You could be mistaken. We should keep moving, head southwest.'

'No, we must turn back,' Vertatis gripped her brother's arm firmly, her gaze ablaze with determination. Before Protheux could voice his dissent, shadows flitted amidst the verdant foliage.

'We meet again…' a voice echoed, resonating through the forest's depths. Meeriah emerged from behind a tree, her presence unsettling yet familiar. 'Red irises of uncommon power, green skin of a cursed race,' she observed, her tone dripping with cryptic knowledge. 'You remember me,' she added, advancing slowly. 'I had your general within my grasp before you intervened.'

'Sister?' Protheux exclaimed, bewildered.

'You tried to kill him,' Vertatis retorted, rising to her feet. 'Why?'

'Because what lies ahead is inscribed in the pages of fate… A future in flux, yet I perceive it clearly now, I wasn't meant to end him…and the idea fills me with satisfaction,' the witch explained, a sinister smile curving her lips. 'When one of us glimpses the future, all are privy to its secrets. My sister has been blessed with a new vision, and it feels…promising.'

'Who are you? What do you speak of?' Protheux demanded, stepping protectively in front of Vertatis.

'Do not fret, Protheux, son of Hypno, born without magic amidst a lineage of sorcery,' Meeriah continued, her words laden with ominous portent. 'You may traverse this forest freely. Your actions will only hasten our inevitable convergence upon the same unalterable future.' A chilling laugh punctuated her proclamation, resonating among the towering, silent sentinels of the woods.

'Let us go, Vertatis,' Protheux urged, tugging at his sister's arm.

'Before you leave,' the witch interjected, her voice carrying a note of grim prophecy. 'Allow me to illuminate the path ahead. You shall tread in circles, over and over. Your fate is sealed within the white towers, their darkness a relentless vortex that catches and releases you, only to ensnare you once more. Beware, for truth shall bring your downfall!' With a gesture, she directed their gaze towards the distant reaches of the forest.

'Foolish babble. We would never venture into our enemy's stronghold.' Protheux scoffed.

'No, brother, she speaks the truth,' Vertatis countered, her red eyes alight with revelation. Stepping away from her sibling, she approached Meeriah. 'Tell me how we may survive this…'

'I'm afraid defiance is futile. None shall escape. We retreat to the outskirts, as darkness here will soon reign supreme. Your daughter will rise, a harbinger of conquest and dominion, and we shall not bear witness to her destruction,' Meeriah declared solemnly.

'Una will survive? That is all that matters. Thank you!' Vertatis exclaimed, reaching for the witch's hands in gratitude.

'Do not thank me, naive greenskin,' Meeriah rebuked, withdrawing her hand sharply. 'The birth of a greater evil begins with a mother's choice. Your choice. From this moment forth, all is set in stone. Now, go. Fulfil your destiny. Rescue the Crown Sunshine. But be prepared for anguish and loss…'

'Are you saying there's hope to save Kareesto? To save Umbra?' Vertatis rejoiced, heedless of the witch's harsh tone. Blinded by optimism, she clung to the promise of salvation.

'Four shall depart the City, but only three shall emerge alive. And you, magicless male, when the time comes, seek him out in his chambers...' With that cryptic utterance, Meeriah turned away, ignoring Vertatis's pleas for further elucidation, and vanished into the depths of the forest alongside her coven.

'We have an opportunity we may never encounter again, brother. We must journey to the crown city, free Kareesto and Umbra.'

Protheux recoiled in disbelief, his gaze locking with hers.

'Have you lost your senses?' he exclaimed. 'Of all places to seek refuge, you propose to listen to the mad words of a witch and march straight into the Humans' city? Our sister is gone, Vertatis. Kareesto is likely lost to us.'

'You cannot be certain of anything,' Vertatis countered, her voice unwavering. 'I sense your doubts, lingering beneath the surface. Why do you refuse to listen to them? She spoke the truth. This is our chance. With most of the soldiers deployed at the temple, we might slip in unnoticed. If not now, then when?'

Protheux wrestled with his sister's fearless plan and the doubts plaguing his own mind. The risk loomed large: even if they managed to infiltrate the city unnoticed, they lacked vital information on Kareesto's and Umbra's whereabouts. Yet, Vertatis pressed on, marching downhill towards the northern gates, steady in her determination. After a brief internal struggle, Protheux relented, falling into step beside his sister.

'How do you propose we breach the walls?' he inquired as they approached the gates.

'There's a way through. The same route I've used whenever Kareesto and I met,' Vertatis answered, her stride purposeful as she made for the barracks on the western side, where the walls curved southward.

It had been yacs since they had begun their clandestine rendezvous, shrouded in the cloak of night. Yet, for Vertatis, the memories felt fresh, etched into her heart alongside the resilience of their bond, a beacon driving her forward.

The crown city stood resplendent in the early morning, its ivory towers gleaming in the violet hues of the sky. Erion bathed the city in an otherworldly glow, casting a luminous sheen upon its marble edifices. Streets lay deserted, the city's denizens shielding themselves from the star's piercing rays behind tightly drawn shutters. As Vertatis had anticipated, much of the army was absent, engaged in battle against the Leonty in the hills. The siblings navigated the labyrinth of streets and alleys, their movements stealthy, their senses alert for any sign of danger.

'Sister,' Protheux murmured, halting Vertatis before she descended a winding staircase towards the city center. 'Look, Human cloaks. We'd do well to conceal ourselves before proceeding further,' he suggested, retrieving two grey capes hanging from the wall of a nearby dwelling.

'Kareesto and Umbra must be somewhere in the heart of the city, this way,' Vertatis affirmed, adjusting the concealing robe over her form. Her gaze swept over the vast courtyard unfolding below. 'I've never ventured to this side of the city,' she confessed, 'but that towering structure there'—she gestured towards a grand palace nestled amidst the pale edifices—'is the king's residence.'

'I highly doubt they're held within those walls, sister. And even if they were, storming the king's stronghold is sheer madness,' Protheux cautioned. The distant clank of armoured footsteps echoed from a nearby street, prompting the Leonty to swiftly pull Vertatis behind a nearby wall. Pressed against the cool stones, they huddled together, striving to remain concealed.

'Did you hear that priest?' the voice of a nearby soldier reached the Leonty's ears. 'Dictating our very moves as if he were our general…'

'If the king doesn't put an end to their experiments, we will end up dead,' another one replied.

'Experiments?' Protheux queried, his voice barely audible amidst the gust of wind; nearby guards exchanged positions atop the citadel walls.

'Kareesto once mentioned a place he called the Dungeon of Madness. The so-named scientists keep their prisoners beneath the library for their twisted experiments,' Vertatis disclosed in a hushed tone.

'Tell the guards atop we need to open the golden fountain of the Radhal Daíuh,' the first soldier told another one who had just met them on the paved road. 'They are ready to use the Leonty's power.'

'Umbra?' the two siblings exclaimed simultaneously.

'How far is this dungeon?' Protheux added.

'I'm not sure. The Radhal Daíuh is the same place where the great library is.' Vertatis moved slowly, sliding along the wall, peeking around its corner. A gentle breeze swept across the narrow street, causing the long tail of her cloak to flap over the edge.

'Who's there?' a soldier shouted from afar, his eyes fixed on the grey cloak. 'You know the king's decree. No work nor walk before Erion-dát. Show yourself!' But his request went unanswered.

'We need to move, now!' Protheux urged, his eyes darting to both ends of the street. Pulling Vertatis by her arm, the Leonty led her down a set of stairs, towards a large opening where a grand fountain spilled a bright, golden liquid from a tall statue. Four guards trailed closely behind, their gazes fixed on the fleeing strangers. Ahead lay the gates of the enormous palace, exposing the Leonty to the open.

To their left, along the citadel inner wall, a dangerously narrow street stretched at the hill's peak. To their right, another set of stairs descended towards the coast. As they chose the safest path forward, a vast, glittering blue landscape unfolded before them.

'Stay right there and turn around!' a guard shouted from just a few feet away.

'Pull your hood down and show your face,' another one added.

'Sister,' Protheux whispered, his heartbeat accelerating. 'Find them. I'll hold them off.' Before Vertatis could object, he turned around. As instructed, he slowly removed the cloak from his shoulders and stared at the Humans.

'A Leonty!' one gasped, his eyes widening.

'Inside our city...' another one continued. 'How did you pass the walls, unseen? What power do you possess?' The four guards advanced cautiously, their right hands gripping the long swords hanging at their sides.

'I'm a male of my kind, you fool. Are you just stupid, or are you blind as well?' he retorted, sharp.

'What about you? Pull it down, immediately!' The only guard brave enough to stand in front of their most feared enemy stepped close, his hand reaching for Vertatis's hood.

'Hands off my sister!' Protheux acted promptly. In the blink of an eye, he grabbed the Human's arms, pushed him around, and kicked his legs, causing him to fall to his knees. A sharp blade glinted in the air as it was turned against its owner, pressing against the guard's throat.

'No, brother!' Vertatis exclaimed, gripping his arm. 'We are not here to cause trouble,' she continued, finally revealing her face to the Humans. 'We need to get to the Radhal Daíuh...'

'What business do you have with the priests? The Radhal Daíuh is open only to those who are invited. Release the soldier immediately, or face death at our hands!' The guards' tone was demanding, but their actions betrayed their worries. Their feet were glued to the stone steps, and fear prevented them from moving.

'Where is your general, the Crown Sunshine?' Vertatis asked, taking the soldiers and her own brother by surprise.

'Our general?' one guard laughed. 'Kareesto is dead.'

'Where is he?' Vertatis repeated, her eyes blazing red. The guard's lie had flashed in her mind, shrilling loud, exposing him; she finally knew he was still alive. The only thing left to discover was where they could find him.

'He… he…' one of the Humans stammered, stepping back, terrified by Vertatis's face. The other two guards suddenly fled, leaving him alone. 'He is… in the dungeons…' he finally confessed.

But before the two Leonty could run and resume their rescue mission, a loud horn echoed throughout the city. The soldiers at the walls had been alerted to the intruders, and a small army quickly assembled at the entrance of the palace. It was only a matter of moments before Vertatis and Protheux were surrounded, from both the top and the bottom of the staircase. Protheux held the sword tight; drops of blood started to flow down the guard's neck. Amongst the crowd, a whisper ran from one part to another. On the ground, a grey smoke rose slowly, slipping through their legs; the many soldiers were petrified by that new, surging magic. The Leonty quickly gazed at his sister, his expression sharing a silent agreement.

'She is alive… She is near,' Vertatis let out, happiness slipping through her words.

The light of the large sun was gone. The smoke had turned to fog and raised high above their heads. Dark clouds built up in between the soldiers, turning day into night, hiding the Leonty from sight. With Umbra's power reaching from below, Vertatis pulled her brother away and ran downwards, following the trail her sister's magic left behind. Soon enough, they reached the large doors of the Radhal Daíuh where two more guards stood still with their hands on their faces, their eyes itching from the thick mist. The defenceless library opened up to the two strangers who, concealed by the darkness of the Leonty's power, moved inside unseen.

Inside, a few harmless Humans moved around. Their long brown habits dragged on the cold floor; they held lanterns up in the air, attempting to shed light into what clearly was to them a bad omen. Three of them had gathered together in front of a rusty gate closed shut. As Vertatis and Protheux moved closer, they heard the exchanging words of danger and excitement.

'This is what the Aver talked us about... This is their magic.'

'We have been testing and forcing the female for rhocs, she has never manifested any power...'

'I'm telling you, this is it! Let's go down below. This is our chance to extract her magic from her mind. You,' one of the priests said to another, 'call the Aver, tell him we are ready to turn on the Machine of War.'

The three moved at once. Without hesitation, two of them pushed the gate open and descended into the dungeons. Turned blind by Umbra's magic, unaware they were being followed, the priests reached the end of the path. There, an enormous cave extended wide and deep as if it had no visible end. At the centre, a large construction stood incomplete, wooden beams and iron pillars holding it upright.

'What are they doing in here?' Protheux asked, his voice muffled by their sister's magic.

'Looks like they are building something, look at that dark stone over there...' Vertatis replied, hurrying her steps while the Humans moved further ahead. Inside a short, wide well, a rounded, metallic construction stood a few inches from the water. At its top, the sky peeked through an opening; a tall, shining pole ran all the way up to the outside. Electric blue flashes darted all around, magnetizing the space. As she stepped close, her hair lifted, shivers crawled on her skin.

At the centre of the Human artefact, a black stone spun on its own. Its edges shifted from solid to dark fluid, a random sequence of grey flares flashing around its surface.

'Hurry up, sister. We are going to lose them in this labyrinth.' Protheux rushed her, following the Humans into a corner. Several cells lay one beside another. Some were empty, some held the white remains of prisoners long gone. But the one where the two priests had stopped by, kept someone captive still. Umbra's hands on the ground, rusty handcuffs on her wrists, she was kept kneeling down. All around her, water flowed in and out of her cell, reaching the large machinery nearby.

'I can't see her, but she must still be here...' one of the priests murmured, his hand resting on his ample belly as he selected a key from the cluster dangling at his side and deftly unlocked the gate.

'The Nucleus is active,' the other one affirmed. 'Her power streams through the waters, just as we anticipated. Let us wait until all her energies have been drained. Once life has left her, we can examine her safely.' Vertatis glanced towards her brother, her own magic confirming the grim truth; swift action was imperative.

'Sister, I'm here. Let me in, I can't see you,' she implored, her voice lost on ears devoid of power. A moments later, a rift materialized within the murky fog, revealing the anguished form of Umbra.

'Vertatis, Protheux,' Umbra breathed, weariness evident in her voice. 'You came...'

'We didn't expect to find you alive,' her brother exclaimed, enfolding her in his arms. 'How do we remove these restraints from your wrists?'

'They have the key... Hurry, brother. I can't endure much longer...' Umbra faltered.

'What horrors have they inflicted on you?' Vertatis moved to support Umbra, while Protheux approached the priests, his hands deftly navigating through their heavy brown robes.

'They have discovered a way to channel their Flare through magic...' Umbra muttered weakly. 'They call it the Machine of War. Inside, the Ergon Déil spins constantly, absorbing our powers. Not only ours, but Garughals', and I swear, I glimpsed two Aqualymphs imprisoned in a cell not long ago.'

Vertatis was aghast. Humans wielded the divine gift of Flare as a weapon against other races, harnessing their victims' magic to wreak havoc upon the inhabitants of Runae. Protheux returned to his sisters, key in hand, poised to liberate Umbra, when she collapsed, unconscious, into Vertatis's arms. Abruptly, the magic ceased, the fog dissipating. Under the petrified gaze of the two priests, the Leonty materialized out of thin air.

Like thieves caught red-handed with the most coveted treasure, the trio found themselves trapped, with no escape in sight. They had walked willingly into a prison that would soon become their tomb, their fate racing towards them, their final breath destined to fuel the sinister machinery of war, just as it had for countless others before them.

# Chapter Seventeen

*The Price of Freedom*

∞

Umbra's essence and power instantly drained from her body, leaving a trail of sparkling matter creeping along the cold, paved ground. As it penetrated the surrounding waters, her magic briefly lingered, waiting to depart. Guided by the magnetic pull of the Ergon Déil, her soul transitioned from her inert form to the malevolent war machine, unleashing a blinding surge of energy upon the surface. Several of the pristine white structures quaked, shedding ivory dust from their walls and rooftops.

With the weight of Umbra's head resting in Vertatis's embrace, Protheux rose, his fists clenched in readiness to confront the two feeble priests. Bereft of any magic and lacking combat prowess, the panicked Humans turned tail and fled the dungeons, their cries for aid echoing in their wake. Supported by the Leonty, Umbra was raised from the damp ground, her arms draped over their shoulders, as they sought a way out. Amid their search, a male voice startled them.

'Vertatis?' he queried. 'Is that you?'

'Kareesto!' The Leonty hastened to his cell, tears welling in her eyes as she gripped the rusted bars. The general's hands were trapped in heavy handcuffs, his arms stretched upwards by chains.

'How did you find your way here? You must leave; they'll find you and end your lives,' he pleaded, his face smeared with dirt and dried blood, bearing the scars of prolonged torment.

'No!' Vertatis retorted firmly. 'We've come to rescue you and my sister from this wretched place. Protheux, give me the keys…'

The Radhal Daíuh soon teemed with soldiers, their clamour reverberating through the library, reaching the quartet below. With their adversaries descending upon them, the Leonty and Kareesto had to seek an alternate escape route. Guided by the general's weakened yet sharp mind, they trailed him through a labyrinthine passage at the dungeon's rear.

Round after round, they navigated cramped, dim tunnels where water and filth coursed towards the crown city's outskirts and the sea beyond. Emerging into the open,

Protheux and Vertatis halted their flight, their sister's weight becoming too burdensome to bear. Under the shining light of the large star, a pall of grey overshadowed Umbra's eyes; death had drained the colour from her pallid visage.

'What are you doing? We must keep moving,' Kareesto urged from a few paces ahead.

'Sister…' Vertatis choked back a sob as she and Protheux gently laid Umbra's body upon the dusky sand. 'I'm so sorry…'

'We must leave her, Vertatis… Umbra's soul has departed for the beyond,' Protheux murmured, kneeling beside his two sisters. Tears streaming down his cheeks, he surveyed the towering walls and the boundless sea.

'She did not deserve such a fate, such suffering…' The Leonty seethed with resentment.

'No, she did not,' Kareesto agreed, drawing nearer. 'But you have freed her, brought her body from that abyss… She understands. Her spirit can now find peace, here beneath the open sky, beside the sea.' His hand tenderly closed Umbra's eyes. 'Let her journey on the Sacred Waters. There, her form will reunite with the Gods.'

The trio hoisted Umbra's body from the sand and guided her into the embrace of the sea. The warm water lapped at their waists and their hearts as they gently propelled Umbra towards the boundless azure expanse, her form swaying with the gentle rhythm of the waves. Before their resolve faltered, her body descended into the depths, vanishing from sight. Thus, the one who had endured agony and torment to save them all bid her final farewell, her magic dispersing across Runae as a forerunner of trials yet to come.

Leaving the sandy white beaches behind, the fugitives at last arrived at the outskirts on the eastern fringe of the Human kingdom. With desperation propelling them forward, they pressed on through treacherous terrain, their bodies weary but their resolve unyielding. As the verdant hills of the Chomps loomed into view, Kareesto broke the silence.

'The Aqualymphs' Sea stands as a barrier before us. We cannot simply traverse it. To reach the silent forest, we must follow the coastline upwards…'

'But we're still too close to the outskirts. Venturing into the village bordering their territory is too risky,' Protheux interjected, his eyes scanning the landscape.

'And what alternative do you propose? Entering the domain of those who align themselves with the king? The Aqualymphs harbour no warmth towards your kind. We must navigate through the Crown's End district. If we proceed cautiously, the Chomp's hills will be within reach,' the general countered, quickening his pace along the coast.

'Look! There are a few structures atop that ridge,' Vertatis pointed out, her gaze fixed on the distant silhouette. 'They appear abandoned. Perhaps we could seek respite there for a moment?'

Fortune briefly smiled upon them as they found the houses devoid of life. With their roofs ravaged by storms long past and their walls bearing the scars of time, the structures seemed frozen in a state of abandonment. Within, scant remnants of former inhabitants lingered—a few forgotten belongings left behind. Amongst the sparse traces of bygone occupancy, heavy cloaks hung in eerie silence, their once-vibrant hues muted by a layer of dust, rendering them a ghostly grey.

As they settled in for a brief rest, the weight of recent events pressed heavily upon Vertatis's mind. She could vividly replay the haunting moment when her sister's essence departed, drawn inexorably towards the sinister machinery.

'Kareesto…' she began, her voice echoing softly against the cracked walls as she settled onto the cold pavement. 'How many others have you witnessed being sacrificed to that malevolent device?'

'Too many,' he replied gravely after a prolonged silence. 'They have devised a method to harness the Dark Flare, absorbing any power it encounters.'

'Is that the Humans' Flare?' Protheux inquired, stealing a glance outside through a small window, where distant buildings loomed into view from their secluded refuge.

'Indeed, it is. The Ergon Déil. The Flare of Power. Initially bestowed upon my people by Time itself, it granted us the ability to manipulate matter and extract its energy. In the beginning, it served to sustain our city and foster its growth. But King Lohan's ambition knew no bounds. He coveted what others possessed. Thus, he assembled a cadre of scientists to unlock its full potential. Over time, they discovered that the Ergon Déil resonates with the magic inherent in other beings. Unable to wield a Flare against another, as they are all facets of the same original source, King Lohan sought to wield it against those blessed with magic instead…'

'So, this is what they did to my sister? They stole her life, her magic, to fuel their Flare?' Vertatis asked, her voice trembling with horror.

'I'm sorry…' Kareesto's sorrowful gaze met hers, traversing the expanse of the room where they sat, distantly connected yet now grappling with the final trials of their forbidden love. Their bond had weathered countless trials, yet in this crucible of adversity, they found themselves struggling to remain close.

'What will they do with it?' Protheux interjected. 'Now that they've siphoned my sister's power… What comes next?'

'Her magic will accumulate within the Machine of War. Soon, it will be unleashed. If her power is as formidable as I suspect, we will soon hear the thunderous echoes of that unleashed magic, regardless of how far we flee.'

'Alright, we must press on. The cloak of night no longer veils our movements, and the land is bathed in Erion's light. If your words hold true, then we must put as much distance between us and that moment as possible.' With resolve, Protheux strode outside. In a twist of fate, the trio found themselves on the brink of a familiar destination—near the very tavern where Kareesto and Vertatis had first encountered one another, a reminder of the tangled web of fate that now trapped them.

'Vertatis,' Kareesto whispered, his hand finding hers as they followed Protheux uphill. The general's once-shimmering silver hair had dulled, his eyes bearing witness to the cruelty inflicted upon his body. Yet, within them still flickered the flame of a powerful bond with the one he loved. 'Our baby…where is our baby?'

'Una,' the Leonty replied, a gentle smile gracing her lips as her hand tenderly caressed Kareesto's face. Traces of scars and dried blood marred his features, causing her heart to ache. 'Her name is Una. She bears the features of my people but the eyes of yours. Her skin mirrors mine, yet a delicate pink hue adorns her completely.'

'Where is she, Vertatis?' Kareesto's voice betrayed his worry.

'She's with my sister Lethya at the temples. I know, I'm worried too…' she added, noting the concern etched upon Kareesto's face. 'Lethya is using her magic to cloak both herself and our daughter, erasing all memory of their presence.'

'My love, Romohan's forces march against your people!' he exclaimed, his voice rising with urgency. 'We must retrieve her at once!'

'Your king is already there,' Protheux interjected, joining them once more. 'Now, keep your voice low…there are Humans walking around.' With a swift motion, he pulled the hood over his head, concealing his distinctive green skin beneath the heavy fabric.

'These lands were already rife with thieves, traitors, and criminals,' Kareesto murmured as they hastened behind buildings and homes. 'I dread to imagine their state now, with the crown corrupted by power and madness.'

'We ought to linger at the edge of this village; drawing attention is unwise,' Protheux suggested, veering around a corner and ascending a narrow street flanked by dilapidated cottages. Nearby, a small group of Humans emerged from a house, their movements furtive. Suddenly, two more were violently ejected from their home and dragged into the open, their weathered faces meeting the wet, soiled ground with a sickening thud.

'There's no room for begging, you wretched scum. You were warned. Pay up or get out!' one of the attackers bellowed in a thick accent, delivering a brutal kick to an elderly man's stomach. A handful of coins clinked and scattered onto the street, coming to rest at Kareesto's feet.

'We heard you called upon the king's army for protection…truly foolish. The king cares naught for you nor these lands,' another spat, delivering a vicious blow to an old woman's face.

'No, don't,' Kareesto murmured to Vertatis, whose hands had clenched into fists, poised for action. 'These are Leeches, the vilest of criminals. Let's go…'

'What are you staring at?' one of the Leeches growled, fixing his gaze upon Vertatis. Suddenly, the entire group turned their attention to the three strangers.

'Let's move,' Kareesto urged, pushing Vertatis and Protheux up the alleyway, hastening their steps away from danger. 'They won't leave us alone. We must vanish immediately. Come with me; I know someone whom I hope we can still trust.'

Turning the corner of a looming structure, they passed through its cavernous interior, emerging onto another narrow street where a small, grey cottage stood in silence. Kareesto rapped on the door four times in rapid succession, a secret code concealed within his gesture. Moments later, someone appeared at the entrance, wordlessly ushering them inside.

With all the windows sealed shut, the interior was shrouded in darkness, so thick that they dared not move a step. The air was heavy with the acrid stench of dust and mould, assaulting their senses with a nauseating force. A small candle flickered to life in the far corner, casting feeble illumination as their host finally emerged. Her visage was weathered and worn, her wrinkled skin darkened by time, a single eye piercing through the gloom while only a few remaining teeth stood as sentinels in her mouth.

'The general, back here in my humble home...' she murmured, her voice laced with a mixture of surprise and suspicion. 'So, it's true what they say, you're still among the living...'

'Doria, where's Mort? We need assistance,' Kareesto pressed, his tone urgent. Vertatis and Protheux exchanged puzzled glances, noting Kareesto's lack of reaction to the woman's appearance or the putrid odour permeating the air.

'Mort is no more,' she replied flatly before retreating into another chamber. 'He was taken, along with all those loyal to you and your army.'

'Kareesto, something feels wrong about this place...' Protheux remarked once the woman had vanished. With his hand resting on the warm candle, he gestured around, casting a flickering light into the dim space. A scene of horror unfolded before them—dozens of severed heads hung upon the walls, their vacant eye sockets and gaping mouths bearing silent witness to unspeakable atrocities. Traces of dried blood crisscrossed the walls, vividly displaying the grim testament to past tortures. Vertatis recoiled and sought refuge behind Kareesto, whose expression was frozen in shock.

'Doria,' Kareesto's voice trembled as he called out. Moments later, she reappeared, her form emerging from the shadows as she approached Protheux. 'What in the world is the meaning of all this?'

'This...these are the handiwork of the Leeches. They've been tormenting me with reminders that my dear Mort was deemed a traitor to their cause...' She trailed off, her gaze drifting to the side as if she were listening to unseen whispers.

'She's lying!' Vertatis's accusation cut through the air, her eyes ablaze a righteous red.

'They're all yours...' The old woman's voice echoed through the darkness, her words a grim harbinger of impending danger. Suddenly, hands and bodies materialized from the shadows, launching a frenzied assault against the three fugitives. In the chaotic melee, fists flew amidst the darkness, mingling with the sounds of fear and the triumphant shouts of their assailants.

Amidst the chaos, a forceful shove sent Protheux crashing against the cracked front door, the impact causing it to splinter and creak open. Disoriented, he stumbled a few steps onto the street. The fight seemed futile, their bid for escape brief and ill fated. Overwhelmed by sheer numbers, they were soon subdued, forced onto their knees in defeat.

In a final, desperate plea for salvation, Vertatis's anguished cry pierced the tumult. 'Brother, please, my daughter!'

In that moment, Protheux faced the defining choice of his life: abandon his beloved sister to the clutches of their enemies, or honour his vow and race to Una's side. With countless pairs of eyes fixed upon him, he acted swiftly, his resolve steeled by determination. He fled the village with every ounce of strength he possessed, his heart pounding in his chest, tears of anguish clouding his vision.

In the depths of his being, a tempest of emotions raged — a maelstrom of rage and sorrow, love and hatred intertwined. With grim determination, he vowed to return, to liberate his sister from captivity, regardless of the sacrifices demanded.

As the two lovers were forcibly pulled outside the traitor's abode, a deafening blast rent the air, reverberating with a force that shook the very foundations of the earth. A cloud of grey smoke billowed from the distant crown city, accompanied by a surge of potent energy that rippled through the air like a tidal wave. The shockwave slammed into the Leeches and their captives, hurtling them violently across the street, their bodies crashing amidst the sea of shattered glass strewn from the devastated windows.

Just as Kareesto had forewarned, Umbra's power had surged to its zenith within the Machine of War, unleashing a cataclysmic wave of energy that rippled across the land, leaving destruction in its wake.

On the far side of the hills, the forceful blast found another fugitive in its path. Pursued by a formidable army of Aqualymphs, Aura's form dissolved into pure steam as the relentless wave surged towards her. Several paces behind, the surrounding soldiers were thrown to the ground by the sheer force of the blast.

Amidst the chaos, one figure remained untouched by the destructive tide, floating serenely on the verdant grass, her gaze fixed upon the distant western horizon. Queen Eah's narrowed eyes scanned the scene, focusing intently on the spot where Aura had vanished moments before. In a fleeting instant, a pair of wings had briefly materialized just before dissipating into nothing.

# Chapter Eighteen

## *A Truth Worth Dying For*

∞

The journey to the crown city morphed into a harrowing march of shame and impending doom for Vertatis and Kareesto. For two rhocs they had journeyed amongst their enemies. As they approached the towering east wall and passed through the imposing gates, a multitude of guards and soldiers observed the two fugitives with a mix of disdain and curiosity. Some hurled insults and jeers, their contempt palpable in the air. Others, still loyal to their esteemed general, averted their gazes, the weight of Kareesto's downfall heavy upon their hearts.

For Vertatis, the toll of her relentless pleas echoed loudly in her mind. She remained resolute in her determination to reunite with her daughter, even if it meant sacrificing the fragile peace they had hoped to find within the sanctuary of the Chomps' dome. The precious moments shared with Kareesto before the war now passed before her like fleeting memories. He had welcomed her into his arms and into his hearts, transforming two strangers into allies, lovers, providing a sense of safety and belonging. While their early days were filled with moments of peace and joy, her present nights were plagued by tormenting visions of her daughter's tears and anguished cries echoing in the silence of her dreams. She was their daughter's, the fruit of a forbidden love they had both steadfastly pledged. In exchange, Kareesto had sacrificed his name of the Crown Sunshine, forsaken his dreams of glory, to instead seek a life of eternal refuge with the Chomps—a hope that was short-lived.

As they slowly walked towards the city centre, Vertatis grappled once more with the vision of herself and Protheux departing from the temples, parting ways with her daughter. Una's face haunted her, etched against the backdrop of the high, white walls she wouldn't dare to look at. With each passing moment, Vertatis's yearning intensified until it breached the barriers of reason.

As they crossed the threshold into the king's palace, inching closer to their formidable adversary, the vivid scene replayed in her mind once more. Even as Romohan's most formidable ally emerged in the cold expanse of the grand chamber, standing beside the king's throne, Vertatis wasn't pay attention to Lëogan's diabolical smirk; only the tender smile of Una remained etched in her memory. There, the two outcasts were forced to their knees, their heads yanked up by the calloused hands of the Leeches who had proudly escorted them, bearing the king's most coveted prize.

'Where is the king? We have brought him something he wants,' one of the Leeches bellowed, yanking at Kareesto's sandy locks, thrusting his head before the Aver. To their surprise, Lëogan paid no heed to the Human; instead, his unwavering focus was fixed upon the Leonty.

'We have just returned from the temples. The king has no interest in looking at another one of those beings…and certainly he does not entertain himself with such low-level Humans like yourself, especially if not informed in advance,' the Aver replied, moving closer to Vertatis.

'Very well then,' the Leech retorted. 'If you don't see what is in front of you, we won't be wasting your time.' He nodded to his dodgy companions as if they were all about to leave, bringing their prey with them.

'Hold it,' Lëogan interjected, almost in a whisper. 'This one you brought with…our former general. This one, where did you find her?'

'They were together. They entered the outskirts with a third one, a male Leonty. He fled like a coward, leaving these two behind,' the Leech laughed.

'Tell the king we want our reward, as promised. Twenty thousand róans for each one of those, like it says here,' another one in the far back shouted, waving an old flyer, the Leonty's face on it deforming with the movement as he swung it in the air.

'No more, we brought the general too!' a third one added. 'Or we walk!'

'The king doesn't have any interest in this one any more,' Lëogan replied, his hand on Vertatis's face, pulling her chin up. Her eyes secretly burnt red; his lie had reached her ears, triggering her magic. She kept them closed shut, but tears had found their way out, down her green cheeks. 'But you can leave her here anyway. We have a special place for beings like her. And it's two thousand róans, can't your people even read?'

'What is the meaning of all this?' an old woman asked, entering the throne room. Her long, dark hair was pulled up and adorned with a golden tiara. Her face looked tired, her eyes dark like night, she had immediately recognized her son's most wanted offender. As she walked right beside Lëogan, the many Leeches suddenly bent on their knees, their faces revealing that the respect they were bound to show came only reluctantly.

'Queen Shahara, these…people brought our king a present. They found the general in the outskirts, together with this Leonty,' Lëogan explained.

'It's a she!' the queen gasped. 'Get that thing out of here, now!' And she moved back, slowly retracing her steps out of the room. As she approached two guards standing at a door to the inner rooms, she added, 'Call King Romohan, tell him it's extremely urgent! And tell him it was me who sent you.'

'Now, are we getting paid or what?' a Leech asked.

It wasn't long before Romohan arrived. After rewarding the Leeches with their craved payment and sending them away, Lëogan and Queen Shahara smiled at the arrival of the king. He moved cautiously around the two who were still on their knees, their faces staring at the cold, square pavement. There was much he wanted to say, much he wanted to ask, and yet, he was keeping silent, his mind packed with thoughts. Addressing the lesser menace first was the way forward.

'Take him away where he belongs. His cell craves to be reunited with its guest,' he told the two guards standing a few feet away. Afraid the three could not oppose the magic of the Leonty, as the guards left the room with Kareesto, Queen Shahara moved a few steps back.

'You are the one we could not find at the temple... The one that sees the truth, aren't you? You are the one called Vertatis,' Lëogan asked.

'So, tell me,' the king continued. 'Tell me the greatest truth of them all...' The Aver was caught by surprise. Of all the questions Romohan could ask for, he had asked the most dangerous one. If Vertatis told him she knew about his true nature, it would be the end of his master's evil plan.

'Sir, I'd proceed with caution. She is a Leonty. A spell is all she needs to set free.' And Queen Shahara nodded in agreement. Her eyes quickly glanced at a guard who had just entered from the main doors. His wide shoulders bore a long cloak and his heavy helmet covered his face. A feeling of protection slightly comforted her.

'Liar…' Vertatis whispered; her eyes opened, shining red. 'Who are you really? You are not Human…why do you carry such a formidable disguise?' And on her face, fear mixed with anger.

'The evil still speaks through her!' the queen shouted, her hands covering her ears.

'Quiet, Mother! I want to know…' And Romohan moved closer; an unexpected soft touch found Vertatis's face. 'We have been looking for you. Your name and your magic seems to be at the centre of everything that concerns me. You will tell me the greatest truth…as it's true I'm King Romohan, son of King Lohan.'

'No, you are not,' the Leonty replied, after a moment of hesitation. 'But this is not the truth you seek…'

'Tell me. We have brought your kin to their knees because of you. It was my father's kindness that spared you the day we first conquered your lands… Now, tell me the truth I seek and your life might be spared once more,' Romohan repeated, his eyes only a few inches away from Vertatis's.

'You know deep in your heart you have been deceived,' Vertatis replied, her eyes shining like rubies. Her face almost touched his as a great secret was about to move from one bearer to the next. 'The one you trust the most is your true enemy. The one who seduced your father before you with words of false wisdom and will seduce the king that will come after. Look behind you…' But her words broke off in the cold air. The fiery glare left her eyes at once as she spilled purple blood from her mouth.

A long, shining blade had pierced her chest through and through, the dripping pointed end stopping close to King Romohan. At the other end, a proud old queen stood with a sharp face and a firm hand. She had acted quickly when her son could not. A guard stood close to her; he had let her take the weapon of death against his will and let her use it as she pleased. In Shahara's eyes, a dark shadow twirled, mirroring Lëogan's gaze as he held her mind gripped in his evil magic.

'It's you!' the king roared to his mother, his face in shock. 'She was about to tell me, it's you!' but the queen looked back at her son in disbelief, her eyes and ears dull to her recent act. 'You lied about my father and she knew. What else have you lied about?' But Queen Shahara could not answer. As she quickly released her hand from the hilt, shock rose in her mind.

The tall guard still had his face hidden in the shadow of his helmet, tears clashing against the enemy's magic he had been enslaved under. He had defied his sister's prayers and moved inside the city the same way she had shown him a few rhocs earlier. There, after defeating a lone guard in a silent street, he had taken the shape of a soldier, entering the palace without trouble. And there, he had come to rescue Vertatis, only to become the very instrument of death at the hands of Queen Shahara and through the dark magic of Lëogan. His mind was trapped in the evil spell, but his heart spoke of sorrow and desperation. Unable to move, he could only stare at her lifeless form.

On the cold floor, Vertatis's last breath had left her body behind, in the hands of her enemies. Her last thought was of the one whom she loved the most. Una looked back at her as she lay in her arms, a different kind of power growing between a mother and her daughter. Their bond was made of blood and spell beyond limits, merging their magic as if it was one. In the secret of the newborn's mind, Una had learned and absorbed her mother's craft as if it was hers. She had tied Vertatis to an enchantment beyond the one of a mother, turning her blind to the extent of the power she held in her tiny body.

As Vertatis's soul departed, a final glance of magic travelled through the lands: a last truth to be confessed to the ears of the one who would listen, who would care. Miles away, by the temple, a beautiful Leonty gazed at the purple sky. Her tiny body lying in Lethya's embrace, her eyes were fixed on the invisible, distant crown city as a whisper reached her. Her heart trembled as she suddenly started to cry, her eyes ignited with the first powerful spark of revenge.

Her destiny had just been written before her, by hands that would soon pay a tremendous and dire price. In that moment, the quiet determination in her eyes spoke volumes of the storm that was about to be unleashed upon those who had wronged her kin.

# Chapter Nineteen

## *A Brother's Revenge*

∞

'Tell the truth for once, Mother,' King Romohan said as Queen Shahara sat on a rusty old chair. Her hands were bound behind her back; she sat in the centre of a cold, stony room. To her left and right, two soldiers waited for instructions on an imminent torture.

'I told you already,' she cried, profuse sweat covering her face, her eyes darting between her son and the Aver who stood right next to the king. 'I don't know why I did it… One moment I was beside you, the next I saw my hand holding that sword.'

'Whatever you are hiding, it will come out,' Romohan replied. 'It's up to you to decide if you want to talk freely or under torture. You know what we do to traitors of your kind…'

'I'm your mother!' she shouted, desperate. 'And I'm the Queen Mother. Do you think I'd do something like this of my own will? Something happened to me. You need to find out what it was before they do it again!'

'Tell the scientist to come over,' the king told one of the two soldiers. 'She is right. After all, she is the Queen Mother…' And he walked beside her, his hand slowly moving her messy hair from her face. There was no tiara adorning her head, indicating the terrible fate that was to be hers. 'We won't use brute force on you,' he continued. 'We will get what is inside your mind with that little potion you invented yourself…'

'No!' she snapped, violently trying to set herself free. 'It's them! It has always been them!' Her gaze on Lëogan, she was horrified to see he was not coming to her rescue. The one who had been all along agreeing with her hatred for the Leonty was suddenly keeping quiet. 'Tell him, tell him!'

'What's wrong, Mother?' Romohan asked, sarcastic. 'You were our greatest scientist, after all. Isn't it you who taught them all the subtle art of confession through potions and poisons? If what you say is true, they can help, can't they?' And he moved away, pulling Lëogan out of the dark room. 'Who knows, we might finally find out what truly happened to Father…'

Under the shrill cry of a terrified woman, they departed from the eerie screams atop the western tower. Her desperate pleas for aid mingled with fury and loathing.

Once again, Romohan tasted the bitter conflict within his own mind. Deep within the recesses of his troubled psyche, he struggled against an unknown oppressive force, to no avail. A dark shroud had descended over his eyes, concealing their true golden hue beneath a perpetual veil.

Several floors below, another tormented soul wandered the labyrinthine palace, searching for the king's chamber. After swiftly avoiding the few guards standing in protection of the building, fearful that his disguise would soon be unveiled, Protheux hurried to the eastern wing, seeking the solitary space where he could confront the king without the protection of his soldiers. Within his mind, Vertatis's voice echoed incessantly, repeating the same haunting words. The names of Una and Kareesto vied for dominance in his thoughts, tearing him apart. *I should leave the crown city at once and honour my promise I made to my sister,* he pondered, *or should I instead rescue her loved one, once again? Una needs a father now more than ever...'*

Driven by a burning thirst for vengeance, Protheux found himself standing within the confines of the king's chamber. Concealed behind voluminous dark drapes, he awaited the return of his most-wanted enemy. Moments later, as his mind drifted amidst the myriad memories of a bygone era of peace, when he revelled in the company of his sisters, a deep voice resonated from beyond the chamber doors. Romohan's tone was tender and affectionate, bidding farewell to two beloved souls before retiring for the night. Barely a heartbeat later, after his fearcel Fariah and their son exchanged wishes for a peaceful rest, the king withdrew into his inner room. Driven by a thirst for revenge, Protheux prepared to emerge from concealment and enact his vengeance, when an unexpected knock interrupted his intentions.

'Your Majesty,' Lëogan began as the king admitted him into the chamber. 'Our scientists are fully occupied with the Nucleus device. With another female in our possession, it's imperative we focus on extracting her power and feed it into the Machine before it's too late.'

'I need to understand what has overtaken my mother, Lëogan. Despite her actions, I refuse to believe she's the one the Leonty was referring to,' Romohan asserted.

'Ah, my liege, I comprehend the difficulty of this situation,' the Harpy responded, his hand gesturing subtly. A faint grey mist billowed from the floor, drifting towards Romohan. Unseen behind the thick curtains, Protheux's eyes widened at the unfolding magic, recognizing the handiwork of the one who had tricked him into submission and bewitched Queen Shahara.

'Which one of the many we took prisoner do you speak of?' Romohan inquired, his tone shifting abruptly from sorrow to hate-fuelled resolve.

'It's the female we took from the temples. They call her Mementhya, the last one of her family…' Lëogan divulged, causing Protheux to stiffen at the mention of the name. 'She wields immense power, my king. She may indeed be the one we seek.'

'Very well then. Inform the guards my mother can wait. I want that machine operational. We shall demonstrate to all of Runae who rightfully commands these lands,' Romohan declared as he made his way to a smaller room filled with garments.

'Yes, Your Majesty,' Lëogan murmured, feigning deference. 'We shall indeed reveal to this entire realm who holds dominion. However...'

'What else?' Romohan interrupted.

'Of the seven sisters, we know the fate of six only... One died by the hand of Queen Eah. Two died right before our eyes and one was taken by the Machine of War before her body was carried away by the general. Queen Shahara might have taken care of the most-wanted one, while we keep another one in the dungeons, but I wonder...' And as Lëogan paused, Protheux started to silently cry. The cruel recounting of his sisters' fall tested his anger to the limit.

'What is this obsession you have with those Leonty? Have you not gotten what you wanted? I should be the one concerned. The one who could tell me the truth is gone. Now, leave. I'm tired and I need to rest.'

'As you wish, my king.' With a sinister grin, the Aver departed.

The ensuing silence clashed with the screaming thoughts raging in Protheux's mind. Despite his readiness to sacrifice himself to eliminate Romohan and rescue Kareesto, he couldn't bear the thought of another sister enduring the horrors of the dungeons. He needed to succeed in his assault, and to do so, he reluctantly bided his time for a more opportune moment. Thus, Protheux remained motionless until Romohan had succumbed to slumber, then stealthily made his way to the small room where his adversary had left his armour and weapons. With every step guided by the imagined presence of his sister Vertatis, and the desperate pleas of Mementhya echoing in his mind, Protheux prepared for his fateful act.

As Romohan departed the realm of the awakening, the Leonty's sword pierced his heart, ensuring he would never lead another army nor another war. With hands firmly grasping the gleaming hilt, Protheux stood transfixed for a moment, tears tracing down his verdant cheeks. Strength and grace mingled with pride and shame in a tumultuous whirl of emotions. Despite his innate gentleness, over the past yac, he had transformed into a figure of villainy, a murderer, a seeker of vengeance. The love for his sisters, the yearning for peace, and the burden of his heartache had woven a dark enchantment akin to that wrought by Lëogan upon Humankind.

Cloaked in the darkness cast by the sealed windows, Protheux slipped stealthily out of Romohan's chamber, vanishing from the palace unnoticed. At the front gates, sitting on the ground, two guards lay asleep, their minds and body tired by the weary embrace of Erion, their misplaced confidence betraying their lack of vigilance. Like a ghost gliding on air, the Leonty traversed the expanse, skirting past the grand fountain and descending the sweeping staircase; it was a familiar path, fragmented echoes of a recent history. Though Vertatis was absent this time, like rhocs before, another sister's voice beckoned him from the depths beneath the Radhal Daíuh.

As he reached the entrance, a deafening roar erupted from below, reverberating through the very foundation of the edifice. Dust cascaded from the lofty walls, and fractures ran across the pavement, rending the once-imposing white stones. The colossal doors groaned on their hinges, one crashing to the ground, catching Protheux off guard. The notion of an ambush flickered in his mind like a fleeting shadow.

Without pause, he hastened into the library, his strides purposeful as he made for the dungeon gates. A pallid mist swirled in the air, as if the essence of every stone in the crown city had been pulverized and gathered in a single space. With the path ahead obscured, Protheux halted, his hands instinctively shielding his itching eyes. Nearby, figures materialized seemingly out of thin air, their voices raised in heated debate over the safety of the clandestine undertaking unfolding just steps away.

'We were instructed to utilize only the Leonty! What madness is this, employing one of greater power?' one exclaimed.

'The Aver insists that the Aqualymphs possess the potential to catalyse the necessary energy for the machine's activation. We have exhausted all other avenues; why not pursue this?' countered another, prompting Protheux to edge closer, seeking refuge behind a towering stack of ancient tomes. A film of white dust began to coat his helmet, rendering his once-green countenance ghostly.

'The Nucleus demands a stronger catalyst. Yet, I concur with Lorái; these Aqualymphs own a formidable power,' whispered a third, their words barely audible. 'But I'm terrified of the idea of their queen discovering what we are doing to her kin.

'There is no need. She vanished into the steppes, across the desert. Many Aqualymphs have been sighted on the fringes of the Garughals' domain, trailing her alone,' argued another vehemently.

'The Aver said she has been summoned… When she presents herself to the king, she will find out. What's going to happen then?' insisted the final priest.

'How could the Aver conceal what we are doing? How can he coerce her, let alone subdue Queen Eah's wrath? It is rumoured that she alone can wield two Flares…'

'They say she has three!' the priest interjected, but his words were drowned out by a primal scream emanating from below, followed by another thunderous roar that reverberated violently through the chamber. Books and tomes cascaded from shelves, striking the fleeing priests in a chaotic flurry. Two figures emerged from the dungeons, their presence a beacon guiding Protheux onward. Amidst the chaos of dust, screams, and confusion, the Leonty seized the opportunity, racing downstairs towards the source of the impending menace. Before him, an astonishing tableau unfolded.

A radiant brilliance emanated from the heart of the chamber, where the Humans' machine loomed. Bound on either side were two captives: Mementhya knelt, her wrists trapped in hefty handcuffs anchored to the floor, while opposite her, another figure was confined within an electrified cage, his form morphing incessantly. The

Aqualymph's legs were submerged in the very waters that fuelled the war machine, causing him to oscillate between luminosity and darkness in an endless cycle.

'My queen!' the Aqualymph screamed, his body convulsing as darkness consumed him. 'I can't contain it any longer. Please, release it!'

As if all of space and time had converged into a single moment, the anguished cry reached the ears of the one who wielded devastating power. The ground quaked, splitting apart as cold water surged in every direction. Amidst this upheaval, Queen Eah emerged, her form towering over the trembling onlookers. Radiant and resplendent, she thundered in the vast dungeon.

'May you all perish by my hand for what you have done to my kind!' Her voice reverberated with righteous fury as a brilliant wave of energy surged from her outstretched hands towards the Machine of War. In her path lay Mementhya, ensnared in chains, resigned to her fate at the hands of a formidable adversary. Yet, to her astonishment, her would-be executioner stood at her side, warding off the impending onslaught.

Under Queen Eah's incredulous gaze, Lëogan stood with arms outstretched, his silver hair agleam amidst the devastation. A towering apparition materialized behind him, dark and absolute, absorbing the queen's magic with insatiable hunger. The more it consumed, the more it expanded, its ominous form eclipsing even the might of the enraged monarch.

Amidst this terrifying spectacle loomed an even darker, malevolent figure, his arms raised in triumph as a colossal shadow mirrored his form. Laughter echoed through the chamber before he spoke, 'You came exactly as I predicted.' And he laughed again. 'My master, King of Emptiness, the path lies open before you. It is time to reclaim this realm and realize your desires!'

Like a shrill whistle piercing the air, another scream, louder and more primal, assaulted Protheux's ears, reverberating through the grounds above. As if the very essence of Erion had been unleashed within those dungeon walls, an unstoppable energy surged forth from the Nucleus machine, its brilliance and intensity escalating with alarming speed. With a sweeping motion of his arm towards the breach in the ceiling, Lëogan's sorcery unleashed the full force of annihilation.

The entire library collapsed inward, a cascade of debris crushing on those who had been caught within the Harpy's malevolent enchantment. Above ground, structures disintegrated in an instant, consumed by a towering column of white energy erupting from the former site of the grand fountain. With its power ascending to the heavens and beyond, the long-awaited signal was sent. The time had come for Nothing to reclaim Runae as its own.

A sudden eruption of potent energy engulfed the atmosphere, filling the air with searing heat and bathing the land in blinding light. As if a second sun had emerged alongside Erion in the skies, the inhabitants of Runae shielded their eyes in terror. Inside the Chomps' dome, outside Faróel's home Aura was conversing with Treekan when a piercing whistle caught them by surprise.

'What is this sound?' the Chomp bellowed, his hands reflexively covering his ears.

'It emanates from the west, near the crown city!' Aura responded, her form undergoing rapid transformation, resonating with the pulsating energy's vibrations, losing cohesion and reverting to her true essence.

'May the Flare bless us, what is it?' Faróel exclaimed as he exited the house, gazing upon a towering column of light ascending from the distant earth, piercing the heavens. Oscillating from golden hues to pure white, the pillar expanded rapidly in size.

'Do not gaze upon it,' Aura urged, hastening towards their home. 'Seek shelter inside. This is beyond terrible, gravely so! I sense Queen Eah's presence in the air, and I feel the influence of our Flare, intertwined with that of the Garughals'. Move quickly!'

'What about you? Join us inside,' the Chomp implored, extending a hand towards his friend.

'No. I have been hiding for far too long. I must reach the node and beseech Time for help.' Without hesitation, the Gatekeeper ventured outside the dome and entered the waters of the Gochi River.

In mere moments, Lëogan's malevolent magic traversed the skies, propelled by the combined might of four Flares, piercing the celestial expanse like a speeding projectile, reaching the vast void surrounding the planet. After millennia of anticipation, the nefarious King of Emptiness stood poised to enact his sinister designs. Between Runae and his diabolical intent, the God of Time hovered in the near cosmos, arms outstretched, eyes closed, enveloped in radiant power. In his mind, the foretold tale unfolded as expected and yet, he was still unprepared to face the enemy. A gleaming green clepsydra hovered near his chest, ready to manipulate time as his bearer commanded. Within Time's mind, the desperate pleas of countless souls echoed, beseeching aid.

'Where are you? Where is the protector of our world?' Aura's voice surged among the many. 'Time, we need you; something terrible is happening here…'

'All of you, get on your knees and pray!' another one said. Atop a temple in the Leonty's hills a frightened Runer shouted in panic.

But there was no voice loud enough to change Time's mind. He had sworn to protect Runae from evil, and Nothing was only a step away, approaching fast. If the inhabitants of his beloved planet were held hostage by another wicked will, it was something he could not help them with. Something greater was about to strike. Like Health before him, Time was going to face his greatest enemy head on, right outside their doorstep.

The countless discussions my siblings and I had shared regarding the defence of the cherished worlds from the encroaching enemy's onslaught had etched indelibly into his consciousness, piercing through his resolute will. As I had emphasized time and again, our beloved kin needed to harness their own inherent power, to stand united in battle as we had. If the Flares represented their sole chance of survival, there was no luxury of waiting to prepare for the impending conflict. His plan was clear: every living being in Runae needed the time to master their renewed magic. If there was something he could certainly give them, it was exactly a piece of himself.

Disregarding the beings' inclination to squander his gifts in internecine strife, Time swung his right arm in the skies above the planet and turned the wheel of Runae's destiny ahead, hastening the march of rhocs and yacs, surging forward, drawing the inexorable approach of annihilation ever nearer.

# Chapter Twenty

*A Promise Made of Hate and Blood*

∞

'All of you, kneel and pray!' the Runer's command echoed through the temple. Ten yacs had been rushed forward by Time's magic. They had passed in a blink, as if they were mere glimpse of fleeting dreams. And yet, the cruel enslavement of the Leonty had remained the same. More Humans had flooded the hills; under the false pretence of priesthood many commanded the females spared by the war as if they were animals waiting for slaughter.

'I said, kneel!' His visage contorted in anger, he wielded a cruel instrument of torment, lashing out at a defiant female Leonty who refused to comply. While others bowed and began intoning prayers of deliverance, Una resisted. As the act of flagellation couldn't break her indomitable spirit, something deeper spoke of an enduring enslavement. Partially obscured by a mask fashioned from gold and silver, the young Leonty's face bore the mark of her oppression. Cold metal encircled her head, sealing her mouth shut. Despite the fiery defiance burning in her eyes, Una's magic remained imprisoned within an unyielding cage.

'Una, please, submit,' implored Lethya, tears streaming down her cheeks as she shielded her swollen abdomen.

'Your name is on the Radhal Daíuh. You'll be next. Join the others and pray,' the Runer insisted once Una relented. 'But do so in silence,' he added with a mocking laugh. 'We won't allow your dark magic to be spoken again. So, pray convincingly for the God's guidance.'

'Una, my dear, you must be wiser than this,' the other Leonty urged once the Runer had departed. 'We have no other option. It's either this or the crown city.' But Una met her gaze with a defiant glare, anger showing in her eyes.

'I would rather die than endure this any longer,' another Leonty declared. 'The menace of being sent to the Humans' city is has become a twisted dream. Since the young king is on the throne, things have got worse.'

'I wish for this nightmare to end as well,' lamented an older Leonty, tears streaming down her face. 'Look at what they've reduced us to. They keep us alive, force us to mate with our males just to produce more offspring for shipment to the crown city… Lethya, if yours is a male, you know they'll kill him. And if it's a female, they'll take her away.'

'I know,' Lethya replied with a sad smile. 'But I can sense it's a girl. She possesses magic too. She assures me everything will be alright.' Tenderly caressing Una's face, she continued, 'You will be alright too. You and my daughter, Demetra, will live as sisters in a world of peace. I promise you.'

But Lethya's promise held no ground. Although their yacs had been moved forward, the looming present held its spot over Runae unchanged. As Time stood resolute against the encroaching advance of Nothing, the once-purple sky darkened, Erion seemingly obliterated from existence in an instant. Amidst roiling storm clouds, a colossal, hovering entity materialized, a harbinger of destruction descending to claim the denizens of the planet.

The earth quaked violently, driving all Leonty within the temple to flee into the open, leaving Una behind. Between the towering pillars, they stood awestruck by the sheer enormity of the impending calamity. A pall of darkness enveloped the land, the frigid air warping and twisting as if matter itself convulsed in agonized reshaping. Down the hill, three Runers observed the unfolding spectacle, one of them turning to shout, 'What are you doing here? Get back to the temple!' But amidst the frightening danger, their command went unheeded as the Leonty fled the hill without a backwards glance.

'Where are they running to?' one of the Runer demanded upon re-entering the temple, his voice echoing through the sacred halls as his hand struck the young Leonty once more. Although he knew she was rendered mute by the Runers' own making, he asked the same question again and smiled.

Una lay prone on the cold, trembling floor beside the offering stone table within the naos. White dust fell across the large room, on her head, her shoulders. The remnants of her endurance were etched in the lash marks that marred her skin, a cruel testament to the unrelenting punishment inflicted upon her by her captor. Her features were obscured by a heavy metallic mask, a cruel muzzle that silenced her cries but couldn't extinguish the fury smouldering in her eyes, which burned with the intensity of a raging fire. Hate festered within Una, a seething tempest of indignation and defiance, though she remained unable to articulate the consuming rage that gnawed at her soul. As the Runer raised his whip once more, she seized it with bare hands, locking gazes with her assailant in a silent challenge.

'You were warned, your magic can't help you,' he taunted, his voice dripping with derision. 'You cannot wield spells any longer.' Yet he knew even if Una's lips were sealed, her defiance remained unbroken. And still, he struck her, again and again. 'You are just lucky you haven't fully matured yet. But every day you look more like the others… Soon the time will come when we extract one or two monsters from your wretched body, and once you've served your purpose, you'll be cast into the depths of the city… Two of your own clergy are in audience with the king even now. They seek to offer more of your kind to fuel the machine that will deliver us from the clutches of evil…from abominations such as yourself.'

'Roadhon, get out of here before the entire temple collapses!' Another Runer burst into the chamber, his breath laboured, his brow glistening with sweat from his hurried ascent up the hill. As if he was about to faint, he gasped out, 'We've been summoned to the northern gates. Looks like there is going to be a meeting between the king and the Valahans. Rumour has it the Chomps will be there too…'

'You should consider tempering your indulgence in alcohol, Tarasco. Your scent precedes you,' the other Runer quipped, tearing his gaze away from Una. 'It's preposterous. The Valahans haven't met with Humans for yacs, and the Chomps? Ha! They'd rather traverse the depths of the abyss than grace our king with their presence, let alone meet with a mere boy…'

'That 'mere boy' is our king!' Tarasco retorted, his voice bristling with indignation at the slight. 'He is guided by the Aver. If they decree it, we obey. Make haste, meet me at the foot of the hill. We need to depart before the madness in the sky strikes upon us.'

'Did you hear that?' Roadhon turned back to Una, who struggled desperately to rid herself of the oppressive mask. With every shake of the earth, the air turned whiter and more toxic to breathe. 'We have a new monarch. Ha! Yet we all know who truly holds dominion over our realm,' he scoffed, making his way towards the temple entrance. Glancing back at Una's futile struggle, he added, 'Were you not so beautiful, I might look upon you and see naught but a feral beast…'

She looked back at him with rage, her eyes burning with the red of death. 'Your magic is useless, just like you. You can't speak, and yet your eyes tell too much… That's it! Your time in here is finished. You'll come with us to the crown city… If this derelict building doesn't claim you first.'

If punishment was to be meted out, it would be of a nature far removed from the Runer's intentions. Just as his blow fell upon Una once more, he stepped beyond the confines of the naos, only to be met with a scene of devastation and chaos unfolding before him. A seismic tremor, unleashed from a distant epicentre, rent the air with its force, causing a portion of the architrave to succumb, fracturing the entablature and dislodging towering columns from their ancient moorings. Two pillars toppled in succession, crashing to the ground in a thunderous cacophony, the Runer barely evading their deadly descent as he stood atop the pristine stylobate. Staggering backward, buffeted by the sudden collapse, he found himself sprawled amidst a pall of fine white dust, his face obscured from view. Right there, where luck had graced him with salvation, death quickly found him again. Through the hands of a young Leonty, the Runer met his end.

Empowered by a seething desire for vengeance, Una seized hold of a hefty fragment of metal torn asunder from the shattered architrave, unleashing her fury upon the Runer's craven form. Blow after merciless blow rained down upon him, again and again, and again, each strike driven by the weight of her anguish and the echoes of past injustices suffered. Amidst the tumult of her mind, amid the myriad faces of the Leonty she had known and lost, one figure loomed large. The distant memory of a mother who had left her behind emerged in her mind. The recollection of feelings, fragments of a kind motherly visage mixed with the Leonty's power when Vertatis's face clearly formed before her. Una felt the bonds of blood and magic that tethered them together, an unbreakable seal forged in the crucible of fate.

*Why did you forsake me to endure this torment?* she silently lamented, her thoughts a bitter refrain. *Why did Lethya and the others stand futilely by, allowing this travesty to befall me?* Her mother's choice had set in motion a tragic sequence of events, transforming an innocent young Leonty into a tormented soul, a pawn in a cruel game of power and betrayal.

As her gaze lingered upon the fallen Runer, she felt no remorse. Una looked past the marks of merciless death she'd inflicted on him; all she could see was his expression of violence, hatred, and primal terror. Though outwardly Human, he bore the same dark essence as those who had crossed her path before—a collective guilt shared among all warders, each complicit in the agony that rent her fractured heart asunder. Amidst the chaos unfurling around her, Una moved with measured deliberation, her steps a silent cadence marking the solemn rhythm of her resolve. While the tempest of her fury mirrored the cataclysm ravaging the world, her expression remained stoic, imprisoned behind the unyielding mask of metal.

With a steady hand, she reached for the priest's rope, deftly retrieving a gleaming key from the fallen Runer's side. The warmth of his lifeblood, seeping into the earth, stained her hands and arms as she liberated her mouth from its tormenting confines. The rush of hot air upon her jaw and lips offered a reprieve akin to healing balm upon searing wounds. Amidst the onslaught of evil, she found an unexpected solace, a revitalizing touch upon her verdant skin, upon her countenance, within her very soul.

With newfound freedom, the young Leonty departed the Temple of Time, descending the hill with purposeful strides, her gaze fixed upon the distant fray unfolding on the horizon. Whatever conflict raged to the south, it beckoned to her from afar, an irresistible call drawing her forth as if a saviour had emerged to rescue her from the abyss of despair. Yet her faith did not rest upon Time, nor did her trust lie with the deity promised to safeguard all within Runae. He had forsaken her since the dawn of her existence, deaf to the silent pleas she offered within his hallowed sanctuary. The truths and beliefs she once clung to now lay shattered, replaced by the bitter taste of deceit and hypocrisy.

Whoever had come to deliver the final blow to this age of darkness, they were greeted with open arms, a harbinger of hope amidst the encroaching shadows.

# Chapter Twenty-One
## *The Meeting of the Twelve*

∞

Far to the south, at the edge of the Chomps' protective dome, Treekan perched impatiently upon a massive boulder. Instructed by his father to await Aura's return, he trained his gaze upon the protective dome. He had witnessed the same spectacle for many yacs. Every rhoc looked the same: the tumultuous clash of light and darkness and the flickering energies traversing the heavens with no side prevailing. In his mind, he could picture the titanic struggle between forces of great power and unspeakable evil. Somewhere out of reach, Time held his position in the skies, protecting their world, and yet, they could not join him in battle, supporting the one who fought for their survival.

When the Aqualymph finally emerged out of the Gochi River he queried, 'Well?' No other words were added. To a familiar eye, that interaction could be predictable, almost boring. They had been looking for answers, help, a resolution. Although their lives were sped by Time's magic and their yacs had passed in a fleeting moment, they had obtained nothing. The situation stalled with no end in sight.

'I explored the woods again. No signs of Garughals anywhere. I truly hoped a spark of life could bring us hope. A stem, a flower…' she added, defeated. 'The sea remains empty. There is no Aqualymph left, anywhere. Since that rhoc when I heard Queen Eah's voice thundering in the sky, I've felt nothing but emptiness. The Flare of the Sea hasn't returned either. I'm certain it's in the crown city, with the king.'

'If that's true, we might find out soon,' Treekan replied, retracing his steps towards the village. 'Father said to get ready. We are leaving for the city as soon as Varuk and Voishan get here.'

'So the Valahans have accepted the king's request?' Aura's gaze fixed north, towards the giant Mog. 'I thought they wanted nothing to do with the Humans…Faróel,' she continued as they reached his home. 'I know I said you should not get near the crown city, but I understand the two brothers will join you. If you have made up your mind, I'll go with you too.'

'I know you believe it's your duty to protect us, but maybe this time, you could stay behind,' Faróel replied, packing a large bag with provisions from the house. The journey ahead promised to be both lengthy and perilous, and food was the only aspect he felt he could manage. 'After you left, I sought out Varuk and Voishan. You know how elusive the Valahans can be, but I've always had a peculiar connection with Vasheer. Though it pains me to say, he's not quite himself these days…barely recognized me…'

'What's all this rearranging for?' Aura inquired as Faróel shifted the long table away from the dining room.

'The brothers are due to arrive soon. We've come to an understanding that it's time to unite our strengths, especially our Flares…we cannot venture into the crown without tapping into our magic,' the Chomp explained.

'Absolutely not!' Aura exclaimed. 'Combining the Flares is a dangerous gamble. The power they possess individually is overwhelming, let alone together. Remember what happened with Queen Eah and her three Flares? It's all connected. We mustn't bring them into such proximity.'

'Perhaps you should stay and convey your concerns to them directly,' Treekan suggested, acknowledging Aura's apprehension.

'I will. With the throne now occupied by a mere boy, there might be an opportunity to infiltrate and uncover the truths we seek before it's too late. I'll return,' Aura declared, and with that declaration, the Aqualymph turned on her heel and made her way towards the Gochi River.

Inside the Chomp's home, the conversation persisted. Faróel and Treekan found themselves entrenched in opposing viewpoints regarding the impending events. Treekan remained steadfast in his belief that they should wait for Time to intervene and usher in the long-awaited peace. His father, however, harboured a readiness to take matters into his own hands. It was unusual for a Chomp to entertain thoughts of war and conflict, but the weight of waiting had worn him down. While Kasthor's fate had diminished somewhat in his mind, the ache in his heart remained unchanged. Whatever had befallen his fearcel, he yearned for closure. Despite their differences, father and son continued to collaborate to ensure the house would be hospitable for the two sizable Valahans. Within the confines of the Chomps' abode, untouched by the turmoil of the outside world, they pondered over what provisions to offer.

After numerous deliberations between the Valahans and Aura, the five agreed to traverse the streets of the crown city with one condition: the Flares were going to be left behind. Accompanied by Faróel and his son, Treekan, a reluctant Aura trailed behind, her form nearly imperceptible to the Humans as she silently moved along the coastline, the gentle lapping of the sea beckoning to her. After persuading the others that it was safer to circumvent the outskirts, Aura convinced the group to enter the city via the King's Thousand Steps by the seaside. That same path, once trodden by Vertatis, Kareesto, and Protheux as they fled their oppressor, now served as the Aqualymph's ingress.

'Only because you need to stay close to the sea...we have to climb the ceremonial steps all the way up,' Varuk let out, annoyed. His gaze directed at the top of the many steps, he could feel tiredness reaching him fast, even before they had started to walk up the steps.

'There is a dark magic running in the outskirts, Valahan. There are Humans with magic now inhabiting those lands. Witches who have no mercy, cast spells on anyone they could take advantage of. We are entering from the southern gates because it's safer, nothing else.' And Aura glanced at the shoreline. 'Here is where a Leonty said goodbye to one of their own. Her soul is still floating at the edge of the beyond; my home still holds her in a motionless embrace. I can't blame her... Taking the same farewell road of the king who massacred her kind...'

'Do you truly perceive her presence?' Treekan inquired, his gaze searching for a truth that eluded his grasp.

'Let's not indulge in such madness, Aqualymph. The ascent is arduous enough,' Varuk interjected, forging ahead. Before them loomed a towering wall that stretched across the landscape. Between two colossal pillars, a lengthy staircase wound its way up, its end obscured by distance.

'If you possessed the sight of my people, son of Vasheer, you would discern what I do. Darkness pervades everywhere I gaze, particularly here and atop where you all are so eager to ascend. I advise vigilance. There are minds of formidable power exerting their will in this realm...' Aura asserted, striding forwards despite the sceptical glances exchanged by the two brothers.

After the gruelling ascent, nearly at the summit, two imposing golden gates stood closed. Varuk rapped on them twice, prompting a tall guard to appear, surprise etching his features at the unexpected arrival of guests from that quarter of the city.

'Two Valahans and two Chomps…' he muttered, adjusting his oversized helmet atop his small head. His countenance was sharp, his eyes wide, betraying his youth. 'Are you the ones the Aver awaits?'

'We are,' Varuk declared, a touch affronted. 'I am the king's son. This is my brother, Voishan, and our companions, Faróel and Treekan. We seek an audience with your king, not the Aver.' With scant regard for protocol, Varuk flung the doors open and strode inside.

'The Aver has expressly summoned you to the Radhal Daíuh. Or what remains of it… Follow me,' the soldier directed, leading the way to the right, towards the library.

'What does he mean by "what remains of it"?' Treekan murmured to his father, a sense of foreboding settling over him.

As Treekan's gaze swept across the space, he found the answer to his query. Around the bend of a grand courtyard, a scene of devastation unfurled before the stunned guests. Every edifice in sight had been stripped of its once-pristine, adorned façades, their inner workings laid bare for all to witness. White dust danced through the air, as if still echoing the cries of the past tormented structures. At the far end, the entrance to the Radhal Daíuh lay in ruins, its absence a stark testament to the destruction wrought upon it. Several soldiers patrolled the area, while others toiled to

251

clear the path of debris. With a sense of grim familiarity, the young soldier hastened his stride towards their destination.

Upon stepping into the ancient library, the guests were seized by a paralyzing shock. Darkness and dust intertwined in the toxic atmosphere, causing the bearded faces of the Valahans to pale, their facial hair becoming unwitting collectors of the aftermath of ruin. Aura, too, struggled to maintain her concealment amidst the swirling particles, her magic at odds with her desire for invisibility.

Moments later, a figure emerged from the shadows in the distance. Resembling a Human in appearance, he bore the same white hair and beard as the Valahans. Yet, in stark contrast, his eyes gleamed with an abyssal darkness, betraying the malevolence that lurked within. With a flat smile, he greeted the arrivals.

'Our esteemed guests have returned to us at last...' he began, arms outstretched in a mock display of welcome.

'We are here to meet with the young king, not you,' Varuk interjected, stepping back instinctively to evade an unwelcome embrace.

'And meet him you shall, Varuk, soon to be King of Valahans,' Lëogan responded, his voice a haunting whisper that slithered through the space like a sinister enchantment.

Aura silently surveyed the space, her focus fixed on the man she knew to be untrustworthy. She could vividly remember the moment he had crossed the node and was brought in front of Queen Eah. Although the Aqualymph believed him to be the root of all their tribulations, she tamed her desire to confront him right there and dared not risk detection. Thus, her invisible hand landed firmly on Faróel's shoulder, sending him the necessary warning. At the Chomp's subtle reaction, the Harpy redirected his attention from Varuk to Faróel, his eyes narrowing into thin lines as he smiled once more.

'Please accompany me and the other guests below,' he said, executing a shallow bow. 'They await your presence. The king will join us shortly.'

'What other guests do you speak of?' Voishan queried, suspicion tainting his tone.

'The king deems it necessary for representatives of all six races to address the threat that has long loomed upon our heads. He has summoned the Garughals, Queen Eah, and even two Leonty. He believes it's time to set aside old grievances and forge ahead…'

'Lies!' Faróel interjected. 'The Garughals are extinct. All of them. I am certain of it.'

'And Queen Eah vanished yacs ago… What game are you playing, Aver?' Voishan added.

'I speak only the truth…Chomp. And to you, king's son, why not witness it for yourself?' Lëogan countered, gesturing with his left hand towards the dungeon entrance. 'If what you witness displeases you, you are free to voice your objections to our king and depart.'

Under the influence of the Harpy's dark magic, the four guests acquiesced abruptly. Their senses dulled, their vision shrouded in a grey haze, the two Valahans and two Chomps surprised Aura as they followed the Aver without hesitation.

Descending into the depths, they were met by a small gathering awaiting their arrival. At the centre of the chamber loomed the ominous Machine of War, flanked by a youthful king engaged in conversation with one believed to have long departed from the mortal realm. As they stepped into the dimly lit space, Garúth turned, his smile a bewildering sight for Aura. Before her astonished gaze stood the leader of the Garughals, alive and well. Nearby, Queen Eah's ethereal form danced between realms, suspended amidst steam and solid matter.

'As I mentioned, we were anticipating your arrival...' Lëogan remarked. 'The two Leonty called Mementhya and Umbra will join us shortly,' he added.

'Father,' Treekan whispered urgently. 'This is very odd. All the ones we believe dead are here...'

Before the Chomp could respond, the two Leonty arrived, accompanied by another Garughal. To the bewitched eyes of those ensnared by the Harpy's illusion, all twelve attendees appeared present in both spirit and flesh. Two representatives from each race had convened to strategize against the malevolent force that had allegedly besieged the crown city, unleashing a devastating surge of energy into the heavens and paving the path for their adversary.

'Now,' the young king began, his words deliberate yet laden with uncertainty. 'Firstly, I extend my gratitude for your presence in this late hoc. I understand the challenges this situation presents. I realize the scepticism surrounding my ability to lead us against such darkness…but we have survived many yacs since the enemy has presented itself to us. And yet, the power to defeat it lies out of reach.' His voice faltered slightly, overshadowed by the myriad ghosts haunting his thoughts, manipulated by the firm grasp of the Aver, steering him like a marionette.

'We all know this is the site of the incident that triggered all our tribulations. How can you seek our counsel on a matter that originated here, within your own home?' Varuk challenged, undeterred. The veil of Lëogan's enchantment wavered, struggling to maintain its hold over so many minds simultaneously.

'You're not mistaken.' Queen Eah's voice rang softly. 'It began here because it's where the resistance made its stand. The king and I attempted to wield our Flares against our adversary. Ours, theirs, and those of the Leonty who stand among us. Yet, four Flares alone proved insufficient…'

'So, this is why we're convened here? I presume you're about to request the use of our Flares as well?' Faróel interjected, a note of scepticism lacing his tone.

'What a revelation…' Varuk chimed in, a wry laugh escaping his lips.

'The gateway stands open,' Lëogan retorted sharply. 'Your God, our God can't stop the enemy from entering indefinitely. If we hesitate now, we face certain doom.'

'You two,' Voishan interjected, stepping closer to the Leonty. 'How can you abide being here? We're aware of the atrocities inflicted upon your kind. Even within our protected borders, we've heard of the horrors they've endured…'

'He speaks truth,' Faróel added. 'It's highly suspicious, especially considering what we've heard. We believed you were long gone,' he added, looking at Garúth. 'Both you and Queen Eah. What manner of sorcery is this?'

'It's not sorcery, but the very power of our Flares that has brought us back…to wage war for the liberation of all races,' Umbra asserted. Though her voice rang strong and resolute, her form seemed ethereal, her green skin replaced by a translucent grey hue.

'Allow me to dispel any doubt, if you will…' Queen Eah interjected. With a sweeping gesture, a radiant stone materialized before her. The brilliance of the Aqualymphs' Flare pierced through the dungeon's darkness, illuminating the space. Beside it, another figure materialized—a male Aqualymph, his countenance serene. 'For the one cloaked in her own magic…' the queen continued. 'Mareen will attest to the power of resurgence. We've all returned, united in our struggle against our common foe. I implore you, Aura, to see reason and join us in the light.'

In a tumult of emotions, Aura appeared, her form aligning with the shared reality inhabited by the others. Her limbs and visage tinged with white, she had allowed her magic to absorb the heavy dust that permeated the room. Tears welled in her eyes as she beheld her beloved returned to her. Moved by gratitude, Mareen hastened to envelop her in an embrace.

'It's going to be okay, my love. I'm here with you now…'
he whispered, his forms flickering amidst the dusty fog, his
eyes darkened by an obscure power.

'It is time to act,' the Aver declared. 'Whatever terms you
deem suitable, we are prepared to acquiesce. But swift
action is imperative.'

'Agreed,' Aura replied, her smile tinged with a
bittersweet happiness. The Harpy's magic had finally
penetrated her defences, ensnaring her and leading her into
the shadows where others had already found solace. After
the Valahans and Chomps regarded her with surprise at her
sudden change of heart, she continued. 'We shall harness
the power of the Flares, but not here where darkness has
taken root more than once. We will do so in the safest place
of all: the Chomps' village.'

A malevolent grin crept across Lëogan's countenance.
'The location is inconsequential, as long as we stand united.
Very well, we shall accede to your wishes…'

The group embraced Aura's proposal without
opposition. As Queen Eah, the Garughals, and the Leonty
were mere illusions conjured by the Harpy's influence, their
agreement was immediate. Though initially hesitant, the
Valahans eventually consented, their suspicions assuaged.
The Chomps, while pleased to host the event within their
domain, harboured concerns about inviting so many
potential adversaries into their midst. Nevertheless, the pact
was sealed. The twelve would unleash the power of their
Flares together in the heart of the Chomps' village.

# Chapter Twenty-Two

## *The Great Dawn*

∞

The recent unsettling events unfurling in Runae had already pushed the Chomps to a precipice of fear. When the two Valahans had materialized inside their protective dome to seek audience with Faróel, an ominous anticipation settled over them. Now, six more enigmatic figures had breached their sanctuary, defying the solemn pledge to remain apart, twisting their hearts and minds alike.

Alongside the two Valahans strode the young king and his trusted Aver, their demeanour brimming with entitlement as they strode as if the very air belonged to them. Trailing behind were two Garughals, their appearance subdued, as though draped in a dull veil of resignation. Amidst the disquieting intrusion of strangers violating their age-old equilibrium, the Chomps found solace in the presence of a familiar ally and friend. Aura stood at the forefront, accompanied by another Aqualymph, a newcomer to their eyes. Mareen, indistinguishable in form from his companion, blurred the line between substance and ethereal essence, rendering them nearly imperceptible.

'Faróel! What is the meaning of this intrusion?' bellowed an elder Chomp, voicing the collective unease that simmered within the assembly.

'Who are these trespassers, and by what authority do they intrude within our land?' questioned another, his tone laced with suspicion.

'What connection does this have to the trio of Valahans lingering at our northern border for five rhocs now? What do they seek?' asked a female Chomp, her voice tinged with urgency.

Their chorus of inquiries echoed the anxieties that weighed heavy on their hearts. The clamour drew forth a throng of Chomps, emerging from their dwellings to converge atop the hill where Faróel's abode stood. Initially poised to disregard their demands, the one who looked too young to hold any power took the crowd by surprise.

'Chomps, esteemed friends and allies,' began the young king, his voice betraying not only his tender years but also the burdens of his nascent reign. His wavering tone hinted at his inexperience and the arduous struggle against the

Harpy's enchantments. 'Fear not; we come bearing aid. No harm shall befall you—only liberation!'

'What is he talking about?' a bold Chomp interjected, unafraid to disrupt the discourse. His gaze shifted from Faróel to Aura, seeking answers. 'We are perfectly secure within our dome. We have been living all those yacs with no concerns. Why speak of liberation now?' Yet, their queries remained unanswered as the enigmatic ten turned their backs to the amassed crowd, embarking on their ascent towards the old quarter of the village, where the clandestine secret of their invisibility lay concealed.

The clustered houses formed a labyrinthine network, their structures nestled together in a tight embrace around a central courtyard, evoking the ambiance of a quaint, rural hamlet. Illumination emanated from the courtyard's heart, where a blazing Flare cast dancing shadows upon the surrounding walls, its warm, pulsating energy permeating the air. Just beyond the radiant beacon stood a grand edifice of dark stone and weathered wood, awaiting their arrival.

'The Sháten Déil… Your magic bears a distinct essence,' Lëogan remarked, his gaze flitting across the surroundings as if plotting an escape route, should the need arise. Despite his formidable power, the scrutiny of many eyes threatened to unravel his malevolent machinations. Straining to maintain the veil of obliviousness over their minds, he expended every ounce of his energy in pursuit of his nefarious designs. 'We would certainly fail without your Flare.'

'It's fortunate you possess the Leonty's Flare,' chimed in Voishan, his gaze lingering momentarily on Aura. 'Considering their reluctance to join us here. The animosity between our races spans epochs of conflict and bloodshed. It strains credulity to imagine they would simply surrender it to you…' His words trailed off, hinting at the Valahan's ongoing struggle against the magical entrapment encasing his mind.

'As it has been conveyed to you previously, we have reached the mutual understanding that our true adversary lies elsewhere.' Lëogan replied, his tone incisive. 'The Leonty stayed behind with Queen Eah as protection of our lands. Please, esteemed Chomp master, lead the way.' With a gesture of deference, the Harpy motioned towards the imposing doors of the tall structure, offering a semblance of respect. 'Varuk, gather those awaiting outside the dome. If they have been entrusted with the safeguarding of your Flare, they are needed here.'

Without hesitation, the Valahan complied with the Harpy's directive, departing to usher the remaining individuals into the building. As the others filed inside, they were met with a cavernous expanse, its chilly atmosphere stark against the warmth of the Flare they had left behind. The vastness of the room seemed incongruous with the stature of its inhabitants, with feeble candlelight struggling to stave off the encroaching shadows. Balconies loomed overhead, heavy drapes cascading from ceiling to floor, while a semicircular wall at the far end enclosed the space in solemn austerity. Amidst the darkness, a faint glimmer flickered on its surface catching Aura's eye, drawing her focus.

'Those pedestals over there,' Lëogan interjected, gesturing towards a collection of columns scattered throughout the room. 'Can they be moved?'

'They are, but they're quite weighty. What's the purpose?' Treekan queried.

'We'll use them to display our Flares. Let's hurry; the Valahans will arrive soon.'

As the group set about their task with determination, Aura furtively approached the enigmatic shine on the wall. It stirred a sense of familiarity within her, prompting her delicate fingers to trace its surface gently. Though she struggled to recall its origin, a touch was all it took for a long-suppressed memory to surge forth.

Aura found herself teetering on the precipice of the Avalian Deep, locked in a desperate bid to rescue Mareen from the abyss's eternal embrace. An identical flickering had caught her attention before. In that very moment, her queen's command to send her and her loved one to death flooded back in her mind, unravelling a sequence of events in reverse. She remembered her encounter with Lëogan once more, his audience with Queen Eah, and the reverence accorded to him as though he were a deity. And as the mysterious spot on the wall expanded, morphing into a gleaming mirror framed in gold, Aura's reflection gazed back at her, bearing witness to the immutable truths of a bygone era.

'Brother, it's time,' Voishan addressed Varuk as the Valahan entered, bearing a grey, imposing stone. Rays of potent energy pierced the frigid darkness of the chamber, illuminating his grip. 'We are ready,' he declared.

'It's time,' the young king echoed, his words devoid of expression despite their urgency.

'Place your Flare upon this pedestal; our ritual nears,' Lëogan instructed, gesturing towards the designated spot. With a wave of his hand, three radiant stones materialized in the air. The Roshén Déil, belonging to the Leonty, emitted a crimson glow as the Harpy positioned it atop the short column. Next came the Physin Déil, the Beacon of Fire, its fiery essence pulsating with orange vitality. Finally, a translucent white stone followed suit, its luminance captivating Aura's gaze. In the stranger's possession lay the Flare of her kin, prompting unsettling thoughts to swirl within her mind. 'Where is Queen Eah?' she pondered. 'What I witnessed…it's all true. She didn't return with us. Perhaps she was never there at all…'

As her eyes darted around the room, Mareen vanished, the stranger's enchantment fading from her consciousness to reveal the painful reality. Her beloved had never returned. Their last encounter had been fraught with ominous warnings of the queen's malevolent intentions, as he succumbed to a dark transformation. Moments later, the two Garughals dissolved into thin air, leaving Aura bewildered. The remaining figures appeared as mere puppets, manipulated by the deceit of the intruder who had infiltrated their cherished realm.

'My king…' the Harpy intoned, silently urging his master to place the Humans' Flare in its rightful position.

With deliberate steps, the young monarch approached the pedestal, bearing a large, obsidian stone. Its form undulated as if in turmoil, devoid of illumination or warmth. As the Ergon Déil was set in place, a new enchantment unfurled, the five Flares resonating with each other. The chamber trembled as the ground and walls quaked, bathed in the pulsating brilliance emanating from the clustered Flares. Spaced evenly around an invisible circle, they framed the Aver, who stood at its centre with a serene smile.

'Now, Chomp… The final one,' concluded Lëogan. His countenance began to warp, his form expanding as if a monstrous twin emerged from within. Bathed in arcane light, a colossal shadow unfurled from the confines of the circle, reigniting the old dread within the Aqualymph's heart. She was confronted once more with the reality of the peril she had long forewarned—a risk she had pleaded to forestall time and again, to her own queen, to the Chomps, and most recently, to the Valahans. But her awakening had come too late. Faróel advanced towards the lone, vacant pedestal, and the Harpy commenced his long-anticipated ritual.

'As foretold by the Almighty, we return this power unto Him…' Lëogan intoned, his voice resounding with authority. 'Indeed, a vow was sworn—a pact steeped in blood and hate towards those who followed, those who deem themselves Gods…'

'No! Faróel, stop!' Aura's cry echoed, her voice drowned out by the Harpy's incantation and the grip of malevolent influence tightening around the Chomp, ensnared in the clutches of darkness.

'You cannot halt this any longer, Gatekeeper. You have faltered. You have failed in your sole duty. It is time.' The Harpy's laughter reverberated throughout the chamber, its resonance amplified tenfold. 'Now, surrender yourselves to him. Return to the One to whom you all belong!'

'No!' Aura interposed herself between Faróel and the Harpy, seizing the Chomps' Flare from its pedestal without resistance, for the Chomp's mind had already been claimed by the void. With swift resolve, she shrouded the others in the protective aura of the Flare and vanished from view. Without hesitation, she ushered them out of the structure.

Behind them, a towering spire of pure magic erupted from the ground, rending through the stout ceiling and obliterating a swath of the roof. Even in the absence of the sixth Flare, the Harpy's scheme had succeeded. The combined power of the remaining stones was sufficient to breach the barrier once more, this time with enough force to sustain its breach, heralding the return of the One for whom Lëogan beseeched.

# Chapter Twenty-Three

*The Face of the True Enemy*

∞

It's too late…your tricks won't save you this time!' The Harpy's voice echoed through the stormy air, carrying a tone of ominous finality. Within the ancient edifice, a tempest of magic and raw power surged, filling every nook and cranny with its volatile energy. The building quaked as if protesting the intrusion of such overwhelming forces, its very essence trembling under the weight of the malevolent spell.

Drapes billowed and items scattered, drawn inexorably towards the epicentre of the dark enchantment. Amidst the chaos stood Lëogan, a towering figure, his form expanding to fill the space as if melding with the very fabric of magic itself. Each of the five Flares blazed with an intensity bordering on cataclysmic, their flames swirling in a crescendo of power verging on collapse. At the zenith of this arcane display, a pillar of light pierced the roiling atmosphere, unleashing a blinding explosion that seared through the land, leaving naught but devastation in its wake.

Outside the building, those few who had been hurled clear by the timely intervention of the Aqualymph found themselves shielded by the protective aura of the Chomps' Flare, though their bodies still bore the scars of their ordeal. With determination etched upon her features, Aura stood resolute, her hands clasped around the precious stone, a bastion against the encroaching darkness.

'Stay behind me!' she commanded, her voice a clarion call amidst the chaos, even as her form flickered with the strain of channelling the immense power of the Sháten Déil. 'I must extend this barrier as far as I can. None shall survive beyond its reach.'

'Our people…' Faróel's voice wavered, his concern palpable.

'We will endure this,' the young king reassured, his gaze unwavering despite the howling winds. 'This is our salvation!'

'What are you talking about, you silly boy. Look up. We have been deceived!' Varuk's voice thundered, his hands gripping the king's shoulders with a force born of desperation. 'This is your doing!' With a shove, he thrust the monarch aside, his gaze brimming with a venomous resentment that pierced through the chaos like a blade.

Desperation hung heavy in the air as Aura raised the Flare aloft, her very being a conduit for the torrent of magic that threatened to consume her. Her essence seemed to fray under the relentless assault, luminous strands of magic torn from her form and cast into the tempest, each one a testament to her sacrifice. At the brink of despair, a gentle touch fell upon the Aqualymph's back, a silent gesture of support and gratitude amidst the chaos.

'Thank you for standing when I could not,' a spectral voice whispered. 'I am here to shield you, all of you.'

In a flash of ethereal light, Time materialized amidst the crimson haze that shrouded the ravaged landscape, his presence a beacon of hope in the encroaching darkness. With a swift gesture, he bolstered the Gatekeeper's waning strength before striding purposefully towards the heart of the evil spell. As he confronted the Harpy within its altar, the oppressive force of Lëogan's magic faltered, its grip upon the world loosening beneath Time's steadfast resolve. With outstretched arms, he contained the surging power, inch by inch, until his gaze met the one of the Harpy in a clash of wills.

'How dare you pervert my mother's blessing against her own children? Against me, the guardian of Runae?' Time's eyes blazed with righteous fury, their brilliance so intense it seared the Harpy's vision in an instant. 'I will purge you and your corruption from these lands once and for all!'

'As I said, it is too late…' Lëogan's laughter echoed through the chamber, mingling with the wreckage he had wrought upon them. Though his visage was shrouded in darkness, his malevolence remained palpable. 'He is here…'

With a force that seemed to defy comprehension, Time was struck down, his form crashing to the ground under the weight of the onslaught. In the next instant, he was wrenched into the air, his energy forcibly drawn skywards through the gaping tear in the ceiling. Those few witnesses outside the pierced structure watched in horror as their fearless defender was propelled through the skies, buffeted by unseen forces as if caught within the tumult of a storm.

In his valiant struggle against an unseen adversary, Time raised the power of his core and set himself free, descending on the fields just outside the Chomps' village. Yet, even as he sought to defy his assailant, the King of Emptiness closed in once more, seizing Time and hurling him across the expanse with a merciless force.

'Your reckoning is at hand…God.' The words thundered through the air, resonating with a primal authority. 'Join your siblings where you rightfully belong: within me!'

An unnatural darkness swept across the once-serene purple sky, Erion swallowed by the looming shadows cast by colossal clouds. High above the Leonty hills, a swirling vortex of malevolent force unfurled, as though the very fabric of reality had been torn asunder by the voracious maw of Nothing. His tendrils of evil snaked outwards, trapping the land in a suffocating grip of shock and dread, freezing the hearts of all who bore witness.

Time emerged from the scorching earth where he had been cast down, arms outstretched towards the heavens. His cloak billowed wildly in the growing tempest, yet the God remained resolute, a solitary beacon amidst the encroaching darkness. With his hood drawn back, Time's countenance glimmered like a distant star amidst the night, illuminated by the verdant radiance emanating from the artefact clasped within his grasp. The Clepsydra of Time, at last revealed, held every fleeting moment in stasis, suspended between the folds of past, present, and future.

'This is your truth…the defiance born of she whom you once called Mother.' Nothing's chilling voice echoed across the realms, its sinister presence felt from the depths of the Aqualymphs' Sea to the towering peaks of the Mogs. 'But she is gone, as are the others. Your brother Love is about to fall by my hand, and so will you. Embrace my oblivion!'

From the roiling depths of the darkened clouds, two colossal hands materialized, their titanic fingers stretching as though poised to seize entire continents. Nothing's malevolent power bore down upon Time's magic, his divine form too feeble to withstand the onslaught of such unbridled malice. As the enemy unleashed its wrath upon the God, its violent energy surged across the land, uprooting trees and rending the very crust of the planet down to its molten core. Long fissures rent the earth's surface, snaking their way towards the Leonty temples atop the hills, unleashing waves of terror and devastation.

One by one, the homes of countless residents crumbled beneath the relentless assault, followed by the sacred sanctuaries themselves, their white stone structures collapsing into clouds of dust. The few remaining Leonty, survivors of the earlier conflict with Humans, fled in terror, their spirits shattered by the onslaught of this new, more insidious evil.

In the midst of the tumult, shockwaves rippled across the distant hill where Una raced with restless determination, her senses keenly attuned to the unfolding cataclysm. Unbeknownst to her, a chance for retribution lay ahead, nestled within the chaos that loomed before her. As Time's strength waned, crushed beneath the weight of an implacable evil, Una halted in awe before the titanic clash. In that moment, she beheld the full extent of the power she had long yearned for, her gaze transfixed upon the scene of devastation unfurling before her.

The earth trembled beneath her feet, rending asunder as the malevolent force swept through, leaving death in its wake as trees were uprooted from their ancient homes. Yet, amidst the chaos, the stalwart defender of the crumbling world refused to yield. Despite the relentless attack of the enemy, Time fought valiantly, his form contorting and rewinding in a desperate bid to escape the clutches of his inevitable demise. With each defiant gesture, the destruction surged ever wider, defying the very laws of existence and reducing the once-vibrant world to naught but ash and ruin.

While her kin fled in terror, Una remained resolute, her gaze fixed unwaveringly on the heart of the storm. No longer obscured by the mask of shame that had once cloaked her features, she appeared unrecognizable to those who sought to restrain her, their voices pleading for her to preserve herself.

In that pivotal moment, the fates of my brother and I and our respective realms became irrevocably entwined. Whether Time had orchestrated this convergence as a precursor of future resolution or not, it unfolded in synchrony with my own struggle against the enemy on Earth. Within the crucible of my sister's and my own magic, Nothing waged a desperate battle on both fronts, only to falter beneath our combined might.

As he rent my soul asunder and shattered Health's core into myriad fragments, we, in turn, pierced through his very essence with our pure light, our power of making corrupting his very being.

In that moment, Nothing's formidable will was made weak, forced to acknowledge its temporary defeat. Though it could oppose Time, it could not wholly obliterate him. With each passing moment of the battle, the likelihood grew that the God would strike a decisive blow against its dark heart. Recognizing the need for a change in strategy, Nothing swiftly sought an alternative to its original plan, finding its ideal jailer in a being willing to comply with its malevolent will.

As Una's thirst for retribution intensified, he sensed her fearless approach. She moved slowly amidst the destruction, her gaze fixed upon the one who raged across the lands.

'You do not fear?' Nothing's voice thundered from the raging heavens. 'You are unlike the others. What is this…anger I sense? No, it is more than anger. It is wrath, a desire for annihilation.' Yet Una remained silent, her eyes fixed upon the malevolent entity above, a hint of a smile playing upon her lips. 'So you seek it from me… It was you I had seen…'

'Free me…' Una whispered, tears flowing on her green cheeks. Every trace of Human blood running under her skin had disappeared. 'Free me from this pain.'

'And so I will! You come to me in a time of need, as I do to you. I shall transform your fury into a power unlike any other. You shall wield the might of this God and his dominion, bending it to your will, for as long as I require to fulfil my design.'

Even as Time clung to his position, his form trembling upon the unstable ground, a surge of potent magic enveloped him. A crushing force pressed in from all sides, compressing his body and shrinking his heart.

'You call yourself Time…' Nothing's voice dripped with scorn. 'Allow me to bestow upon you an eternity of endless fractions of a still moment, where you shall live and perish…forever. There, amidst the monuments erected in your name by these…beings, you shall languish for as long as my eternity extends.'

A haunting whistle pierced the air, as if every element of the dying planet were being drawn inexorably towards a singular point. In that instant, Time was reduced to naught but a brilliant speck, cast into the abyss below the Temple of Time. Amidst the swirling dust and flames, a clepsydra descended, coming to rest within Una's outstretched hands.

'Others have come to me before, seeking the same power you now crave…' Nothing's voice echoed through the frozen expanse, holding the lands and sky in a dark, motionless tableau. In a world on the brink of death, one heart raced with anticipation; Una's eyes gleamed with a fierce desire. 'But your desire is of a different nature. They sought to conquer; you seek to obliterate…'

'I seek to end it,' the young Leonty declared, unflinching. 'I want to end it all. I have been enslaved, imprisoned by forces I have never even encountered. And for what? There is no reason, no justification at all…'

'You were wrought by the hand of one who shaped all existence. As you were not meant to be, so too is your anguish. This suffering is a…gift, a direct consequence of the rebellion against me. Should you wish, you can undo it all. Strip away everything. With the power I offer, you can erase all that exists. Future, present, past…'

'How?' Una inquired, taking a defiant step forward. Though she could not grasp the entity that lurked everywhere and nowhere, she yearned to possess it at any cost.

'The artefact now in your grasp… It holds the key. As all the power and magic of this world converge upon you, claim it as your own. Consume it, and obliterate all in your path. Once you possess it all, I will return to grant you the peace you seek. It must be done…' Suddenly, Nothing's thunderous voice faltered, muted by an unseen force. The oppressive clouds dissipated, the darkness receding to reveal the light of the distant star.

'No!' Una cried out. 'How am I to accomplish this? Please, don't leave!'

'These…Gods…' Nothing's voice faded to a whisper, as though speaking directly into Una's mind, tinged with a note of anguish. 'Even in their twilight, they defy me… Take the power, take everything. I will return to you…'

Alone amidst the desolation left in the wake of the malevolent assault, Una, the lone soul who had approached Nothing without fear, stood in solitude. Destruction and despair enveloped her like a silent embrace, stretching as far as her eyes could see. No other beings stirred, no other voices resounded. She cast her gaze over the barren landscape, the few remaining temples standing as testament to the lingering presence of her adversaries.

Una's hands tightened around the golden clepsydra, its emerald flashes dimming under the weight of her rage. In her mind, Nothing's words echoed incessantly: Everything… Take everything…

# Chapter Twenty-Four

## *The Rise of a New Queen*

∞

To the far side of the imposing Mogs Mountains, nestled within the Chomps' village, a group of six creatures found their way to Faróel's abode. Their hearts quaked with terror, their limbs trembling as they encountered a gathering of apprehensive Chomps just outside the chieftain's dwelling. Standing a few paces away, the young king observed from a distance, his mind reeling with the unfamiliarity of wars, conflicts, and fear.

Ill-equipped to partake in the weighty discussions unfolding among those whom he knew so little about, he could only recall fragmented stories his father had recounted to him. In his perception, Chomps and Valahans were no longer allies. Bereft of the Aver's guidance, his thoughts were vacant, his tongue unable to articulate any words of reassurance.

'Chomps, please,' Faróel's voice cut through the tension, addressing the anxious throng bombarding him with questions laced with fear. 'Time has returned to our lands. Beyond the Mogs Mountains, he engages the enemy in battle. Here, under the protection of our Flare, we are safe.'

'What happened? The earth shook, and we feared our demise was close!' A female Chomp voiced the collective concern.

'All is calm now… The skies no longer blaze with fury. Erion has returned. Is the ordeal concluded, or do we owe this respite to the dome?' another Chomp queried.

'Truth be told, we cannot say for certain. It may be that the conflict has ceased, or perhaps we are shielded by our own magic. Regardless, I advise against venturing outside to ascertain the truth…' Faróel responded cautiously.

'But we must,' Varuk interjected in a hushed tone to his brother. 'Chomp…we must return to our homeland and ensure our people seek shelter within the caves. We cannot linger here.'

'No. You have witnessed the unleashed power of the evil… You can't leave!' Treekan's apprehension was palpable, his gaze shifting swiftly from the Valahans to Aura, who stood gazing towards the distant north, her thoughts seemingly probing the possibilities of imminent danger beyond the dome.

'They must,' the Aqualymph unexpectedly interjected, catching the Chomps off guard. 'But before you depart, we must ensure the individual who accompanied the king is no longer a threat. We left him to face our God, but his fate remains uncertain. Allowing him to roam freely within your confines is unthinkable. We won't make the same mistake again.'

'Why do you speak of my Aver as if he were the enemy?' the young king finally interjected. His cerulean eyes pierced through the crimson haze of war, gleaming like twin diamonds amidst the chaos. His countenance, pale and adorned with freckles, betrayed his unmistakable youth and inexperience.

'This is not a matter for a Human pup. Leave the decisions to those who have endured the rightful burdens of rulership,' Varuk retorted, mocking laughter punctuating his words. 'He is the one who allowed the enemy to infiltrate, you silly boy.'

'He is also the one who beckoned Time back to our realm. Thanks to the Flare, our God returned to rescue us,' the young king countered, his conviction unwavering.

'Perhaps King Doroas has a point…' Voishan interjected, drawing Varuk away from the Human and restraining his brother from making any further aggressive gestures. 'Why don't we investigate for ourselves? If the Aver still draws breath, we can question him directly,' Voishan suggested, attempting to defuse the tension.

'No!' Aura's response was swift and decisive. Faróel's proposal posed too great a risk to their fragile minds.

Allowing the Aver to speak again could lead to further manipulation. 'We will not allow him the chance to speak. We go, we confirm his demise, and that is the end of it. No discussions.'

Following the lead of the Aqualymph, the group retraced their steps towards the imposing structure at the northern edge of the village. To their astonishment, the building stood empty, devoid of any trace of the Aver or the five Flares. In their absence, the space bore the scars of devastation, with dust and debris strewn haphazardly across the floor. Where once dark magic had held sway, a new presence now asserted itself. Seven mirrors hung upon the expansive wall at the far end of the chamber, their frames glinting with gold and silver. Among them, one mirror loomed larger than the rest, its surface opaque, offering no reflection to the bewildered onlookers.

'He must have taken the Flares with Him...' Faróel murmured, his voice tinged with disbelief.

'They were His to begin with. He bestowed them upon us to shield us from evil,' Voishan remarked, his attention drawn to a large rock on the ground. As he moved it aside, a glimmer caught his eye. Beneath layers of dust and debris lay a twisted, deformed golden crown—the Aver's pin— providing the answer to their most pressing question.

'So he is truly gone...' Faróel's words hung heavy in the air, met with solemn nods from the assembled group.

'And this confirms he was the enemy,' Varuk declared, disdain evident in his voice as he kicked the jewel away. 'Why else would Time have slain him?'

In the wake of this grim discovery, King Doroas retreated towards the grand front doors. Devoid of the Aver's protection and guidance, he found himself alone amidst a populace harbouring resentment towards Humans and all they represented. If they deemed Lëogan complicit in the malevolence they feared, he would inevitably bear the brunt of their retribution for the Harpy's crimes. Seizing the opportunity presented by the group's distraction, the young king slipped away unnoticed, disappearing into the shadows without a trace.

As King Doroas hastened his steps across the rugged terrain to the west, he traversed the fields at the foot of the imposing Mogs Mountains. In that moment, the young Human and Una found themselves intersecting in the sight of a colossal Mog, silently dividing the expanse between the Chomps' village and the steppes beyond the ridge. While the king fled in defeat, Una surged forwards with purpose.

Whispers circulated of a multitude of formidable beings straddling the realms of magic and despair at the fringes of the newly formed desert. These outcasts, once loyal followers of a now-lost queen, roamed the lands like forsaken pariahs, their destinies obscured, their homelands forever beyond their reach. Yet, within them, lay dormant potent power, awaiting the touch of those bold enough to claim it. In the shadows of her vengeful resolve, Una's actions danced to the haunting whispers of Nothing's influence.

Not far from the Valahans' northern pass, where the mountains ceded to the Garughals' forest, the Leonty slowed her stride, her gaze fixed upon the myriad rocks strewn across the field. An invisible divide seemed to cleave the space in twain, suffused with an aura of chill and melancholy. Within the echo of despair, Una moved with a sense of familiarity, her emotions guiding her steps.

'Reveal yourselves!' she commanded, her voice cutting through the silence like a clarion call. 'I am here to bestow upon you the gift of freedom. The same freedom granted to me by one who can surely aid us. Show yourselves, you lost souls…show yourselves!'

As if stirred by a magic beyond her own, a multitude of eery beings emerged from the earth. Their forms, nebulous and ashen, were summoned by a presence they had not anticipated. She was not their queen, yet she exuded a similar authority. Though her substance differed, her allure was just as strong. Where once a leader had faltered, a new one arose in her stead.

'Who are you?' one entity inquired, its essence flickering between existence and oblivion.

'I am Una. Called forth by a great power to deliver you and this world from its suffering. Join me in my cause. It is your sole path to freedom,' she declared, her voice resolute, her countenance stern. Her eyes gleamed crimson, casting a beacon in the darkness for the lost souls before her. Her power finally fully manifesting, she bent the will of the many standing before her.

'We are trapped, unable to return, unable to advance…' another spirit lamented. Stepping forwards from the throng of spectral figures, it approached Una with hesitant resolution. With each step, its form solidified, drawn towards her presence like iron to a lodestone.

'Because with me, with the power bestowed upon me, you shall transcend what you once were. You shall become more than you dared hope,' Una proclaimed, reaching out to touch the spirit's shoulder. 'Follow me, and you shall be liberated to exist in every realm, in every form you desire.'

As one, the hundreds of spirits moved in unison, kneeling upon the dry soil, their forms bowing before the sandy earth. A vast cloud, a mixture of darkness and steam, hovered above them, a harbinger of the dominion they were destined to assert. High above them, Una stood with a regal bearing, surveying the scene with pride and anticipation.

A fleeting smile graced her lips, the verdant hue of her cheeks betraying a newfound sense of fulfilment. No longer a captive, she had shattered the chains of shame and oppression to emerge as the sovereign of a realm in flux. Nothing's will had infiltrated her soul, becoming her own, his nefarious designs weaving through her mind like portents of days to come. A new order was dawning, and she stood poised to usher it forth.

'To you, we swear our oath of loyalty!' the assembly intoned in unison, their voices reverberating across the echoing field. 'In you, we place our trust. Lead us through anguish and despair. Liberate us, our queen!'

'To our queen!' they echoed, their proclamation ringing out with unwavering devotion.

# Chapter Twenty-Five

## *The Mirrors of Time*

∞

A gathering of Chomps moved tirelessly within the expansive, partially ravaged edifice, their efforts focused on clearing debris and battling encroaching dust. Amidst the bustling activity, two Chomps engaged in hushed conversations, their words laden with the weight of hidden concerns.

'I still believe we should venture out, father,' Treekan voiced his dissent against Faróel's decision to remain sheltered within the radius of their Flare's protective influence. 'He might need us.'

'What could a God possibly require from us? From you?' Faróel's voice trembled with emotion as he surveyed their surroundings, his eyes shimmering with unshed tears. 'Look around you. We failed to safeguard even our own sanctuary… It lies in ruins.'

'We cannot afford to remain ignorant of the events unfolding beyond these walls,' the younger Chomp persisted. 'Varuk and Voishan departed ten rhocs ago. Don't you yearn to know of their fate?'

'They are Valahans, Treekan. Resilient to flames and forged metals. We, on the other hand, are half their stature, incapable of traversing even the shortest distance if a single raindrop descends from the heavens,' Faróel lamented, retreating towards the distant semicircular wall, his gaze fixed upon a towering mirror.

'I am well aware of our limitations, father,' Treekan countered, his resolve unyielding. 'But our past has proven our adaptability. Rain or shine, we find refuge when necessary, as we always have.'

With each exchange, the tension between them palpable, the Chomps grappled not only with the physical challenges of their environment but also with the daunting uncertainties lurking beyond their diminished sanctuary.

As if oblivious to his son's words, Faróel remained fixated on the mirror embedded within the wall, his gaze unwavering. Six other companions stood nearby, their presence a silent testament to the allure of the mysterious artefacts. Yet, despite their intrigue, the mirrors offered no reflection to the mesmerized Chomps who now stood before them.

The frames of the mirrors gleamed with an otherworldly radiance, their structure imposing and their surfaces shrouded in an enigmatic darkness that seemed to defy the passage of time. Though they had appeared only recently, each mirror bore the weight of an unexpected antiquity, as if they held within them the echoes of countless ages.

'You ought to be more concerned with what lurks within our own home,' Faróel remarked solemnly. 'These mirrors are not of our making, nor do they bear the mark of our magic. Who placed them here? And for what purpose?'

'This large one has been here since the day we brought all the Flares inside,' Treekan recalled, his fingers tracing the intricate golden frame. As his touch met the cold metal, a shimmering light danced along its edges, catching him off guard.

Before Faróel could caution his son against further interaction, a radiant glow emanated from the heart of the mirror. A wave of warmth washed over Treekan, sending tingles coursing through his body from head to toe. And then, as if awakening from a slumber, words began to materialize upon the darkened surface, illuminating the mysteries hidden within.

*'A yac knokr yac. Tay yacsh knókr tyor yacs, soathár tyor shaclash, sagirath tu'*

'A yac for yac. My yacs for your yacs, to buy your oldest secrets, the beginning of yourself...' Treekan whispered as he read the enchanted spell. 'What secrets?'

As if in direct response to the Chomp's inquiry, a luminous wave surged forth from the depths of the mirror, cascading over its surface and spilling onto the surrounding wall. An otherworldly energy, thick with power and purpose, flowed towards the stunned duo, ensnaring them in its ethereal embrace. Treekan and Faróel stood transfixed, their very beings bathed in the brilliance of the unfolding spectacle.

Before their incredulous eyes, the fabric of time itself seemed to rewind, reversing the ravages of destruction as debris danced backwards into place, reconstructing the ceremonial hall to its former glory. And there, amidst the restored splendour, materialized the figure of their divine benefactor, Time, his form translucent and ghostly, yet suffused with a profound sorrow.

'I seek solace here, Mother, where the shadows cannot reach me,' Time's voice echoed, imbued with a mournful longing. 'Blessed by a fragment of your own essence, this flame of protection burns bright. Yet, even in this sanctum, your presence eludes me.'

His ephemeral visage contorted with anguish, Time's words carried the weight of cosmic despair. 'I do not fear the encroaching darkness upon these lands, though perhaps I should. My concern lies beyond this realm, across the vast expanse of the cosmos, where my sister has vanished without a trace. Her energy, her essence, eludes me. What fate has befallen us, Mother? What fate has befallen you?'

Abruptly, the scene shifted, transporting the two Chomps into the heart of a cosmic struggle, where Time's recent efforts to contain the encroaching malevolence unfolded before them in a blaze of blinding light. A towering column of radiant power surged skyward, Time's outstretched arms straining against the tide of dark magic, his celestial cloak billowing in a frantic dance.

'I have glimpsed the myriad futures, and they do not bode well!' Time's voice reverberated with thunderous authority, his eyes ablaze with the fury of collapsing stars. 'You may prevail for now, but the ultimate victory shall be ours!' Amidst the tumult, the Aver remained conspicuously absent, leaving Treekan to ponder the lurking presence of a more insidious, unseen adversary.

A deep, menacing laughter reverberated through the chamber, slicing through the solemnity like a jagged blade. Time, the guardian prepared to sacrifice all for the people of Runae, found himself the target of scorn and mockery.

'There is no time within me,' the voice boomed, dripping with disdain. 'What pitiful visions could you possibly have witnessed? Mere trickery, conjured by the hand of one now consigned to oblivion. Go, follow the spectre you dare to call Mother, into the void of my domain!'

With a thunderous impact, a surge of energy struck Time's shoulders, driving him to the ground with a force that reverberated through the very fabric of existence. Though the two Chomps bore witness to a mere echo of the recent past, the sheer intensity of the scene sent them sprawling backward, their hearts gripped by a primal terror as they were suddenly expelled by the uncanny vision.

As they struggled to regain their footing amidst the startled murmurs of the other Chomps, Faróel and Treekan exchanged a glance fraught with trepidation. Amidst the rising chatters, Aura emerged with purposeful grace, her countenance a mask of stern judgment.

'What did you see?' she inquired, her voice cutting through the clamour as she approached Faróel, extending a hand to aid the elder Chomp in rising from the dusty floor.

'We saw Time,' Treekan interjected, his voice tinged with urgency as his father brushed the debris from his back, revealing wings now streaked with red and white. 'And we saw the enemy that opposes him. It is a force of unimaginable power!'

'The Aver confronted him?' Aura added, her eyes carefully scanning the mirrors, one by one.

'The Aver wasn't there,' Faróel replied. 'The true evil wasn't him…'

'Maybe, but an evil he remains,' Aura's hand moved to Faróel's shoulder. The fine dust collected on his body and wings started to move towards her arm, descending on her body, hips, and legs. Her skin appearing last, shades of pink and red enclosed the Aqualymph's magic like fresh paint on a large canvas. 'There is something similar to these artefacts in the depths of the sea,' she continued. 'I saw the same magic shining at the bottom of the Avalian Deep. Whatever these are, it's certain we will never recover that one. It's truly impossible to come back from the black death of the abyss…'

'Maybe they are all the same? In that case, these will do?' Treekan showed unusual enthusiasm. It wasn't clear to them what the mirrors were and why they had appeared, but seeing Time in a vision of the recent past sent confidence right into the young Chomp's heart.

'Faróel, I've come to ask you to embark on another risky journey…' Almost dismissing Treekan's question, she had a more urgent topic to discuss. 'Once more I need you to go to the Mogs Mountains and meet Varuk.'

'What for? We agreed it's not wise to venture outside the dome,' Faróel objected. His eyes on Treekan, the old Chomp was terrified at the idea of putting his son's life at risk more than fearing the journey itself.

'We also questioned what might be happening outside the protection of your Flare,' Aura said. 'I crossed the edge just a few hocs ago. Right where the Gochi River turns the hills and runs down towards my home, there I felt it! My Flare… My people's Flare. It's back in the sea where it belongs.'

'What? How? I thought ours was the only one left!' Treekan let out.

'Time must have taken them and placed them back within the rightful owners' homes. I can't imagine any better explanation. But the point is, if that's the case, there are Flares left unprotected, in the open. There is nobody left in the Sea and there are no Garughals left alive in their lands…'

'Why don't you go and take yours and I go to take the other one then?' Faróel asked.

'I thought that too…' Aura's countenance changed. Something else worried her.

'Either way, is it safe to go out? I think that's the most important question…' Treekan added.

'The bright glow has vanished, and the sky has returned to its natural state. The immediate threat appears to have dissipated, but…' Aura's voice trailed off, her gaze drifting towards the broken front doors with a troubled intensity. 'I fear there is a lingering charge in the air, akin to the dark magic I once confronted at the northern reaches of your dome, as I strove to safeguard the Beacon of Fire from the clutches of Queen Eah…'

'You mean the other Aqualymphs?' Faróel's confusion mirrored in his voice. *If Queen Eah is still in the crown city and the malevolence oppressing her has been vanquished, why does Aura still harbour apprehension towards her kin?* he thought. As Aura turned towards the mirror adorning the left side of the chamber, Faróel couldn't help but voice his thoughts out loud.

'The depths are empty of life. I believe my queen has never truly returned. We saw her as the Aver wanted us to see her. I suspect she is gone. Yet, something else now guides their way, leading my fellow Aqualymphs down a treacherous path of corruption,' Aura explained, her words heavy with implication. 'If their aim once lay in the pursuit of the Flares, it's prudent to assume they continue to hold such ambitions. And facing them alone would be madness. We must seek the aid of the Valahans.'

'And let us not forget King Doroas's whereabouts remain unknown. If indeed he has returned to the city, there's a chance he may dispatch his Human soldiers in pursuit of the Flares as well,' Treekan added, his voice tinged with concern.

'I was freed by the Aver's spell thanks to these mirrors,' Aura continued. 'I think we should explore their magic further. Treekan'—she turned around and looked at the young Chomp—'you should examine this power while we are away…'

'I'm going with my father. If he is going to see the Valahans, so am I!'

'No son. Aura is right.' Faróel's hand moved on Treekan's shoulder, love and sorrow mixing on the old Chomp's face. 'It's important we know what the God is trying to tell us through those relics… It'll be a short trip anyway. Isn't it true, Aura?'

'I hope so. You know I can't go with you all the way to the caves. We will travel together to the mountains' feet. There we'll part ways. I'll follow the Gochi stream to the Garughals' waterfall. I'll wait for your return there.'

'Wouldn't it be wiser to secure your Flare first?' Treekan proposed, his voice stained with a quiet determination, a silent plea to remain involved in their collective journey. 'I could journey to see Varuk while you venture to the sea…'

Faróel hesitated, torn between the urgency of their situation and the instinctive urge to shield his son from the dangers lurking beyond their sanctuary's walls. 'Time is of the essence, but I cannot in good conscience allow you to venture out alone,' he replied, his tone firm yet full with paternal concern.

Though his heart ached to witness his son's eagerness to aid their cause, Faróel knew that the perils they faced were too great to risk his safety alone. With a heavy sigh, he turned to Aura, seeking her counsel in navigating the treacherous path ahead.

'Yes, we can leave the Sea for later. If my people have not returned, it is for a reason. They are still possessed by a darkness from which they cannot break free. The sacred waters may now serve as a barrier, repelling them from our realm.'

'For our sake, I pray your optimism holds true…' With a silent understanding, the trio reaffirmed their commitment to their shared cause, steeling themselves for the trials that lay ahead.

With heavy hearts and tearful farewells, Treekan embraced his father with a depth of sorrow that threatened to consume him. In a desperate plea, he voiced his longing to accompany them, to share in their journey and their burden.

'Can I not come with you?' His voice cracked with emotion, a last-ditch effort to defy the inevitable parting. But Faróel's response came not in words, but in a gentle smile, a silent reassurance that spoke volumes.

'I will return before you know it,' Faróel whispered. 'In my absence, remember the wisdom and compassion of your father, Kasthor. His love for you and our people was boundless. If you carry that love within you, time will pass unnoticed until my return. Flioch tu, my son…'

With a final embrace, they parted ways, each heart heavy with the weight of uncertainty, yet buoyed by the hope of reunion. As the rhocs rushed by with relentless speed, urging them to action, Faróel and Aura found themselves on the northern outskirts of their village, ready to embark on their respective quests. And as they ventured on their separate paths, they carried with them the enduring legacy of familial love and resilience that would guide them through the troubles ahead.

# Chapter Twenty-Six

## *The Sweet Taste of Revenge*

∞

The enchanting beauty of what once was a free land lingered only as a distant memory. The green hills adorned with white temples now bore witness to terror and strife. Once symbols of magic and reverence, they had been tainted into heralds of sorrow and persecution by the many wicked hands that had turned against the Leonty in an unyielding war against perceived enemies.

From the day of her birth, Una had known only horror and hatred. The significance the hills held for her kind remained elusive to her. The glory and beauty of the past were experiences foreign to her. As she stood before the Temple of Grace nestled at the foot of the first hill, her gaze pierced through layers of pain and anger. Bathed in Erion's gentle light, her green skin seemed to radiate a reddish hue, casting an oppressive air of despair and demise. In the distance, a few Leonty moved about the temple, ferrying their belongings from dilapidated homes to the sole surviving structure. A cluster of figures congregated at the base of the pristine steps, where towering Leonty exerted their dominance over kneeling compatriots, compelling them to clear rubble and debris.

Though too distant to discern their voices, Una understood the scene unfolding before her. Once again, her people were divided between oppressors and the oppressed. Though physically removed, she stood among them with a fractured heart and a mind entangled in turmoil. A steely resolve etched onto her features as she addressed the void enveloping her.

'Remain concealed until I give word…I shall bring this to an end myself,' Una declared to her followers, advancing slowly towards the crest of the hill. As she drew nearer, faces grew clearer, names resurfaced in her mind. The Leonty who had shared captivity with her struggled to ascend the steps. Pallid and drained, the verdant hue of her skin seemed to have faded. Legs quivering, she pleaded for respite.

'I beg of you, I cannot endure this any longer… I have an infant to care for. Allow me to tend to her needs,' she implored.

'Where would you shelter her with no home left standing? Cease your selfishness and consider the welfare of our people,' a male Leonty retorted, his words tinged with the weight of his own guilt as he observed Runers imposing their will upon their fellow Leonty.

'And if she dies, it's not a great loss, is it?' a Runer interjected, laughing.

'And if you die…well, she's better off gone too,' another Runer chimed in, his corpulent frame and indulgent countenance betraying a life untouched by want or suffering.

'Please, Demetra needs me. Let me rest for a moment. I promise I'll return…' the Leonty pleaded, her outstretched hands reaching for the Runers' legs. In response, they recoiled, their faces contorted in disdain. Just as the larger Runer raised a familiar wooden stick with menacing intent, a voice pierced the air from behind.

'I say this to you once and only once…' Una's voice rang out, mere steps away from the group. 'Drop it.'

'How dare you presume to command me!' the Runer roared as he turned to face Una, his gaze scrutinizing the young Leonty. 'Who are you? You seem familiar… Speak!'

'Be cautious what you wish for… It may not be wise,' Una cautioned, her words dripping with warning. 'But I suppose you wouldn't recognize me without that metal trap on my mouth…' At those words, the large Runer recoiled, dropping his stick with a clatter. Terror etched across his features, his eyes widened in fear of the dreaded crimson sign of magic.

'What madness is this, Tarasco?' the other Runer demanded, his confusion evident. 'Why do you fear this wretched creature?'

Before Tarasco could respond, Una's answer came in the form of her glowing crimson eyes. Almost instantly, one of the male Leonty, under the influence of her magic, seized a large stone and struck the Runer on the head. Empowered by unnatural strength, the blow sent the man staggering backwards, life fleeing his body before he hit the ground.

'Please...' Tarasco pleaded, snatching the wooden stick from the ground. His voice barely above a whisper, his words choked in his throat as another male Leonty closed his hand around the Runer's neck. With Una's will bending minds to her command, the Leonty snapped the stick in two, half falling to the ground and the other driving into Tarasco's throat with lethal force.

The few females stood frozen, their eyes wide with shock. Lethya's gaze shifted between the lifeless bodies of the Runers and Una. Despite the mask that had concealed half of Una's face during their earlier rebellions, her eyes were unmistakable. The fiery determination she had displayed in their early struggles mirrored the hate burning in her gaze now. After a moment of hesitation, Lethya spoke, her voice trembling with uncertainty.

'Una? Is it truly you? Please, tell me it's you...'

'Where is your daughter?' Una's response was chilling, devoid of any trace of compassion.

'She's in the Temple of Wisdom. Another Leonty is watching over her inside the naos...' Lethya replied, her worry palpable. *How far will Una's wrath extend?* she wondered. 'Are you here to save us?'

'I am here to save no one…for no one ever came to save me,' Una's words cut through the air like sharp ice, her eyes flashing red once more. With a swift motion, she turned her gaze towards a male Leonty. In rapid succession, she directed her gaze at each of them in turn. Blood still staining his hands, the Leonty who had struck down the Runer moved towards the other two nearby. Without resistance, they were pummelled, dragged, and stoned to their demise. They offered no fight, their minds clouded by Una's overpowering influence. As the killer vanished into the distance, leaving the female Leonty in shock, Una spoke again.

'He too will meet his end soon enough, do not fret,' Una assured, extending her hand towards Lethya. Terrified yet desperate for hope amidst the carnage, Lethya hesitated before finally grasping Una's hand and rising to her feet. 'Tell me where Demetra is… I will not allow her to remain in this place. She will come with me. And so will you.'

'Where…where will you take us?' Lethya's voice trembled as she glanced anxiously at the other Leonty. 'Are you taking all of us?'

'How many of you are expecting? How many have daughters?' Una's response was terse, her gaze fixed on the Temple of Wisdom shrouded in the mist atop the hill.

'Why? Are you only saving those who do?' another female inquired as the group began to ascend the slope.

'Don't be foolish. Only those who have daughters or will soon. The rest of you can wallow in your own despair...' Una's heavy words casted a pall over the group. A new master had emerged, promising liberation but wielding the same cruelty as their former oppressors. Humans, male Leonty, Runers—they had all played a part in their subjugation, their suffering, their exploitation for the sake of war. Now, one of their own, a female Leonty, emerged as the new tyrant, the new tormentor.

'Why? What did they do to you? We're all victims here, just like you,' another Leonty pleaded, fear mingling with her tears.

'Like me?' Una turned, her expression twisted into a wicked grin. 'None of you are like me. None of you have seen what I've seen, felt what I've felt. Otherwise, you wouldn't ask such foolish questions. Now, how many?'

'T...ten of us,' Lethya stammered. 'No, eleven. Corinthia is expecting a daughter too. She just sensed it...she plans to name her Revelia.'

'Take them and their daughters to the Temple of Wisdom. You may all go. I will extend my welcome as long as my orders are not questioned. Gather them all. I will join you there once I've dealt with the others...' With that, Una turned and strode away towards the western slope of the hill, leaving the Leonty to comply with her command.

'What are you planning to do?' Lethya's desperation lent urgency to her question, her mouth forming the words against Una's demand.

'Once they're all gone, we can't leave our Flare behind, can we?' Una's gaze swept over the terrified Leonty gathered before her. 'I'm going to give you the greatest gift I possibly can…revenge.'

By the time Lethya and the others reached the Temple of Wisdom, Una had already delved into the heart of their ravaged homeland. With her came a host of spectral figures, drifting through the ruins and alleys, gathering the remaining Leonty like discarded remnants. Terrified by the presence of Una's ghostly army, the Leonty obeyed her commands without the need for her coercive magic. Finally, a few Runers were brought forth, flushed from their sanctuaries where they had long wielded their cruel dominion. Confusion and fear gripped the land. Unaware of Una's intentions—whether she came to conquer, destroy, or liberate—whispers and questions swirled among the many terrified faces.

As they all assembled in front of the imposing white Temple, Una ascended the steps and stood beside Lethya and the other females. A dark fog enveloped them from both sides and behind, as the once-gentle and peaceful Aqualymphs now held them captive. There was no escape, no fate but death.

After Una meticulously counted the females and their daughters, she turned to address the crowd. 'Who am I? You ask… What am I doing? Ignorance festers in your midst… I pose a different question: Who are you? What have you done? You are Leonty! Gifted with power and magic beyond comprehension. Yet instead of ruling, you allowed madness to reign. You let Humans assail you. You allowed your own kind, your own flesh and blood, to betray you. And you stood by. They took our females, they slaughtered them, and you stood by. They unleashed this vile evil upon your homes, your temples...and you stood by. They branded you evil in their insipid books. And still, you stood by.'

Una paused, her gaze sweeping over the gathering below. Silence fell, thick with the realization that liberation was not her intent. Some males attempted to flee, only to find their escape thwarted by Una's shadowy army. Two Runers knelt, pleading for forgiveness, their faces drained of colour, tears tracing lines down the slopes of their uncertain future.

'To forgive you?' Una's smile was chilling. 'I can and will forgive you...when you return my mother, my family, my past. Can you do that? Tell me you can, so I can ask them why I was left behind...why you all allowed this to happen.'

'Una...please. Just—' Lethya's plea was abruptly silenced by Una's magic. With a brief turn, Una's eyes glowed red, and her power subdued the will of the Leonty in an instant.

'Spectres!' Una's command pierced the air, and in an instant, the group below was consumed by smoke and fury. The cacophony of screams filled the hot air as pain and death reigned over the once-peaceful landscape. With a grim determination fuelled by growing hatred, Una watched as her kin were reduced to ash and bone, their blood staining the verdant grass. Leonty and Runers alike were erased from existence in the aftermath of the brutal onslaught.

Untouched by the carnage she had wrought, Una turned silently and made her way into the temple, leaving Lethya and the other females in a state of petrified shock. Their new master had one final duty before she would drag them away. Their Flare called to her from within the naos, its magic and malevolence drawing her closer. In the darkness of the cold chamber, a small stone burned with a crimson fire. As Una approached, her eyes and soul drawn to its power, something else caught her attention. At the far end of the room, three gleaming mirrors glittered in the darkness.

Responding to her presence, the mirrors quivered, their surfaces opening to reveal new revelations. In the left mirror, six female Leonty engaged in conversation with a seventh, who also appeared in the right mirror. She held a tall Human in her soft embrace, their faces locked in an intimate gaze, an intense emotion radiating from the mirror's depths. Intrigued, Una moved closer to inspect this new magic, but the largest mirror at the centre flickered, drawing her attention.

From within its core emerged an unusual sight—a tiny island floating in a lifeless sea. Three unfamiliar Humans materialized on the island, their faces distinct from any Una had encountered before. As they wandered, bewildered, an Aqualymph emerged from the waters, catching them by surprise.

'What is this? What magic is this I see?' Una whispered in the hushed room.

In the next moment, the vision shifted, images flashing in rapid succession until they coalesced into one final picture. Una appeared older, her beauty marred only by the darkness of her soul. Alone in a small, rounded room, she stood at the top of a tall tower, her gaze fixed on the outside world through a narrow opening. In her hands, a crumpled piece of paper betrayed the rage that consumed her heart. Whatever lay beyond that window, it was clear that the young Una glimpsed her future, and a warning echoed vividly before her eyes.

# Chapter Twenty-Seven

## *Valahan Mogs*

∞

How many times the Chomp had traversed the walls into and out of the Valahans' kingdom was something Faróel could not even recall; yet the inaugural visit remained etched in his memory and heart. A yac after Faróel and Kasthor's initial encounter, Kasthor had ushered him into the mountains to introduce him to his longstanding companions. Following his proposal to Faróel, Kasthor surprised him by revealing his prior commitment to one of Vasheer's sons. When the opportune moment arrived, Voishan—the younger of the king's offspring—would wed Kasthor, thus cementing an unbreakable bond between their races and lands.

'I must depart,' Kasthor had stated. 'The king ought to hear it from me directly before rumours reach the Mogs.'

'I can't fathom you were promised…you're engaged to a young Valahan and never disclosed it to me!' Faróel had exclaimed, his shock and resentment palpable as he crossed the invisible boundary between the Chomps' hills and the Valahans' territory.

'It was never to be,' Kasthor chuckled. 'Voishan and I have conversed throughout these yacs. He's enamoured with a female Valahan beyond the ridge. He's yet to divulge this to his father. The king can be rather bad tempered at times…'

'So the king remains unaware?'

'He suspects… Regardless, I vowed to Voishan that I would be the one to breach the pledge by informing King Vasheer of my intent to marry another. You must understand, our families—mine and theirs—have shared a longstanding connection spanning many yacs. I've defied the political boundaries dictating our segregation from the rest of Runae to maintain our bond.'

'This explains your extensive knowledge of the lands, the people, and their laws. Your familiarity with the Garughals, the Humans…'

'Yes. A responsibility we'll entrust to our progeny when the time arrives. Steering the Chomps can prove arduous at times. We're obstinate, but we have a good heart. It's imperative we continue to engage with the world, combatting our tendency towards isolation.'

Kasthor's words had reverberated in Faróel's mind for yacs, echoing once more as he traversed the same road they had travelled together in a distant past. His fearcel was gone, and the duty Kasthor spoke of seemed to evaporate amidst the flames of conflict and the ravages of war. Their son, Treekan, was meant to follow in the footsteps of Kasthor and his forebears, *but how can he?* he thought. There seemed little left worth fighting for, and the Chomps were more resolute than ever in their desire to seclude themselves from the rest of the world.

'And yet, here we stand, the solitary guardians of the ties that bind us to others,' Faróel muttered to himself as he passed through the imposing stony entrance of the cave on the southern side.

If his memories held true, the entire landscape had undergone a profound transformation. The narrow pathway flanked by towering rocky walls lay deserted, enveloped in an eerie silence that accompanied Faróel as he approached a crossroads ahead. Some of the Valahans' dwellings on the periphery of their territory stood abandoned, their stone doors left ajar, beckoning darkness. Faróel scanned the surroundings, his gaze darting between the bottom and the summit of the rocky cliffs, when two Valahans emerged from their cave. Leaving their home, situated at a considerable distance from the road, they appeared as mere specks navigating through the dense fog.

'Hey, you two!' Faróel called out, craning his neck to address them. 'I'm Faróel, from the hills to the south. Where is everyone?' But the tiny figures paid no heed to his inquiry, instead hastening along the narrow path ahead. 'Wait! I'm a Chomp, I must speak with your king! Stubborn mountaineers… What's happening?' he exclaimed, watching as the Valahans vanished into the mist.

Bathed in the bright glow of Erion, casting its light through the cleft between the peaks, the crossroads ahead seemed as if divided by arcane magic. The path to the right, ascending towards the highest Mog, gleamed brightly. Conversely, the one veering left, descending into the depths of the mines, was engulfed in impenetrable darkness. As Faróel drew nearer, a peculiar sight unfolded. At the juncture of the two paths, a massive, flat wall loomed in the background, its stony surface trembling. Etched upon it, a cryptic sequence of words flickered fleetingly. Before Faróel could investigate further, murmurs emanated from the depths of the mines. Unintelligible whispers, their language foreign, spoke of anguish and demise.

'Who's there? Come out. I'm here to talk to the king!' Faróel shouted in the dark of the road ahead. A few moments later, a grey fog appeared from deep inside, moving into the open, crawling on the hot ground. Unfamiliar with that new magic, the Chomp stepped back, worried. Whatever power the Valahans had put as defence to their dominion, it was of a new making. Suddenly, the grey smoke lifted in the air, taking forms of creatures he had never seen before. Their bodies slim, their backs curved under the weight of their darkness, a dozen ghosts formed right before his eyes.

'Are you Varuk?' one spoke. With no mouth nor facial features to be seen, it was like that voice had come from all around, as if the fog itself was talking to the Chomp. Faróel's eyes widened in fear.

'The caves are empty,' another one added. 'Where are they?'

'Who are you? You are not Valahans. What are you?'

'We are spectres… We come to take. We come to end it…' And the first one moved slowly, leaving the scary pack behind. His head and face slowly took form. With no eyes to look at, two large cavities stared at the petrified Chomp. The bottom of the creature's face moved as he talked; his mouth turned into a hovering force.

'Which one do you own? You are not a Valahan… Which Flare do you own?' another spectre asked, taking place beside his companion.

'You are the ones Aura spoke of. You are Aqualymphs. What happened to you?' Faróel asked as he slowly walked back, his wings almost touching the wobbling wall.

'There are Aqualymph no more… We follow and answer only to our queen. Runae's new queen…'

'Queen Eah is dead! What queen do you speak of? What did you do to this place? Where are they?' Fear mounted in Faróel's heart. He had come to meet friends and allies. Instead, he had met a new, evil, surging power.

'Take him,' a spectre whispered.

As the fog expanded rapidly, the spectres dissolved to become only one, larger enemy. With his back almost glued to the large wall, Faróel could not escape. His eyes closed, his mind briefly recalling a name, Treekan. There was no warning that could reach the Chomps. Faróel was going to disappear in the silence of an unmerciful mist. Suddenly, two hairy hands emerged from the wall and grabbed his shoulders in a rescuing hug. A moment later, the Chomp was swallowed by the mountains, dragged into the deep layers of rocks and stones.

'In the name of Time, what was that?' Faróel exclaimed, fear and relief blending together as his eyes met those of his saviour. Voishan stood right in front of him, a weak smile appearing on his face.

'It's Valahans' magic, Chomp. You should know better. Did you not read the spell?' And Voishan smiled again.

'I was busy talking to your new guests! Did you see them? Who are they?' Faróel asked as he looked back at the wall through which he had been pulled.

With the hosts' magic at work, the thick skin of the mountain was reduced to a mere transparent veil. The desolate outside was visible to those hidden inside the mountain. The enemy moved frenetically on the other side, anger growing as fast as their foggy nature. The Chomp had been snapped away, rescued by the hands of an enemy they could not find. Fingers formed from the dark cloud slid on a wall they could not penetrate. They knew the Valahans' Flare prevented them from passing through, and yet they kept touching, pushing against a door that would not open.

'They entered our land several rhocs ago. Through the Mogs Pass at the north, by the steppes, they crawled in, pressed by a new master's will...' Voishan replied, taking Faróel's arm and leading him into the depths of the dark cave.

The road ahead ran down to a deep below, twisting in loops towards an unseen destination. With large cavities opening up at the bottom on each side, the narrow pathway looked like a risky descent into the core of the planet. With heat and pressure mounting on his head and body, Faróel's face turned red, sweat appearing on his forehead. After the two had circled down three times, a gigantic cave opened up to the left. In there, a multitude of Valahans moved around; some sat on the hot ground with tiredness imprinted on their faces. At the far end of the opening, a few smaller holes broke the silvery wall into a countless number of homes. As if the Valahans had permanently moved inside the mountains. Faróel wondered how long they had been hiding in there.

'We started the move not long after we cut ties with King Romohan. We knew darker days were ahead so we decided to strengthen our position by hiding in here. At first, we moved our families and the ones who needed protection the most. Eventually, yac after yac, everybody else accepted the idea of a permanent hide. The last ones resisting the idea of relocating inside the mountain changed their mind after what happened to Time,' Voishan explained.

'Can these mountains protect you indefinitely?' the Chomp asked, as they walked inside one of the smaller caves. Under the eyes of the many curious Valahans, the two disappeared inside Varuk's home.

'We hope. They have taken the north pass and the south pass. There is no way out for us…' Voishan let out, sighing. 'Fancy a strong drink?'

'This is…well, claustrophobic…' Faróel said. At the corner of the small cave, a rocky table was holding the weight of a dozen mining tools. To the opposite side, a tall pile of books and maps held their balance precariously. Just beside the improvised small tower, Varuk appeared through an opening in the wall.

'It is for you, Chomp. You are blessed with open skies and fresh air. But I have to admit, the idea of living here indefinitely is not pleasant.' And Varuk moved beside the Chomp, inviting him to take a seat on a large wooden chair. After sitting next to him, he continued. 'We are evaluating the idea of opening a new pass, at the west side, right over the desert. The height of those ridges makes it hard, but if we can break free, we might have a way out through the Leonty's hills… Thank you, brother,' he added after Voishan had handed Faróel a cup filled with a golden liquid.

'I hope for your sake you are right… Thank you, Voishan.' After making a funny face triggered by the sour taste of his drink, the Chomp added, 'Aura asked me to come here because of that very same thing that is hunting you outside. She said they are following a new master and they confirmed it to me, right before your brother saved me. By the way, Voishan, I can't thank you enough!'

'I know, I'm great!' the Valahan replied, laughing. 'To think you took my promised fearcel-to-be…I should have let them take you.'

'Very funny…' Faróel said as the two brothers laughed loud. 'Anyway! The Aqualymph says they are after the Flares. And again, she was right cause that's the question they asked me before they attacked me.'

'Our Flare is safe and yours is pretty much impossible to take. What's to fear?' Voishan asked as he sat beside his brother. Although they were several yacs apart, they looked almost identical. Same blue eyes on their square faces, large and tall bodies covered with a thick layer of hair, they looked like two beautiful beasts.

'The other Flares are back,' the Chomp replied, taking them by surprise. 'The day Time fought the Aver, the Flares went back where they belonged. At least, that's what Aura told me…'

'It's true…' Varuk let out, a worrying thought showing on his face. 'We found our Flare here when we came home. Time must have placed it back, and so He must have done the same with the others.'

'All of them?' Voishan inquired. 'If all of them are back where they belong…'

'Some of them are up for the taking!' Faróel continued. 'The Garughals' is the one we fear the most. The Beacon of Fire is vulnerable in an empty land. Aura is already on her way to the waterfalls. My only consolation is that the enemy seems to haunt this place instead… Sorry, I shouldn't have said that…'

'No Chomp, you are not wrong. We can protect ourselves, she can't,' Voishan replied. His hand moved on Faróel's and a soft smile accompanied his gesture. 'I understand why you came here…'

'And I'm afraid we can't help you…' Varuk interjected, taking the Chomp by surprise. 'You have seen it with your own eyes. We are trapped in here. There is no way out.'

'Assuming they are at the south pass, how many are they? Is it wise to think the steppes might be our way out?' Faróel stood up and moved close to the tall pile of books. After carefully slipping a large map from in between the large tomes, he turned around and placed it on the stony table. 'It's one, maybe two rhocs from here to the waterfalls. It can be done.'

'It could…be done, Faróel. It's a huge risk.' Varuk replied, standing up. His eyes inspecting the old map, he was hesitant. 'We will have to go with you but we can't leave our people alone. Our father is not well enough to lead our miners and we must continue the digging at the west.'

'Brother…' Voishan let out before being interrupted.

'No!' Varuk said, firmly. 'I'm not leaving you here alone. We will have to take our strong Valahans with us if we want to make it to the waterfalls. That means leaving you unprotected.'

'He is right,' Faróel added, sad. He had done the same by leaving Treekan behind. Sorrow mounted in his heart.

'We should have never listened to that silly boy and his Aver,' Varuk stated, angered. As if he was pushing judgment against his own previous decisions, he was afraid to fail again. To fail his brother, his family, and his people once more.

After a few moments of silence, Voishan resumed the conversation. 'Listen to me, brother… Like the many yacs past, we have been called on by events that are far beyond our means. This is our God's war and, somehow, we are called to fight as if we had his same power. Remember what he told us, back when Father was still able to comprehend? He wanted to share his power with us. This is why he gave us the Flares. We are meant to protect everyone, not only our people…'

'We almost lost it all when we gave them to that wicked Human,' Varuk replied. 'We can't risk repeating our missteps.'

'And we won't!' Faróel said. 'This time, it's us. The four of us, nobody else. Me, you, Voishan, and Aura. We trust nobody and no one else. For the good of our people, our families. Like my beloved Kasthor said many times: we need to stay together.'

'Okay, I understand we are called to fulfil a path laid before us, whether we want it or not, but if we do this, we need to come up with a proper plan. We need to tell our families what we are about to do.' Varuk said, acceptance finally conquering his heart. 'Let's get together one last time. A quick dinner, a good explanation for them and a strong plan for us. Then we go!'

# Chapter Twenty-Eight

## *To the Bitter End*

∞

The two brothers stood in silence amidst the murmuring crowd, a palpable tension hanging in the air. Varuk had called upon only five hundred of his ten thousand soldiers, many of whom lacked the experience and prowess expected of an army. Among them were veterans haunted by memories of past battles and novices untested in combat, fuelling whispers of impending defeat throughout the gathering. Some Valahans questioned the wisdom behind the king's son's decision.

'We're safe here. Why risk our lives for a stranger? An Aqualymph, no less,' a tall, elderly Valahan remarked.

'The king has his reasons, Volstock. We must retrieve the Beacon of Fire before the enemy seizes it,' another countered.

'The king is not even here. We haven't seen the king in rhocs! Who gave the order?' another one replied.

'And with only five hundred of us? We may never return home,' sighed another, echoing the collective apprehension. Their anxiety mounted as they awaited Varuk's command.

'My word is our king's word,' Varuk stated from the top of a square rock, at the centre of a courtyard. 'My word is for our people's sake. You might not fully grasp the magnitude of this threat yet, but listen to me. The powerful foe moving against us is shifting form, taking possession of new bodies, but his will remains the same: our end written in stone and our Flares in his hands!'

After countless hocs, the dissent finally subsided. The realization that their move could grant their people and their family the long-sought safety had finally charmed their restless spirits. At the dawn of the following rhoc, the large group moved to the north side of the mountain. While torch-bearing Valahans illuminated the passage ahead, the two brothers inspected the strong wall in the depths of a cavern. Shadows flickered and danced, casting an eerie atmosphere over the scene. Faróel, a trusted ally, paced nearby, his eyes fixed on the radiant Flare grasped tightly by Varuk, its magical light piercing the darkness.

'It's been long,' Voishan remarked. 'I see no sign of the enemy over the wall.'

'Something feels amiss, brother. These lands are no longer familiar to us. There's a malevolent presence lurking,' Varuk responded, his gaze drawn to the horizon. 'The Murán Déil can penetrate the matter and grant us the sight, but this enemy has no body to be seen…'

'Do you sense their nature?' Faróel inquired, drawn closer by the comforting warmth of the powerful glow.

'I cannot, but I feel the risk crawling beneath my skin,' Varuk confessed, his grip tightening around the stone, a beacon of hope amidst uncertainty.

As he held the Flare in his hand, he turned around to reveal a startling transformation unfolding before the eyes of Voishan and Faróel. His wrists, arms, and shoulders lost their colour, his skin turning transparent along with bones and flesh. The Flare's magic seemed to extend inward, pushing against its bearer.

'Is this normal?' Faróel asked, his voice tinged with shock.

'Brother!' Voishan exclaimed, his concern evident. 'What's happening to you?'

'Look at your hands; it's happening to you too!' Faróel added, further unsettling Voishan.

'It's them. Their magic is pressing against ours. The more I project the Flare's power outward, the more they push it back towards us. They're here, I'm sure of it, but why can't we see them?' Varuk explained urgently.

'If only I had my Flare with me… We could sneak out unseen. But I couldn't take it from my people, you know?' Faróel lamented.

'It's fine, Faróel. We'll take our chances anyway. Brother, tell the others we're moving,' Varuk urged.

Amid doubts, fear, and dissent, the crowd reluctantly complied with Varuk's command, inching towards the pass. After a moment of hesitation and a shared glance with his brother, Varuk crossed the invisible boundary between their home and the steppes. The thick, stony wall shimmered with a silvery light as he passed through it, stepping into the perilous unknown. Moments later, Voishan and Faróel followed suit, their senses heightened, ready to flee at the first sign of danger. Yet the tension gripping their hearts proved unwarranted. The world beyond the large Mogs lay silent.

'Looks like you were wrong, brother,' Voishan remarked, gesturing to the soldiers that it was safe to emerge. 'I haven't seen the Garughals' land since the day we met Time. Do you remember the way?'

'I do, but these lands have changed. That large field over the Mogs Pass… Look. It's turning dead,' Varuk observed solemnly.

'I'd heard it's transforming the steppes into a desert, but witnessing it firsthand is sobering,' Faróel added.

'Alright, let's move. Stay quiet, stay vigilant. We take the old road. The mountains' shadow may offer us protection from whatever pursues us,' Varuk instructed the crowd, determination ringing in his voice. When the small army had exited the cave, the Valahan pulled one of the soldiers aside. 'Vushnat, take the Flare back to my father. We risk to take one only to lose our own.' After meeting Faróel's worried gaze, he added, 'The stone needs to stay behind as protection of my people, same as yours.'

Sped up by the fear of an invisible threat, the group moved at a fast pace through the rocky grounds. Afraid of moving away from the giants who had been watching over their safety for millennia, they let go the idea of walking on soft hills in favour of a perpetual shade. With Erion blocked by the large ridge, the Valahans looked like hundreds of shadows sliding along the side of the mountains. At the top of the stretched line, Varuk and Voishan were followed closely by the Chomp, whose gaze was firmly fixed on the faraway destination. Towards the quarter mark of their journey, a sudden heat rose from the ground. Cracks ran from the rocky walls to the harsh hills. A red, piping-hot magma glittered from place to place, revealing an upcoming obstacle to their journey.

'What is this I see?' Varuk asked, his surprise evident as he, Voishan, and Faróel ventured ahead, leaving the rest of the army behind.

'The magma is surfacing this far from Mog? How is this possible?' Voishan added, kneeling on the hot soil to inspect one of the ground fissures. He could feel his skin almost burning at the touch of the steamy crust.

'This must be what the Leonty complained about during that long-gone rhoc when we met Time in council. Father said it was impossible, and yet, here we are. The planet is truly breaking apart…and we did this.'

'We? How? We've been digging since ancient times, and this has never happened before' Voishan protested, surveying the multiplying cracks that created a terrifying mosaic of a world on fire.

'Things have changed since we unearthed the Mother Flare… How many times have we ventured this side of Runae since then? The last time was when we met Vasheela's father, and you asked him to grant you the wish of marrying her.'

'We need to go that way,' Faróel interjected. 'There's a large opening on the ground further ahead. It cuts across from one side to the other. How are we going to cross it?'

After a moment of contemplative silence, Varuk surveyed their options: move north, deeper into the steppes and into the dangerous unknown, or continue alongside the mountains.

'That would add two more rhocs to our journey!' Faróel objected. 'Walking the path of mountains will take us too far south. My home would be closer than the old forest.'

'And if we move north, we'll lose almost as much,' Voishan added. 'And we could expose ourselves to even greater risks.'

'We've been fortunate thus far. I'm not comfortable pushing our luck any further,' Varuk replied, his voice resonating with authority but tinged with sorrow and fear. 'Let me use my own magic to scout the path ahead inside the mountains. My power can do very little without our Flare but if the magma flow isn't too extensive, we might only need to extend our journey by a little.' Returning to address the crowd, he continued, 'The path ahead is blocked. Fire and lava are rending the road asunder. We may need to re-enter the mountain and hope we find an existing path forward. It will take time, so please, take this opportunity to rest.'

'Split into groups of ten,' Voishan continued. 'Lie with your back against the rocks and spread thin along the path. We need to stay hidden in the shadow. If any of you catch anything suspicious, stay calm, keep quiet, and alert the troops. Please remember, keep as quiet as possible.'

With no hesitation, the five hundred moved all at once. Fast on their feet, haste in their hearts, they all obeyed their master's command and his brother's instructions. In the space of a single hoc, they had all disappeared into the dark shade of the ridge. Their skin covered in grey clothes, their faces full of dark hair, they looked like they had fused together with their eternal companion. Varuk moved further east, closer to the edge of a large fissure. With his hands stretched towards the rocky wall, he pushed his hands against it, slowly dissolving the layers of rocks and metals as if they were made of thin, fragile fabric. A few feet away, Voishan and Faróel sat on the ground. With sweat on their foreheads and the heat turning their faces red, they felt as if they could faint at any time.

'Oh, come on! You stubborn evil!' Varuk shouted a few moments later. Penetrating the wall for a good length, he had disappeared into the dark depth of the mountain. His

321

voice muffled by the rocky crust, the Valahan took the sleepy Chomp by surprise, waking him up. A terrified look appeared on his face as his gaze met Voishan's.

'Don't worry about it. This is routine for us… Faróel, what's wrong?'

'The air…I can feel the rising moisture!'

'How long?' Voishan asked, knowing exactly what the Chomp meant.

'One or two more hocs… This is…what am I going to do?' Faróel panicked. He looked left and right, terror growing in his eyes. Heavy, dark clouds were moving fast from the Leonty hills, sliding against the high peaks of the mountains.

'Stay calm…' Voishan replied, taking Faróel's hands. 'You are going to do exactly what you are supposed to. You will take some rest while I watch over you. Don't forget, I've been dealing with Chomps all my life…' And a smile appeared on Faróel's face. 'Well, one in particular… But we won't discuss him. I know it upsets you,' Voishan added, laughing.

'It doesn't upset me. May I remind you that Kasthor chose me? He spent more time with me than he did with you… We had a little mad Chomp together.' Without Faróel noticing it, Voishan's attempt to distract him from the rising fear had worked its charm.

'Only because I fell in love with someone else.' Voishan smiled. 'He could have been a king's brother if we married…'

'I can only imagine…Kasthor living in a smelly cave…'
And Faróel moved towards the spot where Varuk had
disappeared.

'Hey! It's my home you are talking about,' Voishan
replied, following the Chomp inside the tunnel.

'I miss him, you know?' Faróel's expression changed
again. Sorrow was claiming its spot inside his heart. 'He
knew so much. He loved so much. It's safe to say we
wouldn't be here if he were still alive. He would know what
to do.'

'Did he tell you of that time we went to the crown city
and on our way back home we ventured into the outskirts?
It was silly of us to go and roam in such a dangerous land,
but it was nothing compared to what it is now…and we
were young and stupid.'

'What happened?' Faróel's curiosity had taken over. The
discomfort of feeling the air getting wet was easily
dismissed.

'Oh, you can't imagine. We had gone to the crown city
for Romohan's big birth ceremony. *"Bring your fearcel,"* my
stubborn father insisted. He was determined to let the king
know we were promised…' And Voishan rolled his eyes,
showing dissent. 'King Lohan could not care less…
Anyway, on our way back, Kasthor and I decided to take
our own way and leave my father and my brother behind in
the City. We wanted to go and visit the coastline at the
Aqualymphs' Sea. It was said you could see the old souls
departing this world if you took the King's Road and
travelled at the rise of Erion. Well, we didn't see much

because we took the wrong way and entered the outskirts. There we met a few Valahans who were running some dodgy business with some Humans and a few Leonty…'

'This feels very familiar…' Faróel let out as he remembered the day he and Kasthor had brought Treekan to the crown city to be registered.

'In short, we landed ourselves in trouble. We angered a few Humans who weren't inclined to be kind to us in the first place. At one point, it seemed like it was the end for us! Backs against the wall of an old tavern, their fists flying, our faces taking a beating. I'll never forget Kasthor, fighting like a legendary hero. He took out two of them, his strength unbelievable. He grabbed my hand, and said, "To the bitter end!" Then he flew off, pulling me into the sky. It was the first and only time my feet have ever left the ground. Incredible. That's when I knew I loved him as much as I loved my own brother…'

'My Kasthor…' Faróel's voice trembled, tears welling in his eyes as he stared into the hole forming before him.

'Varuk, what's the situation?' Voishan interjected, concern etched on his face as he turned to his brother, who exited the mountain appearing weary and resigned.

'I can't cross it. Take a look for yourself. The stream is too wide and stretches as far as I can see. Magma surrounds us on all sides. I'm afraid we're stuck,' Varuk admitted, his tone heavy with defeat.

'This can't all be because of us…' Voishan muttered as he placed his hands on the rocky wall, his mystic eyes gazing at the vast expanse of boiling red beneath the mountain's surface.

Before they could formulate a plan, a piercing scream shattered the air. Without hesitation, the trio rushed back, their hearts pounding with apprehension. A horrifying sight greeted them. Dozens of large Valahans were flung through the air by an invisible force, their forms obscured by smoky tendrils that swept across the rusty soil. Soldiers scattered in a frenzy, their cries mingling with the roar of sudden battle. Some, blinded by fear, stumbled into the gaping cracks of the earth, meeting a fiery demise. A few managed to reach the brothers, their warnings arriving too late.

'They are here! We can't see them, but they can reach us!' one screamed, before his body lifted from the ground, pulled by whispers and evil magic.

'Run! Run! Run!' another Valahan shouted, followed by a dozen more who sped past their master, their faces deformed by horror.

With urgency driving their every step, Varuk, Voishan, and Faróel bolted downhill, fleeing from the encroaching darkness of the mountains. Behind them, a vast, ominous cloud expanded, consuming the few remaining Valahans in its path. Their anguished cries echoed in the ears of the trio as they hastened their pace, desperate to outrun the encroaching evil. But with each stride, the threat drew closer, the vision of their upcoming end looming ever larger.

Suddenly, a yawning chasm emerged before them, blocking their path. They skidded to a halt at the edge of the steaming fissure, their hearts pounding in unison. And then, a figure materialized behind them, emerging from the swirling clouds. It was Una, her slender form taking shape amidst the grey mist. Beside her, a legion of spectres coalesced from the dark fog, their malevolent presence palpable.

'You won't escape your judgment, Valahans,' Una declared, her voice cutting through the air like a whip crackling with wrath.

'A Leonty? Which one are you?' Varuk demanded, positioning himself protectively in front of his companions, his hands poised defensively at his sides.

'Does it matter? I'm the only one you should fear,' Una retorted, her gaze fixed unwaveringly on the older brother. A crimson light flickered in her eyes, her magic homed in on her prey. Varuk, succumbing to Una's overpowering influence, reached forward, willingly moving towards her embrace.

'Brother, what are you doing?' Voishan gasped, his disbelief evident.

'It's her! She's controlling him!' Faróel hissed.

'Brother?' Una's curiosity piqued. 'Ah, so you must be the one he treasures the most… Kill him!' she commanded, her voice dripping with malice. But before the spectres could descend upon them, Faróel seized Varuk and Voishan, lifting them into the searing air and whisking them away from the brink of certain death.

'To the bitter end…' he whispered to Voishan, glancing at the large clouds covering the sky. He knew rain was about to fall. His action might be the last one he would take, and yet, he pushed his strength to its limits, speeding across the lands as fast as he could.

'Brother, look at me!' Voishan shouted as they flew across the arid land. Varuk's eyes were still held prisoner by Una's magic, twirling with a red shadow. With Faróel's hands holding on to the two Valahans' arms, they floated a few feet from the ground, moving at great speed. Just behind them, the loud screams of death had died off at the hands of both magma and smoke. A few remaining Valahan soldiers had disappeared into the land's large fissure. Some had fallen right into the planet's hungry mouth, while others had been taken by the spectres' fast advance. One by one, all the five hundred had gone, leaving only the two brothers and the fierce Chomp alive. Close by, a few lonely ancient trees appeared at the edge of the Garughals' land. Further ahead, the large forest opened up as if it were welcoming them in a safe, protective embrace.

'We won't go far, I'm afraid…' Faróel said as he slowly descended to the ground. 'It's about to…' But Faróel's voice was suddenly muted. The three crashed down on the green grass, propelled by the speed of their escape, rolling like thrown stones on the soft ground. Varuk stopped right at the feet of an intricate mesh of bushes and trees while Faróel lay still in the open space. With his hairy feet on dry, brown soil, his head and arms on green moss, the Chomp's small body looked as if he were holding the vast partition between the two lands. Voishan gazed left and right. His brother and

Faróel had landed on opposite sides, and the loud whispers of the enemy could be heard getting closer.

The dark clouds shrouding the sky had transformed the already ominous day into a nightmarish night. The Chomp's vulnerability served as a stark reminder of their dwindling hope, a flicker fading in Voishan's heart. He knew Faróel wouldn't wake until the ceaseless rain abated, but the downpour was so relentless that visibility was reduced to mere feet. With fear gnawing at his mind and desperation driving his actions, Voishan dashed towards Faróel. His hands moved swiftly, hoisting the unconscious Chomp onto his shoulders. Moments later, he stood by his brother, who had just roused from his painful slumber.

'Varuk, are you alright? We need to move! They're closing in!' Voishan urged.

'I think I've broken something...' Varuk grimaced, his hand trembling as it traced the source of his agony across his chest. 'And now it chooses to rain. Of course it does!' His frustration simmered beneath the surface, fuelled by anger.

'Brother, we've lost them all. Our Valahans are gone! Faróel saved us, but they're catching up. Don't you hear that...whistle?' Voishan's voice trembled as he helped Varuk to his feet.

'Yes, and it chills me to the bone. Let's move!' Varuk declared, leading the way into the realm of the Garughals, his brother trailing close behind. 'That was a Leonty, wasn't it? It confirms what King Lohan warned us about... The Leonty are orchestrating this...'

'I'm not so sure, brother. If they're Aqualymphs turned malevolent, it's unlikely they'd be under a Leonty's control. Their power far surpasses ours. Something else is at play here…I can feel it,' Voishan countered, his voice heavy with uncertainty.

'This way… The old entrance should be around here. But everything looks different. The guards used to be just beyond those trees. Now, it's all overgrown…' Varuk mused aloud, scanning the unfamiliar surroundings.

'The mist swirling on the ground…it's so warm. What manner of magic is this?' Voishan pondered aloud. 'Are we certain the Garughals are truly gone?'

'I'm not certain of anything any more, brother. But this fog… it reeks of their magic… Ah!' Varuk doubled over suddenly, his arms clutching his chest. A series of coughs wracked his body, splattering ruby droplets onto the dark foliage below. Before Voishan could reach out to support him, a thunderous voice boomed from behind them.

'I was told you were the ones who gave them strength. I was told you were the ones who provided them with stones to keep us apart…with metals to shape their blades. You gave the Humans what they needed to enslave us!' Una's voice resounded across the trees. The two Valahans turned around, gazing at the darkness surrounding them, but the Leonty's presence was undetectable.

'We have done nothing! We have kept ourselves apart from the Humans since King Lohan went to war against your people. We have no part in their actions!' Voishan shouted.

'As if you could erase your evil-making by giving it an expiry date?' Una's laugh could be heard from all around. 'You think you can remove yourself from the past by simply denying it?'

'Brother…' Varuk whispered as he bent on his knees. The pain crushing him down was not only made of blood and broken bones but of pure magic. Una's will was growing inside his mind once more. 'Take the Chomp and run…'

'No!' Voishan replied. 'I'm not denying anything,' he continued, looking at the growing fog entering the woods. 'We are all victims of this evil that doesn't rest. We should be on the same side. We should not be fighting one another!'

'Side? Do you know what side is mine?' Una's body appeared out of nowhere. Her long, slim figure emerged from the fog, a stunning mix of beauty and terror. Her eyes, shining red, mirrored the colour of her long hair. Her green skin looked like soft velvet gently wrapping her flesh. 'Tell me yours, and I'll tell you mine…'

'I'm Voishan, Vasheer's son, and Varuk's brother. We are Valahans, the great diggers. We have been providing the Humans with stones and materials to build their empire…' Voishan let out. As if he were confessing an undeniable truth, Una's spell was extorting words out of his mouth. 'My father sided with the Humans for a very long time. He helped King Lohan and his son, King Romohan, in pushing the Leonty further north, closing them off the lands. We let the Aqualymphs cross our borders as they went to war against your kind…as they took the Roshén Déil.'

'You see? We are really not on the same side, are we?' Una's hand moved on Voishan's face. Her fingers gently touched his chin as her ruby eyes spilled the magic of a mind bender. 'Now, Varuk... Son of King...ah, ah, ah. King of the diggers...the choice is yours to make. Your brother or your Flare. If what Voishan says is true, and we are on the same side, give me your Flare and let me have my revenge!'

'Voishan...' Varuk said again as his eyes teared with pain and agony. At his feet, the strange mist stirred in a circle, its magic rose up his knees and body.

'My queen...' a spectre interjected as he formed out of the smoke, right beside Una. 'The Garughals are here... We can sense their Flare moving in the air...'

*'Voishan, move your feet slowly inside the mist...'* Aura's voice whispered behind the Valahan. *'Bring yourself and Faróel inside the circle...'*

As Voishan complied with the Aqualymph's command, an ethereal wall of vapour took shape between the three fugitives and Una. As if it could shield them from the Leonty's magic, Una's voice became muffled by the powerful spell of the Beacon of Fire. A transparent partition between the two factions held the sign of a new resistance. Una's hands moved up in the air, pushing the spectres against it. Her expression filled with anger, she pressed her army towards Voishan, who stood still, untouched.

*'Meet me at the waterfall! Be quick, their power is very strong...I can't hold them for too long...'* And Aura's voice quickly dissolved amidst the pitter-patter of the heavy rain. With the help of his brother, Varuk stood back on his feet,

their minds fixed on the designed destination. Under the irate look of the new queen, they disappeared inside the forest.

'I have to say, I'm actually changing my mind about this Aqualymph,' Varuk let out, smiling.

'Can you walk on your own, brother? I'm struggling already with Faróel on my shoulder… We need to hurry.'

Whatever magic Aura held in her hands, the two Valahans didn't know how long the Beacon of Fire could keep the evil confined at the entrance of the Garughals' land. If what she said was true, the enemy would soon overcome its power and would find the three unprotected once more. Their only hope was to reach the Aqualymph and run down the hills, following the Gochi River right to the Chomps' village, where their Flare would shield them from Una.

Soon after, the tall trees opened up to a large, partially destroyed structure. Where the large tower holding the Flare once stood, ruins and rubble massed together, spilling over the rounded, white courtyard. Aura stood right in the middle, holding the Beacon of Fire in her hands. Her eyes closed, her body fluctuating between steam and rocky matter, she was pulling a myriad of droplets away from their rightful home and channelling their power forwards, transforming the waterfall at her back into a magic mist.

'Aura!' Voishan said, happiness filling his tone with joy. 'Thank you, we thought we were finished!'

'They are breaking the wall…my brothers and sisters are of a different kind now. I can feel it through the Garughals' magic…they are pure evil. We need to run! There is no path down the hill left standing. The only way forwards is the Gochi River. Don't worry, I'll lead you inside the waters with my magic.'

'Faróel is still asleep. The rain is slowing down, but he could be out for a while longer. Varuk is also seriously injured. Can you help him?' Voishan moved his hand towards his brother, who had slowly reached them by the waterfall. His face was pale, and his body bore the unmistakable signs of a life ebbing away.

'I have no such power… The Chomps might have a medicine of some kind that might help? Let's go!'

As the two Valahans moved their hands towards the Aqualymph, a large sphere formed just beside the waterfall. Their feet standing at the edge of the courtyard, a jump was all that was needed to enter the air bubble and penetrate the river and flee. But as Voishan took Faróel off his shoulders and placed him inside the sphere, a loud cracking sound shook the space. The many trees surrounding the courtyard were snapped from their roots, their leaves scattered all around. A swarm of spectres poured like a second, dark waterfall, filling the space in a blink. The new queen floated on their backs as if she was riding a carriage of death, her arms stretched in the air, her eyes fixed on her prey.

'There it is… the Beacon of Fire… Kill them and take it!'

'Move, brother!' Voishan pushed Varuk inside the Aqualymph's bubble and turned around to Aura. 'Let's go!'

'It's yours, if you want it. Just give me what I lost…what I need the most, and I'll give it to you freely…' Aura said, taking the Valahan by surprise. Her form changed quickly, the dust of the dead rocks filling her body, turning her grey. Like them before, her eyes had turned red.

'Aura, no!' Voishan shouted, pulling her arm.

'And what is that you lost?' Una asked. 'Let me see inside your mind… Oh, I see…' she added, after a few moments of silence. 'Someone you loved… In front of all of this, after all you have witnessed, this is what you want the most? Are you not pathetic?'

'Let her go!' Voishan screamed at the Leonty. 'Let her go!'

'Kill them!' Una commanded, and a wicked smile appeared on her face.

The multitude of spectres moved at once, advancing fast from every direction. With no time to think but only a strong will and an unbreakable love to lead him, Voishan looked at the Chomp and then his brother. The two Valahans' eyes met for a brief moment. A single instant carried a lifetime of memories and the power of a fraternal bond.

'To a bitter end,' he whispered, crying. And his hands moved fiercely on Aura, pushing her inside the sphere as the spectre's hands grabbed the Beacon of Fire from the Aqualymph's hands. Responding to the touch of Aura's essence, the bubble fell far below, right where the waterfall met the Gochi River, disappearing in the waters. In the courtyard, one Valahan stood alone, as his body was overwhelmed with the dark magic of the evil. Not too far from him, Una stood silent, watching her army ripping his body and soul apart, her eyes fixed on the only thing she craved. The Beacon of Fire slowly moved towards her, shining brightly.

'And that's two...' she said, turning towards the edge of the courtyard. Her gaze on the hills below, she stared at the sea glittering at the touch of the warm light of Erion. Her next move was finally set.

# Chapter Twenty-Nine

*Anún Déil: the Flare of the Sea*

∞

As if Aura's magic had a will of its own, the air bubble dived into the Gochi River at a fast pace, speeding downstream with no other control but nature and its wild elements. Through the twirls of the waters, the three companions were shaken and turned, pushed and hit in a nauseating loop. With her mind still trapped in a slowly fading spell, the Aqualymph was unable to steer or lead the way. Beside her, Faróel bounced around unconscious. With the rain still falling on the lands, his body succumbed to its own weakness, forced to stay in an unbreakable sleep.

Varuk, on the other hand, witnessed most of the wild ride as he tried to keep his balance through the impossible. Eventually, the pain from the recent fall at the Garughals' Forest grew tenfold, and after the ethereal sphere had collided with a large rock at the riverbed, he lost his senses and fainted.

A while later, right where the Gochi River changed its course at the Chomps' hills, the air bubble surfaced, and at a sharp turn, it popped out of the waters, rolling a few feet on the green grass. Aura had finally freed herself from Una's enchantment and, in a quick move, she had deviated from the charted course right at the edge of the Chomps' dome. In a loud pop, her protective magic disappeared, leaving her two passengers rolling further away towards the nearby Silent Forest. The rain had suddenly stopped, but angry, dark clouds still pushed their heaviness onto their world. While the recent events replayed in Aura's mind, her feet ran to Faróel. With her hands on the Chomps' shoulders, the Aqualymph begged for her friend to wake up.

'Faróel, please! Oh, this is terrible…' she cried. Her body had turned the same colour as the vivid green grass, but her face was as grey as the stones paving the riverbanks. Under her eyes, two dark shadows clashed against the glittering tears flowing on her cheeks. 'Please, wake up!'

Whether the Chomp sensed a new wave of rain was coming or the one just passed hadn't worn off yet, Faróel would not come back to her. So she quickly moved to her other companion, Varuk's pale face anticipating a new horror. As she bent on the soft ground, she gulped at the sight of the Valahan's body. The clothes around his chest had been torn apart, and a large, black spot covered his entire trunk. After several attempts to wake him up, Aura said, 'I'm not sure if this is going to work, but I have no other way… Please, stay strong my friend. I'll do my best!'

After closing her eyes and tilting her head towards the dark sky, the Aqualymph placed her hands on Varuk. With the right one on his chest and the left one on his mouth, she unleashed a new kind of magic. The entire matter of her body shifted in between solid and ethereal. Steam and flesh mixed together as Aura moved her fingers inside the Valahan's mouth. As if her nature had turned into a flowing stream of vapour, she infused Varuk's bloodstream with her own. Little by little, the colours she was made of started to change. From green to red, from grey to brown, Aura absorbed her friend's trauma, dragging it out in the open, cleansing his body from the excessive blood that was slowly killing him. In the space of a few moments, the Valahan's face came back to its natural state, his breathing slowly resumed its peaceful rhythm.

'What happened? What are we doing home?' Faróel had suddenly woken up. Staring at the familiar landscape, his gaze moved to Aura, whose power had just subsided. Beside her, only one of the two brothers was still with them. 'Is Varuk okay? Where is Voishan?'

'He didn't make it…' Aura replied, looking back at the Chomp. Sadness was spreading around her figure like a second wave of magic. 'And Varuk is not well. I've removed the internal bleeding, but he needs your kind's medicine right away.'

'Tell me this isn't true…' Faróel whispered, sobbing. 'It's my fault. The rain came, and I knew I could not fly all the way to the waterfall. Was it me? Did he fall to his death?'

'No, Faróel. You saved them both from the hand of…this new queen.' Aura lifted Varuk's shoulders from the ground, holding his head close to her chest. 'He is breathing okay now. This Leonty who attacked us… She is very powerful. Her magic is as dark as pure evil. This is not a power the Leonty have ever mastered. This is of a different kind. When she stood in front of us, when I was under her magic, I felt the same oppressive feeling I had felt that day on the Cloudy Mountains, when Garúth and I saw Queen Eah speaking to the evil…'

'What did she do?' the Chomp asked as he moved beside Aura, helping her to lift Varuk's body.

'She's controlling my people. Well, whatever they are now. She enslaved me in her darkness without even touching me. I was just…hers. She took the Beacon of Fire, and as she was about to kill us, Voishan pushed me inside the aldúrin. A moment later, we were at the bottom of the river, and he was left behind.'

'Is there a chance…' But Faróel could not finish the question. In his heart, he knew the answer. Voishan was gone, and the Garughals' Flare was in the Leonty's hands.

After walking for two hocs, the three reached the heart of the Chomps' village. There, a large group of small residents gathered together. A loud murmuring spread quickly from corner to corner. Almost every house emptied; their owners filled the space outside Faróel's home. In shock and saddened by the news of the latest events, Treekan kept quiet, his hands busy preparing the right ointment for Varuk's condition. While the four held their heavy thoughts to themselves, the young Chomp placed leaves and straws of yellow, dry hemp around the tiny dining table. Inside the ritual circle, the large Valahan lay motionless. His legs hanging on one side, his shoulders over both edges, it looked like the table's feet could collapse at any moment. From the low windows and the open door, worried faces and pressing questions ran wild. The fear of a new powerful enemy grew fast among the Chomps.

'A Valahan victim of this evil…if it can overcome them, what are we going to do when it gets here?' a Chomp asked Faróel as she handed him a fresh batch of brown leaves. 'You need to boil them first. Then place them on his head and wrists. You need to keep the body grounded.'

'How did you get these?' Aura asked, surprised. 'These are núntaels. They grow only on the shorelines, at our kingdom doorstep…'

'Dear Time, Dashae! You should not venture outside the dome. Especially now!' Faróel added, worried.

'Calm down, old Chomp.' And Dashae smiled. 'Freesk went to get those. You know he has the gift…'

'What gift?' Aura asked, puzzled.

'Our Flare's gift.' Dashae smiled again. In her opinion, she had said something everyone should have known. 'Freesk can go without being seen. Don't you know a few of us can do that?'

'You are saying some of you can bring the power of your own dome with you? In the open?' Aura shot an expression of judgment across the table. 'Why are these special people staying here, hidden, when they could be out there, helping us?'

'There are only two we know of that can do that. And they are young. What are you suggesting? Have us send our young ones to war? Two of them? To end up like him?' Faróel shouted, his finger pointing at Varuk. By a strange coincidence, the Valahan had just regained consciousness.

'I see you have woken up, Chomp… Lower your voice; my head hurts…' Varuk mumbled.

'Speaking of waking up…' And Faróel's upset at Aura's questions was suddenly replaced with joy. After hugging the large Valahan, he added, 'I thought I had lost you too…'

'Too? What do you mean?' Varuk slowly gazed at the small gathering around the table. 'Where is my brother?'

The difficult conversation unfolded with no mercy. Varuk's broken heart moved from devastation to anger at light speed. His body would not respond to his burning desire to get up and fight against his feelings, against the evil that had taken his beloved brother. All he could do was cry as he lay still, like a stone. Eventually, Aura moved to the back of the tiny house and engaged with Faróel on the new upcoming mission. Unable to get over the latest events as fast as the Aqualymph, the Chomp challenged her.

'No! You can do whatever you like. I understand this is important, but this is enough. We can't afford to lose anybody else.'

'There is not going to be anyone else if we don't take our Flares somewhere safe. The Anún Déil is still in the depth of the Sea. She will take it.'

'And what else will she be able to do she can't do already? She won't have ours; she definitely can't take the Valahans'. The Humans' Flare is protected by a hundred thousand soldiers. Let them deal with her…'

'Faróel, I know it's fear and sorrow talking. Please see reason…' Aura replied, moving a few steps away, exiting the Chomp's home. Her gaze fixed on the hills; her heart was already turning towards the sea.

'I'm sorry, Aura. I've tried everything I could to help you…to help everybody. This world doesn't want to rest. It's an enemy after another. I have to think about my son, my friend Varuk, and my people. I can't help you. Not this time.'

'I understand… Wherever our God is, I hope He'll give us the strength we need. You could be right. Your dome will shield you from any evil. Please, wish a speedy recovery from me to Varuk. I'm sorry about Voishan, truly. I have to go, before it's too late.' After turning her back to the Chomp, Aura said, 'Farewell, my friend. May our eyes meet again when peace finally finds us.'

'Please, be careful… If you can't rescue the Flare, don't fight them. It's just you against many of them. We've seen what they are capable of. Just run and come here. This place will always welcome you, dear friend.'

And so the final goodbye was said. The two long-time friends parted ways, unaware that would be the last time they would talk to one another. Though her heart urged her to cling to their companionship, to resist the pull of an impossible quest, Aura's resolve was firm. Her place was by the sea, guarding the node. If the enemy seized her Flare and her kingdom fell, her duty would end. Swiftly, she hastened her steps, her form dissolving into a mere breeze. Like wisps of steam traversing space, she swiftly reached the shoreline. Casting a fleeting glance at the steadfast barrier erected by Queen Eah to divide the sea and the midlands, Aura plunged into the waters, her destination clear: the red keep.

In the desolate expanse of the deep blue, the queen's residence stood in solitude. The throne room lay abandoned, overrun by untamed sea flora that crept into every corner. Over the countless cycles of the time past, the palace had stood unattended, and red corals had flourished unchecked, transforming the surroundings entirely. The ancient seat of royalty had been engulfed by the relentless force of nature, concealing the secret passage to the Flare's chamber forever. Sensing the pulsating presence of its magic, Aura delved into the material realm, her essence melding with the matter to reach the crystal stone nestled quietly beneath the throne. Untouched and unblemished, the Flare awaited its rightful wielder, its pale blue brilliance igniting a spark of hope in Aura's eyes as she beheld the precious artefact once more.

The moment Aura's hands closed around the Flare, a vision of impending danger seared into her mind. Like a shadow creeping through the depths, darkness surged from the surface to the seabed, spectres spreading like a malignant plague throughout the blue expanse. At the shoreline, the one unable to master the sacred dive awaited the return of her soldiers.

Aware that the Leonty's assault was imminent, Aura seized the Flare and surged upwards through the water. Breaking the surface, she felt the warm caress of the breeze, and a sense of déjà vu washed over her. Across the sea's vast waters, countless spectres floated, their malevolent presence seeking the pure essence of power. At the furthest reaches, Una stood motionless, her arms outstretched. With the Beacon of Fire radiating its energy across the distance, her voice boomed like thunder.

'Behold the Anún Déil comes to me… The Flare of the Sea. The power of eternal sustenance, the power of pure magic,' Una proclaimed.

Suddenly, the calm waters trembled, as if boiling under the intense heat of raging flames. Steam billowed from the sea, engulfing the Aqualymph in a vapour-made prison. Around her, a triple barrier materialized, encasing her in a lethal trap. The sacred waters held her captive, Queen Eah's old magic surrounding the sea reinforced the confinement, and a swirling mass of spectres formed as a final layer. In Aura's mind, Faróel's words echoed, *'Don't fight them.'*

Intoxicated by power and enslaved by dark magic, the sea lymphs had long forgotten their true home. Their former residence felt alien to them, their memories completely annihilated, their souls corrupted by their newfound allegiance to their queen. Moving between Una and Aura, they aimed at the Flare's guardian like a menacing arrow pointed at Aura's heart.

The stone bearer found herself immobilized amidst steam and malevolent magic, unable to shift into her ethereal form and flee. The Anún Déil, her cherished artefact, seemed to fail her in the dire moment. Memories of her encounters with Lëogan flooded her mind, sparking a desperate hope that she could too navigate the sacred passage as he had. *Would it lead me to Time, the one who saved us before? Why he seems so distant now, so powerless, much like the stone I'm holding on to at the risk of my life?* she thought.

'Give us the Flare, lymph!' a spectre demanded, its companions looming nearby, their forms shifting between smoke and sinister entities.

'You can't defeat us or escape. Surrender and we'll leave you be,' another urged, his voice a seductive whisper that enveloped Aura.

'Why don't you take it then? If I'm defenceless, why prolong this?' Aura retorted, feeling the Flare flickering in her hands, its blue light growing.

'You've heard our queen. Submit and join us in the new order,' a larger spectre declared. As his form shifted, his defiled form struggled with the remnants of his corrupted soul. The ghost of a distant past spoke to Aura as he begged her to resist. The visage of the one who long before stood beside Queen Eah as her consort flickered in the air. No trace of his original self remained, only a last glimpse of resistance swirling in darkness and defiance.

'I know you!' Aura exclaimed, her voice tinged with sorrow. 'How did this happen to you? You were meant to protect our queen, your fearcel. You were meant to help her lead our kind to peace, to safeguard this world from evil…'

'This is exactly what we are doing,' he replied, his voice trembling as he struggled against his other will. 'Don't Aura! Please don't! Now, come with us… Join us in the bright future ahead.'

The spectre stretched his arms into the air, releasing a wide, dark vortex towards Aura. The hovering force clashed against the Flare, causing it to shine brightly, magnifying its opposing power. Like night and day locked in combat, a colossal divide widened across the sea, spreading two opposing magics along the waters and into the purple sky. An electrifying layer of pure power transformed into an enormous barrier, reflecting the clashing forces like a mystical mirror. Aura and the spectre appeared as two exact replicas of one another, one dark as the malevolent mind pushing from the shoreline, the other bright as the large star shining above their heads.

'Look at me, King Nuróhen!' Aura's voice fought against the spectre's oppressive energy. 'Return to who you were before all this. I'm Aura, the Gatekeeper, the protector of the node. You entrusted me with this duty. You honoured me. Can't you remember?'

'You speak of things that no longer hold significance,' he retorted, his voice altered, resonating with Una's presence. 'I've grown tired of waiting…'

Una's mystical form emerged from within the spectre, her green hands crossing the invisible boundary between unmaterial and reality. Carried on the back of the many whom she held prisoner, she floated above the waters, her arms stretching over the Aqualymph. Streams of wicked essence slid slowly over Aura's body, crawling on her skin, stripping her power away like caresses on fragile cords.

'Give in!' Una's voice thundered as her magic enveloped the Aqualymph, breaking her ethereal shield apart, squeezing her soul into an ephemeral memory.

'*Time!*' Aura's agonized scream pierced the air like the thousands of green thorns shredding her being. In a final gasp, her weakened hands released the Flare, surrendering to the embrace of death.

'It's mine!' Una cackled, her presence looming larger than the horizon itself. 'Now, leave this world behind!' But before she could deliver the final blow to the one who resisted her, Aura vanished into pure nothingness. Without a sound, without a trace of magic, the Aqualymph simply dissolved before Una's eyes.

'No! I won't allow it. You're the only family I have left!' Faróel's voice echoed in Treekan's mind as he cradled Aura in a gentle embrace. Surrounded by unchallenged dark magic, Una had finally grasped the Anún Déil, wasting no time in unleashing its power. Bright waves flashed from the depths below, drawn forth by the one who now commanded three of the six Flares. 'Wherever you are, I can find you!' she shouted, her eyes burning with a raging fire.

'She's our friend! She's family too. She had no one else. Who will stand for her if not us?' Treekan confronted his father, unwavering. A few paces away, a subdued Valahan remained silent, his thoughts clouded by grief and loss, finding kinship in Treekan's stance.

'Let him be, Faróel…' he murmured.

'What?' the elder Chomp exclaimed, incredulous. 'You, of all people…you've just lost your dear brother…'

'So she could live… So we could survive. And what now? Shall we squander my brother's sacrifice like this? Either we all march into the jaws of death together or none of us will. And my brother has already gone. The path is clear, you obstinate Chomp,' Varuk's words silenced Faróel's objections. Without another word, Treekan departed, buoyed by the Valahan's resolute support.

'Of all of us, my son…my son had to possess the gift. And I must watch him go, acting as if he were our saviour…'

'We each play a role in this. My brother, you, Aura, Treekan, and I. Learn to accept that we've been summoned to battle until our dying breath, Faróel. In one way or another, our fates intertwine. Mine may come sooner than later. I'm returning to my people, before this…queen reaches them.'

'If we manage to keep ourselves safe, mark my words, none of my fellow Chomps, not even my son, will ever leave this place. Ever!' the Chomp declared as he withdrew. From outside his home, he watched the far edge of the village, where Treekan had just departed from the dome and vanished.

With Aura cradled against him, the young Chomp resisted the gravitational pull of Una's magic. His eyes narrowed, his mouth set in determination as he shielded Aura from the Leonty's fury. His tiny body pierced the space like a stubborn, bright dot in a blue, stormy ocean, Desperately resisting Una's growing power, he held the Aqualymph as if she was the most precious Flare of all. Their bodies invisible to the enemy, his inner, unique magic handed Aura the rescue she sought from their God. With a final effort, he broke free from the evil prison and carried Aura to the nearby small island. There, he gently laid her on the soft grass, wiping away tears filled with regret. In his heart, he wished he had acted sooner.

Satisfied the enemy had been erased from existence, Una withdrew her power and recalled her minions from the sea's expanse. Turning her gaze towards the crown city, her desire for victory quickly burned brighter again.

'Treekan?' Aura whispered, struggling to maintain her form. 'How?'

'It's okay, I've got you,' Treekan reassured her, his eyes gleaming. 'I used my own magic to reach you unseen. I saved you before it was too late.'

'You brought your Flare with you, so close to her? What about the others?' Aura's figure flickered.

'No, the Flare remains in the village, where it belongs. The Sháten Déil's magic is within me. Father kept it secret, fearing I'd be sent to war, but I couldn't stand aside any longer.'

'Of all the surprises your kind has revealed, this is the biggest,' Aura said, her form wavering.

'Aura, please, stay with me…' Treekan pleaded.

'The magic of the sea is gone. There is no lymph left for me to absorb. My people's magic is gone with the Anún Déil. Don't cry, Chomp. You indeed saved me…' With tears streaming down his face, Treekan watched as Aura's gaze moved from his face to the beyond, her body dissolving into droplets, slowly sinking in the green grass, merging with the island she had sworn to protect.

Of all the future events my brother Time had foreseen with his powerful sight, I am certain he had witnessed this moment countless times. Each time he peered into the folds of time, he must have encountered this scene, where his chosen one valiantly fought to safeguard the sea and the node from evil. Yet, he allowed it to unfold. Time's actions were calculated, precise, deliberate. His defeat and the subsequent events would pave the way for the arrival of Daniel, Noah, and Anita, right there, on the same island where Treekan had witnessed his friend's sacrifice at the hands of the Crimson Queen.

Somehow, Una remained oblivious to the fact that she momentarily stood at the doorstep of an entire universe. With the node only a few steps away, Una held the key to trespass space and time as she pleased. And yet, blinded by her boundless hatred for her own world, she knew little of the magic surrounding the island and the true purpose of Aura's duty. So she left it untouched, pressing forwards in her quest.

# Chapter Thirty

## *The Crimson Queen*

∞

From the shoreline at the bottom of the ceremonial steps to the high towers of the king's castle, Erion shone its warm light on the Humans' kingdom. To the many soldiers, the day looked like any other in those difficult times, and yet a sinister silence ran from every corner of their land. They had been watching, scanning the edges of their dominion with fear and determination since the day their young king had returned from the Chomps' land.

Their city, once the grand jewel of Runae, lay now in ruins. The white skin of the many buildings carried the weight of a long, tiring war against an enemy that had no face any more. The dust that had spread during the Great Dawn had finally settled, leaving a trail of misery in every street and alley. In their broken hearts, the Humans no longer had an idea who they were up against. Their once-true enemy, the Leonty, was gone. The Aqualymphs and their astonishing magic were no longer; their existence was slowly turning into a myth. Rumours of a surging power by the hand of a new master had reached the many ears in the city, and above them all, one resident feared it the most.

Lëogan stood silent by a tiny window in the throne room. His gaze fixed on the outskirts, his mind inspected the many possibilities ahead. What had he accomplished? What was the true reason why he had left Earth to reach Runae? He had done it to fulfil his master's will. The King of Emptiness had demanded the key of the four worlds, the souls of the four Gods. Time was gone. He knew that much. Right when he had faced the protector of Runae, Nothing had come to put an end to his ruling. Where was his true king now? Why had Nothing disappeared, together with Time and the other Flares? His eyes moved to a pedestal next to the throne. A dark flame flickered in the air, wobbling, whispering of a new imminent threat. *If this is the end of my journey here, I shall depart with a heart buoyed by the notion that I have fulfilled my master's bidding*, he thought. *If I die, Death will bring me back, right beside the other Harpies, where I belong.*

'We still have our own…' The young king interrupted the Harpy's thoughts. Somehow, his inexperienced mind had caught Lëogan's worries as if he had spoken them out loud.

'You have grown much in these last few yacs, King Doroas,' Lëogan replied, looking back at the bright landscape, 'but you still fail to see beyond realities. But don't worry, this is why you have me here. We must be prepared for what is coming, whatever this is…'

'I know you said our God was a deceit…who should we put our hope and trust in then? We can't possibly face this power with our Human hands.' And Doroas moved beside the Harpy, his crystal-blue eyes directed at the same unknown his companion was staring at. 'What is that?' he added, worried.

A wide, grey fog swept all across the shoreline, making the sea disappear. It seemed motionless, and yet it grew fast, devouring lands within its fold. In the space of a few moments, the outskirts disappeared, together with the ceremonial steps and the southern gates. All around the city walls, the darkness of the incoming enemy touched their fear as if it could infect their minds and hearts at once.

'It's wise for you to stay here, my king. Find your mother and bring her here. Whatever this enemy wants, I'm sure it's here, in this room.' And Lëogan moved away, towards the entrance of the castle. His mind fabricating the most horrifying outcomes, he kept his walk steady. He was a Harpy, a soldier of the most powerful master in the universe. He was going to return to Nothing with the most wanted gift, the keys of Runae. Whatever this new sorcery was, it was not going to stop him.

At the southern edges of the city, hundreds and hundreds of soldiers moved frantically in and out of the walls. Their armours shining under the light of the large star, they looked like diamonds rolling towards a dark destination. 'The eastern flank! Behind the first gates. Don't move from your spot!' a tall man shouted. 'Where is the north division? I've said they needed to be here at the inner walls!'

'I've heard the Aver has instructed them to stand at the entrance of the palace, my general,' a soldier replied.

'Under whose orders? Who is running this bloody city?' the general let out loudly. 'Go to the eastern gates. Tell them to keep their position. We don't know where the blow will strike first. Andhúr.' He turned to another soldier. 'It would help to have the west flank down here. There is no threat from the Leonty's hills any more. Go fast!'

Between the Humans and Una's army, the crown city walls stood as if made of thin paper, unable to shield their people from the magic of the enemy. At the top of the ceremonial steps, the Leonty's features appeared amidst the dense fog. The faces of the many spectres appeared and shifted in a continuous loop. Their dark eyes and evil forms swirled around her green body. Una's gaze briefly moved from the rusty, large gates to the nearby sea. Something close to her nature, her true origins whispered from afar; a lost memory of someone who once was her family floated on the waters.

'Once again, I'm reminded of how rightful is my will,' Una let out, almost as if she was talking to herself. 'My mother's sister, another victim of the evil residing within these walls, is still screaming for revenge. Umbra…yes, that was her name…I felt her kind soul through my mother's power, and still, I can't accept their cowards' decision to let it happen, to leave me behind. Anyway, this is not the age of the weak of hearts any longer. In this new world, I come to rule… Spectres, we move now!'

The evil entities responded to Una's command at once. Through the cracks, the narrow chinks, and climbing over the walls, the spectres moved as if they were flooding the space with no material resistance. Their consistency shifting between realities, they turned into a breeze, breaking through the Humans' defences and reappearing right among their enemies. Shocked and petrified by the sudden magic, the soldiers started to shout words of fear and terror. The spectres' hands flashed like arrows darting through the Human bodies, grabbing their hearts, squeezing them to their death. Their silver, shining armours turned grey, covered by darkness as their faces paled. As the southern flank ran in panic, Una's army pushed many soldiers into the air, down the walls, and against the white buildings.

'Run to the inner gates!' the general shouted amid the loud screams. His eyes fixed on the upcoming peril, the general wielded his long, shining sword against the enemy. A large spectre formed right in front of him, a few inches from the pointed blade.

'Ha, ha. How can I possibly face you and your powerful weapon?' the spectre mocked as he moved closer, allowing the sword to pierce his intangible body. 'I'm already dead…' And the evil ghost pulled the general up in the air, freezing his body as he kept him prisoner in his dark magic. A moment later, a moaning sound was followed by a violent snap. The general's body was bent in two and thrown away on the ground. Beside him, many other soldiers lay dead, their eyes still open as fear lingered in the air and mingled with the sour taste of a quick defeat.

Outside the palace, Lëogan stared at the soldiers running from the outer into the inner city, sending him the clear signal of the enemy's advance. 'Soldiers! Gather in the palace! The Flare will protect us all!' he shouted. 'Move inside the palace, now! Gather the others and come to the palace!' he kept shouting. Of the thousands of soldiers fighting in every corner of the crown city, only a few hundred had managed to escape and reach the king's home alive. With terror imprinted on their faces and their hearts on the verge of stopping, they gathered inside the walls of the large structure. The heavy doors shut, darkness engulfed the large room, as the voices of the few men were muted by fear and by the crying and screaming of the many others who had been left outside to die.

The Harpy ran back to the throne room where the young king, his mother, and several other family members stood terrified. Without saying a word, the Aver placed his hands on the Flare, moved to the centre of the large room, and with his eyes closed he enchanted the rescuing spell.

'In the core of every matter, we shall find the key to do and undo our world as we please. Let this power bring their nature to their single elements and reshape them for our own sake!'

A large, dark wave wobbled from Lëogan's hands all the way to the walls, over the ceiling, the stony pavement. Traversing rooms, floors, and the white bricks, a powerful energy released inside and all around the palace. For a brief moment, everything went silent. Smiles of relief had started to appear on the many faces staring at the front doors when the enemy suddenly penetrated the walls like a river overflowing its banks. Una's body emerged from the fog, amongst the terrified soldiers.

'You think the Ergon Déil can do much against me? Against our Flares? Against the Aqualymphs', the Garughals'? Which one do you want to taste first? I'd say the latter…' And Una raised her hand in the air, releasing a burning blast around the room.

Feet were suddenly fused with the stony floor, limbs and bodies were turned to rocks. The many soldiers became one with their surroundings, their faces frozen in a perennial state of stony terror. Before Una could move further inside the palace, another wave of energy left the throne room, travelling across the palace, disintegrating the matter of the ones Una led, and with those, turning the Human soldiers now petrified by magic into fine dust. For a brief moment, the Leonty hesitated. Whatever magic the Humans were deploying, it was working against her power.

'You think you can still rule unchallenged? You think you can still impose your will on the ones that demand answers to the crimes you have committed?' she shouted as her eyes turned red. 'You!' She turned to one of the few soldiers left alive. Moved to the back of the large hall, their minds fought against their duty of protecting the way ahead and their desire to open the doors and find refuge beside their king. 'Let us in!' one screamed.

Without hesitation, a soldier standing at the other side of the large doors complied. Enslaved by Una's magic, his already weak will could not resist the wicked manipulation of minds. His hands moved to the rings, and as he turned them around, the doors flew open. One by one the spectres came back to their ethereal form, reversing the magic of the Humans' Flare in an instant. No mercy was given to the ones who had obeyed and let them through. As the army stormed inside the regal rooms, all the remaining soldiers were killed on their spot.

Up the shining white staircase, Una moved as if she conquered every single corner. Corridor after corridor, the enemy ran without touching the cold ground; the many sets of stairs were climbed in a flash. At the end of the path, the king and his Aver were only a few steps away. In between them and the Leonty two more wooden doors stood shut. With a swing of her arm Una broke through, scattering the fragile wood into pieces all across the throne room. Splinters travelled with the power of her magic, piercing the four soldiers who stood at the entrance. Their eyes still fixed on the Leonty, their expression froze as they crossed the line between life and death. With blood pouring from their necks, they fell on their knees and quickly died.

The hands of the young king pulled on his mother's shoulders as she stood in front of him, shielding his presence from the evil. Right next to her, Lëogan held the Flare in the air, making it glow with an obscure light. His eyes twirled with dark magic as his body started to grow, shifting from flesh and bones to its true, ethereal matter. Before he could act against her, Una moved her hands forwards and, in a snap, Lëogan's magic suddenly stalled. His face turned back to the one of an old man. His white beard and white hair slowly reappeared.

'You know why I'm here…show your face to me…King of the Humans!' At Una's words, Doroas's mother stretched her hands in protection of her son. Before she could even speak, the Leonty turned her gaze to a young girl whose feet peeked from under a large, pompous couch in the corner of the room. With her eyes burning with a deadly red fire, Una's magic found the most innocent mind she could place her magic on and, after penetrating the girl's mind, she told her to come out from her hidden spot.

In the petrifying silence, the young girl moved beside the body of a dead soldier. After taking his sword from his cold hands, she turned around and slowly walked towards the throne. For every slow step she took, the terrifying idea of what was soon going to happen grew large in everybody's mind. And yet, nobody was able to move; nobody was able to fight back. Their minds in the grip of unbeatable power, they could only watch the slow unfolding of Una's revenge. It was there that the little girl raised the heavy sword in front of her and, with unnatural strength, she pushed it against the king's mother's waist. From one part to another, the pointy blade penetrated unchallenged, violently reaching the king. With tears in her eyes and a dull expression on her face, Doroas's mother fell on the ground. Behind her, the young king stood in shock. His side bleeding heavily, he moved a few steps and then fell on his knees.

'You don't understand,' Lëogan said. His words, counted and slow, slipped through his silvery white beard. 'We are on the same side here…we both belong to the same master.'

'There has never been a side that was the same,' Una replied, her eyes on fire. 'I've never been on the same side with any other living being.'

'But we are…you and I were sent by the same one.' And he moved backward, trying to put distance between himself and death.

'Your magic is not working…why do you keep trying?' Una shouted. 'Keep your lies in your defiant mouth. You have been plotting in the shadows for a long time. You have corrupted the souls of the many who lived in these lands, turning one kind against another. You are the one who started the hunt against my people, convincing the Humans we were the enemy. Convincing our own kind to strike the ones like me who had magic in their veins.'

'Leonty…' the young king interrupted, slowly taking his crown off his head. 'If it's our Flare you want, my kingdom, you can have it. But please, spare my family and the few left alive.'

'I was never given any chance, why would I now be the one who gives it? I don't want your crown. I want you to witness the true nature of the evil you and everybody else made me become.' And Una's face turned back towards the old man.

'You think you can kill me, but let me warn you, as I go to the beyond, I shall return alongside many more. You don't understand, we are all here to fulfil his will...' the Harpy said as he halted, his back at the open window.

'You will never set foot here, ever again. Whatever lies your mouth speaks, no ears will be yours to enchant.' Una's eyes fixed on the ones of her enemy; he was immediately entranced by the Leonty's power. Her will becoming his, she moved him like a pawn, dragging his feet against his own will. He turned around, stepped onto the windowsill, and jumped to his death. Determined to accomplish her mission, she showed no hesitation, and with the mere swing of her left arm, she cut through the king's throat, making him fall on the cold floor, his crown slipping from his hand, rolling towards the new queen.

# Chapter Thirty-One

## *The End of Metal and Stone*

∞

Una's army departed from the crown city, leaving a trail of death and misery in their wake. Despite her numerous accomplishments, she found herself unable to fully savour the pleasure of her bloody revenge. As they entered the outskirts, right where the road split in two, the Leonty faced a crucial decision: whether to head towards the Chomps' hills or the Mogs Mountains. *Is it them? Is it their resistance?* she thought. *No, it is not. Some of the spectres are still watching over the caves. Once I reach them, it will all be over…*

'My queen?' a spectre whispered, materializing right out of the collective fog. Their queen hesitated, her gaze fixed on the mountains. They wondered why they had come to a halt. 'Is it your will for us to reach the invisible ones instead?'

*The Chomps…the ones who cannot be seen…is it them, then? Will they halt my advance now that I'm so close to ending it all?* Una's own mind troubled her. Something she had seen in the Mirrors of Time was coming back to her. A threat in her future was calling her from afar. If that was the case, how could she keep the promise she had made to her benefactor? Would the one who entrusted her with the arduous duty blame her for not being powerful and definite enough? *No,* she dismissed her own insecurity. *I've swept through the lands with no match against me. I'll do the same with them. It's true; one Chomp alone stopped me from taking the life of that stubborn, annoying Aqualymph. But it doesn't matter…I'll find them, and that will end it all.*

'No. We'll leave the feathered ones for last. Let them indulge in their own sense of security… To the Valahans!'

Driven by an insatiable hunger for power and the coveted magic of the Murán Déil, the remaining spectres stationed at the cave entrance on the southern slope took matters into their incorporeal hands. In blatant defiance of their queen's orders, they phased through the imposing mountain face. Their relentless efforts to breach the unyielding barrier were eventually rewarded as the Flare's magic gradually shifted towards the western edge of the Mogs ridge. Within the shadowy depths of the caverns, Varuk led his people deeper into the labyrinthine passages, guiding them to the precipice of the massive Mog. There, amidst the unyielding layers of ancient rock, the multitudes of Valahans came to a halt. Despite Varuk's steadfast determination to press onward, the land quivered beneath their feet, and their dusty visages turned pallid with exhaustion.

The desperate invocation of the Valahans' magic, aimed at securing their liberation, exacted a dire toll. The true essence of their power shifted deep within the mountains, relinquishing its hold on the very threshold they were meant to safeguard. With the vanishing remnants of magic, the spectres infiltrated the caves unopposed. Despite the difference in numbers, the enemy held enough power in their hands and evil in their hearts to annihilate the unprotected fugitives.

'Varuk, please… You must rest,' Valiah implored, her hands resting gently on her fearcel's shoulders, beseeching him once more to relent.

'If we do not break through, our fate is sealed,' Varuk replied wearily yet resolutely. Exhausted but determined to safeguard his people, he turned towards the formidable barrier, his gaze unwavering. With arms outstretched and the Flare blazing anew, Varuk directed the miners' magic against the corroded surface, causing it to tremble. The once-impenetrable façade now appeared translucent, revealing yet another layer beneath. A gleaming, obsidian barrier stood in defiance of Varuk's efforts, punctuated only by sporadic breaches of magic that unveiled fresh obstacles between death and liberation.

'My son,' Vasheer uttered softly as he approached Varuk, his frail form swaying with each step. The delicate skin of his face seemed as ethereal as a transparent veil, barely able to contain the weight of his exhaustion. Yet, driven by paternal love, he pressed onward. 'Allow me to shoulder the burden for a time. Reclaim your strength…'

'Strength, father? You have none of your own. I cannot allow you to bear the weight of this dire fate upon your shoulders. You deserve better than this,' Varuk protested, his voice tinged with concern.

'I may be aged,' Vasheer acknowledged with a gentle smile, his weathered hands resting upon his son's. In that simple touch, faith and affection intertwined. 'But I am still your father. You do as I say. After all, I'm the one who has borne the stone's weight for longer. I know its tongue. Perhaps she will heed my words.'

After exchanging a brief glance with his fearcel, whose eyes conveyed a silent plea for acquiescence, Varuk relinquished the Flare into his father's care and retreated to find rest.

All around, a large number of Valahans stood apart from the others. Their armour, made of metal and rocks, appointed them as the sole protectors for their kind. They scattered all across the caves, moving slowly in between the dangerous cracks of the roasting soil, scanning the long, perilous road they had left behind. From the top, all the way down to the descent, they kept watch for any signs of attack.

'Foar tal dú! Foar tal dú!' Two soldiers' cries echoed throughout the vast expanse of the cave, sending tremors of fear rippling through the assembled Valahans. With hearts gripped by terror and bellies empty with hunger, panic seized the throngs, driving them to frenzy. In the throes of confusion and horror, they trampled over one another in their desperate attempts to flee, transforming into a maddened horde.

Amidst the chaos, three colossal spectres materialized at the cave's apex, their forms glowing with a dark sorcery. Descending upon the rocky terrain, they unleashed havoc upon the fleeing masses, casting them into the fiery abyss below. Varuk, stunned by the unfolding tragedy, watched helplessly as his people were consumed by fear and crushed by their own panic.

Summoning his every strength left, Varuk raised his hand, unleashing a torrent of magic that created a chasm beneath the spectres, claiming both enemy and Valahan alike. Yet, the sweat on his brow and the bitter taste of imminent defeat gnawed at his senses as the spectres reformed before his eyes.

'Valahans!' he cried out, rallying his people amidst the chaos. 'For our lives, we must fight!'

A valiant group of Valahans answered his call, their cries of defiance piercing through the clamour. Transformed from captives into warriors, they surged forward, their armour gleaming like beacons amidst the darkness. Forming a barrier between their vulnerable kin and the encroaching threat, they braced themselves for the inevitable clash.

As the sounds of battle erupted behind him, Varuk's gaze shifted to the west wall, where his fearcel and children stood. With grim determination, he grabbed his father's hands, the two Valahans embracing the radiant Flare in a ceremonial circle of magic.

'May I be your stone father, as you are my metal. Together we shape now far more than the mountains. We take our destiny in our hands!'

A tremendous blast of energy clashed against the stubborn wall, breaking it apart. Its foundation losing strength, its matter finally gave in, exploding into fine dust. The fresh air of the open world spread inside the cave accompanied by the serene look of a peaceful, purple sky. It all lasted a few moments. As the Valahans started to smile and rejoice, their thick skin finally regaining its colour, the entire structure collapsed, its majestic, dark ceiling crumbling on them. A brief sense of liberation had filled their hearts and lungs only to be quickly replaced by certain death. There, in the devastating, loud sound of a cataclysm, the west side of the Mogs turned into a landslide.

Several hocs had passed when Una and her army reached the Mogs Pass. A reddish cloud of dust floated in the air from the flank of the mountains all the way down to the far ground. The entire side of the giant had been blown apart; a gigantic hole spoke of a recent explosion of pure magic. Sparkles of power mingled with the aftermath of destruction, flickering amidst the heavy, dense cloud. Here and there, she could grasp a glimpse of the harsh landscape of the desert peeking through spots of clear air. The Valahans had pierced through the mountains, opening a passage from the south cave, leading the eye to the spectacle of the Leonty's hills. Holding her thoughts to herself, Una scanned the space surrounding them. Something was calling her from deep, at the mountain's feet.

'My queen,' a spectre said. 'Looks like they have gifted you with a quick win...'

'Their long hiding within rocks and caves has turned against them...as it should have. For many yacs, they provided the Humans with the means to exterminate us, to eradicate anyone that wasn't them. But when the time came, the Valahans sought shelter from judgment in these very mountains. As if they had no part in their crimes.'

'Well, they are gone now, aren't they?' another spectre asked as his smoky eyes gazed at the many bodies scattered far below.

'They are...but their magic is still at work, all over this place...' she replied, almost as if she talked to herself. 'Let's get the Flare and move. Something important urges my attention.'

They floated down the crumbling path, carrying Una on their shoulders like a carriage of scavengers. In between red rocks and thick dust, Varuk's face popped up amongst the dead ones. His eyes still open, his face locked in the same expression full of desperation, he still had the Flare in his hands. Blood and marks of a crushing death screamed of a defeat too costly to be fully paid. Trapped in his last attempt to save his people, the Valahan had carried the magic with him, down to his end. As the Leonty swiftly moved to grab the precious stone, her eyes ignited, shining red. A crimson vision unfolded in her mind.

She saw herself in the same mirror she held before. Once more, she held a piece of paper in her hands. Anger was moving her lips, twitching them. At whatever point she was in her vision, she wasn't there yet. *This room, this place…* she thought. *Made of stones and the red sand of the desert… This is what I'm meant to build? This place is where he'll come back to me, to tell me I've done good…to tell me I've fulfilled my purpose…*

'My queen, where are we heading next? Do we move southeast to the Chomps?' someone whispered, their voice showing the thirst for a new fight. With the Valahans gone before they arrived, they were prevented from acting upon their wicked desires. They were robbed of the next battle they craved. Something else had to take its place instead.

'No,' Una firmly replied. 'There is much else we need to do first… Now that we have the Mogs' Flare, we can build a home for ourselves in no time. We can raise our unchallenged power to the sky. We move to the desert where the Leonty are waiting for me. There we will erect our new home.'

'Why would we leave the last of our enemies behind?' another spectre asked, perplexed.

'Because they are not like the others,' Una replied, angry. 'They are not fighters; they are more like these ones lying dead under your feet. They will hide until the end of time if they want to. They won't seek liberation, nor war. We will need to flush them out of their protective power. I need to think how. I need to make sure everything else is in place before we act against them. Now, we move north!'

# Chapter Thirty-Two

*The Eradication*

∞

The lands at the feet of the towering Mogs had plunged into darkness as the sinister mist slithered down the rocky flank, swiftly engulfing the distance between the Valahans and the desert. The Crimson Queen's army moved like a colossal cloud, shrouding the once-bright Erion in its chilly embrace. In return, whispers of sorrow spread through the surroundings, transforming them into a valley of mystery.

As Una approached the edges of the newly formed desert, a disturbing sight unfolded before her crimson eyes. The few derelict homes she had instructed Lethya and the other female Leonty to stay in, while awaiting her return, appeared abandoned, as if untouched for ages. Halting her advance momentarily, Una gazed at the verdant hills to her left, their beauty starkly contrasting the arid, lifeless ground below.

'They are not here...' a spectre whispered from behind her. 'They must have returned to their temples.'

'I can hear their foolish prayers emanating from their filthy lips from here,' another added.

'Quiet!' Una snapped. 'These are not prayers...they are lullabies...and it's not only Lethya's voice I hear. How is this possible?'

The bright flame of the Beacon of Fire appeared in the air as the Crimson queen lifted it in her hands. Her emerald, elongated fingers grasped the Flare as if hungering for its power. The reverence for the God's gift was foreign to the Leonty, who instead held the stone with one purpose: conquest. Suddenly, her body shifted, doubling into a spirit form. The glowing twin sank into the dusty ground and sped towards the hills. To her surprise, the place was deserted. Amidst the ruins of crumbling temples, silence still lingered, holding the aftermath of Una's act of revenge. In the far north, shadows of the Cloudy Mountains loomed, echoing a sequence of lyrics bouncing off the grey, rocky walls—a blessing prayer for protection against some evil presence.

Familiar voices called for help, and Una spotted Lethya amidst the landscape. The Crimson queen moved closer, traversing from one tree to the next, bush after bush, rock after rock. Inside an old, partially destroyed shack, a few males stood close to Lethya and another female.

'I'm certain. She is expecting…' Lethya murmured, fear tightening her voice to a mere whisper.

'Good!' one of the males replied with a smile devoid of joy or love. Pride and ruthless indifference drove their actions to a dark end. In a desperate attempt to preserve their kind, they had claimed the few remaining females for themselves, abusing and exploiting them to perpetuate their lineage. 'Now, check the other one. For your sake and hers, I hope you'll have good news once again.'

In the corner of the derelict building, another young female sat in shadows, her face twisted with terror. As Lethya approached and placed her cold hands on her sides, she gulped and began to cry. The two females exchanged looks of terror, anger, and defeat before Lethya turned and nodded to the males. Her response was the same as before, but she couldn't bring herself to declare it good news.

Suddenly, the foundation of the old home shook, dust swirling from the cracked wood floor. Una's rage had multiplied, manifesting openly and closing the distance between them. Dark, heavy clouds materialized in the sky, summoned by the Flare's magic, transforming day into night and unleashing a torrential downpour. Amongst the repeating lightning flashes, the Crimson queen appeared, her unmistakable features ethereal in the stone's power, bearing news of a terrible omen. Though physically absent, her presence was felt, and they knew they had been discovered.

Without hesitation, the two males dashed outside, only to be caught unprepared by the powerful storm. Blind in the deluge, they stumbled, lost amidst the intensifying rain. Then, two flashes struck the ground. One after the other, both Leonty met a swift, electrifying death. Their long hair steamed, bodies convulsing on the flooded ground. The last sight before their demise: the arrival of a few spectres at the Cloudy Mountains.

Not long after, the Queen arrived with her army. After casting a look of disgust at the lifeless bodies, she entered the shack. Lethya and the other Leonty remained in their spots, while the third female lay on the dusty floor. Her intentions unclear, they awaited her judgment. She could have come to punish them all, having declared her disdain for the Leonty's inability to oppose violence. Instead, her voice rang flat, discordant with the crimson hues of her irises.

'Where are the others I freed?'

'They ha…' Lethya struggled to speak, fear holding her tongue, but Una's magic compelled her. In an instant, she confessed. 'They have taken the others to their homes to mate and bring new blood into Runae. Once done, they abandon them here, left only to my care.'

'Where is your daughter? Where is Demetra?' Una demanded.

'They won't let me see her. I don't know…' Lethya began to cry.

'Has she shown the gift?' But the other Leonty remained silent, her sobs growing louder. 'Has she?' Una thundered.

'She is too young, and they haven't let me see her much, Una.' The other Leonty glanced at Lethya, gripping her hands tightly. Why was she asked that question? What did she truly want?

'Don't say that name! I'm your Queen now. I liberated you once, and I'm about to do it again. It seems you have no spine of your own, so I'm forced to do what's right once more. When will your kind ever learn?'

'You *are* our kind, Una,' the other Leonty retorted, terror seeping from her heart to her lips.

'So you do speak,' the queen laughed. 'Good. This is the strength I seek. Pity is not yours to give; it is against me… This is your unborn child's magic already at work, isn't it?'

'Please…Queen,' the third Leonty interjected, her body bearing the marks of prolonged abuse. Shadows marred her face, the vivid green of her skin dulled. 'Set us free… We all carry magic within us. Our little ones will too, I'm sure of it. I see it in the unfolding of our yacs.'

'You are gifted with sight?' Una's eyes widened at the news.

'I'm not. But my little one is… Revelia will be the one with the gift,' she whispered, caressing her stomach, eyes imploring the queen for help.

'Stay here,' Una commanded after a moment of silence. 'Some of my spectres will guard this…home. I'll be back.' With that, she left the shack, heading towards the highlands, closer to the Cloudy Mountains. There, several males hid in the shadows, unaware of the impending arrival of their most terrifying enemy.

As my brother Time recounted Una's most hateful act, he seemed unmoved by the horror she had wrought upon her own kind, just as he sounded indifferent to the atrocities committed by their males. In the millennia we existed, I got the sense that my brother, as is the master of the past, present, and future, emotions do not define his power. However, as I'm Love, the narration of such violence disturbed me deeply and it did it for a long time. It still does to this day.

When Una reached them, she ensured they suffered the most agonizing death. Nature itself dragged them down, swallowed by the earth, torn apart by enraged trees. Their limbs snapped, tongues seized by spectres. One by one, they were consumed by magic and smoke, drowned in their own blood, shredded into countless pieces. Their last sight: the Crimson Queen hovering in the air, five shining Flares orbiting her, filling her with the power of the Cosmos. Two red, glowing rubies marked their passage from life to death, Una's gaze upon them, satisfied with her own righteous judgment.

Once the queen accomplished her goals and her wrath subsided, she took the females with her, deep into the desert. There, using the precious gift extorted from the Valahans, she erected a giant fortress for herself and those she vowed to protect. Foundations and large walls emerged from the sandy ground, awakened by magic. Tall towers marked the four corners of their new homes, spikes and gates surrounding the perimeter. At the centre of the majestic, yet terrifying, structure, a red tower stood taller than the rest.

At its pinnacle, Una's grand chamber formed. Its circular shape remained unbroken, save for an opening through which a smaller tower spiked beside its larger companion. The future of the true holder of the Flares came into existence for the first time. The room where Daniel, Noah, and Anita would enter many yacs later was built with the magic of evil. The room where Treekan would make the ultimate sacrifice to steal Time's key from the Crimson Queen's grasp was ready to host the most precious artefact.

There, where every stone lay, every brick formed, taking her rightful place, Una stood. Her stunning beauty, untouched by the evil of her soul, shone brightest. As she gazed through a tiny, stony window at the landscape beyond, her eyes lingered on the distant Chomps' land. The end was near. She could sense the accomplishment whispering in her ears. Yet, the vision of an expected challenge troubled her. Turning from the window, she faced a grey wall. A small, rounded mirror glowed with an unsettling light. Her irises flashed red, eyes narrowing to thin lines. In her hands, a green light broke through her fingers as she held the grip on Time's clepsydra, determined to keep it with herself at all times.

'Your work here is not finished,' a familiar, incorporeal voice suddenly reverberated around the walls.

'It's almost done. Besides my own sisters, there is only one kind left on this planet,' Una replied, her gaze fixed on the bare stone wall. 'Five of the six stones are in my hands.'

'You better be finished when I'm done with my mission. His power is still crawling across these lands, his magic still lingers in the hands of your own kind. Take it and be done with it!' Nothing replied, disappointment evident in his tone. 'Nevertheless, you have given me time to destroy Creation's stupid Gods. However,' he resumed after a brief silence, 'these Gods are painfully stubborn. It seems I'm prevented from destroying them completely, but sure I can trap them indefinitely. The one you watch over, the one whose power lies in your hands now, might even try to come back to life, with the help of others. If anyone or anything crosses the gates of this world, you must use the power I've given you to tear them down. If necessary, take half of this planet with them, but do it!'

And just like that, the dark entity who had bestowed upon her an unchallenged dominion departed, swiftly quelling her satisfaction. Nothing reminded her she was far from done. A final act would close her quest for good. She had to take the lives of those she had rescued and destroy the Chomps once and for all.

# Chapter Thirty-Three

*The Invisible Ones*

∞

Twenty rhocs had passed since Una had raised her new abode, a grim testament to her dominion of death. The small group of Leonty she had brought under her sway continued to exist in a perpetual state of dread, knowing that their lives hung by a thread under the rule of one who wielded the darkest of magics, devoid of any semblance of love or mercy. Lethya's existence remained unchanged, transitioning from one tyrant to an even more sinister one, imprisoned alongside her kin deep beneath the queen's fortress. Denied the opportunity to nurture her offspring, interactions with her daughter, Demetra, were scarce at best.

Determined to mould the newborns into instruments of her will, Una refused to allow them to be influenced by their maternal bonds. She alone would dictate the shaping of their minds, hearts, and magic. Thus, when Revelia came into the world soon after the birth of the twins Ferhentia and Trasfigea, the young Leonty were swiftly separated from their mothers, consigned to the shadows under Una's oppressive authority, inheriting her venomous hatred for all life.

As the young ones matured and became self-sufficient, Una plotted her final assault against the last bastion of resistance. The Sháten Déil rendered them impervious, necessitating a shift in strategy. She could not simply launch a frontal assault as she had against the Humans and Valahans. The Chomps, cautious and reclusive within their dome, had thus far eluded any direct confrontation. Yet, Una was undeterred; she would find a way. If she couldn't breach their defences, she would ensnare them in a deadly trap.

'I know for certain that at least one of them has ventured beyond the dome…to rescue the one who dared challenge my supremacy,' Una declared, pacing the confines of her sombre tower. Though she was seemingly alone, the cold, grey stones bore silent witness to her scheming, embracing her presence with the same chilling indifference she exuded. She had walked the room countless times, thinking how long she had to wait before finding a way through the dome. Rhoc after rhoc, an entire yac had passed while the Crimson Queen sent her spectres to scout the southern hills, looking for a sign of the enemy. In her mind she could see the defiance of her winged ones challenging her, opposing her attacks.

And so Una waited. She waited long enough to have at her disposal the magic she didn't bear. Although her power had found no obstacle in her thirst for conquest, she feared a war against the invisible ones required the magic the young Leonty displayed since their birth. As she stood next to the same mirror that for long had oppressed her with its wicked omens, suddenly, the wall beside the entrance quivered, as if recoiling from the presence of its queen. Two spectres materialized swiftly, their ethereal forms swirling like dissipating smoke within the chamber.

'No sign of them, my queen,' one spoke. 'I don't think they own the strength to venture outside their protected abode.'

'And yet, we encountered one in the caves, during our attempts to breach the Valahans' realm,' the other spectre objected.

'Can't we utilize the Garughals' Flare to infiltrate from beneath the earth?' the first one suggested.

'Or ours? The Flare of the Sea?'

'Yours?' Una's gaze sharpened as she turned towards the one who still clung to the identity of an Aqualymph. There would be no allowances for reclaiming former identities or laying claim to the Flare she had appropriated for herself. After a tense silence, the spectre's gaze fell, conceding to her authority. 'This is not how the Flares work, you foolish creature! They are all interconnected. While I can wield one against living beings or inanimate objects, I cannot wield it against another Flare. Their powers would avoid each other…'

'How then do we compel them to leave?' the other spectre inquired, moving towards a narrow window. Dark voids replaced where its eyes once were, fixating on the distant mountains.

'I would employ the abilities of the young ones if I could. Some possess unique powers. I could infiltrate the Chomps' domain physically, deceive them into trust…but I cannot afford to wait any longer. I should already have acquired all the Flares…' Una's frustration was palpable, mirrored in the gaze exchanged between the two spectres. While they could comprehend her dissatisfaction with the current state of affairs, they failed to grasp the urgency driving her actions. After all, with no remaining adversaries and the Chomps securely hidden within their dome, there seemed to be little reason for haste.

'It's a comfort, my queen…' the other spectre ventured cautiously. 'Even if all else fails, you will wield formidable magic. And if waiting becomes necessary, the other Leonty will prove invaluable…'

'Enough!' Una's voice sliced through the air like a whip, prompting the two spectres to hasten towards the door, ready to depart.

Una bristled at the notion of being reliant on others, especially those she held in contempt. Though she had woven tales for the young ones, fostering the illusion of kinship and shared purpose, it was all a façade. She harboured no concern for their well-being or happiness;

they were mere instruments, to be wielded at her whim. 'I have no need for them. I have no need for anyone,' she muttered to herself as she approached the small mirror hanging in the shadow of a looming wall. *The sorcery of the one who cannot best me,* she mused, her thoughts swirling with contempt. *A false deity whose magic seeks to undermine my victory… Showing me a past I refuse to acknowledge. But what if…*

'Bring me Revelia. Now!' she demanded suddenly, her voice ringing with authority.

In the blink of an eye, the spectre vanished, dissipating into nothingness. Moments later, they reappeared, accompanied by a young Leonty. Like the others, Revelia had matured rapidly, her skin now a vibrant green, her hair beginning to harden, and her eyes gleaming like crystalline gems bathed in Erion's light.

'Revelia,' Una addressed her as she entered the room. 'I require your assistance… Can you aid your beloved sister?' she added, punctuating the request with a smile. The two spectres who remained by the door watched in astonishment. It was the first time they had witnessed Una donning this façade, the counterfeit guise of a benevolent and humble sibling. Yet, despite the charade, the fire in the queen's eyes remained undimmed. 'Do you see this mirror?' she continued, gesturing towards it. 'I need you to gaze into it, intently. Climb onto this stool beside me. Yes, here.' Revelia, barely half Una's size, struggled to reach Una's shoulders even after ascending the rickety stool. 'Now, focus only on my reflection. Disregard everything else and tell me what you see…'

'I see you, sister!' Revelia exclaimed, her smile betraying her amusement at Una's request. In her mind, Una was being silly

'Look closer. Let your mind wander,' Una urged, her hands guiding Revelia's shoulders.

'I don't know, sister. I see you and me only. Wait...' Revelia hesitated, drawing Una's attention. 'Someone who looks like you is standing next to another figure. I've never seen anything like it. What is it, sister? It has pale skin, taller than you, with bright eyes and wearing shining grey clothes. It's alive, but what is it?' Before Una could interject, Revelia continued, recounting the scene unfolding in the mirror's memories. 'The one who resembles you is embracing it. You're crying... You say, "I want to see my daughter, Kareesto. We need to return and take Una away from the temples." The other one says, "We can't traverse the lands. The Humans are hunting us. We must bide our time until they cease their pursuit. The Chomps will offer us refuge, my love."'

As Revelia recounted the past glimpses from the mirror, Una withdrew, her thoughts racing. Weak, estranged feelings for Vertatis struggled to surface amidst the cacophony of hatred, vengeance, and resentment. Her mother had abandoned her to ally with the enemy—a Human. Despite her longing to reunite with her daughter, Vertatis had opted to seek refuge under the Chomps' protection, yet another adversary. Anger swiftly reclaimed its hold on the queen's heart.

'What you witness is the past, sister,' Una declared firmly. 'It is the deceit of the artefact before you. I need you to focus on the future, not dwell on the yacs gone.' She pivoted, positioning herself behind Revelia. With slender fingers resting on Revelia's chin, Una's eyes glowed crimson as she ensnared Revelia's mind in a binding spell. Instantly, Revelia's irises mirrored the same crimson hue.

'Something is shifting...' Revelia murmured as she peered into the mirror. 'There's a small creature before you. It has...wings? It holds his hands on a mirror like this one. "The Crimson Queen," it cries out. You're both in a large room filled with other mirrors. Wait, there are others... Three figures have appeared. They look like the one I saw before, Kareesto. They, too, gaze into the mirrors, observing you. I can see myself reflected within as well? I look as tall as you... Sister?' Suddenly, Revelia's magic faltered, extinguishing the crimson glow in her eyes.

'So it comes to this...' Una muttered to herself, her thoughts echoing through the dimly lit chamber. 'I suspected they would be linked to the threat I've been sensing incessantly. It seems they possess mirrors of their own. The advantage this grants them is unimaginable. Nonetheless, thank you, Revelia. You've assisted your sister as well as I knew you would. Now, return to the others. There is something crucial I must attend to.' After Revelia had departed the dark tower, Una turned her attention to the walls, commanding the cold stones to heed her will. 'Prepare the army. We are mobilizing against the winged ones!'

As if time and space had converged into a single point, Treekan suddenly gulped. He had been entranced by a large mirror hanging upon a curved wall, seeking answers within its evocative magic. Ensnared by its allure, he was convinced that the artefact held the elusive solution. After being granted a connection to Revelia's magic, offering him glimpses of past, present, and future, he stumbled backwards onto the cold, unforgiving ground.

'Son!' Faróel's voice called out from a distance, laced with concern. 'What happened? What did you see?'

'I...I'm not sure, father,' Treekan stammered, struggling to make sense of his experience. 'I thought these mirrors only showed the past. I saw the new queen in what I believe is her stronghold now. But it didn't seem like a distant past. It felt as though I was catching up with lost time. And then, something changed. I saw another Leonty, a very young one, using a mirror just like this. Somehow, she saw me as I gazed at her. In an instant, I aged, aged beyond measure. Then, Humans appeared in this room, accompanied by a Leonty.'

'As if you were propelled yacs ahead?' Faróel drew nearer, intent on examining the mirror for himself. To his dismay, its magic seemed depleted, its surface rendered inert.

'I believe so. And...Father...' Treekan's voice faltered, a note of urgency creeping in. 'I heard the queen's voice speaking. She wants to see us dead. She is coming!'

Treekan's unexpected revelation afforded the Chomps a glimpse of the imminent peril. Despite being thrust forwards in time, they found themselves ill-prepared for the impending assault. Rushing out of the towering edifice, Faróel raced down the hills towards the heart of the village. Alerting the others to the queen's malevolent intentions elicited panic and dread in return.

After hocs of deliberation on how to confront such a formidable foe, they abandoned thoughts of direct confrontation. They lacked armour to shield their bodies, and they had no metal to wield against the queen's forces. All they possessed was their innate strength, wings, and the power of invisibility.

'She hasn't been able to breach our dome,' one Chomp objected as a small faction broke away to seek counsel from the Flare. 'She cannot penetrate it. We must not venture beyond its protection.'

'What if she does?' Treekan interjected, standing beside the luminous stone. 'This is the last remaining Flare. If she manages to breach our defences…'

'She wields many stones, but it is the Garughals' that fills me with dread,' Faróel remarked. 'Aura traversed our barrier with it. Who's to say this queen won't attempt the same?'

'Father, Aura was only present in spirit. She wasn't physically here,' Treekan countered, offering fleeting reassurance to the others.

'Even so, her influence could seep in, her words driving us to madness,' Faróel reasoned, raising the Sháten Déil from its resting place. A timid green glow danced across the faces of those gathered. 'No, we must be cunning. We must be prepared!'

Inspired by his resolve, the elderly Chomp strode towards the nearby structure, its roof shredded as a reminder of the looming threat. Undeterred, he entered, resolute in his determination to devise a plan to thwart the unbeatable evil. Silently, the others trailed behind, eager to hear the formidable strategy Faróel was about to unveil.

# Chapter Thirty-Four

## *Those Who Withstood the Evil*

∞

Alone in the vacant building, the young Chomp found solace in silence, his sole companion. Despite the vast star piercing the space through the gaping hole in the roof, Erion's light struggled to permeate the stony floor where he sat in quiet contemplation, his gaze fixed on the ancient mirror. Within his mind, a relentless urge gnawed at him, driving him to seek further revelations. While others placed their faith in the Sháten Déil, he, wielding a power similar to the Flare's, maintained that the key to their salvation lay within the artefacts left behind by Time himself.

Distant from Treekan's watchful eyes and keen ears, a formidable assembly of Chomps traversed the village, each entrusted with a crucial task for the mission they all fervently endeavoured to fulfil. They had amassed all available provisions, bearing them laboriously up the hill to their designated waiting point. Una could manifest herself in any guise, at any corner of their domain, posing an imminent threat. As Faróel had advised, unity and proximity to the Flare were imperative.

While a handful of Chomps returned to the village to gather their essentials, a mother and daughter hastened into their home, their anxious conversation betraying their fear and urgency.

'Take only what is absolutely necessary; we must depart at once,' the elder Chomp asserted.

'But Mother, we cannot possibly bring everything we need,' the daughter protested, her voice trailing off as her mother disappeared into the back of the house.

Determination propelled her mother's movements, but weariness etched upon her face revealed the toll of late-stage pregnancy. 'Ouch, Reela...' she murmured, tenderly caressing her swollen abdomen. 'Be gentle with Mama. I am already fraught with worry. You still have another sixty rhocs to go...' As she stooped to gather the dry clothes neatly arranged in a large basket, a foreboding breeze whispered ominously nearby. The lofty trees' leaves rustled in their familiar cadence, yet an eerie undertone mingled with the tranquil melody, heralding danger.

'You shouldn't be carrying such a burden so close to your due date…' a voice intoned. Startled, the Chomp whirled around, her gaze drawn to the violet sky. 'Summon the others to assist you. The Flare possesses ample protection on its own; there is no need for so many guards…'

'Who's there?' the Chomp called out, worried. 'Is that you, Jórah?'

'I am not a Chomp, dear one. I am nature… I sense your distress as you tread upon my grounds. You must abandon all here and return to the others. Where are they? I can aid you in preserving your strength as you go back, if you so require.'

'Areena!' the Chomp exclaimed, darting back into the house. 'Leave everything behind. Something is wrong here. Hurry, hurry, hurry!'

A short distance from their dwelling, two other Chomps wandered along the perimeter of the dome, patiently awaiting the return of their companions. Their gaze drifted towards the riverbank, where three Chomps moved stealthily, diligently gathering the vital Gochi water. As they rotated shifts in venturing outside the dome's safety, those left behind grew restless, their thoughts racing towards the anticipated return of their comrades. Suddenly, a crystalline figure emerged from the waters, hesitating to assume a solid form. Her radiant visage shimmered like a brilliant diamond beneath the caress of the star.

'Oh my,' one Chomp exclaimed, stumbling backward.

'Aura, is it truly you?' another chimed in, a soft smile gracing his features at the joyful realization. 'We feared we had lost you!'

'Where is your master? I urgently need to speak with him,' the ethereal figure inquired.

'Faróel is atop the hill, near the Flare. We are preparing for the impending attack,' the third Chomp replied. 'Come with us. Treekan and the others will rejoice to see you well!' With that, he hoisted a heavy container brimming with water onto his shoulders and began the trek back to the village.

'I cannot leave the waters,' the translucent figure lamented. 'I fear I am not as well as you hope. Please, hasten. Inform him that I will await his arrival here. Tell him I have a way to protect you all. We need the Flare. Go now, bring him and the stone back, quickly!' Shocked by her words, the three Chomps refrained from further inquiry and, without hesitation, swiftly retreated into the safety of the dome, vanishing from sight.

At the other side of their land, Treekan finally succumbed to the irresistible urge to delve deeper into the wisdom of the mirrors. Standing up, he approached the large relic positioned at the centre of the wall, feeling the familiar incantation forming on his lips.

*A yac knokr yac. Tay yacsh knókr tyor yacs, soathár tyor shaclash, sagirath tu*

'A yac for yac. My yacs for your yacs, to buy your oldest secrets, the beginning of yourself...' he repeated, the words flowing as if etched into his memory. This time, something wholly unfamiliar enveloped him. The soft light of Erion vanished, plunging the world into darkness. White walls materialized around him, replacing the sacred confines of the Chomps' sanctuary with a grander, more revered edifice.

Within, three women stood in a dimly lit corner of the room. Flickering candles cast a feeble glow, barely illuminating the regal figure of the queen beside the king, who sat upon a grand chair, his gaze averted. Though subtle, his disapproval was palpable to those familiar with him.

'Please, my fearcel, you must see reason...' the queen implored, her voice laced with urgency.

'Reason?' the king retorted, his anger flaring in a direct confrontation with Queen Shahara. 'You Witches of Fárahal must have known of this for some time. Either you knew, or you are simply woven from lies and deceit.'

'None of us foresaw this until the appointed time,' Shahara countered, sinking to her knees. Her hands sought his, but King Lohan resisted her touch. 'Try to understand, if we hadn't wed, this future wouldn't have happened at all. Now that a yac has almost passed, the only path ahead is taking shape. With it, the omen of this terrible, evil threat has surfaced in our dreams.'

'Suppose I entertain this absurdity,' he challenged, his gaze sweeping over the other three witches, who, scared by his known bad temper, dared not speak. 'How can you be certain we will bear an heir? How can you be sure it will be a boy?'

'I may err in many things, my love, but never in the power of my own blood,' Shahara asserted, her unwavering faith in her magic bolstering her defiance. 'If anything, I am certain that what I witnessed in my dream will come to pass!'

'Describe to me every detail of your vision,' the king demanded, his resolve faltering beneath Shahara's solid certainty.

'A green-skinned figure, clad in chains and a mask, rises against many,' Shahara began, recounting the same tale once more. 'Her eyes pierce the darkness like fiery arrows. She possesses a power we have never encountered. Death follows in her wake. Our home, our kingdom, lies at her mercy. She strides into the throne room, our palace exactly as it stands now. There, the crown passes from the king to her.'

As Shahara paused to collect her thoughts, King Lohan rose from his seat. Though the plush chair had cradled him comfortingly moments before, he now felt ill at ease.

'As she places the crown upon her head, poised to claim sovereignty over our world, a Human hand seizes her wrist,' Shahara continued. 'Eyes that mirror the blue of the sea and the green of our hills penetrate through her malevolent spirit. His dark hair marks him as your rightful heir.'

'His soul eclipses all who have come before him,' one of the witches interjected. 'As our sister foretold in her prophecy, so it unfolds before our eyes. We recognize him for who he is. Your son embodies the spirit of a warrior. His heart beats to a different rhythm. Within him burns the power of a deity, guiding his steps against our enemy.'

'We glimpse only fragments of the future,' added the other witch, Meeriah. 'He ventures into the heart of the enemy's domain of his own will. He endures tortures in a cold jail, yet emerges victorious. Even Time itself casts its light upon him. He will come, whether you accept it or not.'

'Then so be it!' King Lohan declared, retreating to the shadows of the room, his gaze fixed on a flickering candle. 'If this man is destined to be our saviour, he shall be king. He shall be my son. But speak of this to no one, under any circumstances. The law is clear: he must be mine!'

The regal surroundings abruptly dissolved, plunging Treekan to the brink of a new vision swiftly taking shape. Once more, even the most vivid elements failed to evoke familiarity in the young Chomp's mind. The Crimson Queen loomed in the centre of a confined chamber, encircled by five flames swirling frenetically around her form. Her hair, resembling frenzied darts, pointed in every direction; her outstretched hands seemed to grasp at the very essence of their world, ensnaring the spirits and souls of its inhabitants. The scorching air transformed the room into a furnace, Una's power raging uncontrollably like an unquenchable fire.

For a fleeting moment, Treekan envisioned himself darting around the room, the Flare of his people clutched firmly in his grasp. Whatever he beheld, it was no longer a reflection of the past. He felt poised to confront the terrifying adversary looming large. Beside him, three

Humans stood steadfast, their determination speaking of an indomitable will. Before he could fully comprehend the implications of the glimpse into his future, the entire vision unravelled, consumed by a cataclysmic explosion that hurled him back into the silent reality of the empty room. As he struggled to decipher the meaning behind what he had witnessed, Faróel burst into the room, a sense of urgency etched upon his features.

'Treekan, Aura is back! Aura is back!' he let out.

'Father, we need to talk,' Treekan exclaimed urgently. 'It's essential that I share with you what I've just witnessed...'

'Did you hear what I said? Our friend is back...' Faróel repeated; a sparkle in his eyes hinted at tears about to flow.

'It's not Aura, and we need to act fast, Father,' Treekan replied, resolute.

In the hocs that followed, Una's deceiving appearances multiplied tremendously. Shapeshifting into trees, whispers, and visions, she deployed all the Flares she possessed to drive the Chomps insane. Each attempt failed, the magic stones unable to penetrate the protection of the Sháten Déil guarding the little ones. Yet, Una persisted, moving after the dome's inhabitants, instilling fear and panic. Deploying the Anún Déil, she had pulled the waters of the Gochi River over their banks, the river stream changing, clashing against an intangible wall.

Around the invisible barrier, a myriad of fleeting ghosts slid on its surface, stretching beyond perception, merging their efforts like a second, darker dome. The large Erion slowly disappeared from sight, the sky darkening as if the greatest storm of all had approached on the wings of the wind. Whatever enemy they were prepared to face, whatever weaknesses they could overcome, one thought troubled them terribly: if the rain came, they would fall asleep instantly.

They gathered in the courtyard among the ancient buildings, where the Sháten Déil stood, a sea of tiny people squeezed together. The stone was gone from sight, the absence of its light bringing an even darker omen. Further north, Treekan and Faróel stealthily moved at the edge of the dome, their faces troubled by their impending fate. Once again, the young one urged the other to trust his plan.

'Please Father, it's the only way. We must let her see it. She will never stop hunting us if she knows she stands a chance.'

'You are asking to risk the lives of all our people, Treekan. You put your trust in what you saw in those mirrors, but how can you be sure that's not the deceit of the very enemy you want to let in?'

'The relics came from Time, Father. I'm absolutely certain. Please do as I said. When I tell you to run, you run!' Treekan repeated, his gaze fixed upon the old Chomp. In that brief look, he carried his demands with the authority of a rising new master. And yet, profound love and fear mingled together with it. 'Take my hand. We move over the barrier unseen.'

Afraid yet compelled by his son's sense of security, Faróel took Treekan's hand and followed him through the dome. *This couldn't be a worse time to be proud of him, witnessing him grow up so fast. Kasthor would feel the same,* he thought as he closed his eyes, terrified by the presence of the dark enemy. As they quickly passed the barrier, the ethereal dark presence of the spectres slid on their invisible skins. The feathers on their wings frizzed as if struck by lightning.

Overwhelmed by a sense of oppression and terror, his admiration for Treekan was the only thing that pushed the old Chomp forward. *It should have been me, the one with the courage to act. Age and destruction have taken a toll on me... I have to find my strength back, for Kasthor, for Treekan, Voishan, Aura...*he told himself.

A few moments later, the two Chomps found themselves in front of a horrifying spectacle. From the other side, the vision of the enemy enveloping their world displayed right before their eyes. They moved like a wobbling dark pond, with algae and dirt replaced by deformed limbs and obscure souls as the spectres mingled in their own evil. A few steps away, the one who commanded the dark army stood unchallenged, alone. Her hard hair darted in space while a vortex of power surrounded her body. The five Flares spun frenetically as she kept her eyes closed, her mind over the dome, busy trying to trick the Chomps into surrender.

'Hey, you!' Treekan shouted right after he had turned off his magic. Next to him, his father appeared out of nowhere, his legs shaking. 'How much more space do you need? What you took is not enough?'

Una's eyes opened instantly. The Chomp's voice had come with the sweet taste of success. They were out of the dome as she hoped, and now, the easy trick of sorcery awaited them. 'Finally…' she let out as she turned around. 'I started to believe you didn't exist at all…'

'You have the entire planet at your disposal. We don't come to judge your actions, although despicable. Just go away and leave us alone!' Faróel interjected, fear slowly turning into anger.

'Despicable…' Una repeated, smiling. 'Differently from the others, you have done no harm to me…yet. I would concede to your request if you weren't to become a problem to me, eventually. I want the Sháten Déil! Give it to me and you may live.'

Her last words struck Treekan's mind. *Has she seen the future in her mirror too? She knows we will face her again…*he thought. At their side, the spectres had started to move away from the dome, their attention shifting to the two who had dared to venture into the world they now possessed.

'I can't get in,' she continued, 'and you won't get the Flare out. I imagine we are stalling in a very risky predicament,' she said, her tone as if she mocked the two Chomps. 'Perhaps, if I take one of you, the other could be…compelled to do as I say?' And the grey stone of the Valahans moved away from the other four, spinning faster and faster. As Una raised her hands to touch it, the ground started to shake, cracks began to appear on the surface. The green grass quickly turned brown as the inner earth started to surface.

'Son, she is not using her incantation,' Faróel said as they slowly lifted from the ground, their wings flapping fast. 'Why is she using the Murán Déil?'

'Because once we pass the dome, her coercive power would cease. Stay close, remember the plan,' Treekan whispered. They rose in the air like feathers moved by the wind, light and free. If the lands were to break apart beneath their hairy feet, all the way to the planet core, they wouldn't care.

The black Flare of the Humans suddenly left the gathering of stones and moved forward. With her gaze fixed upon the Ergon Déil, Una extended her arms towards the Chomps. A tremendous blow expanded from her to them, traveling fast. Before it could reach the two opponents, Treekan and Faróel disappeared in a snap.

'I'm not here to entertain your games, Chomps!' Una shouted, angered by their defiance.

'Leave us alone!' Treekan replied as they appeared right behind her, making her jolt. Before she could act against the near enemy, the Chomp disappeared again. 'You need to understand you can't get what you don't see...' Treekan's and Faróel's forms popped up and dissolved in a quick sequence, here and there. 'This is the only reason why we came...' And they were gone again. 'To make you understand you better give up and leave.'

'Enough!' Una's voice thundered in the open space, the energy of the five Flares enlarging rapidly. She was furious, worried she would fail her master's command. Her wicked sense of justice, revenge, had become lost in the abyss of a corrupted mind. Now Nothing's will shaped hers completely. Her own inner demons had stopped moving her actions. Someone else manoeuvred her like a pawn. Blind by sorrow, pain, and her thirst for revenge, she had opened up to someone whose malevolence was eternal, unjustified, undebatable. 'I'll get your Flare one way or the other!'

As if a new star was suddenly born in the confinement of a little land, a bright light surged from within the Crimson Queen. Her arms stretched to the side, her head tilted to the sky above, she called upon herself every power she possessed. In the brief moment the two Chomps reappeared in the air, her gaze swiftly locked in with theirs. Her eyes burning with a raging fire, her spell left her body to travel the distance between her and the enemy. Supported by the astonishing power of the Flares, it travelled in an instant, its prey found in a blink of her petrifying eyes.

'Now, Father!' Treekan shouted as he shone the light of a green stone in his hands. The Sháten Déil glowing at the protection of the old Chomp, his son instantly disappeared again. The entire dome immediately vanished, leaving the village exposed. Under the blind gaze of the Crimson Queen, Treekan materialized next to her. His indomitable will sustaining him, he placed his tiny hands on the vibrating stones, taking them away from his enemy, diverting their power to his small, yet strong body.

'How?' Una murmured as her petrified look fixed on the one who had tricked her.

With his own magic amplified by the power of the five Flares, Treekan's invisibility reached the equal power of the Sháten Déil, expanding in the space around, engulfing Una, the spectres, and Faróel under a new, powerful barrier. The reality of the outside had disappeared. Struggling to contain the extreme power of the stones, Treekan started to shake, his eyes tearing from the intense pain. Suspended into a grey nothingness, he called upon every strength left and he spoke.

'Now you know what we can do…. We might not be able to defeat you…but you will never get us or our Flare.'

'You can't hold this power, Chomp!' Una replied as she moved closer. Her hands grabbed Treekan's wrists as she searched for his gaze. 'But you could definitely be of good use to me…'

Right as the young Chomp was about to faint, his eyes met hers, Una's magic ready to disintegrate every trace of who he was. Her evil attack taking her full attention, she didn't see the arrival of Faróel. He moved fast, desperation in his eyes. His son was the one he wanted to protect the most. He had been guarding him all his life, determined to keep his promise to his fearcel, and now the greatest threat lay right before his eyes.

As he darted next to his son, unable to see or think anything else but rescuing him, the words of a lost friend had been forgotten. Aura had warned him many times, and yet, he could only think to save his dearest from a terrible end. He reappeared next to Treekan and Una and swiftly took his son's hands. The Sháten Déil, the last final Flare to join the gathering of an immense power, reached the others.

The stones touched; the quick kiss of a magical assemble released the blast of an explosive star. The two Chomps were pushed far away, towards their home. The Crimson Queen and her evil army scattered around the planet, traveling over the large Mog. In the smallest fraction of time, Creation's original stone had come to exist once more to then reshape into the six Flares Time's magic had generated.

As the two Chomps landed on the field next to their people's village, the Flare departed of its own will and moved back to where it belonged. The protective dome reappeared over the heads of the many who, terrified by being exposed, finally rejoiced at the reappearance of the magical barrier.

After a little while, the excruciating pain woke Treekan up. His limbs still shivered from the magic borne by his body, his head hurt by the fall. A few steps away, lay the one who had granted him the same future he had seen in Time's mirrors. Faróel's soul had departed even before they had touched the ground. His body showed the scars of the violent battle, yet his face looked serene. The last glimpse of memory that had occupied the old Chomp's thoughts was about his son, the only one who he had managed to protect.

# Chapter Thirty-Five

## *A Tale of Time*

∞

The tale of my beloved brother ended right there. As he shared with me how everything came to be, how it continued, and how it ended, I felt like I was getting to know him again for the first time. Word after word, story after story, I doubted him, his intentions, his motives. Yet, I also understood, believed he knew every detail of the unfolding present and future.

After all, as we stood protecting the universe, he was by my side, along with my siblings, fighting for the same people and worlds we all swore to defend. It's peculiar how our stories, our planets, intertwined together. To this day, and many have passed since the two of us departed, I can't help but think about how much he knew about me, about my future.

When Daniel, Anita, and Noah reached Runae for the first time, they found exactly what they were meant to find. The creatures they met, the alliances they forged, it all led to this very moment. Remove even just one piece from this vast recollection of events, and we would have been defeated by Nothing.

As Time concluded his tale, he recounted how the Flares connected together, the moment Faróel moved to rescue his son. For a brief second, our mother's magic was restored. The power sustaining their world, the same power Time had unearthed and gifted to the six races, existed once again.

The magnitude of that event was so immense that Una refrained from attacking once more. Although she spent some time recollecting the Flares that had scattered back to their rightful spots, she never attempted to conquer the Chomps' land again. The absence of Nothing, who retreated after the blow my sister and I inflicted upon him, must have given her the satisfaction she wasn't going to face his judgment any longer. With the yacs, her desire for revenge subsided, her hate for everything she came in contact with became dormant in her corrupted heart.

After all was said and done, after all the details my brother brought to my attention, I finally understand why it all had to happen. Queen Shahara's prophecy wasn't confined to her kingdom, or her planet, for that matter.

Instead, it linked two worlds together. It brought two destinies, two Gods, and two futures under the same path.

Whether we made the right decision, whether we had no other option but one, I find comfort in the idea that Time knew it all along. It soothes my soul and quietens my nightmares a little. We were destined to walk those steps. We gained and lost exactly what we were meant to. And yes, it comforts me to know that, once again, my brother and I were brought together under the same incredible tale.

*The End*

**The Power of Love**

*A Tale of Time*

# The Power of Love

## *A Tale of Time*

Ross J. Kinnaird

# About the Author

Ross Joseph Kinnaird was born in a far land something like one thousand years ago. He moved to Italy as an infant and grew up in the deep south, shaped by the sun and the wildness of the sea. After moving to Ireland in 2010, he began collecting and organizing the many stories he had written. They all seemed to have one theme, one soul. With the Celtic magic that his new home brought to him, Ross finally saw his novel taking shape through the mystical eyes of his mind. And so, *The Power of Love* became the journey of a lifetime, perhaps spanning many lifetimes.

In the realm between reality and fantasy, he fused together the diverse ways life presented itself to him. Through a literary roller-coaster of emotions and feelings—pain, sorrow, happiness, friendship, and love—Ross J. Kinnaird wrote the many stories we tell ourselves in our never-ending search for greater meaning.

*"Art, feelings, music, emotions have always been the strongest part of me. I was only a young teenager when I started transferring my busy mind onto paper.*
*As the years passed, life and experiences enriched my soul to a point where The Power of Love finally took form.*
*With the strongest connection to what I saw life as, the story of Daniel, Noah and Anita became an extension of who I am, of who many of us are."*

**R. J. Kinnaird**

ISBN: 978-1-0686863-4-4

For more info on The Power of Love Series®

www.thepoweroofloveseries.com


First edition: June 2024

First Print: June 2024

Edited by Imogen Howson

Cover by Ardel Media


*The Power of Love Series concludes with:*
**The Power of Love – The Three**